ARIA HARDING

Also by Aria Harding

* * *

Stand-Alone Novels

Chasing Infinity

Everything In Between

Wonderstruck

The Cedar Ridge Series

Loathing Ryan

Liberating Bells

Just Josie

His Perfect Art Trilogy

His Perfect Canvas

His Perfect Muse

His Perfect Melody

Editing: Nice Girl Naughty Edits

Cover Design by: IndieSage

First Edition published 2024

ISBN (E-Book): 9798988378464

ISBN (Paperback): 9798988378471

For anyone who ever feels like they are trapped in a version of their life they don't desire. You have the power to take your life back and make exactly how you want.
Be empowered, be brave, be bold.

Foreword

Below is a list of Content Warnings associated with this novel.
Please read with your own discretion.
Some of these content warnings may contain plot spoilers.

- Physical and emotional abuse by a partner (Domestic Abuse) (Not between main characters)
- Family member going through cancer diagnosis and treatment.
- Feelings of unworthiness / emotional trauma
- Feelings of depression and anxiety
- Parent dealing with cancer
- Mentions of struggle with alcoholism
- Infidelity between main characters

Chapter 1

Ryan

Five Years Later

"IT IS A BEAUTIFUL SUNDAY EVENING HERE IN CEDAR Ridge, Tennessee. We hope you enjoyed your flight and welcome home!" the pilot's voice echoes over the intercom.

I glance up from the long, monotonous contract I've been reading and blink my eyes. My vision is a little blurry from staring at the text for so long. I adjust the glasses on my nose and let the pilot's words seep in.

Welcome home.

I haven't been home for what feels like an eternity. If my memory serves correctly, the last time I was here was Christmas two years ago. I had come home to celebrate my sister's sixth birthday and spend the holidays with my family.

In the years after leaving Cedar Ridge, my visits and phone calls became more and more scarce as time passed. My mom tried her best to be understanding, given the circumstances, but I knew it was hard for her not getting to see me as much.

Germany became my home without me fully realizing it, and work became my outlet.

At that time, there wasn't much left for me in the States. Sure, I missed my family like crazy, but the emptiness I felt every time I landed in Cedar Ridge was enough to keep me away for a while. For a long time, I wasn't ready to face those feelings.

But now, things are different, and not in a good way. I'm needed back home in Tennessee permanently. So once again, I packed my life up and crossed the pond one last time. For good.

Once I've gathered up my carry-on items into my bag, I remove my glasses, rubbing at my eyes a bit to help reduce the blurriness as the plane slowly taxis into the gate.

I'm a little surprised that I feel anticipation instead of heartbreak at the prospect of being home. A part of me is still aware that things will never be the same, but the other part is ready to reclaim my life with my family by my side.

As soon as we receive the all-clear from the flight attendants, I collect my briefcase and grab my suitcase from the bin overhead. The rest of my belongings have already been shipped to my mom's house. I file behind the rest of the passengers through the aircraft and then into the airport terminal.

My feet carry me past the baggage claim and over to where I know my family will be waiting. A huge grin splits my face as soon as I see them. The young girl beside my mother drops her homemade *Welcome Home, Ryno!* sign onto the floor and runs at me at full speed, giggling the whole way. She launches herself at me as soon as she's in range, and I catch her, laughing too, as I spin her around.

"Hey, squirt!" I exclaim, as my little sister clutches my neck in a giant bear hug.

"Hey, Ryno!" she squeaks back, gripping onto me for dear life. "Did you see the sign I made?"

"I did, but you dropped it back there," I tell her, setting her down and rumpling the top of her soft blonde hair.

She looks back and sees our parents walking toward us. Her dad has the sign tucked safely under his arm, and she nods.

I crouch down to get a good look at her. She has blonde hair and green eyes like me. Though my hair has turned more of a dark sandy brown over the years. I'm still amazed at how small she feels. I'm not tall, by any means; my stepdad Derek still has a few inches over me. But next to Thalia? I feel like a giant.

"Geez, you're getting big," I tell her. "How old are you now, twenty-seven?"

Thalia smiles at me and shakes her head. "No, that's you. I'm only eight."

I plant my palm on the side of my head mockingly. "Oh, that's right, you're eight!" Reaching out, I tickle her tiny waist, and she instantly bursts into a fit of giggles.

As soon as Derek and Mom are standing next to us, I smile and stand up. Mom wraps herself up in my arms, hugging me tightly to her. She is also much smaller than I remember— almost frail. When I let her go, I notice she has tears in her eyes.

"Hey, don't cry," I say as I hold on to her shoulders.

She gives me a sheepish smile and wipes her cheeks. "I'm just so glad you're back."

I pull her in for another hug and hold her tight, but not too tight. I'm afraid I might break her. "Me too, Mom."

Derek looks at me with pride as he extends his hand for a shake. I release my mom and accept his offer, gripping his hand tight and shaking it.

"Good to see you, Ryan," he says. Derek loosens my hand and claps my shoulder in the way only a father knows how. He and my mom got married right before Thalia was born, and he's been a constant in my life ever since. I'm honestly happy to see him too. He is the perfect father to my little sister and a fantastic husband to my mother.

Though he and I had a rocky start, I'm glad to have him as part of my family.

After we settle the first round of hellos, we file into my parents' car and start the trek home. Thalia is overjoyed when I sit in the backseat with her. I happily buckle in next to her and play I Spy during the drive.

At my mom's suggestion, we stop to grab a bite to eat at our favorite Mexican restaurant. Over an abundance of chips and salsa, Mom and Derek ask many questions about work and life in Germany.

My life has taken a completely different course than I had initially planned. After moving to Germany right after high school, I started working at a company called Bates Industries, which offered me an internship that coincided with my degree plan.

As soon as I graduated with my bachelor's and master's degrees, I worked full time at Bates Industries as a structural engineer. I quickly became close friends with the company's new CEO and assisted in helping the company grow to new levels.

Teddy just recently got married, so he moved Bates from Germany back into the US. It will be easier for him to run his company with its headquarters back in the same country as him.

This couldn't have been better timing for me. I originally planned to stay with Teddy and Bates Industries, but with our clients spread out worldwide, I would have still needed to travel quite a bit. And at this point, my family needs me.

After all this started rolling, I took some time to contemplate what I wanted to do. At the end of the day, I only saw one option—I couldn't stay with Bates Industries. I approached Teddy with the notion that I would be going off and starting my own engineering firm. To my surprise, he was more than supportive and offered to invest in my business to help kick-start the process.

It was one of those moments in life when everything seemed to fall into place perfectly.

Now that I'm officially home, I plan to start looking into renting office space and setting up an LLC so I can begin the venture of opening my own business. It will be a lot of work, but most things in life worth having are, so I'm willing to go the extra mile.

I fill my parents in on all my plans, and they are entirely on board. Derek's mind starts going off with different ideas and suggestions. I nod along, wishing I had asked his opinion long before today. My stepfather seems to have an excellent business sense.

Once my family and I are all stuffed full of tacos and burritos, we head back out to the car. I open the trunk, rummage through my carry-on bag, and then shoot my sister a conspiratorial look. Thalia laughs and raises her eyebrows.

"Now I know you're probably too stuffed for dessert, huh?" I tease her as I hold my surprise behind my back.

Thalia sticks her hands out in a "gimme gimme" gesture, and I hand over my treat. Her little mouth forms an 'O' as she observes her gift.

"Chocolate! Mommy, Ryan got me chocolate!"

I squat down in front of her so we look eye to eye. "Not just any chocolate," I say, tapping the outside wrapper. "That's German chocolate. Only the finest for you, kiddo."

Thalia throws her arms around my neck and hugs me again. "Thank you, thank you, thank you! You're the best big brother ever!" Then she turns to our mother. "Mommy, can I have it right now?"

My mom looks at the two of us with a soft smile and nods gently. "Maybe just a little bit. We've gotta get you home and into bed, young lady."

I ruffle my sister's hair and then load her into her booster seat again. When we arrive home, Thalia is passed out with chocolate smeared all over her face. I unbuckle her seatbelt and carefully carry her inside and to her room while Derek is kind enough to grab my bags.

Thalia's room is awfully girly. The walls are a light purple with yellow and pink daisies stenciled throughout. Her bed has a canopy and a lot of stuffed animals strewn everywhere. Along the perimeter are twinkly fairy lights that give off a soft, calming glow.

I pull back her covers and settle her into bed, pulling off her shoes before tucking her in. Reaching over to her nightstand, I grab a tissue and wipe off the evidence of her chocolate coma.

Such a sweet little girl.

I watch her for a second, sound asleep, before I head back downstairs. I don't see my mom, so she must have also called it an early night. Derek is sitting in the living room, a golf game on the television. With a glass of liquor in his hand, he looks up when he hears my footsteps.

"Hey, thanks for getting her settled in. Your mom was feeling the effects of the excitement, so she headed to sleep." He nods down at his glass. "Can I get you one?"

"Sure."

He gets up and pours me a glass before settling back on the couch. We both sip at the amber liquid, the heaviness of our new reality weighing over us and seeping into the silence. My throat feels thick as my mind spins with questions. Me and my family have been living with this new diagnosis for the last few months, but it still doesn't make the harsh realization of how everything has changed any easier. I finally get the courage to ask my stepfather the first question lingering on the tip of my tongue.

"So, how is she?"

Derek sighs and takes a deep sip. Suddenly, he looks older, the lines on his forehead and around his eyes seeming deeper, more pronounced. "The chemo is scheduled to start on Wednesday. They diagnosed her with stage three. So treatment will be intense, but it's still treatable."

"Geez," I murmur, chest tightening.

"Yeah, neither of us saw this coming. That's why we're so grateful you were able to come home to help with Thalia."

My eyes burn, and I take another sip of my drink, hoping to dampen down the emotion threatening to rise inside of me. For so long, my mom was all I had. The possibility that I may have to face life without her burns in the back of my mind like a nightmare I can't wake up from. Thalia, still being so young, only makes things worse and leaves a sick, nauseous feeling lingering in my stomach that nothing will ease.

I glance over at my stepfather. "Have you guys explained to her what is going on yet?"

Derek shakes his head. "Not really. She knows that Mommy is very sick, even though she doesn't look like she is, and we've told her that her medicine might make her lose her hair. But I don't think she fully grasps the severity of cancer."

"That's probably for the best," I say. "Let her keep her childhood for as long as she can."

"Agreed."

I watch Derek as we sit in silence. The recent diagnosis is taking a significant toll on him as well. His normally dark hair and beard have gotten gray speckles, giving him the salt-and-pepper look. He has dark circles under his eyes, proof of many nights spent awake worrying about his family's future.

Derek has turned out to be the rock my family needed, someone I respect and value as part of our family. After my dad died in the war, it was just me and my mom. If Derek hadn't come around, I wouldn't have Thalia, and my mom may not have been as happy as she is now.

My eyes travel over to the collection of family pictures hanging on the living room wall. They show the story of our family growing and expanding. Only the first one has me, my mom, and my father. The others have transitioned from just me and Mom, to me, Mom and Derek, then to our family of four once Thalia was born.

I think about what my mom is facing with this cancer, and I am immensely glad that I am home to be by her side. Cedar Ridge hasn't been my permanent place of residence for many years, but it has always been my home.

And while the house looks and feels the same, everything about life here is not how I left it eight years ago.

Chapter 2

Ryan

"Here, Ryno, have some more pancakes!" My mother's sweet sing-song voice rings from across the kitchen.

I chuckle. "Really, Mom, I'm fine. I'm full." I glance at my plate, cleared of all the bacon, eggs, and pancakes she piled on twenty minutes ago.

Of course, Mom acts like she doesn't hear a word I say and skips over to me before plopping another full stack of her famous blueberry pancakes onto my plate. "Eat up!"

I groan as I fold up the newspaper I've been reading and set it on the table. "Are you trying to make me explode?"

Mom's blue eyes twinkle with happiness as she watches me dig in. Her pale blonde hair is pulled into a messy ponytail, with tiny wisps still hanging free. I hate to think she may lose her hair since she loves it so much.

"I know it's been a while since you've had a home-cooked meal, Ryno, so I wanted your first breakfast to be memorable!" she exclaims as she kisses my head.

I am almost twenty-seven years old, but I will never not

accept affection from my mother. I grin between mouthfuls of pancakes, and she laughs.

"So, what's on the agenda for today?" my mom asks as she sits beside me at the table.

I swallow my bite and then turn to her. "I need to find a condo or an apartment or something today, and then maybe start the search for some office space," I answer as I take a sip of coffee. "Then I might see Liam and Juliet if they're free."

"Oh, that sounds lovely. Maybe you'll get a chance to catch up with Izabel too. She's teaching up at Bennett, did you know? I ran into her mother at the supermarket recently and we got to chatting.

The pancakes I just swallowed turn to lead as they travel down my throat. *Izabel.*

"Such a sweet girl. It was a shame you two didn't work out," my mom speculates, unaware of the fact that I'm choking to death right next to her. "It seems like she's very happy with that Mark fellow. He's a good guy, from what I hear."

I scowl down at my pancakes, my appetite now officially gone. "Yeah, I'm sure he's just perfect."

I haven't heard from Izabel in years. Since we broke up five years ago, there have been a total of two exchanges between the two of us. Once, when her sister married Teddy, since we were both in the wedding party. I will never forget that night because Izabel and I fell into each other again. It was as if, for that night, everything was okay. We were okay. But as soon as the sun rose the following morning, we returned to square one. She disappeared without a trace, and I didn't hear from her again.

Both instances left me with more heartbreak than I care to admit. It was pathetic. I'm over it, though. We both made our choices, and we both moved on.

"Alright, girly," my mom says, clapping her hands, addressing my little sister. "Time to get you ready for school."

Thalia wipes her face with her napkin before bouncing away from the table and up to her room. My mom turns to me again and gently touches my shoulder.

"I'm sorry if being home causes you pain, Ryan," she whispers. "I know how difficult things got for you after everything."

I sigh and close my eyes. "It's okay, Mom. I'm happy to be back. And besides, Izabel and I are long over. There's nothing there anymore. She's moved on; I've moved on. It's for the best."

Mom looks at me compassionately before nodding and cleaning up after breakfast. Though I still feel sick, I scarf down the rest of my pancakes and rinse my plate before setting it in the dishwasher. I kiss my mom's cheek and then head to my room to prepare for the day.

After spending hours looking for a condo, I finally settle on one that is relatively close to downtown Cedar Ridge, and thankfully, they have a few available units. I schedule an appointment to speak with the landlord, ready to make the leap right away.

Our town isn't huge, but we still have a significant business district to show for the smaller population. Since I will be starting up my own business soon, I figure it's a good idea to be close to where all the magic happens.

After that's settled, I wander back into my bedroom and poke around in the closet, feeling the need to start purging through some of my old things to get ready to officially move out—again.

On the top shelf of my closet are a few boxes that I haven't gone through in years. I'm sure they're filled with old artwork from elementary school or trophies from my glory days on the soccer team at Bennett. As I'm lifting one down, I don't see the stacks of books piled on top, and they all come crashing down as soon as I tilt the box just slightly.

I swear and duck out of the way so they don't whack me in the head. Once the dust has settled, I look around at the carnage, trying to figure out what exactly just dive-bombed me.

My heart gets stuck in my throat when I see a familiar group photo staring up at me from the open yearbook. Of course, out of all the pages that it could have fallen open to, it had to be the one from Camp Wildwood.

A sour feeling settles in my stomach as I crouch down to get a better look. The yearbook is from my junior year, the group photo from our last day at Camp Wildwood for the summer. The guys from Bennett are intermingled with the girls from our sister school, Hawthorne Academy.

My attention instantly goes to where I'm standing in relation to the beautiful girl with the striking blue eyes who seems to haunt every waking thought. I'm standing off to one side with my best friend, and *she* is on the opposite end of the photo.

My heart pangs at the sight of Izabel from all those years ago. It's hard to think that only a year after that photo was taken, things would have changed for us so drastically. I take in junior Izabel, noting that she isn't smiling in the picture. Camp Wildwood was her worst time of the year, and much of that had to do with me.

If I could go back, I would never have made those weeks so miserable for her. I wish I could have just bucked up and admitted that she intrigued me. Maybe then we wouldn't have had to go through everything we did.

But then again, that's the whole reason we were together.

With a sigh, I give one last glance at that picture, memories of Izabel and my time in that shoddy old cabin running through my mind before snapping the book closed and shoving it back onto the top shelf of my closet.

The past is in the past.

* * *

Later that evening, I find myself back in my childhood room. I'm set to move into my new condo next week, and I have a meeting with a landlord about office space tomorrow. A listing popped up right as I checked this afternoon, and I was quick to jump on it. Things are moving right along.

From what it sounds like, I should be able to get into the space this weekend and begin working by Monday. Now, I just need to submit all the paperwork and find an assistant.

Flopping onto my old mattress, I pull my phone out of my pocket. I quickly make an ad online for an assistant for hire, and then roll onto my back, my mind spinning. There is so much to do.

But still, even with the never-ending to-do list, my mind keeps returning to the thought of the girl with the blue eyes. I wonder what she's doing—I wonder *how* she's doing.

Every so often, my thoughts get away from me and they spiral out of control. Is she happy? Does she sometimes miss me like I miss her?

Eventually, I rein it in, reminding myself that it's over.

I could play the *would've, could've, should've* game until I'm blue in the face. But it won't do any good.

I have new ventures to focus on. That needs to be my primary focus.

I'm back to help my mom through this new chapter of her life. I'm back to support Derek and Thalia through it all. I'm back home to start my own business and make a name for myself outside of Bates Industries. I'm back to get my life back on track.

I am not back for her.

Chapter 3

Izabel

"WHAT'S THE MATTER WITH YOU?" MARK'S HARSH TONE draws me out of my daydream.

I look over at him from the passenger seat of the car to see his eyebrows furrowed in concern. Blinking a few times to reorient myself, I shake my head. "Nothing."

"You're awfully quiet over there."

I force a small smile, and then look back out the window. I don't have the heart to fully explain to Mark what's on my mind. I'm not sure how he would react, and I don't have the energy to figure it out firsthand.

The last few weeks have been exhausting.

Midterms at the high school have just finished, which means I'm pulling long evenings trying to complete the grading on my students' midterm essays, and on top of that, gearing up the class for the final semester of materials.

Mark has been *somewhat* supportive throughout the whole thing. My boyfriend doesn't quite understand my passion for teaching. He does well at his law firm. Well enough that I don't have to work—a fact he never forgets to remind me of.

But what he doesn't understand is that I *enjoy* teaching. More so than anything else in my life. It's one of the only things I have to look forward to every day.

So having him nag in my ear, especially when I'm stressed enough as it is, has me falling into retrospective silence.

"Hey," Mark says again. "Cheer up. You're the one who's dragging me to this dumb birthday party. The least you could do is act like you actually want to be here."

I squeeze my eyes shut and wince at Mark's tone.

"Who even throws a birthday party for a one-year-old?" Mark continues to mutter. I open my eyes and glare out the window as he pulls into Juliet and Liam's neighborhood.

"I think pretty much everyone," I say back, trying to make my tone sound as teasing as possible.

I must succeed because Mark chuckles, and some of the tension in my shoulders relaxes. We don't say anything else to each other as he finds a space on the road and parks his car.

Mark and I have been together for almost four years, but still, sometimes, he surprises me by getting bothered by the most minuscule things.

We each get out and walk together up to my best friend's large Victorian-style home. I still am in awe every time I come over. Juliet has done well for herself. She just finished her residency at St. Helen's, the primary hospital in Cedar Ridge. She is now an attending emergency room physician. Liam works part time at Bennett as the head coach for the soccer team and then freelances for an insurance agency.

"I'll just go set this on the gift table," I say once we're inside, holding up the gift bag we brought for Ashton.

"I'll go with you," Mark says, looking around the foyer uncomfortably.

I give him a tight smile, but make my way through the

living room toward the table adorned with gifts for the birthday boy.

It's when I set the gift on the table that I feel it. The hair on the back of my neck stands on end, and every cell in my body comes alive. Unconsciously, my spine straightens, and I look around the room.

My stomach flip-flops when I see him.

Ryan.

I blink a few times, wondering if it's a trick of the light, but no, he's actually here.

"Why the fuck is he here?" Mark growls from beside me, asking the question that is burning in my mind as well. Albeit, my version was much less crude.

"I don't—I don't know," I breathe, and it's the truth.

"Did you know he was back?" he asks, as his glare snaps down to me, accusing me of something I had no part of.

I shake my head wordlessly, my eyes still glued on Ryan. As if he can feel me watching him, his gaze roams over the room and settles on me. A softness fills those eyes I used to know so well, and he watches me with interest. After a moment, he raises the beer in his hand, saluting me with a dip of his chin, and then takes a sip. His eyes never leave me.

I can't believe what I'm seeing. Ryan is back? When? How? Why?

Next to me, Mark huffs in annoyance. "Great, just what we needed. You should probably steer clear of him. Don't want to put new salt in old wounds, you know?"

"Yeah," I whisper. I hope Mark can't hear the way my heart thunders inside my chest or see the way my muscles have gone rigid. He traces his hand down my side and takes my hand, giving it a small squeeze.

Mark would probably fall over dead if he knew what was running through my head right now, but I can't help it.

Ryan. Ryan. It's Ryan. He's here.

I take a few seconds to trail my eyes her my ex-lover across the room. I observe the broad shoulders I used to clutch and his dark hair I used to tangle my fingers in. That same sharp jawline, now with a bit of scruff that I used to press kisses to. And those eyes I would find myself getting lost in.

He looks good.

He is even more filled out since the last time I saw him, now looking more like a man rather than the boy I loved.

I recall the last time we encountered each other when Ryan's boss, Teddy, married my sister, Sage. We were just as magnetic then as I feel we are now. Though there's a whole room of distance between us, I can feel him as though he were right next to me. My body responds to him being so near, as if no time has passed at all.

Butterflies erupt in my stomach as I remember the last time Ryan held my hand as he led me to his hotel room. How careful he was as he unzipped my bridesmaid's dress, letting his fingers linger longer than necessary on my bare back and over the ridges of my spine. How he—

No.

That was then. This is now.

I finally tear my eyes away from Ryan and look down at the floor. Mark's right. It's probably a good idea to keep to myself tonight. I shake off the memories and allow Mark to lead me into another room. But the entire way, I can feel Ryan's gaze on me until I'm out of his sight.

Mark leads me through the living room and into the dining room, where Juliet is busy feeding the birthday boy spoonfuls of applesauce. As soon as I set my eyes on her son, Ashton, I feel a smile form on my lips.

Juliet glances up as soon as we get closer, and her eyes light up. "Hey, guys! I was wondering when you were going to get here!"

"We got a little...distracted," Mark says, squeezing my hand suggestively. I blush and look away, wishing he wouldn't be so brash sometimes. Not to mention, his superfluous insinuation makes the moment seem a little more thrilling than it actually was.

Juliet raises an eyebrow with a smirk. "I'm sure. Well, help yourselves to some food. I'm just going to finish up here, and we'll cut his cake."

"Did Liam do the grilling today?" Mark asks.

Juliet nods and scoops another spoonful. "Sure did. We've got hotdogs and burgers, so help yourselves. All the fixings are on the counter."

As soon as we're out of the dining room and heading into the kitchen, Mark pulls me to the side. "I think we should probably just wait to have dinner ourselves later."

I frown at him. "Why?"

He gives me a sheepish but serious look. "I don't really trust Liam's grilling. It's always only half-cooked."

I laugh, despite myself, and pat him on the cheek. "I think we'll probably live. If you're worried, have a hot dog. They're pre-cooked."

Mark's hand covers my own on his cheek, and he leans down to kiss me, his lips pressing against mine gently. "You're right. Here, why don't you go back and sit with Jules, and I'll make you a plate."

I kiss him again before heading back to Jules's side. As soon as I'm settled, I scan the room to make sure Ryan hasn't snuck in without me knowing. The last thing I need is a confrontation between Mark and Ryan. That would be one surefire way to ruin a birthday party.

Mark has never been a fan of Ryan's. Even as far back as

when we were in high school. Ryan Miller was always the golden boy, and I think Mark got overshadowed one too many times.

On top of that, Mark was with me throughout Ryan's and my entire long-distance relationship. Not that Ryan specifically did anything wrong, but the distance wore us both down. Mark was always the one there to cheer me up when I was feeling blue.

I think Mark probably still holds a little resentment for Ryan putting me through that. When I told Mark that Ryan and I had broken up, he wasn't the least bit sympathetic. I'm pretty sure his exact words were, "Good, you can do much better than that tool."

"Where'd your loser boyfriend go?" Juliet mutters under her breath.

I look over at her and bristle. Just as Mark doesn't like Ryan, Juliet likes Mark even less. "He's getting food. He said I could come and sit with you."

"You can, can you?"

"Unless you don't want me to," I fire back. Juliet sits up straighter and narrows her eyes at me, sensing the challenge in my words.

The two of us stare at each other until she finally caves. Her shoulders drop, and she gives me an apologetic smile. "Sorry, Izzie. I just don't like the way he controls you sometimes."

I raise my eyebrows. "Mark isn't controlling me. He offered to get me food."

We've had this conversation hundreds of times. I'm not sure what Juliet's issue is. I don't see anything wrong with what Mark's done. In fact, I think it was sweet of him to offer to get me a plate while I hung out with my friend.

Juliet took the news of the breakup between Ryan and me

pretty hard. She's always been holding out hope that Ryan and I could set aside our differences and get back together. I honestly thought she was going to throw me in the lake when I told her I had started dating Mark officially.

She has never gotten along with him. Whenever I bring anything up to her about our relationship, she'll glare at me and say, "Well, he's just not Ryan, is he?"

I understand where she's coming from. I do. Ryan was an amazing first boyfriend, the best I could have ever asked for. I just wish she would let it go. It's been years. Ryan is the past, and Mark is my future. It's not fair to Ryan or me to keep questioning what could've been.

"Hey, baby," Mark greets me as he returns with two plates. He sets one down in front of me: chips and veggies and a hot dog with no bun. I look over at his plate, and it's exactly the same. No sign of a single hamburger. I press my lips together, fighting back an amused chuckle.

I quickly demolish my food and do my best to chat with Juliet. She's not fully engaged with Mark sitting next to me, and she's too eager to run off when someone calls her name. When she excuses herself, I scoot over into her chair to play with Ashton.

I feel Mark's eyes on me and turn around to face him. He's grinning at me with a dopey look on his face. His chocolate brown eyes are warm and gentle.

"What?" I ask, unable to keep myself from smiling back at him.

"Nothing," he says, and his lips twitch. "You just look good with a baby.

I flush and turn back to Ashton, who's now smacking his hands in a small puddle of applesauce on his highchair tray. Mark scoots closer to me and rests a gentle hand on my shoulder. He leans in close and presses a kiss against my hair. I can't help the shiver that shoots down my back.

"Maybe we'll have one or two of our own someday, hm?" he whispers in my ear before pressing another kiss to the side of my head. My lower belly clenches.

I turn to meet his eyes and give him an unsure smile. Babies?

"I don't think we're there yet," I say softly. "But yeah, maybe someday."

"Well, I think we're closer than you think," he says with a wink.

I'm suddenly immensely glad that I still have my IUD. I decide then to double-check my calendar when I get home to confirm when I need to get it replaced. I am definitely not ready for a baby with Mark, no matter how close he thinks we are.

I love Mark. We've been together for years now. The first year was a little rocky, as we went through a lot of petty arguments and breakups, but we made it. We've been happy ever since.

I have mixed feelings about being Mark's fiancée. Mark and I have been together so long, it's the obvious next step. I should be excited about that prospect, looking forward to the moment Mark finally gets down on one knee and pops the big question, but something is holding me back from feeling that full-blown enthusiasm toward wearing his ring on my finger. Though the idea makes my heart race, I'm not entirely convinced it's from excitement.

Juliet finally comes back in, holding a single-serve chocolate cake. Liam is hot on her trail, holding his phone up to record. She plops it down on Ashton's tray and lights a candle shaped like a number one. A small crowd of party guests has gathered, and we all sing *"Happy Birthday"* to Ashton, who has no idea what's going on. Juliet and Liam help him blow out the candle, and then they set the little boy loose.

Ashton looks at his parents as though asking permission, and then goes for it. Icing and cake crumbs are everywhere as the kid takes giant handfuls, pressing them into his mouth greedily. The crowd murmurs with laughter.

Juliet excuses herself again to go cut the real cake while we all watch her son in amusement. Ashton now has chocolate all over his face and his clothes and isn't even close to calling it quits.

I follow my friend back into the kitchen to see if I can help with anything. She's got the big sheet cake on the counter and a knife in hand. It's a white-frosted cake with tie-dye icing flowers squeezed into the corners. In the middle, it says *Happy First Birthday, Ashton*, in bright blue icing.

The paper plates are at the ready as she makes the first cut. We talk mindlessly, her about work and me about school, as she plates the pieces of cake. Then she has me set them out on the table in the main hall for people to grab. I take a few at a time, walking into the hall and safely setting them down with no issue.

As I turn around after my latest trip, a band of boys flies in from the living room, chasing each other with fake swords.

The kids rush around me, pushing and pressing, and I stumble back, my feet getting tangled. I can't catch my balance soon enough, and I'm sure I'm going to wipe out on the floor. I can't wait to hear what Mark will have to say about that. As I start to fall, I'm already dreading that conversation.

But I don't fall.

Instead, I find myself caught in a pair of strong arms and swept up until I'm pressed against a firm chest. My heart stutters as Ryan looks down at me, giving me a wide grin.

"Gotta be careful around here," he says, his voice rumbling low in his chest. "There are some wild creatures in these parts."

I blink at him before common sense takes over. Quickly, I stand up and straighten my shirt. Amusement is still sketched across Ryan's face as he watches me, his eyes twinkling.

"Thank you," I say under my breath.

"You're welcome, Bells," he responds, and I think my heart goes into full cardiac arrest.

Bells.

I haven't heard that nickname on his lips in years.

Ryan observes me for another moment or two. Both of us stand there in silence, taking each other in. Ryan, with his hands stuffed in his pockets, and me, with my arms wrapped protectively around my waist.

My chest hurts as I realize we're practically strangers. It hurts even worse with that realization, knowing how much he meant to me once and vice versa. But I don't know him now. I don't know anything about him other than that he looks gorgeous standing before me.

I want to wrap my arms around him, just to be close to him, to feel him against me one more time.

But I can't.

"Well," he says finally, breaking the silence. "I was actually on my way out, so... It was good seeing you, Bells. You look good." His lips tighten into a smirk. "Tell Marky Mark I said *hi*."

My eyes widen at him as he turns on his heel and walks away. I want to call after him, make him stop, and draw me into his arms again, but I don't. He grabs his coat out of the closet and walks out the front door without another glance. Then, feeling another set of eyes on me, I turn to see Mark sitting in the living room. His eyes are narrowed, and I instantly know he witnessed the whole exchange.

My shoulders slump, defeated, as I know Mark will let me know just how much he's bothered by our little interlude, no matter how innocent it was. Instead of waiting around for him to say something, I head back into the kitchen. I'm sure Juliet is wondering where I disappeared to.

The party continues on. We all enjoy our cake—maybe not as much as the birthday boy—and move into the living room for presents. It's a big show, and while Ashton loves the toys his parents help him unwrap, he keeps getting distracted by the wrapping paper.

We all watch and cheer him on as he moves from present to present. Mark sits next to me, a hand over my knee. He grins widely when Ashton loves the toy we picked out for him. I smile too.

His hand tightens as soon as Ashton turns his attention to his next gift. I look over at Mark to see him watching me, his eyes narrowed ever so slightly.

He leans forward and murmurs, "Don't think I've forgotten what I saw, Izabel. We *will* be discussing whatever that was."

A chill runs down my spine, but I nod my head. Without a response, I turn back to Ashton and force myself to have fun for the remainder of the party. It works, and I do enjoy myself immensely, but still, I catch myself glimpsing back at the front door every few minutes, wishing the only person I want to see right now would walk back in.

Chapter 4

Izabel

THE FOLLOWING MORNING, I WAKE UP TO THE FAMILIAR smell of coffee brewing and the delectable mix of pancakes and maple syrup. I stretch out in bed, noting a slight soreness to my muscles. I slept terribly last night, unable to quiet my racing mind, which resulted in me tossing and turning all hours of the night.

I reach for my phone sitting on the nightstand on my side of the bed and check the time. Surprise rises through me when I realize I've slept late into the morning. It's almost ten-thirty already.

The sound of a crash and Mark's familiar deep voice swearing in the kitchen finally has me tossing the covers off and sliding out of bed. I pad through the already opened bedroom door, down the hallway and into the kitchen.

After the party yesterday, Mark practically insisted that I come over to his place to spend the night. My head and my heart were a mess after seeing Ryan, so it wasn't my first choice, but Mark had been so persistent that I couldn't say no.

I'm surprised when I see my boyfriend standing in front of the stove, wiping up a mess of spilled white powder.

I make my presence known as I saunter up to him, wrapping my arm around his side and leaning my head on his shoulder. He looks down at me, a bit startled, but his expression morphs into one of fondness.

"Good morning. I was wondering when you were gonna wake up." He leans over and presses a kiss to the top of my head. My stomach flutters at the gesture.

"What's happening in here?" I question, pulling away and looking up at him before turning my pointed gaze to the mess of flour all over the stove and countertop.

Mark clears his throat and chuckles sheepishly. "I thought I'd surprise you with a nice breakfast. But turns out the pancakes got the best of me."

I pat his shoulder before walking over to the sink and wetting a rag. "It was a nice thought, really. But do you want me to take over?" I fight off the smile threatening to pull on my lips.

"Maybe that would be for the best."

With an amused shake of my head, I do just that. I reach for the bowl and the whisk and start from scratch, measuring out the proper amounts of each ingredient before mixing it together into a batter with perfect consistency. Mark steps away and lets me take the helm, choosing to sit over at the kitchen table. He watches me with a satisfied smile, and I can't deny that it makes everything seem better this morning.

I wasn't sure what version of Mark I was going to wake up to after yesterday's events. He had been in a foul mood all night following the run-in with Ryan, even after I had agreed to stay the night to quell whatever possessive feelings he was experiencing. But it's a relief to know that I get the sunny version of him rather than the broody, irritable one. This more playful side of him doesn't come out very often anymore.

When the pancakes are perfectly golden and stacked onto a plate, I shuffle over to where he's sitting. After setting the pancakes down, I grab each of us another plate and utensils, along with the syrup and butter so we can dig in.

Mark eagerly picks up his fork and knife before shooting me a grin. "These look great, babe."

I settle in my seat and smile back, a sense of pride blooming in my chest. Mark digs into his breakfast, making a satisfied sound when the first bite of pancake hits his tongue. He gives me an appreciative nod, and I smile even wider before taking a bite of my own.

As we eat our breakfast, I watch him closely, waiting for the ball to drop. Mark hasn't been this pleasant in what feels like days—weeks. And even though I'm enjoying it, I can't help but feel like there's a giant *but* waiting to drop.

It finally comes as soon as Mark has finished his breakfast and has pushed away his plate. He turns to me, studying me with those brown eyes in a way that makes me squirm. Once I finish my own breakfast, I shoot him a questioning look.

"What is it?" I ask, my voice hesitant.

"You know, I got to thinking yesterday." I bite my tongue, not liking where this is going already. "We've been together such a long time."

Blinking at him, I nod, still waiting for him to get to his point.

Mark stares at me for a moment, a wide, disconcerting smile apparent on his lips. He finally reaches into the pocket of his sweats and pulls something out, palming it right onto the table. When he removes his hand and reveals what he was hiding, everything comes to a screeching halt.

A giant diamond ring stares up at me and sends my mind rushing into a tailspin.

I can hear my heartbeat echo in my ears and my vision jars just slightly as my brain tries to catch up with what my eyes are seeing.

I realize I'm silent for a bit too long when Mark's voice rattles me out of my stupor.

"Well?" Mark asks, pulling me out of my whirlwind thoughts.

"What?" I ask weakly.

He gives me a sharp look that instantly has me feeling foolish. "Are you going to give me an answer?" His eyes fall to the enormous diamond ring sitting on the table, as if to give me a not-so-subtle hint as to what he's talking about.

"Oh, um—" I stare at the diamond now too, watching as it glints from the overhead lighting.

"Come on, Izabel," Mark groans. His voice is impatient now. "This is the next obvious step for us. It's not like this hasn't been coming. It's not spur of the moment, out of the blue."

Well, it kind of is, I want to say, but I don't, knowing that would only set him off.

"The fact that you look even remotely undecided right now is like a knife to the heart, baby," Mark pleads. He hits me with wide eyes, and my heart softens a bit for him. "Please, just say yes. I know you love me just as much as I love you. This is the next step for us."

I take a deep breath, feeling conflicted. The timing of this whole thing has me on edge. But he's right. We've been together for years; this was going to come at some point. I look down at the ring and slowly nod my head. "Okay. Yes."

Mark jolts out of his chair with a *whoop*. The sudden action has me flinching and backing away. He doesn't seem to notice my unease because he wraps me in his arms and pulls me up until I'm standing right against him. He hugs me so tightly that my feet leave the floor.

"See! I knew you'd say yes." He sets me down and cups my face in his large hands, tilting my face up to his and pressing a firm kiss on my lips.

When he lets me go, his face is beaming. It's a sight that has me smiling back and finally getting excited about the prospect of *saying yes*. Mark reaches for the diamond ring still sitting on the table, and then takes my left hand before sliding it onto my ring finger.

He whistles, grinning boyishly at me. "Yeah, I knew that rock would look good on your hand. You deserve some bling like that to make sure everyone knows who you belong to."

I smile tightly, looking down at the ring on my finger. Something about his sentence rubs me the wrong way, but I bite my tongue, not sure how to verbalize it.

Mark gives my hand one long, lingering look before he gives a satisfied nod. "Well, I'm sorry to bail on such a momentous occasion. I didn't think you were going to sleep in that late, and I have a ten-thirty tee time with my dad." He looks at his watch for emphasis before leaning in and kissing me on the cheek. "Maybe we can get dinner tonight and celebrate, though."

What little strand of excitement I felt quickly deflates when I realize he's leaving. To go golfing. Not even spending five minutes with me after asking me to marry him.

So romantic.

I know that asking him to stay would be useless. When he makes his mind up to do something, all bets are off. So I give him another wane smile and nod. "Sure, dinner sounds great."

He kisses me again, his grin still set in place. "You pick, whatever you want."

"Okay," I murmur.

Within the next fifteen minutes, Mark is gone.

More recently, Mark has prodded me with questions asking how I wanted to be proposed to. If I wanted something lavish or simple, extravagant or to the point. And each time he brought it up, I got so flustered that I could barely give him a straight response.

So really, I suppose this lackluster engagement is because I couldn't make up my mind.

But even then, I can't help but be a little disappointed that he apparently put little to no effort into the ordeal.

Now that I'm alone, I can't help but wonder about the timing of the proposal too. Last night after leaving Ashton's birthday party, Mark had been in a foul mood. He didn't seem to believe me when I told him that I had no idea Ryan Miller was back in town. He had yelled at me as soon as we were on our way home, and I tried to convince him that I wasn't lying.

Because I wasn't.

I was still reeling a little bit from seeing him standing there as if it were the most normal thing ever. A little warning would have been nice...not that I expected it from him, but Juliet must have known he was back, and she didn't give me any type of heads up.

Curiosity is getting the better of me, and I'm dying to know *why* he's back.

And I want to know what's going to happen. Where do we go from here? Is he going to join in our friend group again, just like old days? Of course he will. After all, it was basically *his* friend group to start with. I was just an add on with my friendship with Juliet.

Speaking of Juliet, I suppose I have to share the exciting news of my new engagement with my best friend. But knowing she'll be less than ecstatic puts a damper on the whole thing.

So, I don't.

Instead, I clean up the kitchen and grab my things to go back to my apartment. On my way home, I stop at the park and decide to go for a brief walk, hopefully to clear my head and get my thoughts straight.

With every step, rather than thinking about wedding related things like invitations or wedding dates or dresses, my mind returns to Ryan.

I try not to think about how backwards that fact is, but it's no use.

Is he as twisted up about seeing me again as I am about him?

It's so strange feeling so unmoored when it comes to Ryan. For so long, we were perfectly in sync, the second half to each other in every possible way.

But then that ended, and ever since then, I just haven't felt that grounded feeling that I became so used to whenever he was around.

By the time I decide to go home, my head is throbbing, exhausted from spinning around in circles, all having to do with Ryan Miller.

I decide that I'm going to have to get to the bottom of his return, one way or another. If not for anything other than closure. I feel like that's not too much to ask with his returning to our small town.

Doubt blooms in my chest as I catch sight of the glittering ring. I wonder how he'll react to the new piece of bling sitting on my finger.

Maybe I should get him a present? A welcome home gift? That might help ease some of the inevitable tension.

The thought surprises me, but once it settles in, I don't think it's a terrible idea. I start brainstorming about what he might like, and for some reason that brings me more excitement than what I've felt all morning.

Once I'm back home, I settle in on the couch and pull out my phone. I bring up Juliet's contact information and then press the call button.

She answers on the second ring with an airy, "Hey."

I take a deep breath. "I need you to tell me everything you know about why Ryan Miller is back in Cedar Ridge."

Chapter 5

Ryan

I'm having a bad morning.

As I walk into my new office, I scowl as Lori, my secretary, raises amused eyebrows at my appearance. "What the hell happened to you?" she questions.

I frown as I remember the car that swerved directly in front of me right as I was taking a sip of coffee. I slammed on my brakes and my coffee went all over my shirt. Now my white button-up has a lovely coffee stain all down the front. I didn't have time to go home and change before my first meeting this morning, so here I am.

Instead of filling Lori in on this tale, I grumble, "I'm having a Monday," and stride into my office, shutting the door behind me.

Lori and I have only been working closely together for a few weeks at this point, so this is the first time she's really gotten to see me in a morning slump. Typically, I try to leave everything out of the office, but today seems to be an exception.

It definitely is the Monday-est of Mondays, but if I'm honest, it has been a rough few days in general.

I had not been prepared for the effect that seeing Izabel Sanders again would have on me. Being that close to her again wrecked me from the inside out. I'm not sure if it was worse holding her in my arms, knowing that I might never get to again, or having to watch her be all cuddly with her boyfriend for the entire afternoon.

The hot fire of jealousy burned in my stomach at the first touch of his hand on hers, and I nearly reverted to caveman instincts whenever he kissed her. I knew he was doing it to taunt me. Every time Mark would lean over to press his lips to her cheek, his eyes would dart up to mine, letting me know exactly what he was trying to do. It was as if he knew where I was at all times yesterday during that party, and he never hesitated once to stake his claim on her.

Even thinking about it now has a ball of fury welling up in my chest.

I had been on my way out, unable to stomach seeing Mark draped all over Izabel anymore. But then she was there, falling clumsily backward and into my arms after being run over by kids.

It was as though the earth finally righted itself on its axis and all the stars and planets were aligned simultaneously.

We are both older now, but I was surprised at how familiar holding her felt. How having her weight against me and her hands clutching me brought a sense of peace I had almost forgotten. It was too much.

Even now, it's too much for me to think about. I shake my head and throw my briefcase onto my desk, flopping back in my chair and getting settled for the day. I let my face fall into my hands and close my eyes for a second, my head still spinning over the events of the weekend.

After I left that god-forsaken party, I went straight to the liquor store and got some liquid comfort. That evening, I indulged in one too many, trying to ease the pain of seeing Izabel again. Before I knew it, half the bottle was gone. Yesterday, I did my best to shake it off and keep busy. I ran errands and did some chores over at my mom's house. But once evening fell again, the thoughts came chasing back, and I threw the rest of the liquor back like it was nothing.

I groan at the thought of it. That was a serious lapse in judgment. I'm too old to be doing that.

A hesitant tap on my door has me glancing up. Lori cracks open the door and peeks her head in before allowing herself entry. She's holding a mug of steaming coffee in her hands and raises it like a peace offering.

I give her a weak smile and beckon her farther into my office.

"That's a hangover if I've ever seen one," she speculates as she comes up to my desk and sets the coffee down. "Must have been a really shitty weekend to have you looking like this on a beautiful Monday morning. Want to talk about it?"

Lori has been my saving grace. When she sent in her application almost a month ago, I never realized just how vital of a team member she'd become. She has been pivotal in helping me get my small office established, even going as far as bringing some old, unused furniture and home decor from her home to help furnish the space and make it more inviting. Thank goodness, because I wouldn't have thought of that.

I take a grateful sip of the coffee, appreciating the familiar burn down my throat. This is exactly what I needed. If only my last cup hadn't ended up all over my shirt.

"Thank you, Lori, but I'd rather not talk about it," I say with a shake of my head.

Lori nods in understanding. "Alright, well, if you ever need an ear, I'm right out front." She heads toward the door before turning around to face me again. "And you tell that girl who's got you all twisted in knots that she doesn't know what she's missing."

I laugh, even though it's not funny, and she tosses me a wink before heading back to her desk. Setting my coffee mug down, I open my laptop and get to work. I have a meeting in just a few minutes, and I have to get my head right.

The work sucks me in, drowning out any other lingering thoughts of the terrible weekend. Lori runs to lunch and grabs me a sandwich and another coffee from the café next door. Before I know it, I've checked off almost all of my tasks for the day. All I have to do is return some phone calls and I'll be on my way.

I'm jotting down a note on a sticky-pad when I hear a commotion out in the lobby. Lori is talking to someone, rather loudly.

"Excuse me, you can't just go in there!" Lori hollers as my office door flies open.

Next thing I know, I'm staring wide-eyed at Izabel. Her eyebrows are bunched together in confusion as she takes me in. I stand up immediately and she takes a step forward.

"What are you doing here?" I ask.

"Why do you have coffee all over your shirt?"

I glance down at my stained shirt and grimace. Running a hand through my hair, I look back at her and give her a sheepish smirk. "It was a long morning."

Her lips twitch. "And you have glasses?"

I chuckle now, and pull my glasses off my face, tossing them onto my desk. It takes a moment for my eyes to adjust. The glasses are just for work. Staring at the small print and screens for hours on end was starting to give me headaches, so I got these to fix the issue.

"I'm almost twenty-seven, Izabel. That's only three years away from thirty."

Izabel rolls her eyes. "You're so dramatic."

I step around and desk and lean on the edge, crossing my arms over my chest. Her gaze falls to my arms, and I watch her eyes flare. "What are you doing here?"

"I think I should be asking you the same thing, Ryan."

I motion around the room. "This is my office."

Izabel rolls her eyes again and gives me an exasperated look. "I mean *here*. I didn't know you were coming home."

"Why would you have?" I ask bluntly. Izabel rears back a bit at my hard tone. "We haven't spoken in what? Two years?" Memories of how beautiful she looked at her sister's wedding flash in the back of my mind, but I dampen them, focusing more on the present.

"I just thought I would have heard about you coming back through the grapevine. I mean—" She swallows. "It just took me by surprise. Seeing you. Then to find out you've been home for a while was an even bigger surprise."

"Were you expecting me to call you personally to let you know?"

Izabel flinches and then balks. I feel a little bad. "No, of course not—"

I stick my hands in my pockets and observe her. "It was a family matter that brought me home. Nothing to do with you, so if you were worried about that, don't be."

Izabel looks a little relieved, and I can't deny that hurts. Even if I was back for her, would she even want me back? She and Mark seem to be doing just fine.

Izabel reaches up to tuck a strand of hair behind her ear. A bright sparkle catches my eye, and I reach for her before I can stop myself, my heart sinking.

I grab her left hand and splay her fingers. Her fourth finger now adorns a giant diamond that wasn't there two days ago. My blood boils, and I clench my jaw at the sight. Swallowing down my irritation, I force myself to keep it together. The timing is a little too convenient for me to ignore. Even though I have no proof, something tells me this has everything to do with me making an appearance.

"Well, looks like congratulations are in order," I mutter as I twist her hand left and right, inspecting the gaudy ring.

She snatches her hand back and looks at the ground. "Thanks."

I go back to my position against my desk and cross my arms again. "It's a bit much, don't you think? The ring?"

The rock is enormous. As if a beacon from her hand, letting every other man within a 50-mile radius know she's spoken for.

Izabel's eyes meet mine, and she stays silent for a moment too long, giving me my answer.

It is a bit much.

If I know anything about Izabel, it's that less is more. She is more concerned with the intimacy of things rather than extravagance. When I planned to propose to her, I would've made it just the two of us—candles, champagne, soft music. In my mind, I picture the simple solitaire set ring sitting in my sock drawer. That was her ring, and it would've looked perfect sitting on her finger.

A wave of nostalgia and regret sweeps over me as I observe the beautiful woman in front of me. She could've been my wife. Weekend mornings, she would've been the first thing I saw when I opened my eyes. Weekday nights, getting home from work and having meals together before cuddling on the couch and watching our favorite shows. Proudly introducing her as *Izabel Miller*, my *wife*.

I shake my head, pulling myself out of the spiral I'm quickly falling into.

"How'd he do it?" I ask, torturing myself further.

Izabel shakes her head. "It wasn't anything big. He just asked me over brunch yesterday."

"Were you surprised?"

"Definitely. I mean, we've talked about it. And he alluded to something on Saturday. But I didn't see it coming." Her eyes grow wide, and she shakes her head again with a breathy laugh. "I don't know why I'm even telling you this."

I shrug as if I'm not dying on the inside. "'Cause I asked."

When her eyes meet mine, they twinkle, gutting me. She reaches for the strap of her bag on her shoulder. "I almost forgot, I got you something."

"Me?"

Izabel nods and then holds out a small gift bag. It's blue with a silver ribbon tied around the handles. "Think of it as a welcome home gift slash office warming present." When I don't immediately grab for it, she urges forward. "Just take it already."

I reach for the bag. It's heavier than I anticipated, the weight sagging in the middle. My fingers nimbly untie the silver ribbon, letting the bag fall open. Inside, I see the present wrapped in blue tissue paper but surrounded by pieces of confetti.

My eyes narrow as I grab a piece of the confetti, realizing they're actually small pieces of folded up paper.

I set the bag on my desk and unfold it. I'm surprised when I see Izabel's own handwriting scrawled across the paper. Her penmanship looks the same as it did all those years ago—her hand's gentle swirl, looping letters together in a neat half-cursive pattern. I'm sure I still have some of her handwritten letters stashed away somewhere.

I eye whatever she's written curiously.

There are three towns in the United States called 'Santa Claus.'

I look to Izabel, confused, and she grins. I reach into the bag and grab another piece of confetti.

Ketchup was sold in the 1830s as medicine.

I now look at her in amusement.

"It's forty-five things you don't know," she explains. "I thought it would be funny since it's been years since I've riddled you with fun facts. I have to make up for lost time."

I bark out a laugh and grin at her, appreciative of the thoughtful gift. I look over each fun fact a little more, struck by how much time she must've put into this, finding each fact and piecing them together with care. Her fun facts are something that might be meaningless to anyone else. Even after all this time, there's something nostalgic about her sharing this side of herself with me. "Thanks, Bells. I love it."

"That's not the actual present, though. That was just for fun." She urges me to go back into the bag. I do and pull out the heavy object. I can tell it's a book the minute I pick it up. Its hardcover presses into my hand. I tear off the tissue paper and read the front cover.

"*The Obstacle is the Way: The Timeless Art of Turning Trials into Triumph.*"

"I wasn't sure if I should even bother getting you a book since, you know, you don't read as much as I do. But I've heard a lot about this one, and I thought it would be a good office warming gift," Izabel rambles as I peruse the back cover.

"This is great," I say. "I'm sure this will be a great reference. Thank you so much, Bells."

She glows at the nickname. I noticed this same reaction at the birthday party too. Softness fills her eyes for a second and I'm drawn to her. Before she has the chance to protest, I've pulled her into my arms and pressed her against my chest in a warm hug.

Izabel stiffens for a moment before she allows herself to

relax in my embrace. Her head rests against my shoulder as her arms wrap around my waist. I hold her against me, relishing the feeling.

With her in my arms again, I finally feel like I'm home. Her heartbeat strums against my chest, the pulse rapid just like mine.

I know I should let her go. I have to draw the boundary line in the sand. For us, I suspect the line from friendly to intimate could easily be crossed. *She's engaged*, she's not mine.

I know this, but I don't want to let her go. It's as if while I'm holding her close to me, all those years of loneliness and desperation are slowly fading away. Maybe it's the way she's clutching me, or how her scent engulfs my senses, but for the first time in a long, long time, everything feels right.

We stay in our embrace for a moment too long. My heart aches at the thought of releasing her, but I do.

When I step away, I meet her eyes to see her watching me from under her lashes. A soft flush is creeping up her neck, and her lips are pressed into a thin line. I shove my hands into my pockets so I don't reach for her again.

The line has been drawn.

The silence is deafening, but when I open my mouth to say something, anything, a knock on the door reverberates through the room. Both of us startle, not expecting the interruption.

Lori cracks open the door and glances between the two of us, a knowing smirk on her face. Izabel blushes and digs into her bag, trying to look busy.

"Sorry to interrupt. Ryan, Ms. Stevenson is on the line for you," Lori says, amusement in her tone.

I rub the back of my neck and nod at my assistant. "Thank you, I'll take it in here."

Once Lori steps away, Izabel looks at me with a guilty expression. "I guess that's my cue. I'll get out of your hair."

"Thanks again for the present."

Izabel gives me a small smile. "You're welcome. I'm glad you're home, Ryan."

My chest warms with her admission. Izabel observes me for another second before she turns and leaves. As soon as she's gone, the emptiness within my chest reopens. I rub my fist against my sternum, trying to relieve the ache.

Izabel has always had this kind of effect on me. That woman could wreck me, single-handedly.

My pulse thrums as I walk around my desk, replaying every moment of that interaction in my head. What I would give to go back in time and hold on to her as tightly as I could. If I had the chance, I'd never ever let her go again.

But now she's engaged.

To *Mark.*

Nausea sets root in my stomach, and I take a deep breath in through my nose to try to quell it.

As soon as I'm in my chair, I reach for my phone, picking up on line one. Back to work. "Ms. Stevenson, this is Ryan Miller. Thank you for returning my call."

I force myself back into business mode, focusing on my job. I have to think about this rationally, so I don't royally fuck everything up again. Izabel loves Mark, she must. Otherwise, she wouldn't have said yes to his proposal.

So then why does it bother me this much?

Because it's her.

No matter how much I try to convince myself or anyone else, it's useless—I'm definitely not over Izabel, even after all this time.

Chapter 6

Ryan

LIAM'S GROAN REVERBERATES THROUGH THE BAR AS I SINK the 8-ball into the pocket. I look over at my friend and grin victoriously. He glowers at me as he leans over our table, his head buried in his arms. Walking over, I pat him on the shoulder.

"There, there."

Liam shrugs my hand off his shoulder and stands up, shooting me a glare. "That's the third time you've beaten me, Miller. You sure you ain't a pool shark?"

I lean against my pool cue and smirk. "I'll never tell my secrets."

Todd watches us with amusement as he refills his glass with beer from the pitcher. We've been here for a few hours now. The guys offered to take me out for my birthday: nothing terribly exciting, just a few guys in a bar with beers and pool.

I'm honestly having a blast.

It's been a while since I had a guys' night with anyone other than Teddy. Liam and Todd are so busy these days that it's been hard to get us all together. They concocted the plan without me knowing until the last moment. Much to my surprise, though, they fully delivered on a good birthday celebration.

"Rematch," Liam growls, standing up and stalking back over to the table where he re-racks the balls. "I break this time."

I shake my head as I watch my friend. "That's not going to give you an advantage. You broke last time."

"Bet?" he all but snarls in my direction. I know it's in jest, but it amuses me greatly that he's so bothered. "I'm onto you, Miller."

From what I've gathered, it's been a while since Liam was allowed out of the house. With his wife, Juliet, just now getting out of her residency and into an attending position, and a one-year-old at home, he's been booked solid. Thankfully, a lot of Liam's work can be done from home, which allows him the chance to spend time with his son during the day.

Todd chuckles from his seat. I've offered to let him play, but he says he's having too much fun watching me hand Liam's ass to him.

"How's the biz going, Ryan?" Todd asks, as Liam positions his cue and breaks the pool balls with a *crack*. They scatter across the table in a mess of solids and stripes.

"It's good," I say, watching Liam scowl. He takes aim and sinks a solid. "I've got a few projects lining up."

"I heard Izabel paid you a visit," Liam says and sinks another solid.

I raise my eyebrows at him. I hadn't told anyone of her impromptu raid on my office. "How'd you hear that?"

Liam glances at me after he misses his next shot. "Your turn. Try not to miss. And Jules and Izabel tell each other everything. Mostly."

"Mostly?" I line up my shot.

My opponent stands to the side and rocks back and forth on

his cue. I hope it falls out from underneath him. I would laugh for days. "Izabel is not allowed to comment on Jules's parenting techniques, and Jules is not allowed to talk about Mark, other than to ask how he is."

Mark.

His name thunders through my head, and I miss my next shot. Liam rubs his hands together in glee, no doubt thinking about how he's two up from me.

"What's with that guy? For real."

Liam looks up from where he's aiming and glances over at Todd. Todd shrugs, and Liam's attention goes back to the game at hand.

"Mark's a jackass," Todd answers.

"And he will never eat my damn burgers. I can grill a mean burger," Liam grumbles. I ignore him and respond to Todd's assessment.

"I know that already. I've known that from day one." Every encounter I've had with him since high school has been less than ideal.

"Yeah, well, now he's a next-level jackass."

"How so?" I prod him.

Todd looks at me warily. "He's super type-A. Loud. Arrogant. Controlling. And he's a lawyer who thinks he's got all the answers."

"It will be even worse once he makes partner at his firm," Liam chimes in. "Your turn, Ry."

"Oh, he's going for partner?" Todd asks, frowning. This is clearly news to him. "Great, that's just what his ego needs."

I bite the inside of my cheek as I line up a shot and miss again. Liam gloats from his position. He's got a massive lead on me. "Is he—does he always treat her the way he does?" I ask him, thinking about the close eye Mark was keeping on Izabel at the party. Though I haven't witnessed this side of him much since I've returned, I remember this being a dominant trait of his while Izabel and I were dating. He didn't hesitate in letting her know when he didn't like something she did. I have no doubt that this carried over from their friendship into their relationship.

Liam stands up straight, all amusement lost from his face. Todd is still frowning as well. They look between each other again, and then Liam pats me on the shoulder consolingly. "He's not a good guy, Ryan. None of us know why she lets him stick around."

I lean back into one of the chairs at our table and try to ignore the dread lingering in the back of my mind. "Yeah, I was afraid that would be your answer."

The Izabel I've seen since being home is vastly different than the one I knew all those years ago. It's something that has been making my mind spin, trying to reconcile the fiery, take-no-bullshit version of her I fell in love with, with this new accommodating version who is all too willing to step back and watch the world pass with no say in the matter. It's somewhat unsettling, and I'm not sure what to do about it.

The guys fall silent for a minute. Liam purposefully misses a shot, his attempt at cheering me up. The admission hangs around us like a dark cloud. I can't say I'm surprised, but I wish I could be.

I'm not sure what to do about it either.

Izabel once meant the world to me. She still does. But is it my place to step in and confront her about it? Probably not. We haven't been in each other's lives in years. And I keep having to remind myself that just because she comes to my office and gives me a "welcome home" present doesn't mean she wants me back. We grew apart. It's not her fault, or mine. It was just the way things worked out between us.

I try my best to ignore the sympathetic stares I'm getting

from my friends. They can't possibly know what's going through my mind, but they know that seeing her again with Mark is hard for me. It would be hard to see her with anyone. But especially Mark.

I was always suspicious of him from the first day she told me they were hanging out. Izabel assured me it was all platonic, so I bit my tongue. To give her credit, she and Mark didn't start dating for a few years after she and I broke up. He was just waiting for the opportune moment.

"You know…" Todd mutters from next to me. I still haven't gotten up to take my shot yet. I peer at him with an eyebrow raised. "They do say that the best way to get over someone is to get under someone else."

He motions with his head over to the bar where a beautiful girl sits, alone, sipping on something out of a martini glass. I roll my eyes—what a typical *Todd* thing of him to say. "That brunette has been staring at you all night."

"She has not," I say incredulously, though my eyes remain on her. Sure enough, once she thinks the coast is clear, she glances at us over her glass's rim. Her head snaps away quickly once she realizes I'm staring back.

"See?" Todd says, grinning. "You should go buy her next round."

Liam's watching this whole exchange with unbridled amusement, but he doesn't say anything. Todd shoves my shoulder, and I groan.

"Fine. I'll go buy her a drink, but that's it." I point to Liam. "I'll know if you cheat."

Liam rolls his eyes. "Whatever, dude. Just call this one already. I'm one shot away from finally kicking your ass."

I chuckle as I walk away from my friends. My eyes are locked on the beautiful woman at the bar. She sees me coming and sits forward in her seat, trying not to meet my eyes. Settling into the chair beside her, I lean my elbows on the counter and get the bartender's attention.

"Hey, I'll have a Jack and Coke and another one for the lady," I say, smirking at the girl next to me.

Her eyes widen, and she turns to me. "Well, that's kind of you. Whatever did a girl like me do to deserve your attention?"

"Please, you were practically mind-tricking me into coming over here," I tease her, giving her a wide grin.

She shrugs a shoulder and smiles back. "So what if I was?" She pauses, and then extends a hand. "Josie."

I take it and shake. "Ryan."

The bartender brings us our drinks, and we fall into a natural conversation. She asks what the occasion is, looking extremely pleased when she discovers it's my birthday.

"What brings you out all by your lonesome?" I prod, taking a sip of my drink.

Josie follows my lead and sips on her Cosmo. "Oh me? To quote the esteemed Meredith Grey, 'I'm just a girl in a bar.'"

I chuckle, even though I have no idea who she is talking about.

Josie is beautiful, I can't deny it. She has long chocolate brown hair that is slightly curled and gorgeous hazel eyes that scream mischief. A light smattering of freckles covers her nose like someone tossed a sprinkle of cocoa powder on her. Her olive skin is clear and glows underneath the dim bar lights.

She's the obvious sort of beautiful. Totally different from Bells, who is gorgeous, even though she doesn't know it. I don't mean to, but I look at Josie and see how different she is from Izabel. I don't mean it maliciously, but she's not Bells. No one will ever be Bells.

Izabel is quiet and reserved unless you get on her wrong side—which I happen to be an expert at. From what I've already gathered, Josie is the opposite. She would be a handful, I already know.

Maybe that's just what I need.

She notices me observing her, and I see a faint blush start on her cheeks. "Why are you looking at me like that?"

"You're beautiful," I say honestly.

Josie looks me up and down, assessing me, the flush now fully set in. "You're not so bad yourself." She tosses her head, whipping her hair off her shoulder and raising a perfectly sculpted eyebrow. "So, what do you do for work?"

"I'm a structural engineer."

She throws her head back and laughs, a light, cheerful sound. "I knew this was too good to be true."

"Why's that?" I ask, a smile playing on my lips from her infectious laugh.

Josie looks at her hand as if she's expecting her nails. "I'm an architect. I don't think we're supposed to get along."

"That's just a rumor. I know many architects who I get along with just fine," I say, still smiling.

She grins as she finishes the rest of her drink. "Well, I guess there's only one way to find out. You wanna get out of here?"

I feel conflicted, and I turn my head toward my friends, looking for support. Todd took my place against Liam. They both look over at me and give me encouraging nods and a thumbs up. Todd's words clatter through my brain. *The only way to get over someone is to get under someone else.*

"Don't worry, I think your boyfriends will be fine. They look like they can handle themselves," Josie teases, grabbing my attention again as she shoves my shoulder.

I turn back to her and give her a smirk; my decision already made. "Your place or mine?"

We stumble into my apartment, lips locked together, hands flying every which way. I lead her to my bedroom and shut the door behind me as Josie starts to grab at my shirt, pulling it over my head and then working on my belt.

When our clothes are gone, Josie presses against me, arching her chest into mine. I press my lips against hers and move toward the bed. She falls against my mattress, and I follow her, running my lips along the edge of her jaw now.

Her hands tangle into my hair, and she moans my name.

And suddenly, it's as if I'm drenched in cold water. A chill covers my skin, and I pull back and look down at her.

This feels wrong.

"What is it?" Josie asks softly, watching me watch her. I'm propped up on my hands, hovering above her, our lower halves pressed together.

I look down at the woman below me. She's here, she's beautiful, and she wants me.

So what the fuck is the matter with me? What is this trepidation consuming me out of the blue? I've never had any qualms hooking up with someone before, so what's changed?

As soon as I ask myself that, Izabel's face pops into my mind. The way her blue eyes have lost her sparkle and the way something about her still calls to me.

Josie's hands trail up and down my back gently. "What's wrong, Ryan?"

"Nothing. It's nothing," I say as I shake my head, convincing myself of that fact as I lean down to kiss her again. I pull her tightly to me, closing any remaining distance between us. Skin against skin. I meld my lips to hers, feeling her move against me. She sighs into my mouth, and I continue where we left off, forcing memories of a brown-haired, blue-eyed woman out of my mind.

I let myself get lost in Josie.

When we're both sated, she rolls onto her side, propping

herself up on her elbow. I turn to look at her, noting her hazel eyes watching me intently.

"What?"

"Nothing," she says back, a little too quickly.

I arch an eyebrow at her. "Tell me."

"I can just tell you've got a lot on your mind."

What the—is she talking shit on my performance now? Before I have the chance to protest, Josie holds up a hand.

"It's *okay*, Ryan. I'm no stranger to being tangled up in knots. I understand. I'm just saying if you need someone to talk to, I'm here. Okay?"

"Yeah, okay," I respond.

Josie gives me a smile, and then closes the distance between us, snuggling up in my arms and resting her head against my chest.

Her fingers trace patterns over my skin until she falls asleep. Even as her breathing evens out, I think about her words.

She's right; I am tangled up in knots inside. It has nothing to do with the beautiful woman lying in my arms tonight, but rather about the woman I'll likely never get the chance to hold again.

There's something to be said about regret, how it eats you up inside and festers until it consumes you.

That's how I feel right now.

I close my eyes and lean into Josie, resting my nose against her forehead and praying to all the stars above that I can maybe, someday, get over Izabel and find someone to fill the void.

Chapter 7

Ryan

THE NEXT MONTH PASSES IN THE BLINK OF AN EYE AS I stay busy with work. Clients start pouring in, thanks to the referrals I keep getting from Teddy and my other contacts at Bates Industries. I am quickly getting to the point where I may need an associate—not necessarily a bad thing.

When I'm not working, I'm spending time with my mom and Derek or babysitting Thalia. Mom is still going through her chemotherapy regimen and being monitored closely by her doctors. Her next scan is in a few weeks, then we'll know whether cancer has diminished or spread. All we can do is wait.

And when I'm not busy with work or with my family, Josie keeps me occupied.

Josephine DiMarco turned out to be just the firecracker I initially pegged her as.

We went on a total of two dates before she gave it to me straight. We were walking at the local park, hand-in-hand. Only knowing each other for a little over a week, she had stopped our walk abruptly and turned to me.

"This isn't going to work," she said, looking at me straight in the eye. "You're handsome and kind, Ryan Miller. But," she paused, taking a deep breath, "I know you're in love with someone else."

I let out a rush of air and squeezed her hand. It was no use denying it, I'm sure she would've seen right through me. So instead, I was truthful. "I'm sorry. I wish I wasn't."

She shook her head and gave me a small smile. "Don't be. If I'm honest, it's just as much me as it is you. I wish you were the guy for me, but I don't think you are. There's no," she paused, waving her hand around, "spark."

When I didn't reply, she looked at me wryly. "I mean, don't get me wrong, you're great...but I don't think it was meant to be between us."

I reluctantly agreed. There was nothing I wanted more than to feel for Josie the way I felt for Izabel. But I was confident that no matter how many dates we went on, or how often we hooked up, it wouldn't happen. Josie was beautiful and funny and literally everything I could ever want in a woman, but she wasn't Bells. And I hated myself for that.

It had been decided then. We would still hang out and spend time together since we both enjoyed each other's company. But we wouldn't continue to pursue any type of relationship other than friends.

And Josie turns out to be a great friend. And a great business partner. I hired her on as a private contractor right after we defined our relationship. She is proving to be an incredible resource for some of my projects. Josie brings a lot more to the table than I can offer on my own. I can see our teamwork morphing into a highly successful partnership.

Her primary focus right now is to head up the Stevenson project. A project that I wouldn't entrust to anyone else. I'm supposed to meet her for lunch in about an hour to go over some sketches and ideas. I appreciate her being willing to meet me on a Saturday. This past week was stupidly busy, leaving me with no openings. The Stevenson Project has to start getting underway, as I've been sitting on it for over a month.

My fingers fly over my keyboard as I type out an email to another client and hit send. Then I sit back in my chair and take a deep breath. What a crazy few months it's been. It's hard for me to believe that I was still living in Germany and working for Bates only three months ago. Now I'm home, getting a chance, and so far, succeeding at building my own business.

I've been so busy with everything that I haven't had time to breathe. Though I wouldn't have it any other way. The insane schedule has thankfully kept my mind off other things. Namely, a blue-eyed beauty who haunts my every waking moment. I haven't crossed paths with Izabel since she visited my office last month. Which may be a blessing in disguise.

I've divulged my entire depressing history to Josie, who, as usual, didn't beat around the bush with her assessment. She looked me dead in the eye and said, "You need to make a decision. Either you're all in, or you're not. If you want her, go get her. Or don't."

"I don't know if it's that easy," I said, shaking my head.

"If you love something, set it free. If it comes back, it belongs to you. If it doesn't, it was never meant to be yours in the first place."

And so, I put all my energy into work and family. And I reluctantly let her go.

Izabel will always be a part of me; I'll always have a place for her in my heart. I'll always love her. But she's engaged to be married to someone else. There are some lines that I won't cross, and that's one of them. I will not put myself into a situation where I'm not wanted. We put ourselves through too much pain and heartbreak already once before. I'm not sure it's worth traveling down that road again.

I check the clock and determine I can start heading to the restaurant where I'm supposed to meet Josie. I shut down the computer and turn off the office lights before heading that way. We're meeting at a small café just a few blocks down. It's a beautiful day, so I decide to walk.

My feet tread down the sidewalk, scraping against the concrete. Saturday morning has brought out a bunch of people who are window shopping or walking their dogs. The weather today is warmer than it has been. A hint of summer is in the air, giving hope that the winter months are behind us.

I make a mental note to get in touch with Todd over the next week to discuss tryouts and training schedules for the Bennett soccer team that I volunteered to coach. That would be another busy commitment, but hopefully, one that I would enjoy.

Todd seemed to be in a bind when the school's soccer coach backed out last minute. I offered to step in for the next season. Tryouts weren't for another few months, but he and I had to get together to talk schedules and the finer details of me joining the payroll as a new coach.

As I come up to the café, I see Josie already settled in at a table outside. Her long brown hair is curled in her usual style, falling past the back of the chair and swaying slightly in the breeze. She's hunched over the table, scrolling through her phone, facing away from me. I smirk as I quietly walk up behind her and clasp my hands on her shoulders, giving her muscles a slight squeeze.

Josie yelps, startled, and whips around to glare at me. Her hazel eyes cut into mine, and I can see the fire blazing behind them. She extends a hand and whacks me in the gut, causing me to double over and grunt. "Ryan! You could have given me a heart attack, you jackass." I chuckle as I straighten up and walk around the table to sit opposite her.

"Sorry, babe, couldn't resist," I respond.

She rolls her eyes and puts her phone down as her arms cross on top of the table. "How's your day been?"

"Busy," I tell her as I grab the water she's already ordered and take a sip. "Lots to do. The projects keep rolling in, and I'm not sure what to do with all of them."

"That's a good problem to have, Ryan," she says with a smile. "I'd be happy to take over more if you want me to."

"I might just take you up on that. If you can impress me with what you've got for the Stevenson Project."

"Oh, don't you worry. You'll love it." Josie reaches into the tube that's slung across the back of her chair for the blueprints.

She lays them across the table and goes over all the fine details with me. The layout is exactly what I was envisioning, and I'm honestly impressed. I knew Josie was up for the challenge, but she nailed it on the head.

"These are perfect, Jos," I say, not even attempting to keep the awe out of my tone.

She looks at me smugly. "I know. I told you I'd take care of it."

Josie rolls up the blueprints as the waiter comes and takes our orders. Then Josie opens up her notebook and begins going over other construction matters with me. I listen, nod along, and make my own notes, offering corrections or different ideas. When our food comes, we put the business away for a minute while we eat.

Josie is telling me a hilarious story about a nightmare client of hers, when my attention is pulled away. I hear my name whispered by someone a few feet to my right.

"Ryan?"

The sound of that familiar voice has me whipping my head around to meet Izabel's gaze. She's standing a few feet away, hand-in-hand with her fiancé. My throat thickens as my eyes roam over her. Wearing a sundress, she's taking full advantage of the almost-summer weather we're experiencing today. Her hair is swept back from her face in a high ponytail, blue eyes widening as she stares right at me.

Beautiful. Like always.

My heart skips a beat. I dart my attention back to Josie and reach for her hand before I know what I'm doing, lacing her fingers with mine. Her fingers wrap around my own as she watches in amusement.

"Izabel, Mark," I acknowledge them with a head tilt. Mark sneers at me as Izabel looks back and forth between Josie and me.

"Beautiful day for a lunch date, huh, Ry?" Mark asks, malice dripping from his tone, a smirk plastered on his face.

I shoot him a glare as I nod hesitantly. "Sure is." I would give anything to wipe that smirk off his face, preferably with my fist.

Izabel stays silent as her gaze locks on my entwined hand. Mark gives Izabel's hand a slight tug and addresses me again. "Well, sorry for the rude interruption. We'll leave you two love-birds to it. We've got a meeting with our wedding planner."

"Great," I say with no emotion in my voice. "Have fun."

Mark pulls Izabel away behind him, her eyes lingering on me and Josie for a second too long before she turns and follows him. I watch them leave, my heart still pattering too fast to be comfortable.

As soon as they're out of earshot, Josie yanks her hand from mine and hits me with a hard look. "So that was her, huh?"

I look at her sheepishly and nod. My throat still feels thick, and I'm not sure I can respond without my voice cracking. How embarrassing. I'm a grown-ass man, and still, that girl can bring me to my knees just by whispering my name. I think I need therapy.

"I'm sorry, Josie. I don't know what came over me."

Josie presses her lips together, and then moves her napkin from her lap to her table. "Let's get one thing clear, Ryan. You are my friend. I like being with you, and I am happy to work with you. But I will not participate in any more of whatever this was." I wince as she lets me have it. "I told you before, either you're all in with her, or you're not. But I am not going to sit here and let you use me. Do you understand?"

"Yes, I'm sorry."

She sighs from her spot across from me. "I forgive you. This is your one freebie, Ryan."

I nod. "I understand. It won't happen again."

"I like spending time with you. But I won't be part of your ploy to win her back, capeesh?"

"Yeah, I get it. I promise."

Josie's stern expression falls from her face, and she smirks. "Good." She picks up her fork and digs back into her salad. "I gotta hand it to you, Ryan. That Izabel is a looker. No wonder you're head over heels for her."

I groan and bury my face in my hands, knowing that I'm never going to hear the end of it now.

Chapter 8

Izabel

"Hey, babe," Mark grabs my attention from across the dinner table. "Are you okay?"

We're at a fancy restaurant, a celebratory treat after a successful first meeting with our wedding planner. It's a beautiful place that Mark has brought me to a few times. Ritzy. He ordered the filet mignon for both of us, which normally would be a delicacy. Instead, I haven't been able to stomach the steak. I've been mindlessly pushing the food around on my plate with my fork for the last few minutes. My mind is obviously elsewhere.

I snap my eyes up to my fiancé and give him a tight smile. "Hm?"

"Are you okay? You've barely touched your dinner."

"Oh yeah," I say quietly, suddenly fascinated by a piece of roasted broccoli. "I'm fine. I guess my head is just swimming with all the information we got from the planner."

Mark gives me a knowing smile. "Yeah, it was definitely a lot. Finally starting to feel real."

I nod in agreement. It was true, the wedding planner did

give us lots to think about. Things I wouldn't have even considered. As the planner pointed out, our planned date of September is less than five months away. But I felt off throughout the whole meeting.

My day was thrown off-kilter after running into my ex-boyfriend on our walk. Seeing Ryan with his new girlfriend had more of an effect on me than I'm willing to admit. Mark, of course, doesn't need to know about that. But I've been feeling nauseous since we ran into them at the café, like I'm waiting for the other shoe to drop.

Juliet had mentioned that Liam set Ryan up with someone last month. So it isn't as if I didn't know he was dating again. But seeing it in real time is a lot different than just knowing about it. I can't hold it against him; his new girlfriend is beautiful. And it's not like I expected him to be single forever.

It's just...different.

A part of me is surprised Mark hasn't brought up the encounter. Though I'd be lying if I said I didn't notice his attitude perk up a bit after running into Ryan and this other woman. I am curious if Mark is now appeased, knowing Ryan is with someone else. Maybe he'll stop viewing him as such a threat.

"Izabel."

The sound of my name again pulls me out of my thoughts, and I look back at Mark. He's frowning at me. Gone is the concern that laced his voice the first time, instead replaced by familiar irritation.

"Sorry, what?"

"I was trying to ask you a question. Are you sure you're okay?"

I nod and put my fork down, now making an effort to give him my full attention. "Yes, I'm sorry. What were you asking me?"

Mark narrows his eyes for a second, but then his expression lightens. "The firm is having a happy hour next Wednesday. Do you think you can be there?"

Now it's my turn to frown. "Next Wednesday?" He nods. "I have a committee meeting for the Historical Society Gala that night. I told you that last week. I have to be there."

Eyes darkening, he sits forward. "Izabel, this get-together with work could ultimately decide whether I make partner. I need to attend functions like this so that they know I'm committed."

"Well, you are more than welcome to go, but I have my own commitments."

"You have to go with me."

"Why?" I ask and immediately regret it. Mark's expression turns thunderous at the challenge.

"Why?" he questions, the volume of his voice increasing enough to get his point across, but not enough to make a scene. "You're going to be my wife, that's why. And when I need you to go with me to work functions, you will go. Understood? You'll reschedule the meeting and come with me to the happy hour. End of discussion."

I feel my spine compressing in my chair, and I pick up my fork again, stabbing a piece of steak forcefully. My stomach contracts, and I'm suddenly more nauseous now than I was before. "Fine."

Mark sits back in his chair, the clouds and thunder disappearing from his features almost immediately. "Great. Thanks for understanding. It's important they see us as a committed couple as well. All of the partners are married, and family is a big deal to the firm."

"Okay."

He goes back to his dinner, quickly polishing it off before he calls for the check. I still don't touch my food. I'm too busy thinking about how I'm going to reschedule my meeting *again*. This will be the third time I've had to reschedule. They've been accommodating the past few times, not asking questions when I lied through my teeth about my conflicting schedule—or rather, *Mark's* conflicting schedule. But I get the feeling that this time the committee isn't going to be thrilled about it.

The Historical Society Gala is the biggest event of the year. I accepted the opportunity to head it up myself this year, and I seem to be flubbing it at every opportunity. The gala is less than a month away, and we haven't even finalized all the details yet.

Mark pays the bill, and then we head out. My gut is roiling as he puts his hand on the small of my back to lead me out to the car. Neither of us says much as he drives. I keep my eyes trained out the window, watching the buildings and people rush by. The days have started to get longer, one of the sure signs summer is fast approaching.

Pulling the car into his parking space at his condo, he gets out, coming around to open the door for me. I crawl out of the car, making sure my sundress doesn't fly up with the wind. My car is parked a few spaces down in guest parking, and I gaze at it longingly.

As if he can read my thoughts, Mark brushes the back of his hand down my cheek and asks, "Do you want to come up?"

I can hear the implication in his voice. It was a big day for us, and his idea of prolonging the celebration includes getting naked in his massive bed. While I usually wouldn't turn him down, the thought of it tonight makes me want to throw up.

Glancing back at my car, I shake my head. "I'm not feeling good, Mark. I think I should just go home."

Mark pushes a strand of hair behind my ear. "Okay," he says softly, then leans forward to kiss me. I kiss him back, feeling him smile against my lips.

"What's funny?"

"Just thinking that there won't be a 'your place or my place' in a few months. It will be *our place.*"

I can't help but stiffen as he cups the back of my neck and pulls me in for another kiss, his tongue tracing the seam of my lips. As I reluctantly open for him, he dives in, his tongue brushing my own. I feel him take a step forward, until my back presses into his car's passenger door, the length of his body aligning with my own. Mark's weight is crushed against mine, one hand on the back of my neck and the other resting on my hip.

He rolls his hips against mine and pulls back slightly. A low grown releases from deep in his throat, eyes dilated with desire. "You *sure* you don't want to come up?"

I can feel my lips tingling from the increased blood flow. I press against his shoulder, trying to give myself space. "I'm sure. I'm sorry. I just don't feel good."

Mark releases a frustrated groan, but then pulls away from me. "Fine. I'll let you go. I don't want to, though."

"I know."

He kisses my forehead and then gives me a smile. "Drive safe, baby. Call me when you get home. I love you."

"I love you too, Mark." I return the endearment and reach for my keys in my purse. Mark stays in the parking lot. He slides his hands in his pockets and keeps an eye on me, making sure I get to my car okay. Then he waves as I pull out of my spot and drive off.

My hands grip the steering wheel as I drive farther and farther away. Living separately is one argument that I held firm on immediately after the engagement. If Mark had it his way, we would have been living together right from the start. But I convinced him that I needed to have my own space. Thankfully, he conceded. My apartment is closer to Bennett anyway, making it easier for me to get to work. Mark lives on the other side of town, so it would have doubled my commute time.

Mark and I hope to start house hunting in the next month, neither of us wanting to live in a condo or apartment once we're married. But until then, I am happy to have the sanctuary of my own home. My apartment is my safe place, where I'm surrounded by my favorite books and comfy blankets and trinkets that share memories.

I'm not ready to go home tonight, though. My mind has not been able to stop thinking about my encounter this afternoon.

At a stoplight, I pull out my cellphone and call Juliet. I'm sure I'm going to hear all about what I'm about to ask her, but it's the only way.

She answers on the second ring. "Hey, gorgeous, what's up?"

"I need Ryan's address," I tell her abruptly. "Please, don't ask questions. Just give it to me."

A pause, a rustle of paper, and then... "5573 Birchwood Lane, Unit G."

"Thank you," I whisper and hang up. I type the address into my maps, and I'm on my way.

This is crazy. I don't even know what is possessing me to think this is a good idea. It's the last thing I should be doing, knowing my fiancé wouldn't be on board with me seeing him more than absolute bare minimum, but I have to see him. Even if it's just for a moment to apologize for the awkward encounter this afternoon. To maybe meet his new girlfriend...

Closure. That's what this is. Or at least that's what I'm going with. If I'm going to move forward with my life, I need closure.

God, what if she's there? What if they're having a date night? What if they're in the middle of *something else*.

I hadn't considered that. I glance down at my maps and

realize I'm almost there. I can still turn around. I can still go back to Mark's condo; he would be more than thrilled to let me spend the night.

All in the name of closure.

I pull into a parking space and hop out of the car before talking myself out of it. My stomach is still churning as I find the correct building and go in. The lobby is quiet. Decorative wallpaper and pieces of art line the walls. The entrance smells like citrus and vanilla; I notice a wax melting contraption on a side table, the source of the aroma. This place is a lot nicer than mine or Mark's.

Up the stairs to the left...There. Unit G.

My feet carry me down the hallway until I'm standing right in front of his door. I train my ears to see if I can hear any movement inside, but I don't. My trembling hand raises, and I rap my fist on the wooden door.

No answer.

I knock again—still nothing.

My heart feels like it's about to pump out of my chest, and I still believe I could throw up any second. I spin around and lean my back against the door. Then I let gravity do its thing and allow myself to slide down until my butt's on the floor.

Why am I even here?

I think about the travesty this day has been. It started off great. Mark picked me up and brought flowers. We decided to go for a stroll before meeting with the planner. Then it rapidly went to shit the moment I spotted Ryan on his lunch date.

Maybe I was jealous. It wasn't my right to be...I mean, given our history. But it was a huge world shift. Ryan and I dated for a long time. Even though I'm in love with Mark now, some histories are hard to let go of.

Then we met with this wedding planner, who was rattling off this and that: deadlines and to-do lists, and recommendations on caterers and photographers. My head was spinning before I knew it. Wedding this and wedding that. Make sure you talk to an officiant, and you might be asked to do counseling if you're getting married in a church. Don't forget to get your wedding license, so it's official with the state.

Then the whole dinner argument. Nothing new there, as Mark's shit is *always* more important than mine, but still. It was the cherry on top of my disaster of a day. His drive to make partner with his firm is starting to become an obsession. I know it's the next big step for him and his career, and I'm happy for him. But at what expense?

I feel my hips beginning to ache from my position on the ground. What I need to do now is get up off this floor and go home. I need to run myself a hot bath, find something to settle my stomach and watch some mindless show. Then hopefully, tomorrow will be a fresh new day, and I can get on with my crazy life.

I just cannot seem to get myself to stand up. My brain gives the instructions to my muscles, and they flat out ignore it. My eyes begin to sting, and I suddenly don't care that I'm wearing a dress and looking like a hot mess. I bring my knees up to my chest and bury my head in my arms. I focus on my breathing, and my heart rate settles slightly.

In, two, three, four. Out, two, three, four.

I do my breathing exercises, when my ears pick up the sound of footsteps on the stairs. And then they're walking toward me. It's probably a security guard. I noticed cameras monitoring the hallways when I walked in. Someone probably thought I'm a deranged homeless person and called it in, so now they are here to kick me out.

My pulse picks up again, just out of self-preservation. Maybe if I don't move, they won't see me. I have no desire to be manhandled by a power-tripping security guard tonight.

Just keep walking. Just keep walking.

Instead, of course, the footsteps slow and then stop right in front of me. I squeeze my eyes shut and start to prepare an excuse.

But instead...my flight-or-fight response goes into overdrive when I hear:

"Bells?"

Chapter 9

Ryan

THE BARBELL FALLS ONTO THE FRAME WITH A METAL clang. I stand up from beneath it and reach for my t-shirt, hanging loosely on the rack. Running the fabric across my forehead, I gather the drops of sweat dripping into my eyes. I let out a sigh as I feel my heart rate drop back down from the physical exertion.

I hit a new personal record this evening on back squats. Now I feel like my legs are jelly.

Grabbing my water bottle off the ground, I make my way out of the workout room. I desperately need a protein shake and a shower. I wrap my t-shirt around my neck like a towel and head up the stairs to my unit, taking the stairs two at a time, pushing my leg muscles just a little longer before calling it quits.

When I reach the top landing, I'm out of breath again, and I slowly walk down the hallway. I rub at my eyes with the edge of my shirt and then glance down the hall. I'm startled when I see a crumpled heap curled up in front of my door.

My eyebrows furrow as I walk closer. I'd know that woman anywhere. *What in the hell?*

"Bells?" I say out loud, my voice laced with surprise.

Izabel pops her head up in shock, her blue eyes focusing on me. I frown when I see them tinged with red.

"What are you doing here? What's wrong?"

Her jaw slackens as her eyes roam over my sweaty skin, taking in the post-workout glow. I catch her attention tuned in on the scar above my left hipbone. I can still remember sliding down the cliff and catching on a rock, feeling it tear into my skin. The scar has faded over the years, but the mangled skin still stands out; the physical reminder of our time spent together at the cabin in the woods.

"Bells," I say softly, pulling her attention back to me. As if drenched in cold water, Izabel scrambles up to her feet and looks at me sheepishly.

"Hey, I'm sorry. I don't know what I'm doing here. I just needed to see you, and I—"

I step closer to her, unsure of what is giving me this kind of confidence. Maybe it's how flustered she is, or the red-rimmed eyes that are making my heart hurt. She looks like she's unraveling at the edges. I cup her cheek and hold her eyes with my own.

"It's okay. You're okay. Do you want to come in?"

Izabel inhales deeply and presses her lips together, nodding wordlessly. She steps aside when I pull my key out of my pocket and reach around to unlock the door, leaving it open for her to follow me. I hear her footsteps, hesitant, but they trail my own.

"Can I get you anything to drink?" I ask her, tossing my keys onto the stand by the door. I yank on the shirt hanging around my neck and pull it on, effectively hiding the scar on my abdomen that Izabel was staring at. Walking over to the fridge,

I pull out the protein shake I had prepared before heading to the gym.

Izabel grips her fingers together in front of her, knotting and unknotting them. "Do you have a Sprite?"

I peek over my shoulder at her with a confused smile and then back at the fridge. "Uh yeah, I do, actually." I grab the can off the shelf and hand it to her. She wraps her small hands around the drink and pops open the top.

Ushering her over to the couch, I sit down next to her. I take a deep swig of my shake and watch as she takes a teeny tiny sip of her Sprite. Her eyes glance around my condo, trying to take it all in.

"This is a nice place," she says by way of small talk.

I rub the back of my neck. "Uh yeah, thanks. It's not fully furnished."

What is even happening right now? *It's not fully furnished?* Who am I, a Property Brother?

A smile plays on Izabel's lips, and she glances at me, her eyes sparkling.

"How's school going?" I manage to ask her.

"Oh, it's good. We've only got a few weeks left. I'm working on grading research papers and then writing the final. Summer will be here before we know it."

I clear my throat and take another sip. "That it will. So what brings you here?"

Smooth transition, Ry. Smooth.

"I, um, wanted to apologize for this afternoon."

"What happened this afternoon?" I ask, unsure of where she is taking this.

Izabel looks at me like I've lost my mind. "You know when Mark and I interrupted your lunch date. I hope your girlfriend wasn't mad."

Oh, I get it. I chuckle as I shake my head and look at her in amusement. "No, Bells, Josie isn't my girlfriend."

"Oh," she says, "I thought I saw you two holding hands."

"Yeah...I think I need to apologize to *you*. It's stupid, but I was jealous when I saw you holding hands with Mark, and I think I might have had a stroke 'cause I reached over and grabbed Josie's hand in response." I pause and rub my neck again. "Don't worry, she kicked my ass for it. But to answer your question, no, we're not dating."

"Juliet told me that Liam set you up with someone."

I try not to let it get to my head that Izabel is actually here, asking me about my relationship status. Is she jealous too? That has to be the only explanation.

"He did. Josie and I *did* date for, like, two weeks. Then we decided to quit while we were ahead. I hired her as a business partner," I tell her.

I owe Izabel nothing, I remind myself over and over again. I owe her nothing. But I can't get over the glassy look in her eyes or how small she suddenly looks to me. She came *here* tonight. She came to *me*. The least I can do is be honest.

"That's what we were doing today at lunch. Going over plans for an important project I hired her for."

Izabel's eyes brighten at my admission, and she looks down at the soda can in her hands. I narrow my eyes as I watch her closely. I see her shoulders drop slightly, the muscles losing their rigidity. Her hands unclench, and she lets out a sigh.

"Izabel," I start warily. Her eyes snap to me. They are clearer now, but I can still see the hurt in them. "What happened? Why are you here?"

I know it can't just be about my date with Josie. Or maybe it is. Jealousy can consume a person.

"Today was just—" She pauses and shakes her head. "It was

not a good day, and I don't know. I thought seeing you would help sort everything out. It always used to."

I sit up straighter at her admission. Memories flood my thoughts. Izabel and I had a very short period of time during our relationship that we were physically together. The rest of it we were countries apart. It wasn't unusual for us to reach out to one another on bad days, simply to hear each other's voice, and get some perspective.

"And has it?" I ask her.

She shrugs a shoulder and looks at me with a small smile. "I don't know yet."

I lean back onto the couch, extending one of my arms across the back. I notice that my hand rests on the edge of the couch right behind Izabel. It would take one little movement of my fingers to brush the skin of her shoulder or twirl a strand of her hair.

I should move it, but I don't.

If she notices, she doesn't say anything. She just sits quietly, sipping on her soda.

Time ticks by as we sit in silence.

"Want to tell me about it?" I'm aware that I'm asking about something I likely don't want to hear, but the quiet and our proximity is starting to get to me.

Izabel lets out a deep breath and looks me fully in the eye for the first time all night. I see the resolve etched in those beautiful blue eyes. The redness is gone, and instead, there's determination.

"I got into a fight with Mark."

Oh boy. "About what?" I prod her, going for another sip.

"Or...well. It wasn't *really* a fight. It was about our schedules next week. I have an important meeting for the Historical Society Gala that I need to attend on Wednesday. It just so happens that his firm has a happy hour that night that *he* needs me to be at."

"And you caved?" I ask, already knowing the direction this is going, but still dreading hearing about it.

She shrugs. "It's an important function for Mark to attend. He's really trying to make partner, and every little thing counts."

"Don't do that," I growl at her, bringing her attention back to me abruptly.

"Do what?"

"Act like your shit doesn't matter."

Izabel looks down at her drink again. "I know. My work does matter, but there's just a lot going on right now. He's not always this way. Things have been stressful at work for him and—"

"*Jesus Christ,*" I grumble as I stand up from my seat and begin to pace, unable to keep myself still.

"What?" she snaps, jumping to her feet too.

I wave her off with my hand and continue to march a hole into my floor. "You! You should hear yourself right now!"

"What does that mean?"

I spin around to face her with a scowl. "What the hell happened to you, Bells?"

"Nothing! I don't know what you're talking about."

I shake my head, frustrated. "The Bells *I know* wouldn't let something important to her get pushed to the side. The Bells *I know* would stand up for herself when someone is trying to bully her into submission."

I give her a hard look. "Or at least that's the Bells I *used* to know. I don't know who you are anymore. You're just this *shell* of who you used to be."

"You don't know anything!" she shoots back at me, her eyes

a blaze of fury. I see her start to tremble, her arms wrapping across her chest. "You don't know me, Ryan! Not anymore."

"Then why are you here!" I exclaim. "Why are you here? In my house? Telling me all of this? Acting like you don't see what he's doing to you!"

"You're just like Juliet," she whispers brokenly, her shoulders slumping and her eyes going blank.

I feel myself jolt at her words, at her tone, and I immediately know I've fucked up. I observe her close in on herself, completely shutting down. My heart stutters, and I come back to the present, the anger and frustration melting away.

What was I thinking, yelling at her like that?

Bells stares at me as if I'm a ghost, and then she walks around the couch. "I should go."

"Wait," I say softly. She turns back around and faces me. I observe her. She looks small, scared. "I'm sorry," I plead. "I shouldn't have yelled at you."

"Yeah."

I offer her a hand. She looks at me warily, but takes it. I lead her back over to the couch, and we sit down. Neither of us says a word. We just sit together, her hand in mine as I give her space. The condo is deadly silent. I hear the ticking of the clock in my study and sirens outside. But I don't say anything, yielding to her.

"You don't know anything about me," Izabel says finally, her eyes still blank. "You don't get to decide how I live my life."

"You're right," I acknowledge. "I'm sorry."

"Things are different now, Ry," she says.

"I can see that."

Izabel goes quiet again. I let her be, offering her comfort through the hand wrapped around mine.

"Do you hate me?"

I'm taken aback by her abrupt change of topic. I stare at

her, trying to read her mind. When I get nothing, I let out a deep sigh and drop my weapons for good.

"No, Bells, I could never hate you." I look at her wryly and aim for a joke. "I think that's more *your* department. What did you used to say to me? You *loathed* my very existence?"

She doesn't laugh as she curls her legs up underneath her, making herself even smaller. "I loved you, you know."

I didn't miss how she used the past tense. *Loved.* As in she *used to* love me. Arrow straight through the heart. I guess we're having this conversation now.

I carefully adjust in my seat next to her on the couch, putting my own drink on the table. I rest my hand on her knee. "I know."

"I didn't mean to hurt you. I was just drowning on the inside," she mumbles. "I couldn't take it anymore."

"It's okay."

Her blue eyes meet mine, and they're brimming with tears. "It's not okay. How can you say that? I ruined everything."

I cup her jaw again. "Bells, you didn't *ruin* anything. We had some good years. But it wasn't meant to be. We may have been right for each other, but it just wasn't the right time. It took me a long time, and trying to move on has been the hardest thing I've ever done. But we both made our choices."

"And have you? Moved on?"

I look at her but don't say anything. I can see the crossroads in front of me as clear as day. Both paths lead to different outcomes, neither of them good for either of us. I remind myself of who I am, who she is.

My Bells.

I can feel her holding her breath, waiting for my answer. My eyes search her face, looking for some clue as to how I'm supposed to move forward.

She shifts her face ever-so slightly into my hand, and that

does it for me. I move toward her in rapid motion, claiming her lips with mine. Izabel freezes in shock, but then quickly responds, arching her back into me.

My lips trail over hers, testing, learning. I trace the outline of her mouth with my tongue, and she opens for me with a surprised gasp. I don't hesitate as I move forward, taking her for myself. My hand moves from her jaw down her neck and shoulders, across her chest to her rib cage, then to her waist. I grip her there, pulling her into me.

Izabel's hands are doing their own exploring. She tangles them in my hair and gives a slight tug, making me ache for her. I don't let up as I kiss her like a man starved. Starved for years. I only pull away slightly to catch my breath.

"Bells," I whisper her name across her lips.

She opens her eyes to meet my own. Then, she freezes.

As quickly as the moment comes, it passes. Izabel puts distance between us and covers her lips with her hand, her eyes wide.

"I-I'm sorry," she says, standing up and walking away from me. "I shouldn't have done that."

"Hey, hey, hey," I repeat, grabbing her hand and halting her movements. She turns around to face me. Tears are brimming in her eyes again as I smooth her hair over her head. "You didn't do anything. This was all me."

I'm kicking myself internally.

I was at the crossroads, and I picked the wrong path. Now she's blaming herself.

She shakes her head. "I can't do this, Ryan. I'm with Mark. I'm marrying him."

I pull her into my chest and hug her close, feeling her body shudder against me. "I know. I'm sorry. I'm so sorry."

Izabel pushes away from me. "I have to go."

I hold on to her for as long as I possibly can. I debate not letting her go, but I see the look in her eye and know I need to. I don't say a word as I release her.

She gives me a parting glance, and then heads toward the door. Before she leaves, she turns around and gives me one last glance. I feel like she wants to say something else to me, but she must think better of it. Without a word, she's out the door and gone, leaving me alone in my condo.

I stand there looking at the door for a minute, kicking myself for being such an idiot. What good could have possibly come out of that? What, did I think she would just drop everything and come back to me after I verbally attack her?

She's engaged to be married.

Married.

Today was just a bad day. She needed a friend, and I blew it. I lost my temper, and I alienated her even more. I cannot let that happen again. I'm no better than I believe Mark to be if I trap her in a situation like that.

I have to be better.

It doesn't matter that having her against me was the best feeling in the world. It doesn't matter that I was two seconds away from throwing her over my shoulder and taking her to bed, showing her just how much I *wasn't* over her, how much I *love* her right now, not only in the past. Feeling her against me, in my arms, has me going crazy. I haven't wanted anyone or anything as badly as I want her for a long time.

It doesn't matter because that's not what she wants.

She's not mine. Not anymore.

I want her back, but I am not going to force her into anything. I just have to let her know that I'm here. I'll always be here for her. I need to get my emotions in check next time she comes to me with something. I won't allow myself to get mad and push her away again.

Maybe if I can control myself and show her I'm here, she'll

come around for good. Perhaps she'll remember what it's like to have someone love her like she deserves.

I don't know what Mark has done to her. I don't know how life brought her here, but I will get her back. I'll bring back that version of Bells I love so much. But I have to be smart. I don't care how long it takes, I'm in for the long haul. I'll be whatever she needs me to be for her, and maybe someday she'll see that I'm it for her, like she's it for me.

I didn't come home for Izabel, but now I realize that maybe there isn't home without her.

Chapter 10

Ryan

"And then I said, just because I'm younger than you doesn't mean I can't still fire your ass!" Teddy rants on the other end of the phone.

I roll my eyes at my friend, thankful he can't see me. "You really showed them, Teddy," I say, attempting to sound supportive.

Teddy called this morning to tell me all about his newest venture. He's trying to add another corporation to the Bates Industries umbrella.

"I hope so. Just because my dad was old as dirt when he started the company doesn't mean that I have to be old and gray to know what I'm doing! I mean, geez, I've been in the industry since I was in high school." He groans. "And I'm almost forty, for Christ's sake! It's not like I'm some spring chicken!"

"I hear ya, buddy," I say as I mindlessly scroll through my emails, swiveling back and forth in my desk chair. I'm only half-listening to his rant. The rest of my brain is still stuck on this past weekend. Izabel storming my condo, our fight. The kiss...

It's been on a constant replay since she walked out of my house that night.

Teddy sighs. "These stuffy old guys are getting to me. But anyway, I digress. How's business going for you?"

"It's good," I tell him. "I've got groundbreaking coming up this weekend on a personal project of mine, and I've been having other projects rolling in one after the other."

I hear Teddy mutter something on the other line to his secretary. "That's great. Hey, speaking of projects. I'd like you to come to Nashville to speak with the board about the HQ deal."

I nod, although he can't see me. I've been expecting this. Teddy has been on board with my start-up business since I first approached him. The Board of Bates Industries? Not so much. When Teddy approached them about hiring me to help re-design the Midwest branch, they weren't terribly thrilled. They would much rather go with an established company with a good rapport. I can't really hold it against them. I technically have been hired already, but they just seem to be dragging their feet with the full green light.

"Yeah, when were you thinking?"

Teddy rustles some papers. "Probably closer to the end of June. We're booked solid until then, and it's not like the project needs to be rushed."

"I'll have to check those dates. I need to see when soccer tryouts and practices are supposed to start."

A pause lingers on the other end of the phone. "Soccer tryouts?"

"Yeah, I'm going to be coaching my old high school team," I tell him.

"You're really adjusting well to small-town life, huh, Ry?" Teddy teases me, amusement lacing his tone. "Speaking of...how is my little sis-in-law? I'm guessing you sought her out right away."

I groan and drop my forehead into my hand. "She's fine, Teddy. I don't know. You know she's getting married, right?"

Teddy was well aware of the Izabel drama. He was one of my closest friends while I was living overseas, so he had a front-row seat to the aftermath of our breakup.

Not to mention, he's married to Izabel's sister.

"Yeah, I know. Sounds like her future groom is a real winner. Sage hates the guy. But what are you gonna do? Sage hates most men."

I chuckle. Before I get the chance to respond, I hear the front lobby door ding. I sit up straight and peer out my door. Usually, Lori would be the one to greet any visitors immediately, but she is out sick today, leaving me the only one in the office.

Mark's tall form comes into view as he steps farther into the lobby. He glances around the office, and then his attention catches on me sitting at my desk. I narrow my eyes at him. Speak of the devil.

"Hey, Teddy, I gotta go. Izabel's fiancé just walked in," I mutter into the phone, my voice low so Mark doesn't hear me.

"Oh, fuck. Good luck, man. Catch me up later!" The line clicks dead, leaving me and Mark Snyder alone.

"Marky Mark," I say as the culprit walks into my office, his signature sneer on his face. "What can I do for you?"

Mark comes in and stands a few feet in front of me. He's dressed in a neatly pressed suit, his hands stuck in his pockets, thumbs sticking out toward me. He frowns as he observes my workspace.

"Just thought I'd come see where all the magic happens," he says, contempt laced in his tone.

I stand up so that he's not talking down to me and step around the desk to lean on the edge. I'm hit with déjà vu as Izabel was standing in the same spot not too long ago. That conversation was much more pleasant than I'm sure this one is going to be.

"Well, here it is," I say and motion around the room. "Now, why don't we skip the formalities, and you tell me why you're really here."

Mark hits me with a steely glare. "I know she went to see you Saturday night."

Shock reverberates through me, but I keep my face neutral. Did she tell him? Does he know I kissed her? No, she wouldn't have done that.

"How could you possibly know that?" I ask him, not giving anything away with my expression.

Mark frowns even more at my question, his dark eyebrows pulling together. "*That* is none of your business."

The hair on the back of my neck stands up. I do not like this guy one bit.

"Is that all you wanted to say? I have work that needs to get done. So if that's it..." I growl.

Mark smirks. "I'd like you to stay away from Izabel. I don't think she needs you as a distraction. We both have a lot going on, and I don't need her ex-boyfriend sniffing around."

I cross my arms over my chest. "Did she say that? I'll be happy to stay away as long as that's what *she* wants."

"*I* am who she wants now. Look, Miller, just because you didn't know how to keep her in line doesn't mean I'll allow the same thing to happen," he snarls at me. My spine goes rigid at his words.

"*Keep her in line?* She's not your pet to train, Mark. Or have you forgotten how a relationship works?"

"All I know is that things between Izabel and me were perfect until you came back to town. So I need you to stay away from her. We're getting married, and I won't have you jeopardize that."

"If that's what she wants, then I'll stand down. But until then, you don't get to control me like you do her."

Mark takes another step toward me and sneers. "Do *not* mess with me, Miller. I promise you won't like the outcome."

I stand up straighter and step forward as well. We face off nose-to-nose like a pair of territorial dogs, threatened by each other's every movement. Mark's taller than I am, but still, I've got muscle where he's lankier. In a showdown, I'm pretty sure I could take him.

"Is that a threat, Mark?"

He chuckles deep in his throat. "You always were such a cocky little shit. Always used to getting exactly what you wanted."

"And?"

"And now I have the one thing you don't. So just remember that next time you want to cross paths, Ryan." He turns on his heel and heads toward the door. Then he stops and faces me again. "And no, Ryan. It wasn't a threat. It was a promise. Stay the fuck away from Izabel. Otherwise, things are going to get messy."

I watch him walk out of my office, my upper lip curling, and my skin crawling with his *promise*. Energy courses through my veins—a raging fire trying to burst through my skin. I growl and stalk over to the closest wall, throwing my arm as hard as possible. My fist goes straight through the plaster as I let out a yell of frustration.

Shoulders heaving with my breath, my body trembles as I let the anger flow and dissipate. I glare at the hole in my wall.

Mark is a raging asshole. Stalking in here and telling me to stay away from Izabel, acting like she's his *property*. I can't blame myself for my outburst as I remember the threats falling out of his mouth as if it was a regular conversation.

I brace my arms above my head on the wall and lean forward until my forehead touches the plaster, letting the coolness from the paint ease the remaining anger.

How did it come to this? How did beautiful, sweet, gentle, smart Izabel end up with Mark? How did I lose her to *him*?

How do I help her, knowing that staying in this relationship will suffocate her fire more than it already has? How do I convince her of that, too?

I inhale a shaky breath to make myself calm down. Just as I told myself after Bells ran away the other night, I have to be smart about this. I'll get her back. It might take time, and it might get messy, like Mark said, but it will happen.

Taking another breath, I open my eyes, and I'm shocked to see a liquid crimson trail dripping down the wall next to my arm. My eyes snap to my throbbing hand, and I find the source of the bleeding. Blood trickles down the side of my hand and drips onto the floor below me.

Fuck.

Grabbing a tissue off the small table, I press it against my wound, trying to keep from bleeding everywhere. I head over to my desk and kneel on the floor, my free hand going toward my bottom drawer and pulling it open.

Where is that damn first aid kit?

My non-injured hand digs around, looking for the plastic box with bandages and gauze. I know I bought one when I first got here. Did Lori take it for something? Where else could it be? Instead of plastic, my hand brushes against cold glass, and I hear the familiar sloshing of liquid.

I pull out the bottle of whiskey Derek gave me as an office warming present and stare at it for a second. Whiskey is an antiseptic, right? I hold the bottle between my knees and twist off the cap. Keeping it tightly in one hand, I head into the bathroom positioned off my office. The amber liquid flows over my wound as I tilt the bottle over the sink, leaving a trail of fire as it seeps into my exposed skin.

With a curse, I bite the inside of my cheek, watching the alcohol wash the blood down the drain in a disgusting mixture of red and brown. Adrenaline is still coursing through my veins, now only increased by the sting. The bottle clangs against the counter as I set it down and reach for some paper towels to wrap around the cut.

I lean back against the wall and slide down until I'm sitting, my knees drawn up to my chest, holding on to my cut-up hand. What a disaster of an afternoon. My eyes dart up to the now half-empty bottle of whiskey. Before I know what I'm doing, I grab it and bring it up to my lips, swallowing a deep swig, just enough to take the edge off. The liquor burns my throat as I let my head fall against the wall and try to focus on my breathing.

I don't know how long I sit there, but I take a few more gulps of the liquor before I convince myself I have to get back to work. Stumbling to my feet, I manage to get back to my desk. My laptop is still open to my email correspondence, and I start to mull through those again. With heavy and blurry eyes, I try my best to focus. It's all I can do to silence the ominous leering of the hole in my wall and the echo of Mark's threats in my memory.

A few days later, I'm sorting through the mail that Lori has just set on my desk. One letter catches my attention. It's a shimmery silver envelope, the seal stuck down with a fancy sticker. I use my pointer finger to tear across the edge, careful not to rip it. Inside, I find an invitation to the Cedar Ridge Historical Society Gala & Silent Auction. The letter is printed on premium card stock, the script standing out in metallic silver. I run a finger over the bright green Post-it note that was placed on top of the invitation. Written in familiar loopy handwriting, is:

Ryan,

I'm so sorry about the other night. I hope you'll be able to attend the gala. Bring Josie along. The rest of the gang will be there too. It will be fun!

Yours,

Bells

I frown at the apology. I told her it wasn't her fault, but I let her signature soothe the hurt. *Yours.*

"Hey, Ryno!" Josie saunters into my office, briefcase and sketches in hand. "Who's your favorite architect in the world?"

Dropping the invitation on my desk, I stand and give her a grin, my hands pushing into my pockets. "What do you got for me now?"

Josie does a twirl across my office floor. "Just the finalized plans and permits for the Stevenson project! You, my handsome friend, are as good as gold!"

She stops mid-twirl as she comes face-to-face with my less-than-golden moment from the other day. Josie's eyes dart between me and the hole in the wall.

"What the hell happened there? I didn't think my plans were that bad."

A gruff laugh escapes my chest, and I feel embarrassment set in. "Let's just say I got into a few disagreements the other day. Some ended better than others."

"Well, if it was that bad of a disagreement," Josie says hesitantly, "I'd hate to see the other guy's wall."

I force a smile, but I don't give details about the pathetic temper tantrum I threw after Mark walked out, or the subsequent pity party that included a fine bottle of whiskey. She doesn't need to know that. No one needs to know that.

Her dark eyebrows bunch together, hazel eyes narrowing,

but she doesn't ask any further questions. She comes closer to my desk and lays out the plans. Her attention snags on the invitation with the green sticky-note, her eyes quickly reading the jotted message.

"What's this?"

"Oh, I got that in the mail today. Izabel's Historical Society is hosting a gala and silent auction," I explain with a shrug.

"That sounds *fancy*," Josie says, her lips pulling up into a smirk. "I see she had the decency to invite me too. So are you gonna ask me or what?"

I smile at my friend. "What, are you expecting a promposal?"

Josie waves me off with a brush of her hand. "No, I think a simple '*Please, Josie, will you be the Cinderella to my Prince Charming and come to the ball with me?*' will do."

I roll my eyes and chuckle. "How about just, will you go with me?"

She gives a big dramatic sigh and then grins. "Okay, fine, you've convinced me! But I'm not going anywhere near any type of glass slippers!"

Chapter 11

Ryan

Josie and I roll up to the banquet hall where the gala is being held this evening. I park the car and leave the keys in the ignition. Strutting around to the other side, I pull open the passenger door and hold out a hand for my date. She places her dainty hand in mine and steps out, her floor-length red dress swishing around her.

I nod to the valet, and they hustle to move my car out of the driveway. Tucking Josie's hand into my elbow, I give her a grin.

"Ready for this?" I ask her.

She smiles back, her white teeth glinting against the red stain of her lips. "Only if you are.

I straighten out my tux with my free hand and nod forward. "Let's do this."

My heart is racing. I don't think I've ever attended a function this fancy in my life. I'm immensely glad Josie is next to me, keeping me steady. This seems more her scene than it does mine.

We walk through the doors, and I'm blown away by the intricacies of the event. White gossamer banners are draped across the ceiling, covering twinkle lights crisscrossed across the exposed beams. Round tables are dotted across the floor, each with their own satin tablecloth and blue and purple flower centerpieces. On the other side of the room, in front of a stage, a large floor area remains open. A band is set up on the stage, softly playing melodies.

Josie and I aren't late. We're fashionably on time, yet a few couples stand on the dance floor already, swaying gently to the music.

On one long wall, rectangular tables are filled with a variety of gift baskets and other high-priced items—the silent auction. People are meandering down the line, observing, and reading what each item contains. Across the room, staff members set up the buffet table, all dressed in black uniforms.

I tighten my grip on Josie's hand as I look around and spot my friends at a table at the other end of the room.

"Oh, there's Izabel," Josie whispers in my ear, bringing me to a halt. My head whips around, looking for her. And *there she is*. "She's beautiful."

Indeed, she is.

Izabel walks toward us, her hand tucked into Mark the Asshole's elbow. She has a soft smile on her face, her eyes twinkling underneath the lights above.

She's wearing a dark blue strapless dress that hugs her torso tightly. The gown is skin-tight until it reaches her hips, where it flares out like a waterfall, reaching the floor. Dotted along her top half are tiny rhinestones, making her glitter like starlight.

Her hair is pulled up tightly, with a few twirled strands hanging loose. What I wouldn't give to have those pieces of her soft hair wrapped around my fingers. The brilliant blue hue of her eyes stands out against her blue dress as they similarly roam over me.

My mouth goes dry as the couple walks closer. When a

waitress strolls by with a tray of champagne glasses, I hail her down and grab one for myself and one for Josie. I keep my eyes on Izabel as I take a sip of the bubbly drink.

"Close your mouth, you dummy," Josie scolds. "You look like a fish."

I snap my jaw shut and stand up straighter, trying not to meet Mark's eyes as he gives me a harsh look. Our conversation from a few weeks ago rings through my ears, my skin crawling as I remember his threat.

"Hi, Ryan," Izabel says softly once she's standing in front of us. My eyes trail over her body once more, drinking her in and noting any possible change in her since I saw her last—the night I kissed her. "I'm so glad you could make it."

"Wouldn't miss it for the world," I tell her honestly, meeting her gaze. "I know how much this means to you." Then I shoot Mark a glare, and he frowns.

Izabel is beaming, the verbal daggers appearing to go right over her head. She turns to my date and offers a hand. "You must be Josie. It's nice to officially meet you. I'm Bel—Izabel. I'm Izabel."

I feel my chest swell with pride, and I slide my eyes to Mark, who is clenching his jaw so tightly I can see the muscles protruding out of his cheek.

Josie gives her a big smile and takes her hand. "It's nice to meet you, Izabel. Ryan's told me so much about you."

I smirk as Izabel blushes, and Mark gets closer and closer to having a coronary. His fingers whiten around the champagne glass he holds and the muscles in his jaw twitches.

"Oh, uh, that's good. This is my fiancé, Mark Snyder," Izabel introduces. Mark steps forward, taking Josie's hand, raising it to his mouth, and pressing a kiss to the back of it.

"Pleasure to meet you, Josie. Short for Josephine, I'm guessing?"

Josie's eyes widen for a second before she snatches her hand back and steps closer to me, pressing her side against mine. "Yes. Josephine. But please call me Josie. Just Josie."

"Well, please make yourselves comfortable," Izabel interrupts the awkward introduction and motions around the room. "The buffet will be open in a little while. And make sure you check out the silent auction! Ryan, I think there are a few things you might want to bid on! We'll be by the table with everyone in a bit."

I grin and dip my chin toward her. "I will, thank you."

Mark starts to pull her away. She says goodbye and leaves us with one last lingering look. When they're out of earshot, Josie turns to me and shudders.

"That guy is a *creep*."

I wrap an arm around her waist and pull her into my side. Her own hand wraps around my waist, accepting the comfort. "I know. Why do you think I hate him so much?"

She shudders again as I lead her over to the table where our friends are sitting. Besides them, I'm not seeing anyone else I know: mostly old stuffy professors and history nerds. Definitely not an event I would actively go out and attend by myself, but I'd do anything for Izabel. This society is clearly important to her, thus making it important to me.

We get the usual round of "hellos" once we make it to the table. Juliet stands and fawns over Josie's dress while the guys watch in amusement. I sit down next to Liam, making sure there's an extra seat for Josie beside me. She'll be stuck next to Todd, poor girl. Though based on the fact that Todd can't tear his eyes off that red dress, I don't think there will be an issue. I'm silently rooting for my friend; he and Josie would make a good match. He could use a good ass-kicking from her.

Liam nudges my arm with his elbow, grabbing my attention. "Hey, man, did you see Izabel yet? She's looking awfully gorgeous tonight."

I don't miss the inflection. I shoot my friend a questioning stare. "Yeah, I saw her."

"I heard you guys reconnected on a physical level a few weeks ago," he says, looking around to make sure no one can hear him. "You know, with *the kiss*."

I rear back, and alarm bells go off in my head. My eyes dart around the room to make sure Mark isn't close enough to overhear our conversation. "How do you know about that?"

"Juliet. The girls talk. I always get the gist of it after the fact," he says with a shrug. "Don't worry, man, I won't say anything to Marky Mark. But does this mean you guys are back together? Jules is beyond thrilled about that."

"Getting ahead of yourself, there, buddy," I respond as I clap my friend on the shoulder. "No, we're not getting back together. She's still very much Team Mark."

I have to chuckle at the crestfallen expression my friend takes on. Most likely because he'll have to break the news to Jules.

Josie finally gets away from Juliet and comes to sit by me, immediately striking up a conversation with Todd. He seems to have brought his A-Game. Good for him. The buffet opens, and we all get up and make the rounds, filling plates with chicken and potatoes and buttery rolls. The table falls into a comfortable discussion as we stuff our faces.

Izabel and Mark join us at our table, plates in hand. Mark moves to sit closer to me, forcing Izabel into the seat right across from me. He pulls out her chair for her and then pushes it in slightly as she settles. After shooting him a grateful smile, she focuses on her plate.

Mark's eyes catch mine, and his lips curl up into a cruel smile. I feel my shoulders tense as I hold his gaze, not willing to be the one to back down first. Mark seems to catch on to my game, and he doesn't waver. The hair on the back of my neck stands on edge.

Josie puts her hand on my shoulder as if she can feel the tension, easily giving me an out from the stare-down. I reluctantly turn to look at her, and she half-smiles my way. Josie casually asks me if I tried the potatoes, and suddenly the tension is gone.

I exhale sharply and reach for my champagne glass. My throat feels dry, my tongue heavy in my mouth. I take a big sip and relish the warmth. It gives me the courage that I usually wouldn't possess.

"So Bells," I begin, loving how those blue eyes come to rest on my face, and the worry instantly vanishes from her features. "I spoke with Teddy a few days ago. He was telling me the story about Sage and the dog-grooming incident."

Izabel grins and shakes her head. "I heard about that too. My sister has never been good at any type of art. I feel bad for their dog."

"That sure sounds like Sage, though!" I laugh and shoot a sneer at Mark, who is glaring at me. I know it's immature, getting in a pissing contest with him like this, but I can't help myself.

"I'm sure Teddy is as scandalized as their dog! The poor thing is practically naked!" Izabel laughs. Her laugh is like music to my ears—Mark grits his teeth.

The conversation morphs organically after that. We chat about dogs for a bit, then back to work. Someone asks Juliet about Ashton, which triggers the kid conversation.

"Do you and Josie want kids, Ryan?" Mark asks me before taking a bite of chicken.

I nearly choke on my champagne, and Josie looks at me with wide eyes and pink cheeks. "We're um, we're not together. Definitely not having babies anytime soon. Or ever."

"Well, that's a shame," Mark says, his expression darkening in a way as he looks over at Izabel. I catch the malice in his dark gaze, which makes me want to throw up. He glares at her for a second before his expression morphs into one that appears loving. It's so smooth that it makes my unease amplify with how quickly he was able to switch his mood. "We're hoping to start trying right after the wedding. Who knows? Maybe we'll have a honeymoon baby."

Izabel looks down at her plate with a blush and bites her lip in a way that I want to believe is how any fiancée would react to her future husband's suggestion. My stomach roils, making me feel ill. I force it back and take another sip of my champagne, finishing off the glass. Josie watches me like a hawk, her eyes narrowed. I stare back at her with a look that hopefully tells her to get off my back.

The conversation dies after that. We all finish eating in silence, a few mutters here and there. After we eat, everyone disperses off to do their own thing. Juliet and Liam get up to check out the silent auction. Izabel gets up to go check that everything is still running smoothly, and Mark goes with her. Josie strikes up another conversation with Todd.

I stay in my seat for a while, observing. A while later, I notice Mark pull his cellphone out of a jacket pocket and frown as he lifts it up to his ear. He walks out of the banquet room doors and disappears as he takes the call.

The band strikes up a slower melody, and before I know what I'm doing, I'm on my feet. I put a hand on Josie's shoulder and lean over to whisper to her. "Mark just walked out of the hall on his phone. I'm going over to dance with Izabel. Cover me. Do whatever you have to do to distract him."

Josie's hazel eyes dance with the responsibility of the

assignment. "On it." She stands up and strides closer to the doors, striking up a conversation with a random person so she can catch Mark as soon as he comes back in.

I make my way toward where Izabel is. She startles when I approach her, but quickly relaxes when she sees it's me. A small smile plays on her lips that are painted with a nude lipstick.

"Hey, Ry," she says. "Did you get a chance to look over these auction items? They're going to go quick."

I reach out a hand. "Dance with me." Izabel's blue eyes widen a fraction, and then dart around the room in concern. "He's out of the room on a call, it's all clear. Dance with me."

Though she's hesitant, her left hand finds mine. I notice her fingernails are painted in a blue shade that matches her dress. Her engagement ring sparkles, looking much too gaudy for her beautiful hands. I grip her fingers and lead her behind me.

When we're on the dance floor, I turn around and capture her in my arms. One hand holds hers outright, while my other finds the small dip in her lower back. I apply gentle pressure there, pulling her into me until our fronts are flush. She's so close to me now that our cheeks are almost touching. Normally, I'm much taller than her, but the heels she's wearing tonight seem to level the playing field. I hold her close as we sway with the music.

I'm consumed by everything Izabel. The way her small body fits against mine like the missing piece of the puzzle. Her warmth pressed against me. The swish of her dress against the floor. Izabel's perfume wafts up, invading my senses—a sweet-smelling blend of pears and vanilla. I lean my face into her and breathe her in.

"You look gorgeous tonight, Bells," I say softly against her skin. I see her try and fail to hide the shiver that tingles down her spine.

She pulls away slightly until we're face to face. "I shouldn't be doing this, Ryan." Her eyes dart around again. "Mark said I should try to keep my distance tonight."

"Ah, of course. Mark," I mutter. "Did your sweet fiancé mention that he came to visit me at work the Monday after you stopped by my house?"

Izabel freezes, her panicked eyes meeting mine. "No. No, he didn't."

I press my lips together and hum. "Oh yes, he was spewing a lot of big, bad threats. But don't worry," I say, shooting her a smirk, "I told him I wasn't scared of him."

With an expression of horror, she shakes her head and looks me dead in the eye. "Do not push him, Ryan. Mark is a lot stronger than he looks."

My heart skips a beat, and not in a good way. My attention scours every inch of her face, searching for any type of clue. I narrow my eyes at her, my blood heating, and growl, "What the *fuck* is *that* supposed to mean?"

She shies away from my tone, and I curse myself internally. *Keep it together, Ryan. Calm. Cool. Collected.*

"I'm sorry," I say softly, pulling her in close again and rubbing my nose against her jaw. The action is horribly intimate, and I know I'm playing a dangerous game with Mark wandering around here somewhere, but I can't seem to stop myself. Our kiss from a few weeks ago still lingers on my lips, and I'm dying to get another taste of her.

"It's okay," she whispers back, sounding breathless. "I just mean that he might look lanky and weak, but he could hold his own if he had to. Even against you."

"Ah."

I flex my hand against her lower back, bringing her even closer to me. The song ends, and they begin another slower one. Izabel tightens her hold around my body and leans her head against my shoulder as we move together. I close my eyes, pressing my cheek onto her hair. This is heaven.

I don't let myself relax too much, knowing the line we're skirting. Another song comes and goes. My eyes catch Josie's near the door. She's watching us, a knowing smile on her face, and she shoots me a thumbs up. We're still in the clear.

"Tell me something I don't know, Bells."

I feel her smile against my shoulder. She takes a moment as she thinks of a good one. "Since 1945, all British military tanks have the essentials to make tea inside of them."

I chuckle against her, loving the nostalgia our game gives me. It all feels normal, it feels right. And then I see Josie stiffen from across the room as Mark comes barreling inside, a scowl on his face. Josie intercepts him, walking right in his path and spilling a glass of champagne all down his pants.

Smirking, I give Izabel a squeeze and then step away. I give her a mock bow, making her smile—*a real smile*. Unbridled joy and amusement play across her face, her eyes twinkling brighter than I've seen in a while. "Thank you for the dance, my lady."

Izabel dips into a curtsey, pulling at the edges of her dress, still grinning from ear to ear. "The pleasure was all mine."

I grin and stand up straight, giving her another lingering look, taking in her beauty and just Izabel. Then I walk away from her and head back to our table, but I don't see Josie. My eyes do land on Mark, who is watching me with a look so dark it makes my hands clench into fists.

I don't know if he saw anything, or if he knew precisely what Josie was doing. But he's not happy. Biting the inside of my cheek, I look away from his glare.

I don't care. He can bark and bite at me all he wants. I'm not scared of him. All that matters is that I got a real Izabel smile tonight. I could die a happy man after that. It was the first real glimpse that the her I used to know still exists deep inside herself.

It was a beacon of hope for me. The light at the end of the tunnel that assures me that My Bells is still there.

It's just a matter of time. I don't know how, and I don't know when. But I know that it's going to happen.

She and I are inevitable.

Chapter 12

Izabel

As I watch Ryan saunter away from our dance, he holds his shoulders tall, displaying his confidence. Passing a waitress, he grabs a champagne glass, giving her a big smile, before finding his seat at our table again.

I place my hand over my heart and feel the rapid rhythm. I am in way over my head. After the kiss a few weeks ago, I thought space would help me clear my head. If I would just take some time away, maybe these weird feelings I have would disappear.

But now...after that dance? I feel like I'm floating on cloud nine.

I still feel the grin Ryan conjured as he strolls over to the table of our friends. The muscles in my cheeks ache. I'm not sure when I last smiled this big. Being in his arms again, even just for a few slow songs, leaves me with more questions than ever.

I'm standing in the middle of the dance floor when I shake my head and come back into the present. Taking a deep breath, I head back over to the auction table to resume my perusal of the items. They all seem to be bidding reasonably high, which is excellent.

The band begins playing a more upbeat song, and I smile at a few guests who greet me. My eyes dart around the room, catching on the figure of my fiancé walking toward me. I plaster on another smile as he approaches.

He has his hands in his pockets, and his earthy brown eyes are cold. I noticed he had to step out earlier to take a phone call; I wonder if everything is okay. Things have been stressful at work lately for him. One of the partners assigned him to a complicated case. Mark thinks it's just another test before they'll offer him a partner position, but I'm not sure. This career seems to be consuming him.

Turning to him, I give him a small smile and place a hand on his arm. "Hey, is everything okay?"

He shies away from my touch and shoots me a menacing glare. "No, Ryan's stupid *date* just spilled champagne all over me."

I press my lips together and look him over. I feel like I'm treading in uncharted territory. Mark has never been in such a foul mood over something so inconsequential before. Thankfully, his suit is dark enough that any type of stain won't show.

Dejected, my hands flutter over the edges of his jacket, straightening out the invisible wrinkles. "I'm sorry. I'm sure Josie didn't mean to. I saw you ran out of here to take a call. Is there something going on with work?"

"No. Look, we need to talk."

My heart stutters in my chest at his low tone and menacing expression. "Okay."

His eyes dart around, and then he reaches for my hand. "Come with me. I don't feel like making a scene here."

He wraps his big fingers around my wrist, fully encasing me. Giving a slight tug, he heads toward the entrance. I stumble, my heels getting caught on the tulle skirt of my dress. The tall strappy heels I'm wearing were not made for this kind of walking. I can feel my ankles protest.

"Mark," I say as he pulls me along. "Slow down." Guests step out of our way, seeing the warpath that my fiancé appears to be on.

He doesn't respond. He just keeps walking, dragging me out the main banquet hall doors and then down the hall away from the gala. I'm still trailing after him, my wrist aching in his tight grip. I can feel the strength of his fingers digging into my sensitive flesh. Mark stays silent as he suddenly turns on me, pulling and twisting me until he has me cornered in a tight dead-end hallway.

When he releases my wrist, my fingers come up to rub at the hurt right away. I shoot him a glare. "What is this all about, Mark?"

His face is stormy. "Why don't you answer that for yourself?" I frown, my eyebrows furrowing in confusion. Mark steps closer to me, his face inching up to mine. His breath smells like champagne, his eyes wide with anger that I can see boiling. "Were you dancing with Ryan?"

His voice is deep, lower than I think I've ever heard it. The baritone timbre makes goosebumps rise on my skin.

"Mark, you're scaring me," I whimper, which only makes the situation worse.

Mark's upper lip curls at my silence, and he steps impossibly closer. "Oh, I'm scaring you? Poor Izabel. Let me rephrase since you *forgot how to fucking speak*. Were you dancing with Ryan? After I gave you specific instructions not to go near him tonight?"

His voice gets louder and louder as he yells at me, echoing off the walls surrounding the area where we're standing. Mark quickly takes this discussion from a zero to a ten. I clutch my wrist to my chest and cower away from him. Again, I can't get myself to answer him, which is unacceptable.

"Were you, Izabel?" he asks again, slamming the palm of his hand against the wall right next to my head. "It's a simple question. Yes or no." I yelp and flinch away, blurting out my defense.

"It was only a dance!"

Mark backs up slightly, his hand still braced on the wall, caging me in. His eyes narrow at me. "Only a dance? What about when *I* asked you to dance earlier? Hm?"

I look at him warily, still worried his hand is going to strike me like it hit the wall. Mark's never hit me before. I would never imagine that he would, but I haven't seen him this agitated in a while.

"I was busy. I had to work."

"But you'll always have time for Ryan, I see."

"No, that's not what I mean. I—"

He interrupts me with a scoff and pulls away as he begins to pace. His fingers pinch the bridge of his nose. "You know what I don't understand, Izabel? I give you *everything*. I give you everything you want. A trip to Italy, a relationship, a fucking rock to wear proudly on your finger, a wedding to look forward to! And this is how you act?"

Mark motions with his hand back toward the ballroom, where the gala is still happening, and says, "The way you act is a fucking embarrassment!"

"I-I'm s-sorry," I stutter, guilt creeping into my bones. I messed up tonight. I shouldn't have danced with Ryan. I knew it was wrong, but I did it anyway.

Mark turns his head to me, and I lose my breath. His eyes are frostbitten, cold and detached. He takes another step and grabs my chin in his hands, tilting my face up toward his.

"*Sorry?*" he growls. "I don't want you to be sorry. I want you to be better, *Bells*."

"I will," I squeak. My stomach churns with the use of Ryan's nickname. It sounds so foreign coming from Mark, almost as if it's dripping in poison. "I'll be better. Please, can you calm down? You're going to attract attention. Why don't we talk about this?"

Mark is glaring daggers at me. "Fine, let's talk. I'm not enough for you. You always make me feel like I'm never enough."

"You are!" I exclaim. I feel like the situation is slowly getting out of my control. I glance around, apprehensive and worried someone from the Historical Society might round the corner and bear witness to this scene. Mark's obvious hurt and anger are tearing at my heart. I never wanted to hurt him. Tears sting my eyes, one tear trickling down my cheek. "You are enough. You're everything I want."

He hits me with a hard frown. "I know you went to see him that night. Did you fuck him? Is that why you didn't want to come up to my apartment? Would you rather go sleep with him?"

Dread crashes through me as I study him, trying to see through his anger, but I can barely recognize him at this moment—and that thought is frightening.

"No, of course not! Where is this jealousy coming from? What is going on with you?" I plead again, tears now streaming freely down my face.

"You know, I try really hard for you, Izabel. I try to be everything you need. Instead, you go off galivanting with him in public—dancing and flirting over dinner. Making me look like a *fool*. But I still try for you. I try to get your friends and your family to like me, but it's just never good enough. I'm never good enough."

His eyes glint with something I can't name, and it has the hair on the back of my neck standing up. Against my will, my body trembles, and I take a step back.

"I *love* you, Izabel. But you don't love me back. You'll never love me like you love him." Mark trails his nose up and down my jaw, the same way Ryan did only half an hour ago. But it's different. Where Ryan's intimate gesture made me feel tingly down to my toes, Mark's movement makes me want to vomit.

"I do love you, Mark. I love you!" I cry. "I don't love anyone but you."

Mark whimpers, burying his face in my neck. I feel the bile rise in my throat. I love this man, I do. Memories of all of our good times flicker across my vision—Italy, graduating college, Mark getting accepted into law school, summers abroad. All those good times are what led me to fall in love with him.

"But you don't. You don't love me the way you should. Otherwise, you wouldn't even be giving Ryan a second thought. He's in the past. I'm your present, your future. That ring on your finger proves it."

I think about what he says, and I let it sink in. I would give anything to be anywhere else but here right now.

Mark's fingers trail up the back of my neck and creep into my hairline. He grips the back of my head and cranks my neck back, so I'm looking up at him. I yelp as he pulls my hair from their roots. In a swift motion, Mark smashes his lips onto mine, smothering my cry. As he moves his mouth roughly against me, I try to push him off, desperation and fear clouding my vision as I struggle against him.

He pulls away, his breath heavy. His fingers tighten in my hair, and I cry out again, beginning to feel helpless.

"Ow, Mark. You're hurting me."

He grips harder and glares at me, and my stomach tightens with anxiety. "I just want what's best for you, Izabel. I want you to be happy. I want to be everything you need—the only one you need. You must understand that, right?"

"Yes, I do. Please, let go. That hurts."

Instead of listening to my pleas, his fingers stay gripped in my hair, and his free hand travels down to my hip, where he holds me tightly, digging into my sensitive skin. I grit my teeth in discomfort. The fear and panic steadily increase by the second. My ears ring as Mark pulls me into him until his chest presses against mine, stepping forward until my back is flush against the wall.

"I love you so much, Izabel. You don't even know what you do to me."

I struggle against him as he kisses me again, trying to get loose. He's too close. "Mark, back up. Get off. Please," I say, my voice shaking. He groans into my neck but still presses closer to me. I continue to struggle. Panic gives way to full-blown terror, and my body trembles uncontrollably.

Then he's gone, ripped from my body. I feel the roots of my hair being split from my head as his fingers are torn away. Mark shouts as his tight grip catapults me sideways into the corner as he releases me. The muscle of my shoulder strikes against the angle of the wall, my arm going numb with the collision. I stumble over my heels and fall to the ground. My arms reach out to catch myself, and another sharp pain shoots through my shoulder joint.

I groan from my position on the floor, my hand reaching out to hold on to my aching shoulder. "Izabel!" I hear my name being shouted as Juliet and Josie run to my aid. They both crouch down beside me. "Izabel, are you okay?" Juliet runs her hand over my shoulder and my arm. I shy away from her touch, afraid she's going to hurt me. I can't hold back my tears, a mixture of physical and emotional pain from the hurtful words Mark threw at me taking over.

"What happened?" Josie asks gently, but I can't answer her. My eyes are trained on Ryan. He's shouting at Mark, who is yelling right back at him. Mark shoves Ryan's shoulders, and Ryan stumbles but rears back with his fist flying through the air. It connects with Mark's face with a sickening sound.

"RYAN!" Liam shouts as he runs toward his friend. Todd trails close behind him, grabbing hold of Ryan and keeping him from lunging again. Ryan struggles against his grip as Liam pushes against Mark's shoulders. "Take a walk, Mark."

"But he—"

"Take a walk!"

Ryan stands there for another moment, watching as Liam directs Mark away from us. As soon as Mark's back is turned, he spins and comes back in my direction. He falls to his knees next to Juliet and begins fawning over me.

"What's wrong with her?" he asks. "Why is she crying?"

Juliet responds for me. "Nothing's wrong, she's conscious. I think she's just shaken up."

"I hurt my shoulder," I tell him. His forest green eyes survey me, landing on my hand that's holding my shoulder. His face darkens.

"Come here, Bells. I'm taking you home."

I feel myself being hoisted up into a pair of familiar arms. Ryan is careful not to jostle me too much, leaving my injured left shoulder turned away from his chest. I instinctively wrap my free arm around his neck. Burying my face there, I breathe in his cologne—a mixture of cedar and spice. I smelled it when we were dancing together. I grip him closer, and his hold tightens on me as well. The realization that I feel safe in his arms creates another wave of tears that blurs my vision and streak down my cheeks.

"You probably shouldn't take her home," Juliet suggests hesitantly. She hands me my clutch purse that holds my phone and all my other necessities. I grab it weakly with my free hand and tuck it against my stomach. "Mark knows where her apartment is, and that will be the first place he goes."

"Can you take me to your house?" I ask him against his neck. He stiffens and holds me tighter, if that's even possible. My head is throbbing from Mark's grip in my hair, wrist aching, and I feel like I could completely be taken over by sobbing any second.

"He knows where I live, too," Ryan mutters, clearly unhappy about the fact. "I know where I can take you." I feel him lean over and press his lips to my forehead.

"Ryan, wait!" another female voice says. I peek an eye open to see Josie storming up to Ryan and grabbing his chin, forcing his eyes on hers. She has a fierce expression on her face, a woman on a mission. "Look at me."

She stares at him for a moment, searching his eyes. When she finds what she's looking for, she nods and motions to the door. "Okay. Go. I'll get a ride home with Todd."

Ryan stands there for another minute before I feel him start to move. I sway with his gait, but he holds me as if I weigh nothing. He doesn't say anything to me. I stay quiet as well, just breathing in his scent. My body is trembling with aftershocks from the whole event.

I keep my eyes closed as he sets me in the front seat of his car and buckles the seat belt around me. My forehead leans against the window, and I feel my body relaxing in the coolness. Ryan settles in his seat and starts up the car. Before he pulls out, though, he turns to me, eyebrows pulled together.

"Give me your phone."

I don't ask questions as I unzip my handbag and unlock my phone, handing it over. Ryan flips through my screens, looking for a specific app. Tapping the screen a few times, he gives it back.

"Should I even ask?" I murmur.

"I disabled your location settings for a little bit. Just a precaution." I nod and look out the window, feeling vulnerable. That must have been how Mark knew I was with Ryan the last time. I had never even considered him tracking my phone, but it makes sense that he would do something like that. Ryan shifts the car into drive and works on putting some distance between us and the gala.

After I've fully caught my breath again, I open my eyes and am pleased to find everything back in place, no blurriness. I glance over at Ryan, his hands tight on the steering wheel. So tight his knuckles are white, except for the fist that he punched Mark with. Those knuckles are busted open and look red and angry. He clenches his jaw so hard I can see his muscles straining against the tension. His focus is on the road; irritation etched over his expression.

"I'm sorry," I whisper to him.

His attention is immediately on me, the car slowing down a fragment. His green eyes trace my outline. How pathetic I must look—my dress has torn, my makeup likely running down my face from the tears, and my wrists are red and bruised. I'm a hot mess.

With a soft voice, he asks, "What could *you* possibly be sorry for?" He shakes his head. "Bells, this was not your fault."

I turn my gaze back out the window, knotting my fingers together as tears start to prick at my eyes again. "It kind of was, though. If I had just done what Mark asked, he wouldn't have been upset in the first place."

Ryan lets out a frustrated groan. I look back at him, and he runs a hand through his hair. "Trust me, Bells. If anyone's to blame for this, it's me." I look at him, confused, and he lets out a big sigh. "I knew dancing with you tonight would royally piss

Mark off. That wasn't the only reason I did it...but it was part of it."

I don't try to hide the hurt that flashes across my face. I decide against saying anything else, looking out the window. Raindrops fall, painting them with abstract designs. All I can see through the water is the streetlights and headlights of other cars zooming by since it's so dark outside. But right now, I don't feel like looking at Ryan.

Such a guy thing to do. I mean, really? Ryan knows I'm engaged to Mark, and despite the douchebaggery of this evening, he's still my future husband. So what game is Ryan playing?

"Where are you taking me?" I ask softly.

"My mom's house. Mark shouldn't know where she lives. And if he does, I'm getting a fucking restraining order."

I fall into silence for the remainder of the drive. Ryan stays quiet as well. When he pulls into his mom's driveway, he steps around to the passenger door, offering me a hand. I ignore him and struggle out of the car myself. My head is still aching, and I don't have the energy to fight with him. I opt for the silent treatment.

As I head up to the front door, he follows behind me. I can practically feel him stewing in his thoughts. Once he unlocks the door, I step in and look around. The house is dark and quiet, but mostly the same as when I last saw it all those years ago.

Ryan drops his keys on the entrance table and shoves his hands in the pockets of his slacks.

"Everyone here should be asleep already. Do you need any water or anything?" he asks me awkwardly. I shake my head and tremble. He eyes me warily with those green eyes I love, and then bobs his head toward the hallway. "I'm sorry, Thalia is occupying the extra bedroom these days. You can sleep in my old room, and I'll take the couch." He walks past me, barely brushing my shoulder, and moves down the hall toward his childhood bedroom.

I bite my lip and reluctantly follow him. Ryan's old room. How many nights have I slept in this room? A queen bed fits comfortably with two end tables on either side, a dresser located on the wall across from it. Besides the necessary furnishings, the room is stark. No artwork or anything signifying hinting to his years growing up here.

Ryan steps over to his dresser, and I notice him flip a picture frame down, hiding the contents. I wrap my arms around my middle and wait for his instructions. He rubs the back of his neck and looks at me sheepishly before opening a drawer and pulling out an old gray t-shirt. He holds it out to me.

"You can wear this, probably more comfortable than that dress."

I take the shirt out of his hands, feeling the smooth fabric. I glance up at him from underneath my eyelashes. "Um, could you unzip me?"

Ryan swallows roughly. "Oh yeah, of course."

I turn around, exposing my back to him. My eyes close involuntarily when I feel his fingers against the skin of my back. Rain is pattering against the balcony doors, thunder rolling in the distance.

Ryan carefully unzips my dress, trailing his fingers down the length of my spine as he does. My breath hitches as I remember the last time he unzipped my dress for me. At Sage's wedding in his hotel room, he unwrapped me just for his pleasure. I feel myself burning up where he touches me. The memories and our proximity are too much.

His fingers pull away once the zipper's down, and I let the dress fall around my feet and step out of it. I hear Ryan groan from the rear view of me only in black lacy panties. Pulling his shirt over my head in a swift movement, I wrap my arms across my chest, feeling bare even though I'm fully covered.

"Here, let me look at your shoulder," Ryan offers, holding out a hand to me like he's approaching an animal. His goal is to appear non-threatening, I know, but I hate it. I let him step closer, closing my eyes as he rolls up the sleeve of the shirt, exposing the skin of my shoulder.

Ryan tenderly takes my arm in his hand and moves it around, testing the range of motion. I open my eyes and stare at the floor, unseeing, but I can feel his eyes watching me carefully. I try not to wince when he stresses the joint a certain way and white-hot pain erupts through the tendons and ligaments, but it's no use.

Ryan immediately lets go of my arm and steps away. His fingers drag down the skin of my arm as he puts distance between us. I look up at him helplessly, unsure of what to say.

His eyebrows pull into the middle of his forehead, and he rubs the back of his neck. "You should probably ice your shoulder. To help keep the inflammation down. I think my mom has one in the freezer downstairs I can get for you."

I nod and cross my arms, hugging myself. Ryan hesitates for a second, as if he's afraid to leave me, but he finally steps out of the room. When he returns only a moment later with an ice pack, he gives me a pained look before walking over to his bed and pulling the comforter back from underneath his pillows. He fluffs one, and then motions for me to crawl under. I do, and he bends over, situating the ice pack over my throbbing shoulder. When he's satisfied with its placement, he pulls the covers over me, carefully sitting on the edge of the mattress once I'm tucked in.

"Will you be okay here tonight?"

I snuggle up under the comforter and nod, already feeling

the soothing effects of the ice. I'm so ready to sleep this evening off. My head is still pounding, and my sinuses feel stuffed up from the tears.

Ryan runs his hand over my forehead, brushing away a few stray strands of hair. "Good." He gives me the most tender look, and I want to cry again.

"Thank you, Ryan. For everything tonight," I say, my voice coming out weaker than I want it to. "I don't know—"

"It's okay," he shushes me. "We can talk about it tomorrow. Just get some sleep, okay?" I nod again. "I'll be downstairs if you need anything."

He leans down and presses his lips to my forehead, breathing me in. My eyes close as I accept his comfort. Pulling away, he makes sure I'm settled before heading out to the living room.

The glass of the window shakes with a roll of thunder. My fear of storms dissipated over the years, but after the events of tonight, my nerves are fried. I'm on edge, replaying Mark's hurtful words over and over. I do my best to focus on my breathing, trying to calm myself.

I hear the TV turn on in the living room, though the volume is low. Then the clatter of glass as Ryan rummages in the fridge. The rain keeps coming. I squeeze my eyes shut, trying to purge the image of Mark's vengeful sneer out of my head.

He was so mad. I can still feel his grip on my wrists and the feel of him grasping a handful of hair at the back of my head. His words echo in my mind, *"A fucking embarrassment!"* He couldn't have meant those words. He loves me—more than anything.

Guilt and anxiety knot in my stomach. Mark's embarrassed by me. I made him look like a fool in front of our friends and his colleagues.

He asked me to be better. I can do that. I can be the perfect wife for him. I thought I was good enough, but now I know I just have to try harder.

I roll onto my side, being careful to keep the ice over my injured shoulder, and bury my head into Ryan's pillow. I know this isn't the side he used to sleep on. He's more of a left-side of the bed guy. And even though he doesn't live here anymore, his scent is still all around me. I breathe it in, letting it wash away the bad memories and wait for sleep to consume me.

Nothing.

Rolling onto my back, I stare at the ceiling. I feel like I lie there for hours, staring.

This is useless.

Throwing the covers back, my toes find their footing on the floor. I pad my way over to the door and pull it open. As I tiptoe down the hallway and down the stairs, I'm careful not to make too much noise. I don't want to wake up his parents or sister.

I'm not sure what I'm after. Comfort, maybe? Ryan has always been the best at being there for me when I need him. As my foot hits a squeaky spot on the floor, his head snaps up, eyes meeting my own. My breath hitches at his surprised face, which quickly morphs to understanding.

He extends his arm across the back of the couch he's settled on, wordlessly inviting me to him. I take a deep breath and approach the one man I feel safest with.

Chapter 13

Ryan

"Hey," I say to Bells. She stands in the doorway of the living room, playing with the hem of my old shirt. My arm extends across the couch, welcoming her to me.

Izabel gives a soft sound, and then scurries over. I try to ignore how she looks running across the living room, only wearing one of my old t-shirts and her black lacy panties. Tonight was an emotional night for both of us. The last thing she needs is for me to push the boundaries again. "Why aren't you sleeping?"

Izabel snuggles into the crook of my side, leaning her cheek against my chest, and I wonder if she can hear my rapid heartbeat. I let my arm fall around her in a comforting embrace. My hand lands on her bare thigh, and I try my best to think of anything else but the fact that we're skin on skin.

"I can't sleep," Izabel responds quietly, fingers knotted together in front of her. She lifts her eyes up to mine, and I take a deep breath. Her eyes are charmingly timid, the blue irises shining like the moon reflecting on the ocean.

"Is it the storm?" I ask her, wondering if her fear of storms had come back. She shakes her head, still looking incredibly unsure as she nuzzles further against me. "Want to talk about it?"

She lifts her uninjured shoulder in a half-shrug and looks at the TV to see what's on. I'm mindlessly watching a soap opera just for background noise. Then her eyes find the glass bottle of beer I stole from Derek's stash. "Can I have one of those?" she asks.

I get up and wander into the kitchen, where I grab her another bottle and pop off the cap expertly. Handing it back to her, I reposition myself in my seat. Izabel snuggles into my side again, taking a big gulp of her beer and letting it ease away the strain of the evening.

I want answers, but I'm not going to push her tonight. I could, and in doing so, I run the risk of her shutting down again. Tonight, my focus is simply being present for her. I hope she feels safe here. As far as I know, Mark hasn't cyber-stalked my parents' address, and since I disabled her cell phone location, we should be safe. I don't doubt that Mark could find her if he wanted to. But I'm hoping he has enough sense to leave her alone after what happened tonight.

Biting the inside of my cheek, I recollect the events of the evening, one after another. A fire burns in my chest, and I rub at my sternum, attempting to ease it. After dancing with Bells, I wandered back to our group, grabbing another glass of champagne to sip on. Josie came over to the table, looking awfully triumphant with a job well done after spilling her drink all over Mark. She eyed my glass, probably noting that it was my fourth of the evening, but she didn't say anything.

I knew that was what she was looking for when she grabbed my chin and forced me to look at her before she let me whisk Bells out of there. She was checking my eyes to make sure I wasn't plastered before getting behind the wheel.

After seeing Mark's filthy hands all over Izabel like that, drunk was the last thing I could ever be. No, the adrenaline of hearing her pleas for help ate any type of buzz right up. I couldn't control myself as I pulled him off her and socked him right in the jaw.

I flex my fist just thinking about it, relishing the ache. At least I got one good punch in tonight.

I don't know what the argument was about. I didn't hear much other than Bells asking Mark to let her go repeatedly, but I don't think it would be too far of a stretch to assume it was about me.

I poked the bear tonight, and Izabel paid for it. Reaching for my own beer, I take a drink, forcing down the guilt that threatens to rise up inside of me.

"Do you think I'm an embarrassment?" Izabel asks so quietly that I almost don't hear her.

I set the bottle down and pause for a second, wondering where this question's coming from. "Why would you ever think that?"

She shrugs again and looks at me sheepishly. Her hands are wrapped around her beer bottle, her feet tucked underneath her. She seems small, so small. That's all she is these days. "It's nothing. Sometimes I just wonder..."

I narrow my eyes at the beautiful girl pressed against my side. "You could *never* be an embarrassment. Hey, look at me," I say as I lift her chin with my finger, drawing her attention to me. "You are the smartest, most beautiful girl I know. Anyone in their right mind would be glad to have you around, regardless of the setting."

She smiles, her cheeks lighting up with a blush, but she doesn't respond.

My eyes travel over her face. Her makeup is smeared from her tears, her eyes ringed with red, and her hair torn to bits. But she has honestly never looked more beautiful than in this moment right now, sitting curled up next to me in only my t-shirt and her panties.

Izabel notices my staring, and her lips turn up again awkwardly. "What is it?"

I shake my head. "Nothing, I'm just thinking."

"About what?"

I inhale deeply and brush some hair off her face. "About tonight. What a mess it turned into."

"Oh," she says, looking down. Her fingernail picks at the label on the bottle. "Yeah."

"Izabel, has he ever *done* that to you before? Like…does this happen a lot?" I ask her hesitantly, afraid of the answer. I'm treading carefully.

If her answer is yes, I swear nothing will keep me from hunting down Mark and breaking all of his fingers. If it's no, I'm afraid I won't believe her, not after what I saw tonight.

Izabel presses her lips together and looks at me with wide eyes before shaking her head fervently. "No." I let out a loud breath, my chest deflating. "I mean, he's never spoken to me like that before, or grabbed me like that."

Her delicate hand finds its way to the back of her head, and she winces. I saw him holding a fistful of her hair before I shoved him off of her.

"What was his deal? If it's okay to ask."

She shrugs again, her eyes back on the TV. "He was really upset with how I've been acting. He said I shouldn't have been dancing with you because it makes him look bad."

I knew it. It was my fault.

"I mean, he's probably right. I'm his fiancée. I don't know what I was thinking, dancing with you like that," she pauses, "like how we used to."

"You should be allowed to dance with whoever you want."

"Yeah, but I'm his. I have to respect that."

My eyebrows knit together, and I give her a hard look. "You're not property. You don't belong to him. You are fully capable of making your own decisions."

"Yeah, and look where that gets me, Ryan. Besides, you always used to tell me I was yours. I don't see how Mark doing the same thing is any different."

I tighten my hold on her. "I used to say that you were mine as in a *how the hell am I such a lucky bastard* type of way. Not in the *I'm going to keep you hooked on a short leash, so you don't disobey* way."

She tilts her head. "To-may-toe, to-mah-toe."

I emit a low growl from my chest but let it be. I'm not going to win this conversation. All I can hope is that someday she'll see the difference.

"You should be asleep," I say as I take another sip of beer. "Why don't you go on up?"

She looks at me with wide blue eyes and gives an involuntary tremble. "Will, um...will you come with me?"

"I don't know if that's a good idea," I mutter. Isn't she in this whole situation because I didn't know my own boundaries? Maybe it is time that I take a step back.

"Please? I don't think I'll be able to sleep by myself. And I'd feel awful making you sleep on this couch."

This is most definitely not a good idea. But I ignore the inner warnings and relent.

I take our beer bottles, both only half empty, and dump them down the sink. Then, grabbing her hand, I lead her back upstairs to my childhood room. She follows behind me and crawls back into bed, pulling the covers up over her shoulders. I observe her in the dark room, softly illuminated by the streetlights shining through the blinds.

Izabel is definitely babying that shoulder of hers. Maybe in the morning, I'll suggest that she go get it checked out. She might have sprained or torn something.

I pull off my dress shirt and slacks, dumping them on the ground. I don't care if they get wrinkled. I leave on my boxers and climb into the bed next to her. We put as much distance between us as the bed will allow. She's curled up on her side, facing away from me. I lie on my back, staring up at the ceiling, hands resting on my stomach.

"Hey, Ryan?" she whispers after a while.

"Yeah?"

"Tell me something I don't know."

This is the first time she's spun the game around. I'm not that smart. Give me numbers or geometry, and we're good, but random facts? No way. I wrack my brain, trying to come up with something, anything, that could take her mind off whatever it's mulling about.

"I uh...I wrote you letters when I was in Germany. Or emails, actually. After we broke up. I didn't send them, but they're all still sitting in my drafts box on my email."

I haven't told anyone that. I deny it to myself most of the time too. It's embarrassing. Pathetic. Weak.

I hear her sniffle, and then she squeaks, "Why?"

"You're my favorite person in the world, Bells. I missed you. There was so much going on that I wanted to tell you about, but I didn't want to hold you back. So I wrote it all down, but didn't press send."

Izabel sits up and inches closer to me on the bed. She crawls on top of me, being careful of her shoulder, and straddles my waist. My hands find her thighs on their own, running up and down her skin, feeling the baby hairs that are there.

Mark would murder me if he found us in this compromising situation.

"Hey, Ry," she whispers again, leaning down so I can feel

her t-shirt brushing against my chest. Her lips touch gently against my cheek, and my heart takes off in a sprint.

"Yeah, Bells."

She presses her lips to mine in a feather-like kiss. "Will you help me forget? Just for tonight. Please."

I groan as she moves toward me again, now fully claiming my lips. Her breasts press against my chest as she grinds her body over mine. My hands trail up from her thighs up underneath the t-shirt and run along the edge of her lacy panties that have been torturing me since I first saw them. She gasps against my mouth when I smooth my hands up her sides, holding her around her ribs lightly, my fingertips brushing the undersides of her breasts.

Izabel grinds her lower half against mine in maneuvered thrusts, and I jerk my hips up to meet hers. My body is on fire for her.

"Jesus, Bells, *fuck*," I mutter against her lips, and she throws her head back with a moan, allowing me access to her neck, where I pepper kisses along her collarbone.

She gasps at the feel of my lips on her sensitive skin, her fingers digging into my chest, and I suddenly feel myself coming back to the present. This can't happen. Not here, not now. The evening comes crashing back onto me. I can't do this to her, to me. I can't.

I move to push her off, being gentle of her injury. "Bells. Stop."

She keeps grinding against me and whines in displeasure. Her blue eyes look at me, betrayed.

"Stop," I whisper, and she does.

Her dark eyebrows furrow, and I see tears start to well up in her eyes. "Why do you always do this? You always say no. Always turn me down. Is there something wrong with me?"

"Trust me, Bells," I say, my voice thick. "There will never

be a day that I don't want you like that. But sex is not what you need right now. I know you're hurting, and you want to forget, but this isn't the way."

She's still straddling my hips, and I shift under her, moving from the right side of the bed to the left side. Izabel looks at me, confused, until I remove her from on top of me and settle her onto her side, pressed against me, lying on her good shoulder, her wounded shoulder exposed.

I don't fault her for this. I've never seen my headstrong Bells so lost before. She looks at me as if she has no direction, no purpose in her life, and she's grasping onto anything she can to keep her grounded. It kills me to know that she is so untethered.

"Just let me hold you tonight," I murmur. "Let me hold you close and keep you safe. Let me help you this way."

Izabel sniffles, and soon the tears consume her. Each one guts me, searing into my soul. I hold her tightly, letting her cry into my chest. With each sniffle and sob, I squeeze my eyes shut, wishing things were different. Wishing she was mine. Wishing that she would never have to experience this kind of pain ever again. I hold her until the tears subside, and her breathing evens out. Until she's fast asleep, and her fingers, resting gently against my sternum, twitch with dreams.

I turn my head slightly, pressing my lips against her forehead, breathing her in. I want her more than anything, but I would hate myself just as much as she would come morning.

So I hold her.

Even as the storm passes overhead, the rain disappearing. Even as the sun starts to creep above the horizon, I hold her. And I offer her myself in the only way I can for now.

I just pray that's enough.

Chapter 14

Izabel

I WAKE UP TO THE SUN STREAMING THROUGH THE curtains. Warm puddles of sunlight cover my face and my shoulders. Squinting, I sit up and look around, confused by my surroundings. I wince as I feel my shoulder screaming at the movement. When I'm sitting, I take my injured joint through its range of motion, feeling which actions cause the muscles to protest the most.

My eyes observe the room, the events of last night slowly coming back to me. The gala, Mark, the fight, Ryan...Oh, God, Ryan.

My cheeks heat as I recall how I mounted my ex-boyfriend and tried to get him to have sex with me. Thankfully, he was cognizant enough and refused. Now that my head is feeling clearer, I know that turning me down was the best thing for Ryan to do.

Speaking of. Where is he?

The clock on the bedside table reads eight o'clock, but I'm alone in the room. Ryan's suit jacket and white dress shirt are still crumpled in a heap by his closet door. Next to my cell phone on the nightstand, a pair of athletic shorts are folded neatly. They're women's. I suspect they belong to his mom.

I stand up and pull them on over my black panties, adjusting the oversized t-shirt I'm wearing. Tucking my cellphone into the waistband of the shorts, I walk over to the dresser in the room, which has a mirror sitting atop it. I nearly yelp in fright at what stares back at me.

Eye makeup is smeared underneath my eyes, making it look like I have two black eyes. My hair is a knotted mess, and my cheeks are flushed from my earlier thoughts. Heading over to the door, I carefully open it and peek my head out into the hall. When I find that the coast is clear, I dart across the hall into the guest bathroom. There, I dig in the drawers and find a hairbrush, and I wet a tissue to use as a form of makeup removal.

When I'm satisfied that my appearance is no longer trollish, I venture downstairs. I tiptoe into the kitchen that has been remodeled since the last time I was here many years ago, taking in the warm, homely sight.

Lara, Ryan's mom, is slightly bent over a griddle at the kitchen counter. She slides a spatula underneath a cream-colored pancake and flips it over, revealing the golden-brown underside. She's wearing a purple bandana around her head. I'm thrown off by how frail she looks. Ryan hasn't mentioned anything about her health, but I immediately wonder if she's okay. I'll have to ask him about it later.

Over at the breakfast bar, a little girl stabs at her scrambled eggs with a fork and looks up at her big brother with awe —*Thalia.*

Ryan sits next to her, elbows resting on the breakfast bar, a mug of coffee in front of him. He's wearing a Bennett soccer shirt—one he wore all the time when we were younger. It used to be blue, but now the color has faded into a blue-ish gray from overuse and age. I notice that the sleeves are pulled tighter against his biceps than they were when I last saw him wearing it. Ryan is definitely not the high school boy I used to know.

His deep green eyes find me at the kitchen's threshold, and he offers me a grin. "Morning, Bells."

I grip the hem of my shirt awkwardly and shift from foot to foot. "Um, good morning."

Lara sets her spatula on the counter, and then comes toward me with her arms stretched out wide. "Izabel, my goodness! It is good to see you, dear!"

I don't mean to, but I flinch as she moves closer. But I play it off and then wrap my arms around the woman. "You too, Lara. I've missed you."

We step back from our embrace as Lara goes back to her pancakes. Ryan motions his head toward another stool at the breakfast bar, and I shuffle over to his side. Thalia is eyeballing me as I get comfortable. Pulling my phone out of the waistband, I set it next to me on the counter just as Thalia takes another forkful of eggs and narrows her eyes—the same green as Ryan's.

"Who are you?" the little girl asks.

I look at Ryan, and he smirks. "My name is Izabel. And you're Thalia," I say with a smile.

"How do you know my name?"

"I knew you when you were very small—just a little baby."

"Oh," she says, shoveling eggs into her mouth. Lara delivers two plates stacked with pancakes and eggs to both me and Ryan and another mug of coffee for me. The pancakes are steaming, fresh off the griddle.

My stomach rumbles, and the hunger sets in as the scent of pancakes hits my nose. Sunday breakfast is a big deal in the Miller household, and there is nothing in this world like Lara's homemade pancakes. I haven't had them in years, but I can still recall the taste before I even take a bite.

I grab the butter and syrup and set to work doctoring them

up. Once my pancakes are seeping with syrup, I fork off a piece and shove it in my mouth. Ryan looks at me with amusement, knowing how much I love these pancakes.

"Are you Ryno's girlfriend?" Thalia asks out of the blue.

I startle and feel a piece of pancake get lodged in my windpipe, making me cough and choke. Ryan's big hand pounds on my back, enough to dislodge the pancake, but gentle enough he doesn't jostle my shoulder too much. Amusement is etched all over his face, but he remains silent, leaving this one to me.

"Um. No, I'm not. I used to be, but now I'm with someone else," I try to explain.

Thalia goes silent for a moment before those green eyes go wide, and she looks between Ryan and me rapidly. "You were Ryan's girlfriend he was going to marry!"

Ryan makes a strangled noise beside me, and I look at him with an eyebrow raised. This is news to me, yet I'm not surprised.

"Thalia, I never told you that," Ryan reasoned with his little sister. "I told you we were together for a while, but then broke up." He takes a bite of his pancakes and muffles out, "Sometimes things just don't work out the way you plan." Then he glances at me. "But at least we can still be friends."

I know Ryan means well, but his sentiment doesn't feel as good out loud as I know it should.

Lara, as if reading my mind, looks at me apologetically, and I offer her a small smile. Derek chooses that moment to join us, sauntering in and planting a kiss on his wife's covered head. Derek is a tall, broad man who makes Lara look teeny in comparison. I notice his dark hair is now peppered with gray, same with the beard that dons his face. He gives me a nod and a friendly grin.

"Good to see you, Izabel. Heard about the engagement. Congratulations!"

"Oh," I say, moving a piece of pancake around on my plate. I notice Ryan stiffen beside me. "Thank you."

Lara moves over to her husband and says something under her breath. Derek's eyes venture over to me again and then away as he grabs his coffee and walks out of the kitchen without another word. I wonder how much Ryan chose to share with his parents about the circumstances of my attending Sunday breakfast for the first time in years.

Sensing my discomfort, Ryan places a hand between my shoulder blades, effectively pulling my attention. "Did you sleep okay?" he asks as I look up at him. "Was your shoulder hurting you at all?"

I shake my head and move for my mug of coffee. I think it's cooled down enough now that I can drink it without singeing my tongue. "I slept fine...thank you." I know that being curled up next to Ryan had something to do with that. I always slept better next to him than I ever did alone. I'm sure that goes all the way back to our days spent together in that cabin. "And no, my shoulder didn't bother me through the night, but it's really sore today." I move it slightly and wince as if to prove my point.

Lara notices and rushes over. Gently, she rolls up the sleeve of my shirt and gasps at what she sees. I glance down to find a giant bruise covering my deltoid muscle. It's deep and purple, and the edges seem to go on forever.

"Oh, my dear, I'll get you some ibuprofen to help take that edge off," Lara mutters before hurrying over to the medicine cabinet above the kitchen sink. She shakes out three red pills, and I swallow them without argument, knowing they will help. I'd forgotten what a sweetheart Lara is. She's so different from Mark's mother. His mom is a country-club regular, always has her hair curled perfectly, and is never seen in public without her grandmother's pearl earrings. And here's Lara, fussing over me with pancake batter on her cheek, pajama pants, and a blue fuzzy bathrobe. Two completely different ends of the spectrum.

"What happened?" Thalia asks, her neck craning over her plate, trying to see what her mom is fussing at. I glance at Ryan, who's watching me closely already. His eyes harden, and shame and embarrassment fill me.

Before anyone has a chance to concoct a story appropriate enough for an eight-year-old, the ringer on my phone goes off, the screen lighting up with Mark's name.

Ryan's shoulders stiffen again, and he locks eyes with his mom. She nods once, and then grabs Thalia's hand. "Come on, sweetie. Let's give them some privacy."

"But I'm not done!" Thalia protests as her mom leads her out of the kitchen.

My phone is still ringing as Ryan takes another bite of his pancakes. He leans back against his stool, any and all amusement wiped from his face. "You better answer that. Put it on speaker."

I take a deep breath, my stomach in knots. My finger swipes across the screen, and I press the *speaker* button.

In a hesitant tone, I say, "Hello?"

"Izabel?" Mark asks. His voice is raspy, broken. I can tell he didn't sleep a wink all night, as if he was waiting for the sun to be up to call me.

My fingers find the edge of my shirt again, and I grip the hem. "Hi, Mark."

"Baby," his voice cracks. "I am *so sorry* about last night. I don't know what got into me."

Ryan lifts his coffee mug up to his lips and takes a gulp. He doesn't meet my eyes and instead goes back to his pancake. Although he seems uninterested, I know he's listening intently to every word.

"Yeah," I whisper.

"There was just a lot going on," Mark says. "The stress of the whole thing, being around your friends, plus you dancing with *Ryan*." His voice starts to rise, but he quickly gets control again and lets out a sigh. "But it's no excuse. I'm so sorry, baby. It will never happen again. You know I'd never hurt you."

I hear Ryan snort next to me. Looking at him out of the corner of my eye, I pick up my phone and walk to the edge of the kitchen. I leave it on speaker, though, so Ryan can still chaperone, but I feel like we have a little more privacy.

"I know," I say. "But you did. You hurt me. Mark, this can*not* happen again."

"Yeah, I know, I know," he mutters back at me. "It won't. I promise."

"I think—" I pause, choosing my words carefully. "I think we need to maybe look into couples counseling. Before the wedding."

"Anything," Mark assures me. "Anything you need, I'll do it. I just can't lose you. You're everything to me, baby."

You're everything to me. His words trigger memories from last night. Mark trying to convince me that I don't love him the same amount as he loves me. His hand gripping the back of my head and pulling at my hair. His forceful kissing.

"Where are you, Izabel? I need to see you."

I find Ryan's eyes again, and he gives a firm shake of his head. *Do* not *tell him.*

"I'm at a friend's house. I think it's probably best that we have some space for a while."

"Which friend?" I can hear the suspicion in his voice.

"Juliet."

The lie flows out of me seamlessly. I know Juliet will cover for me without a moment's notice, so I feel safe doing it. Mark would flip his lid if he knew I was with Ryan after everything. If he knew that I shared a bed with Ryan last night...

But he won't know. He won't find out.

"Okay," he concedes. "Just...Izabel, promise me you'll give me another chance. I swear, the only reason I acted that way was because I care about you *so much*."

"I know. I promise."

"Good. I love you, baby."

I let my eyes close and relish the sound of his words. They don't warm me like they usually do, but I convince myself that I'm still shaken up from last night. We'll get through this. We've already been through so much together.

"I love you, too, Mark."

He lets out a sigh of relief and tells me he'll speak with me soon. Then he hangs up, and I'm left alone in the kitchen with Ryan again. He's polished off his breakfast and is leaning back against the stool, coffee mug in his hand. He's watching me, but his expression is blank.

"I'm sorry," I tell him, wrapping my arms around my middle, careful not to over-extend my shoulder.

He pulls his eyebrows in. "Why are you apologizing?"

"Because I feel like that's what I should do."

"Well, don't," Ryan says as he sets his mug on the counter and stands up, walking over to me. Without my heels on, I only come up to his shoulders. Ryan carefully runs his hands down my arms and unlocks them from around me. He links our fingers together and bends his head slightly, capturing my eyes with his own.

His gaze is sincere as he looks me up and down. "Izabel, all I care about is that you're happy and healthy and *safe*. To be perfectly honest, I am not thrilled about what I saw last night. You deserve so much better than that."

"Mark's never been like that before. He said he just got overwhelmed."

"And what's to say that he won't get 'overwhelmed' again?"

he asks. "You should never, ever be in his line of fire, and I'm worried that you will be. These things don't usually just happen once."

His intense stare makes me feel like I'm being stripped bare. Ryan has never looked at me so seriously before. A part of me deep down knows he's right, that statistically, abusive partners will revert into the same patterns. But Mark's not abusive. Before tonight, Mark has never even physically hurt me before. It was just a fluke. I have to give him the benefit of the doubt based on everything else I know about him.

"He promised to be better."

Ryan drops his hands from my arms until we're no longer touching. "If that's what you want..."

I look him square in the eye and muster all my courage. "It is."

He presses his lips together and takes a step back. "Then, by all means, go get it."

"Ryan, about last night...when we were in bed..."

He waves his hand and shakes his head. "Forgotten. You were going through a lot last night. Emotions were high. And I think there will always be that connection between us. But it's in the past."

"Yeah." I bite my lip and look him over. Standing there with his hair perfectly mussed up, his old soccer shirt, and his slacks from last night wrinkled, he is still gorgeous. Where Mark is clean-pressed, Ryan will always have that rugged handsomeness to me. I can still see that younger version of Ryan, jumping into the river to save me from being swept away. The way his messy hair clung to his forehead as he dragged me back to shore and pushed me up the river bank. The two of us will always be connected because of that experience.

"Look, Bells," he starts. "I will *always* care about you. And I want the best for you. But I think that if you're going to continue to be with him, we need to set some boundaries."

"What do you mean?"

"I mean that I can't keep being *this* guy for you."

"Oh." Regret and longing rush over me. Does he not want to see me anymore? Is it because I'm choosing Mark?

"I just mean—" Ryan pauses before rubbing his hands over his face. He's frustrated, and I hate seeing him like this. "I can't just stand by and watch you continue to go through this and pretend that everything is okay. I will always be here for you, but I can't watch you choose him and go through more nights like the gala and just do nothing. You deserve better."

I don't know if I have it in me. We'll always share our experience, but on top of that, Ryan was my first love. And everyone says you can never forget your first love.

When Ryan and I broke up in college, I mourned for him for what felt like an eternity. It was as though a piece of me was missing. Finally, I found myself again, especially when Mark and I started dating. But even now, Ryan fulfills a part of me that no one else can.

And for that reason, I understand where he's coming from. I've run to him far too many times for comfort, and that's not fair. To him, or to me. We each need to learn how to live on our own, separate from each other.

As if he can see every thought running across my features, Ryan takes a step forward and cups my cheek with his palm. I lean my weight into his hand and smile as he strokes my cheek with his thumb.

"I love you, Bells," he whispers, and I look at him with wide eyes. "I will always love you." Something warm explodes in my chest and nearly knocks the wind out of me. It's not a phrase I've been missing in my life, but there's something so remarkably different when hearing it from Ryan. For a moment, I feel whole as I let those words wrap around me.

Ryan's eyes dart to my lips, and before I can fully grasp what's happening, he leans down and presses his mouth to mine in a chaste kiss. I stand up on my tiptoes and attempt to deepen it, feelings from last night flaring alive again. Before I can, though, he pulls back and puts distance between us.

He gives me a smile, sadness clouding his eyes. I look at him with a blush, and then hold up my phone. "I should probably go home."

He nods. "Okay, go get your things, and I'll drive you."

I move past him and bolt upstairs, grabbing my dress and the rest of my things. Then I head back downstairs to find him by the front door, keys in hand. Neither of us says a word during the drive until he pulls up in front of my apartment complex.

Ryan puts the car in park and then turns to me. "Look, I know I said I can't be that guy for you, and I stand by that. But if you need anything, I want you to call me."

I frown at his contradiction. But I know what he means. We need to establish space—boundaries—but he'll always be there for me if I need him.

"Thanks, Ry," I whisper. "For everything." I lean forward and press a kiss to his cheek, letting my lips linger for just a second too long before getting out of the car. Walking toward my apartment, I don't turn back, even though I feel his gaze on me with every step.

Chapter 15

Ryan

"ARE YOU EVER GOING TO PATCH THAT HOLE UP?" JOSIE asks me from across my office. I glance up at her over the rims of my glasses. She's lounging on the couch with her feet propped on top of the arm. Her brown hair cascades around her shoulders, making it look like a waterfall of curls.

I take my glasses off and set them on my desk, rubbing at my eyes. I've been staring at these project stats for hours. Josie is supposed to be working too, but she apparently is too distracted by my drywall. "Yeah, eventually. What, you don't like it?"

Josie sits up and looks at me wryly. "Mmm, no. It's messing up your Feng Shui."

I steeple my fingers in front of my face and stare at my friend. "My Feng Shui?"

"You know," Josie trails off as she stands and meanders over to my desk. "The energy of your environment."

"I know what it is. I just didn't realize I had any."

"Oh, Ryan, come on," she whines. "You've been such a

grouch since the whole gala thing. Time to lighten up, buddy, and move on."

I scowl. The "gala thing," as she used air quotations to emphasize, happened to be one of the worst nights of my life. Forgive me if I'm not entirely over it. I haven't seen or heard from Bells since she walked into her apartment from my car without even a backward glance.

That was over a month ago.

This was what I told her needed to happen. I established this distance between us because I wasn't prepared to watch her fall victim to him over and over again.

And every day I wonder if I made the right decision.

I will never be able to forget the sound of Izabel begging for Mark to let her go, crying out in pain from him grabbing her. That night haunts my dreams. There have been a handful of times when I've woken up in the middle of the night in a cold sweat, worried that someone—namely, Mark—is hurting her.

But Josie's right. Perhaps it is time to take another step forward instead of looking backward. I kind of feel like the hole in my drywall is a good source of self-reflection. A reminder of what happens when I let my emotions get the better of me. Not exactly one of my finest moments.

"Yeah, you're probably right," I admit to Josie, begrudgingly.

She crosses her arms and tilts her hip, giving me the signature Josie look. "You need to give up on the numbers for today. Go to the hardware store and get some supplies to patch this shit up. Call it a day, then go home and rest so you can be bright-eyed and bushy-tailed for our field inspection on the Stevenson project tomorrow morning."

"You got it, boss," I mutter. "I'm supposed to have lunch with my mom today, but then I'll run to the store and take care of it."

Josie nods, satisfied with this plan.

A few hours later, I'm sitting on the patio with my mom, finishing up lunch. She's giving me a knowing look, that familiar glint in her eye that can only belong to a mother who's onto her son.

"What is it?" I finally ask her, knowing she'll let me hear it one way or another.

Mom shrugs innocently, though she gives me a suspicious side smile. My mother is still the same, but so different still. It's hard for me to reconcile the two versions of her that I know—her from before the cancer diagnosis, and now her after. She's still got the same spark that I associate with her, but it's also muted, from the exhaustion of fighting a relentless disease.

"*Mom,*" I drag out when she doesn't answer right away. But even I can't fight the smile off my face.

"It's nothing, really." She waves her hand.

I tilt my head and let out an exasperated sigh. "Whatever it is, just say it."

"It's just," she pauses, folding her hands in her lap and hitting me with a meaningful stare, "I want to make sure you're happy."

"Of course I'm happy, Mom," I say, blinking. I wasn't expecting this.

"You haven't really been yourself ever since that night," she says. I don't have to ask to know she's referencing the night I smuggled Izabel into her home after the events that transpired at the gala. Mom doesn't know all the details, but she's keen enough to know it wasn't good.

"And I just want you to be happy. You deserve to be happy. And ever since then, I can tell that you're not."

"I'm fine, Mom," I say, trying to sound sure of myself. "It's still just kind of weird right now, trying to figure out the business-owning world and everything."

"Ryan, that's not what I mean. I'm not talking business," she says, her lips pulling into a frown. "I might not be around forever."

"Mom—" I protest, but she holds her hand up, cutting me off.

"Let's not beat around the bush. I'm sick, we all know it. And every day is still a gamble. So while I'm here, I'm going to do everything that I can to make sure that you're happy with your life. Do you understand? Even if that means harping on you about things you don't want to talk about, because that's what mothers do."

I watch her closely, listening as she delivers her speech. And fuck it all, my eyes start to burn.

I clear my throat and sit up straighter. I'll be damned if I start to cry right here on a café patio with my mom sitting across from me.

"I'm working on it."

"Good," she says sharply. She picks up her fork, and then points it at me. "I expect status reports."

I laugh now, grateful she broke the tension with a joke. Reaching for my drink, I take a long sip and hoping it will clear the ball of emotion now lingering at the back of my throat.

I don't want to think about my mom not being around for some of the biggest milestones of my life, but she's right. It's a possibility.

And that thought is scary. If anything, it's a call to action to get off my ass and start taking the life I want for myself.

Her words still linger in the back of my mind as I stand in the middle of Darby's Hardware store only an hour later.

I'm in the middle of the aisle, rubbing the back of my neck, way out of my element here. Usually, I hire people to do this kind of work. My eyes wander the different brands of plaster kits, and I'm unsure which one I need to get. I also need to grab another gallon of paint while I'm here to cover up the considerable patch-job I'm about to do.

I narrow my eyes at the display when I hear a crash and a string of swears from the next aisle over. Taking a few steps, I peek around the edge of the partitions and am utterly shocked to see Izabel.

She's standing on her toes, trying to reach something on the over-stock shelf. Her arm is stretched as far as it can go, but her fingers are barely brushing the edge. On the ground next to her, I see a metal paint pan, the source of the crash.

"Maybe if you jump, you could reach it, shorty," I tease her, stepping into the aisle.

Her head spins around until her gaze lands on me, and she acknowledges me with an instant smile. "It's a serious character flaw. Why couldn't I just be a few inches taller?"

I shrug and walk up to where she's standing, easily reaching up and grabbing the three-pack of paint rollers she's after. "I don't know, Bells. Maybe talk to your mom about that one."

She huffs and rolls her eyes. "Thank you," she says, taking the rollers from me.

"Doing some painting?" I ask her like an idiot.

Izabel tucks a strand of brunette hair behind her ear and nods. "Yeah, Mark and I found a house. We're moving in in a few weeks. I just wanted to make sure I have all my ducks in a row beforehand."

"Well, congratulations, homeowner!" I try to be upbeat for her—a *house*. Things are moving right along for them. I guess that's a good thing. But even still, I can't deny that I'm disappointed. A part of me had hoped what happened the night of the gala would have been enough of a wakeup call for her to leave.

But I suspect Mark was able to weasel his way back in and exert his control over her even more so.

"It is pretty exciting," she responds, not sounding at all excited.

I shove my hands in my pockets and watch her for a second. "So, what color?"

"Hmm?"

"For your walls. What color did you decide on?"

"Oh," she pauses and rummages in her purse before pulling out a paint swatch, "I think I'm going with this forest-y green color for the living room."

"That's nice, Bells. I'm sure it will look great."

Izabel offers me an appreciative grin. "Thanks, Ryan. So what are you doing here?"

"I had to pick up a plaster kit. I have a hole in the wall to patch at the office."

She nods as if that's the most normal thing in the world. She doesn't ask where it came from, and I don't care to tell her. That would lead to nothing but embarrassment.

I quietly study her, and I wonder how she's been these last few weeks. She looks well enough. Her hair is slightly curled, and her eyes bright. Has he hurt her since? I trail my gaze over her arms and legs and don't see any exposed bruises. But I know that he'd just as likely hurt her from the inside, emotionally. Those kinds of injuries aren't always visible, but can be just as painful, if not more.

Izabel bends down and grabs the paint pan, placing the rollers inside of it. "Well, it was good to see you, Ryan. I hope you have a good rest of your day."

Wow, just like that, huh?

As she's walking away, I feel myself start to panic. I'm not ready to let her go again. I need more time with her. I take another step forward. "Hey, Bells." She turns toward me, those blue eyes mesmerizingly wide. "Would you want to grab a coffee or dinner sometime? Just to catch up?"

What am I doing? I told her I didn't want to stand around on the sidelines, yet here I am, asking to be back in her life again. Gosh, she probably thinks I'm stalking her or something. The last time I saw her, I told her I still loved her.

To my immense surprise, and unexplainable pleasure, another smile graces those beautiful lips of hers. "Yeah, that would be nice. Um..." Izabel reaches into her bag and pulls out her cell phone. "I'm actually free tonight if you don't have any plans."

I feel a surge of happiness, and the corners of my mouth tilt up. "Tonight sounds great. Want to do Siriano's?"

Her favorite Italian restaurant.

My brain is yelling at my heart, *What are you doing, you dumbass!* But for once, I have zero qualms about following my heart. It's only dinner, what's the harm in that? Bells and I have had dinner hundreds of times.

Just dinner between two friends.

"Siriano's would be amazing," she says, and I feel my stomach flip-flop at the wistful expression on her face. "Around six-ish?"

"Six, it is," I say, grinning widely. "I still don't know how such a tiny girl like you can put away a whole plate of pasta con broccoli."

She shrugs a shoulder and smirks. "It's a gift. Okay. I'll see you then."

And when she turns away this time, I let her go, knowing I'll have the chance to spend some more time with her this evening. I grab what I need and checkout.

When I hop in the car, I see that it's almost three already. I don't have time to patch up that wall today, but I swing by the office to drop off the supplies and tell Lori she can head home. Then I go back to my condo to shower and get changed for dinner.

I can't exactly explain why I'm so deliriously happy. I was the one who cut ties between Izabel and me after the gala incident. Boundaries had been set, and she adhered to them, which I appreciated. But the distance didn't turn out to be the all-powerful healing I was looking for.

I'm hopelessly head-over-heels for Izabel, and unfortunately for me, I'm not sure if anything is going to help that.

I rush through my shower and try my best to tame my hair, throw on a fresh pair of pants and a nice shirt, and head out the door. I arrive at the restaurant fifteen minutes before six. The host shows me to a table for two and places two sets of silverware and two menus, and the waiter swings by the table only a minute later with a basket of fresh-baked bread. He looks young, like he must still be in high school.

"Can I get you something to drink while you wait?" he asks me, pulling out his little notepad.

I lean back in my chair slightly. "I'll do a whiskey neat, and a Pinot Grigio for my date. She should be here shortly."

I remember her mentioning white wine is her favorite. Red gives her a raging headache.

The waiter runs off to put in the drinks, and I glance around the restaurant, craning my neck to see if she's at the front of the restaurant. When I don't see her, I pull out my phone and shoot her a text.

Ryan: Hey Bells, I've got a table for us. Just come on in whenever you get here.

No response. A different waiter comes back with the drinks, carefully positioning the glasses on the table. I pick up the whiskey and take a generous sip, my eyes still glued to my phone, waiting for the screen to light up.

Six o'clock comes and goes.

Six-thirty.

I scroll to her contact information and press the green call icon. It doesn't even ring, just goes straight to voicemail: *"Hey, it's Izabel, sorry I missed you. Leave me a message, and I'll call you back!"*

"Bells, it's me. Just wanted to make sure I got the time right. I thought we said six. Just give me a call and let me know if I messed up!"

Six-forty-five.

The waiter comes by and refreshes the basket of bread that I've demolished with a fresh basket. And he drops a few butter packets beside me. He stands awkwardly for a moment. "Anything else I can get you, sir?"

I hold up my glass of whiskey that is mostly empty. "You could put another one of these in for me."

He nods and disappears without another word.

When I look down at my glass, I feel sick to my stomach. Here I thought we'd get to have this pleasant dinner, just her and me—a lame attempt at nostalgia. I didn't even consider how desperate it made me look. Izabel was probably looking for an out, but couldn't find one.

So she just shuts her phone off and ghosts me. Sounds about right.

The other waiter, who I've deduced, is the bartender, strolls by with another whiskey neat, and sets it down.

Getting trapped in the cycle of my own loathing, I quickly down it and then hold it out for him to replenish. His eyes widen just a fraction, but he pats me on the shoulder and heads back to the bar, returning with a fresh glass only a minute later.

Seven o'clock.

By this time, I've sent her two more texts. It is a mixture of confusion and concern that she's possibly gotten into a car accident or held up in another way—namely that asshole fiancé of hers. But still, no response.

I go back and forth between feeling worry that something's happened to her, and irritation with the prospect that she's standing me up. I finally settle on the resolution that if she had been having difficulties with Mark, she could have sent me a text.

Seven-thirty.

I send her one more text. The last attempt. This is bullshit. I feel like Ross on *Friends*. I glance around, making sure the rest of the dinner guests aren't throwing me pitiful glances. Throwing back the rest of my drink, I wave the waiter over. He comes and hands me the check. I look it over, even though the words and numbers are blurring together.

"Do I have to pay for the wine, even though she didn't drink it?"

Now I do get a pitiful look from the waiter. "Unfortunately, yes."

I shrug, hand him my card, and grab the wine glass meant for Izabel. I offer him a toast, "When in Rome," and then get to work emptying this glass too.

He returns with my card and puts it into its space in the wallet I hold out for him. I feel like my fingers are made of cotton. They don't seem to want to function right at the joints.

I try to make a move to stand up, and I stagger back.

Well, fuck me.

The world spins, and I put a lot of effort into not falling flat on my face. My brain is able to control my fingers long enough that I can scroll through my phone and find another contact I'm looking for. Again, I press the green button and bring it up to my ear. It rings and rings, and then...

"God, this better be good, Ryan. I'm at the part where Westley is fighting off the ROUS-es to save his lady love."

My inebriated brain cannot even begin to process the weird words that just came out of her mouth. My own words are slurred when I ask, "Jos, can you come pick me up? I'm at Siriano's, and I don't think I can drive."

Silence. Oh God, I hope she was able to understand what I said. I feel a wave of relief when she lets out a disappointed sigh. "As you wish. I'll be there in ten." Then she hangs up.

I manage my way out of the restaurant, waving goodbye to my friends, the waiters, on my walk out. I lean my back against the firm wall of the building, my head falling back against the bricks. Crickets chirp in the bushes next to me. I feel like I'm spinning, and I command myself to not throw up.

I don't know how long I'm out there waiting, but finally I see Josie's car turn into the parking lot and stop right in front of me. I stumble over to the passenger side door and settle myself in the front seat, slumping against the window as she drives me home.

I vaguely remember her helping me walk up the stairs to my condo, then unlocking the door. Josie pushes me onto my bed, pulling my shoes off but leaving everything else. I settle my head onto the pillow, groaning as I bury my face into it. Why did I do this? I know what happens when you shoot whiskey and chase it with a full glass of wine.

"What did you say?" Josie asks, her voice just a whisper in the darkness.

I didn't even realize I said anything. "I'm an idiot," I mutter, pulling my face out of the pillow just long enough to get that out before flopping back down.

Another low sigh, and I feel her stroke her hand through my hair. "Yeah, Ry. Yeah, you are. An idiot in love."

Chapter 16

Izabel

My reflection stares back at me out of my bathroom mirror. I give myself a good once-over and decide that I'm happy with the result. I don't want to come across as desperate, but I want to look nice for our dinner tonight.

For Ryan.

My hair is still slightly curled from this morning, so I spritz on some hairspray to bring some more life to it and call it good. I'm wearing my favorite shade of lipstick and apply some mascara on my eyes.

Not too much, but just enough.

I think this is the most I've felt like myself in a long, long time.

I smile at the mirror, making sure I don't have any lettuce stuck in my teeth from lunch, and then head back to my bedroom. My feet carry me over to my dresser, where I pull out my jewelry box, digging through it to find one of my most prized possessions. My fingers delicately hold up the silver heart necklace that Ryan gifted to me all those years ago. I run my thumb over the engraving on the back, feeling the ridges underneath my skin. *R&B*. Would it be too much if I wore it tonight? I don't want to give off the wrong kind of message. I bite the inside of my lip, unsure. Laying the necklace down on top of my dresser, I stretch the silver chain out straight.

Anticipation pools in my belly. I don't think I've ever been this eager to go out to dinner before. It's been over a month since I last spent any time with Ryan, and the last time didn't end on such a happy note. His request to put distance between us hurt, but I understand. And I've tried my best to give him that distance he was looking for. But I can't deny that I miss him.

For a long time, Ryan was my best friend. The one person I felt closest to in the world. After all those years, having him back in Cedar Ridge has rekindled a yearning for that kind of connection. That was one of the hardest parts of our breakup. Besides not having him as my boyfriend, I missed having him as my friend.

I don't have that kind of connection with Mark anymore. He used to be the light in some of my darkest days, but now I find that there's more distance growing between us as time passes. I love him, but Ryan and I had a connection that was initially built on trust and friendship. I suppose surviving a life-or-death situation together would be the reason that kind of bond was formed. I don't know if I'll ever be able to recreate that kind of experience with anyone but him.

My eyes dart down to the gaudy engagement ring on my finger. I allow myself to imagine what it would be like if it were someone else's ring, or if it was someone else in general. I always used to dream that I would marry Ryan. It was the next chapter for us. I think about how scandalized Ryan looked last month when his little sister blurted out something about him wanting to marry me. Maybe at one point in the past, he felt the same.

I have to wonder if we made a mistake letting each other go. At the time, the distance was suffocating, and we were hurting each other more than we were helping. We each needed to go and discover our own paths, but I question if that was the right decision.

The sound of my doorbell brings me out of my daydreams. My eyebrows pull together as I walk out of my room and toward the door. I thought Ryan was going to meet me there. Maybe I got confused. It's about a quarter after five, so perhaps he decided to swing by here and pick me up instead.

I open my front door with a big smile on my face, but it instantly drops when I come face-to-face with my fiancé. He's holding a few grocery bags and a bottle of wine.

"Mark," I say, surprised. "I thought you were working a case tonight."

He shrugs and offers me a cheeky grin. "My client canceled at the last minute, so I thought I'd come by here and make you dinner. It's been a while since we've had a quiet night in." Mark looks me over, and then narrows his eyes. "You look dressed up. Were you expecting your other boyfriend?"

My hands feel clammy as I quickly shake my head. I know he's teasing, but the joke hits too close to home. I blurt out, "No, of course not. Come on in."

"Great, oh, I brought you this too! It's your favorite." He holds out the bottle of Zinfandel. Red wine.

I bite back a groan, anticipating the pounding headache I'm going to have later tonight, but I offer him a tight-lipped smile. "Thank you."

Mark moves by me and into the kitchen. I follow him, unsure of where else to go. Ingredients are laid out across the counter: lasagna noodles, red sauce, Italian ground sausage, mozzarella cheese. It looks like he had Italian food on the mind too.

Ryan.

I place the bottle of wine in the freezer to let it chill. Red wine is gross enough as it is, but *warm?* No, thank you. I reach for my phone sitting on a side table next to my couch and begin typing out a text to Ryan.

"Hey, no phones. You know the rules." Mark shoots me a teasing wink.

It was a rule. The two of us had come up with it almost a year ago after Mark started at the law firm. He was always getting texts and calls while we were trying to spend time together, so we made a 'No Cell Phone' rule on date nights.

Shit. I suppose I can explain it to Ryan tomorrow. Surely, he will understand. Hopefully, it won't take him too long to catch on to the fact that I'm not coming. God, he's going to hate me after this. Maybe I can sneak away and send him some kind of message in a few minutes. I place my phone face down on the counter, already plotting my next move.

Mark comes up to me and wraps his arms around my waist, his hands landing just over my rear end. Leaning down, he presses a kiss to the tip of my nose. "You do look lovely tonight."

I offer him a smile, my first genuine one all night. "Thank you, Mark."

"Were you going somewhere?"

"I was just going to meet a friend," I tell him, knowing he'll see through it if I outright lie. He is a lawyer, after all. But even he is not so good at seeing through my lies of omission—what he doesn't know won't kill him.

"Oh well, you can always hang out on another day," he says, melding his lips with mine. He kisses me for a moment before letting me go and heading back into the kitchen to begin preparing our meal.

"Yeah, it will be fine. I'm actually going to run to the restroom," I say, reaching out for my phone resting on the counter. I can send a quick text Ryan while I'm in there.

"With your phone?" Mark asks me incredulously. "I think you can survive a few minutes without it."

I blush but leave my phone where it was, scurrying off to the restroom. Taking care of business, I wash my hands before heading back out to the kitchen.

"So, what are you making me?" I ask him as if I haven't figured it out already.

"Lasagna," Mark looks at me proudly. "And a salad. I thought we could watch a movie while we wait for it to bake."

I'm reminded in this moment of how I fell in love with Mark in the first place. He's looking at me with those big puppy dog eyes the color of chocolate. There is no malice, no superiority in them, just love and tenderness.

Since the night of the gala, Mark has been making a valiant effort to keep his emotions under control. We've been to a few counseling sessions, both together and then on our own, and I honestly think it's helping. Or at the very least, they've given Mark an assortment of tricks to try to get his control back.

If we get into a tiff—which happens more than I like, but still—Mark will turn to those tools and use them. I've seen him straight up walk out of a room, or take a few minutes to catch his breath before responding to me.

Honestly, it's refreshing. Mark is a motivated person, and when he puts his mind to something, nothing can get in his way. It's how he did so well in law school and then got such a great job right after graduating.

I feel myself relaxing at the warm look in his eyes. "I think that sounds great. What can I do to help?"

Mark looks down at the spread of ingredients on the

counter. "Could you start browning the meat and combine it with the sauce?"

I do as he asks but keep eyeballing my cell phone, trying to devise a plan where I can sneak off and try to explain to Ryan why I'm standing him up. Mark seems to notice.

"Will you just turn that phone off? You keep looking at it every two seconds, and it's getting on my nerves."

He holds out his palm for me to hand it over. I press my lips tightly together as I pick up the phone and power it down. My eyes glance at the clock on the screen: five-forty. Ryan's probably almost there. He wraps his fingers around the device when I hand it to him, and then he puts it down by the table next to the front door, placing his own on top of it. No interruptions. No distractions.

I sigh, but turn back to the sausage I'm trying to cook. Ryan will just have to wait. Mark goes back to chopping onions. A few minutes later, I hear him swear and reach for a paper towel.

"Shit. I just sliced my finger instead of the onion," he hisses. "Do you still have Band-Aids in your bathroom?"

I nod, and he hurries off, holding the towel tightly to his finger. I keep stirring the meat. At first, I hear him rustling around in my bathroom closet, but then it goes silent. I peek down the hallway, but I don't see him.

Turning the stove down to a medium-low, I trail after him. "Mark, is everything okay?"

Weird, he's not in the bathroom. I turn the corner into my bedroom and see him standing by my dresser. He quickly sticks his hand in his pocket and looks at me sheepishly.

"I didn't find any in the bathroom, and I know you keep a stash in here. Sorry."

I smile at him and move closer, taking his sliced hand in my own. The towel is stuck to the wound, and I pull at it. He hisses again, and I can't help but roll my eyes at my fiancé. It's not even that deep of a cut. But still, I wrap the Band-Aid tightly around his injury and take his good hand, leading him back to the kitchen to finish cooking.

When the lasagna is fully assembled and layered with mozzarella, we stick it in the oven to bake, along with the loaf of garlic bread I found in my freezer. Thankfully, Mark bought the instant noodles that don't have to be pre-boiled. We settle on the couch together while we wait.

Mark stretches out in the corner, extending his arm over the back of the couch. I shoot him a smile and curl up next to him. He wraps his arm around me, letting his hand fall onto my hip. "So, what should we watch?" he asks.

I reach for the remote to my TV and turn it onto Netflix. I don't give it much thought and just select one of the first titles that pop up on my home screen. Mark doesn't comment.

The movie begins; the characters are introduced. When the kitchen timer goes off, Mark strolls into the kitchen to pull the dish out and let it sit for a moment. I pause our movie, so he doesn't miss anything. While waiting for the food to cool, Mark takes the wine out of the freezer and pours us each a hefty glass. I try not to grimace when he hands me mine.

He sits down again and holds his glass up to mine, offering a toast. "To a lifetime of wonderful evenings like this together." I clink my glass with his and take a sip, feeling the bitter red wine coat my tongue. I force myself to swallow it.

Mark sets his glass down on the table and then turns to me, taking my hand. "Hey, I just wanted you to know that everything I said in session the other day I meant with my whole heart." He squeezes my fingers. He's talking about our last couple's counseling session, when he spoke words to me that I never thought I'd hear from him. "You are the most important thing in my life, and I want to make sure that you know that. I love you."

"I love you too, Mark," I say softly, feeling my heart stammering against my chest. This time, I take the initiative and lean forward to capture his lips with mine.

He kisses me back, but then leans back slightly, pressing his forehead against mine. "I can't wait to marry you, Izabel. I can't wait for you to be my wife." I don't respond and kiss him again. He cups the side of my neck and inhales deeply.

"Speaking of weddings," he mutters against my mouth. I pause for a second before putting distance between us, not liking the sound of where he's taking this. "My mom wants to take you to a wedding expo tomorrow. You're not busy, right? I told her you would go."

I tilt my head and frown. "I mean, no, I'm not busy. But I wish you would have asked me before you told her yes."

He shrugs. "I figured it would be good for you. To bond with her. I know things between you two haven't exactly been...smooth."

I look at him incredulously. "*I* have no problem with your mother. *She* has a serious problem with me, though."

"No, she doesn't. She loves you. I wish you would just give her a chance. She's my mother, Izabel."

I sigh, knowing that no matter what I say, he will not change his stance on this matter. "Fine. I'll go to the stupid expo."

"Great. I knew you'd understand." Pecking my lips again, he runs into the kitchen to serve up our plates. He brings them out, both piled high with cheesy lasagna, a slice of garlic bread, and a fresh-looking salad.

The movie resumes, and we both dig in. I find myself spacing enough that I'm not entirely sure what the movie is even about. I can't help but feel sick to my stomach, knowing I'll have to spend most of the day with Mark's mom tomorrow.

She's the definition of *Smother-in-law.*

Everything has to meet specific standards, otherwise, "What will the club members think?" She has never liked me since the very beginning of our relationship. A high school history teacher didn't seem to meet her high expectations for her sweet Marky-poo.

Barf.

Oh well. I'll attend this expo with her, and hopefully, then she'll leave me alone. We're coming up on the end of June, meaning our wedding is only three months away. There's still lots to do, but soon it will be over, and I won't have to worry about setting examples or following traditions. I'll just be married, and life can go on.

Hopefully.

After the movie is done, Mark takes our plates over to the sink to rinse them off. I stay on the couch, forcing down another sip of this god-awful wine. Once they're dried and put away, he advances over to the table to grab our phones. Our date must be over. I watch him power mine on, and before I can seize it from him, the alerts start rolling in, the phone chiming with the multiple notifications, one after another. His eyes narrow as he reads them, one by one.

My heart pounds harder as Mark turns his glare toward me. His expression is thunderous. The instant I see his expression, I feel the wine-headache coming on. All notions of love and tenderness that he expressed less than an hour ago are gone without a trace. "Wanna tell me why the *fuck* Ryan is blowing up your phone?"

My jaw drops open, and words fail me. Not that it matters.

Mark doesn't give me a chance to explain before he's dropping my phone to the floor and advancing on me. His hand grabs my throat as he pushes me against the wall, his grip squeezing and tightening as he crushes my windpipe.

My eyes go wide as I struggle against him, but his hold is too tight.

Fear explodes within me, and my fight-or-flight kicks in as I claw and kick at him. But still, it's not enough.

I make out Mark saying something to me, and vaguely I recognize him swearing and calling me horrible names. I still try my hardest to get away from him, but his hold is still far too tight. I hate that I'm not strong enough to match his strength.

My mind races as I try to reason my way out of this situation. Should I just let him expel his anger? Get it out of his system so we can move on? If I continue to struggle, could I end up hurt worse than if I didn't? Like the last time I tried to get away from him and he sprained my shoulder?

At some point, the reasoning becomes pointless.

I can't breathe.

Black spots play around my vision as I make the decision to continue to fight. Panic makes my skin prickle and I know I'm about to lose consciousness any second now.

Finally, without realizing I'm doing it, my arm swings up, and I clock him on the side of his face. Mark swears, but lets me go.

I crumple to the ground in a heap, though I catch myself with my hands, sputtering and coughing, gasping air deep into my lungs and feeling the burn. Tears stream down my face and my heart feels as though it's about to explode out of my chest.

Mark sits a few feet away, still cursing and muttering under his breath. Distantly, I see him cupping his cheek.

I blink a few times, staring at the wooden floor, though not seeing anything. My body trembles uncontrollably and my arms give out from underneath me. I press my cheek against the cool floor and allow myself to breathe.

Every insecurity floods me as I lie there, broken in the aftermath of what just happened. In those few minutes, I seem to experience every possible emotion; fear, hatred, disappointment. Yet none of those are as strong as the self-loathing I feel for myself.

How could I have allowed this to happen? I should have known better than to push the limits. I should have been better. I hate myself for being so weak, so broken. And finally, the most fearful thought of all...

Maybe I deserved it.

Chapter 17

Ryan

"Wake up, sleepyhead," a female voice sings to me. I feel my shoulder being shaken in an attempt to rouse me.

With a groan, I roll over to find Josie sitting on the edge of my bed. I rub my eyes, trying to decide if I'm still drunk. My head is pounding, and my stomach feels like I've been on a rollercoaster for hours. When I glance at the clock on the bedside table, I am mortified to find it's not even six in the morning.

"What are you doing here, Jos?"

She gives me a sweet smile. "Well, since you so kindly interrupted my evening with your tomfoolery, I decided to crash here last night. We have a big day today, and I wasn't about to let you ruin that."

Ah yes, my brain miraculously puts two and two together. We have the Stevenson site inspection today. This project is a big deal for Josie. And for me.

"You slept here?" I ask her. My eyes dart to the other side of my bed. It looks undisturbed, but I couldn't be too sure. "We didn't—"

"No, don't worry. I'm not that desperate," she says with a smirk.

Relief crashes through me, and I stretch my arms above my head.

As if she's had enough of my shit, Josie claps her hands to get me moving, and the sharp noise makes me groan as it reverberates through my ears. "Okay, you need to get up, shower, and put on some better-looking clothes. Then we'll get you some super unhealthy breakfast and the blackest coffee possible. Come on. We gotta be on the road by seven. You know how far that site is, and we're supposed to be there by noon. Up and at 'em!"

She tugs on my hand, forcing me to roll out of bed and pushing me into the bathroom. I do my best to shower as quickly as possible, cleansing myself of the aftermath of last night. The steam helps clear my head, and I feel a ton better.

When I step out of my en suite bathroom, I find that Josie's laid out a fresh dress shirt and slacks for me, and has even made my bed. This woman is too much. Stumbling out of my bedroom, I find her scrolling on her phone on my couch. My eyes dart to the overnight bag on one of the chairs in the room. She really is one of the most prepared people I've ever met. She stands when she sees me and allows her gaze to travel me up and down, giving me a nod of approval.

"That's better. Drunk is not a good look on you, Ry. Let's go, I'm driving." She grabs her purse and struts out the door.

Josie looks like a million bucks. She must have packed new clothes to change into, 'cause I vaguely remember her showing up to get me in pajama pants. She's dressed to impress today in a black pencil skirt and a red blouse, and her hair's pulled into a bun on the top of her head. The red of her shirt contrasts with her olive skin perfectly. Red is really her color.

I glance down at the outfit Josie chose for me and am

immensely grateful that I have her as a friend. If it were up to me, I probably would have slept straight through this meeting. And as a startup company, that's a mistake I can't afford to make. Either that or I would have rolled out of bed and thrown on the first thing I could find. Josie seriously saved my ass.

When we're in her car, she selects a playlist on her phone to listen to and then turns to me. "What do you want for breakfast, Boozy?"

I shrug and lean my head back against the headrest, letting my eyes fall closed. "Anything greasy will do it."

"Mickey D's, it is then."

Josie goes through the drive-through, getting me a large black coffee, three McGriddles, and a hash brown. All she gets is a yogurt parfait and a café latte for herself. She's obviously not nursing a hangover, so she doesn't need the good stuff like I do.

Once we hit the highway, I unwrap my first sandwich and try not to groan at how good it tastes. I polish off the rest of my breakfast, taking sips of the scalding coffee periodically. The fast-food settles in my stomach, soaking up the reminder of my poor decisions the previous night.

Josie keeps her attention on driving, quietly humming along to her music. At some point, I think I doze off because I startle awake when Josie has to swerve the car to avoid someone who didn't see her.

"Sorry," she mutters, reaching for her coffee. "Idiot drivers."

"It's okay," I say, relaxing back into my seat.

Josie is quiet for a beat, and then she drops the bomb. "Sooo, are we just not gonna talk about the elephant in the car?"

"What in the world are you talking about, Josie?"

"I'm talking," she says, keeping her eyes on the road but tightening her grip on the steering wheel, "about you getting trashed at Siriano's on a Wednesday night and calling me to come pick you up."

I groan and thump my head back, squeezing my eyes shut. I'm embarrassed, to say the least. "It was nothing. Just a dumb mistake. You can drop it."

"You've been making those mistakes a lot, Ry. You think I don't know about the bottle of Jack you keep in your desk? Or the *cases*—as in plural—of beer I found last night in your fridge?"

"Why are you going through my desk?"

"I was looking for sticky notes!" she defends. "But that's not the point. We need to talk about this, Ryan. Seriously."

"Just drive, Josie. I don't have time for this."

"Actually, you do have time. We've still got at *least* an hour and a half together in this car. So unless you want to jump out...we're talking about this."

I don't respond, and she goes silent for a minute.

"Did you know my brother is an alcoholic?" she asks.

"Josie."

"I'm just saying. I've seen the struggles, and I know what it can be like when you have a vice like that. You're safe with me, Ry. I get it. But we need to address this before it becomes something more."

"I'm fine," I insist.

"No, you're not."

My chest feels tight. I stare out the window, stewing, keeping my eyes off of Josie, ashamed to look at her. In our silence, my phone buzzes in my pocket. I pull it out and glimpse Izabel's name scrolling across the top. My heart twists, remembering how disappointed I was when she didn't show up last night. I click *decline* and put it back into my pocket. Almost right away, it starts buzzing again. With a scowl, I pull it out of my pocket, clicking *decline,* and then shut the thing off for good measure.

I definitely have no interest in hearing Izabel's excuses this morning.

I hear Josie sigh, and then she goes for a different approach. "Look, Ryan, I know being around Izabel is hard, and I know that Mark really brings out the worst in you, but you are better than this."

"You think I don't know that?" I ask her, venom dripping from my tone. "I'm well aware that I turn into a love-sick fool around her. She's all I can ever seem to think about, but even that's not enough. She won't leave him. I'm not enough for her to take that risk."

My honesty surprises me, and I blink a few times. Josie gives me a calculating look, processing the truth I've just spilled.

"First of all, you're wrong. You are enough. And second of all, I know you want her back. I know what she means to you, and frankly, I know what *you* mean to *her*. That's why we're doing this, right?" She nods to the open road in front of us.

I don't respond.

"So it's established that Izabel is what you want. But I think you need to start worrying about your own toxic situation before you get involved with hers."

I stay quiet.

Her words hit me somewhere deep, though. It's time I face the music. At first, it was an extra drink, then two. Now, just like Josie said, it's become a vice that I can't seem to shake. Any time I find myself stuck in a situation that has me feeling inadequate, drinking is what makes it better. It numbs the ache.

"I don't think you need to quit cold turkey, but if you want, I can help you find an AA meeting to help you get on the right path again."

I grind my teeth together, and my jaw muscles scream in response. "I don't think that's necessary." Josie opens her mouth to protest, but I cut her off. "But, I will consider what you've said."

Thankfully, she leaves it at that and then changes the topic. "Wow, this place is way the fuck out here."

I lean my head against the window, watching the trees go by. "No, kidding."

We drive in silence for the rest of the way to the site. I'm still busy processing her blunt intervention, or whatever the hell that was. I know she's right. I've let myself slip on this one too many times. And if Josie's noticing, I'm sure others are starting to as well.

I don't want to be this guy. I need to be a better man, for Izabel, for myself. It starts today. As soon as I get home, it's all going down the drain. Time to start fresh. It won't be clear cut and simple like I'm hoping, I'm sure. But the least I can do is make an attempt to be better.

Josie continues to sing along with her tunes while I'm lost in my thoughts. I only snap out of it when we pull into the drive of the construction site. I'm out of the vehicle before it's fully in park, itching to see the progress.

The Stevenson Project.

Just like Josie said, we are *way* the fuck out here. I always forget just how far it is. The old walls have been completely replaced, a new framework of 2x4s standing proudly. The trees are all the same, and they tower overhead, their leaves rustling in the wind. I stick my hands in my pockets, feeling a smile playing on my lips, and walk up the old gravel pathway.

The things these trees have seen.

"Not exactly how you remembered, huh?" Josie asks from beside me. I look down at her and grin.

"No, not quite." I look back up at the skeletal frame of the soon-to-be livable house and recall what used to stand in its place. Quite the improvement, even now. "But it's going to be so much better when it's done."

The site coordinator comes to greet us, extending a handshake to both me and Josie. Josie takes the lead since she's the architect on the project. She knows all the ins and outs of the minor details. I'm really just her client in this case. He walks us around, showing us, mostly me, where everything will be located by the end of the construction.

I point out a few things I'd like differently, and Josie jots them down for me in her notebook, so they don't get lost in the madness.

"This will turn out to be an excellent investment for you, Ryan," the coordinator tells me proudly. "Much better than that piece of junk that was here before. I don't even know how that thing was still standing."

I shrug. "The owner died a few years ago. His family didn't even know it was still in the family until I reached out to them. It got a little neglected over the years."

The guy nods. "Yeah, well, it won't be that way anymore. We kept the integrity of the space like you wanted. It's basically the same, just more fundamentally sound, and bigger. You got more than a one-room cabin now."

"That sounds perfect," I tell him with a smile, and I mean it. He shows me a couple more things and then heads off to check on his crew. The construction should all be finished in about two months. Then it's all mine.

As I look around the area, I feel more at home than I have in a while. The fresh air is doing wonders for the hangover. The McGriddle soaked up most of it, but this fresh air and the trees are taking care of any lingering effects. I could stay out here forever.

I'm not sure what possessed me to actually buy this place.

My real estate agent was questioning my sanity when I told him I wanted to purchase this property. I had been thinking about it for years, nonstop. The place has been haunting my dreams since we left. Its architecture took up at least one page in all of my sketch pads. What it was, what it could be.

Memories flood my mind as I observe the area: injuries, truths, laughter, jokes, first kisses, fights...love.

This was where loathing turned into a friendship and then into more, much more. Where fears were addressed, and trust was built at a level that could never be reproduced for either of us. Where my relationship with Bells began. Mac Stevenson's cabin.

Now, my cabin.

Josie shakes her head as she comes to stand by me. Her hands are on her hips as she follows my lead, looking around. "I can't believe you bought this place. It sure looks like a whole lot of nothing."

"Yeah, but it means everything."

Chapter 18

Izabel

"Are you sure you're okay?" Mark asks me timidly as I step out of my bathroom the following morning. He decided to stay over last night, and I hate myself for letting him.

I stare at my fiancé for a moment and wrap the towel tighter around my torso. I hope he can see the bright purple bruise located at the base of my neck. I hope it hurts him just as much as he hurt me.

After striking him, he finally let me go and I fell to the ground, utterly defeated.

And then he was there. As if a flip had been switched, his anger turned into concern. Mark fell to his knees, careful to give me enough distance as he told me repeatedly how sorry he was.

"Izabel," he gasped. "I'm so sorry. I didn't mean to. When I saw those text messages, I just lost control. You know how I get when it comes to him. You shouldn't have been texting him behind my back. I'm sorry, I'm sorry."

Mark's breathing was almost as labored as mine, and he hesitantly reached out a hand, his fingers trying to brush my skin. I cried out and swiped at his hand, feeling my skin hit his. I didn't want him touching me. Not while I was still working through the aftermath of the events that had just transpired. He jerked his hand away from me and paused.

A moment later, he pulled me into his lap and rocked me back and forth. My body sagged with submission, and I allowed him to comfort me. My tears turned to sobs as he held me close. When they subsided, Mark picked me up off the floor, carrying me into my bedroom, setting me onto my bed—the mattress sagging under my weight. Mark's fingers went to the zipper on my dress and pulled it down. I let him lift the dress off me, the fabric rustling as it fell to the floor.

He sat on the bed behind me, his lips pressing against the edge of my shoulder, then in the hollow space of my collarbone. As his kisses trailed up my neck to my jaw, I could feel his hand snake around to my bare belly. His fingers traced along the edge of my panties, dipping under the thin seam.

I lurched away from him, my skin crawling from the contact. "No," I snapped as I pulled my knees up to my chest. Sex was not going to fix this. Not this time.

Mark looked at me sheepishly for a second before scooting off the bed and reaching for my brush on the dresser. I watched him like a hawk as he held it up like a peace offering. He crawled back on the bed behind me and ran the bristles through my hair.

I was still stiff as a board, but I started to relax as the brush against my scalp soothed me on a more intimate level. He dragged the brush through my hair, whispering sweet words and apologies. His kind actions brought on another wave of tears that I let consume me and drag me into unconsciousness.

This morning when I woke up, Mark was already awake, gently running his hand over my hair. I stretched underneath the covers and then rolled out of bed. He gave me space as I walked into the bathroom and flicked the light on. As soon as my eyes found my reflection in the mirror, my stomach dropped.

The red and purple bruise took me by surprise. I didn't think it would be that bad. My hands shook as I traced the outline of Mark's fingerprints on my neck. Pulling myself away from the reflection, I turned the shower on and put the water on the highest setting. Stepping under the spray, I let it burn away the events of last night until my skin was bright red. As I let the hot water cleanse some of my shame, I replayed last night, going through different scenarios and wondering what would have happened if I'd responded differently.

I found it cathartic, pretending that I was strong enough to stand up to him. Even if it was in my imagination, I found the exercise to be a good funnel of my anger. It helped me process it better, gave me clarity.

Now, I stare at Mark wordlessly. I know my skin is blotchy from the hot water and that there is an ugly bruise around my neck. A bruise that *he* put there. The sight of Mark still in my bed has bile rising in my throat, and I'm suddenly spinning around and running back into the bathroom to spew up my dinner from last night.

He said it wouldn't happen again. He *promised.*

Even if I set myself up for his anger, he promised it would never happen again and he lied.

I feel Mark crouch beside me by the toilet, pulling my wet hair away from my face as I gag and throw up again. He rubs slow circles on my back, and as much as I don't want to admit it, I find the action comforting.

When I decide I'm not going to throw up anymore, I fall against him. He wraps his arms around me, holding me tight. Mark's hand brushes over my forehead, which is beaded with sweat from the vomiting, and presses a kiss into my hair. Sighing, I let the kiss soothe me.

As much as I love Mark, those are not the kinds of feelings running through me right now.

I pull away from him, re-wrap my towel tightly against my chest, and walk back into my bedroom. With a heavy exhale, I begin digging through my dresser and closet to find a suitable outfit for my outing with Mark's mom.

Mark steps into the room after me. His movements are careful, as if he's walking on eggshells, afraid of my reaction.

Except he should know by now that detonating into a fit of rage is more *his thing*.

"What are you doing?" he asks me quietly.

I've selected a modest outfit: a pair of blue dress pants that go to my ankles, a white blouse, and a blazer. I double-check to make sure nothing is wrinkled, otherwise, I'll never hear the end of it.

"I'm getting ready for my day with your mother," I tell him, my tone flat.

Mark comes and sits on the edge of my bed as I pull on my bra and panties. "I can call her if you want. Maybe you should just stay in today."

I shoot him a glare. "Why? Because I have a bruise on my neck from where you strangled me last night? Afraid Mommy's not going to be too pleased?"

He rears away from me as if I've just struck him. I'm not one to usually let my temper show, and I've taken him by surprise. A small part of me, buried deep down, remembers that I used to be this fiery all the time. Somehow, I let him dampen that spark within me, so it's no surprise he's shocked to see it flare again.

"No. I was just saying 'cause you didn't seem to want to last night. But yes, after everything, maybe you should just rest. I can stay with you if you want. I'll call into work."

I close my eyes and take a deep breath, buttoning the few buttons at the top of my blouse. "Honestly, Mark, I can barely look at you right now. Why would I want to spend the rest of the day with you?"

"Izabel," he says brokenly. "I said I was sorry. What else do you want from me? I don't know what came over me."

I square my shoulders and look up at him, hoping I come across more confident than I actually feel. My hands tremble and my pulse thunders in my ears. I draw whatever remaining strength I have and pray my voice doesn't waver as I say in a firm tone, "What do I want? I want us to be capable of having a conversation without you throwing me against a wall when you get mad. I told you that this couldn't happen again. And yet here we are."

"I know," Mark whispers. "Maybe we should try to go to a counseling session today? I could call her—"

"No." The forcefulness in the word takes me off guard, reminding me of last night, when in the same tone, I turned down his sexual advances. Mark steps back another inch from me and I feel empowered by the slight act of submission. "I need space, Mark. I'll go to this stupid expo with your mom, but honestly, I don't even know if there will be a wedding after this."

My words surprise me just as much as they appear to surprise him. My breath catches in my throat, but I buckle down and hold my ground.

"I don't want to see you today. Or tomorrow, for that matter. Don't call me, don't text me, just leave me the fuck alone until you get your shit straightened out. Do you hear me?"

"I understand," he says dejectedly. He holds his hands out,

begging me. "I know I fucked up again, Izabel. I know I did. I swear on my life this will be the last time."

"Can you leave now?" I ask through gritted teeth.

Mark stares at me with those wide chocolate eyes that, on any other day, I could get lost in. I can see the hurt etched there. My heart twinges, but I just cannot bring myself to care. He gets up off my bed and sticks his hands in his pockets. I'm grateful he doesn't try to touch me.

"I really don't think you should be alone. I can stay, Izabel, it's fine."

"Leave," I plead with him, desperately, my body trembling. "I don't want you here."

"Okay. Okay," Mark responds, holding up his hands. "You remember I'm going out of town next weekend for the holiday with my dad?" I nod. The Fourth of July is next weekend. Mark always goes to the smoky mountains to fish with his father for the holiday. "Maybe we can touch base once I get back."

I don't deign to respond, instead crossing my arms over my chest and watching him leave without another word. As soon as he's gone, I take a few deep breaths.

Once he gets back. That would give us a little over a week of alone time. Maybe I can have my thoughts sorted by then. Maybe the distance will give Mark a little perspective too. I meant what I said; I don't know if I even want to marry him after this.

I'm not about to enter into a marriage where I get thrown around whenever I do something he doesn't like. Maybe by standing my ground now, I can nip this whole anger-thing in the bud before it truly becomes an issue. I know Mark. I've known him for years. And because I've known him for so long, I know he's better than this. I deserve better than this.

When I hear my front door close, I allow my shoulders to

slump. I reach for my phone, sitting on the nightstand and pull up Ryan's phone number. First thing's first, I have to apologize for bailing on him last night. Not to mention, I have an overwhelming need to hear his voice.

The phone rings and rings before being sent to voicemail. I grumble and then hit the call button again—ring, ring, voicemail.

Fine.

I want to speak to him when I give my spiel. Trying to explain myself over text is just not good enough. I type out a quick *Call me, please* text and hit send. Then I put the phone down and walk back into my bathroom to inspect the bruise at the base of my neck. It is a mix of colors, looking as angry as I feel.

Reaching for my makeup, I apply some foundation and concealer over the bruise with a blending sponge. I wince at the pressure, the area sore.

Makeup isn't cutting it. Though it helped conceal some of the bruising, the injury is still noticeable. I'll have to cover it with clothing to minimize the apparent damage. Although if I wear a turtleneck sweater in the middle of summer, I will make a spectacle of myself.

I head back into the bedroom and find a lightweight scarf that I can tie around my neck over my blouse. It looks out of place, given that it's almost July, but it will have to do. I'm very much not looking forward to this, but I suppose I can grin and bear it, even though I look like I should be employed by Delta Airlines.

I drive over to the convention center in complete silence. I am not in the right headspace for music today. Once I pull into a parking spot, I send his mom a text, letting her know I'm here. While I wait for her response, I lean my head back against the headrest and take a few deep, cleansing breaths.

How different would today be if I had made it to dinner last night with Ryan? If only I had left just two minutes before Mark showed up. I would have had a lovely night with my old friend, probably sipping wine that didn't make me gag and laughing at old memories.

Now instead, I'm sporting a wounded heart and a beat-up neck. Distance will be good for us.

I pull up Ryan's contact information again, making a last attempt to reach him. This time, the phone just goes straight to voicemail. He hates me. I'm sure of it. The thought makes me nauseas.

My phone chimes with a text alert. It's Mark's mother letting me know she's at the front doors, and I groan. As I'm walking to the entrance, Mark's mother spots me and waves. When I get closer, I see her plastered smile slowly morph into a scornful sneer as she takes in my flight attendant outfit.

I bite my tongue and force a smile. Let's just get today over with.

A few wretched hours later, I find myself pounding at my best friend's door. Juliet opens it with a flourish, smiling at me.

"Ugh, I literally *cannot* with Mark's mother," I shout as I storm past her into the house. My friend gives me a concerned look at my rampage.

I stalk into her living room, Jules trailing after me, her son Ashton sitting on her hip.

"Oh Lord, what did she do now?" As my Matron of Honor, Juliet has seen Mark's mother's full intensity a few times. There was almost a showdown at my engagement party between the two of them.

"She just feels the need to nit-pick every little thing I do. If I have an extra glass of champagne or one cookie too many, she always has to comment on it." I throw my hands in the air. "And I swear if I had a dollar for every time she said, 'Izabel, darling, are you *sure* that's what you want?' I wouldn't have to accept her money to pay for my own damn wedding!"

Juliet just stares at me with her blue-ish green eyes in amusement.

"What!" I snap at her.

"Nothing," she says quickly, shaking her head. "That's just the most you've sounded like yourself in...a while."

I feel my anger dissipate into confusion, and I my eyebrows furrow. "What does that mean?"

Jules shrugs and sits down in one of her living room chairs, placing Ashton on her knee and bouncing him up and down. "I don't know. You just sounded like the old Izabel just now. Instead of whatever Mark has turned you into over the last few years."

I sigh and pinch the bridge of my nose. I don't have the mental capacity to get into it with her today. Not after everything else I've had to deal with over the last twenty-four hours.

"I do have a question, though," my friend says from across the room. "Why are you wearing a scarf?"

I shoot her a glare. "I can't accessorize?"

She holds up her hand that isn't wrapped around her son in surrender. "Just an interesting choice."

I bite the inside of my cheek. Juliet would lose her mind if she found out what the scarf was hiding. She fussed enough after the gala incident. The last thing I need is her on my case about this too. I can handle Mark and his temper by myself. I'm done with people trying to save me all the time. I'm a grown woman about to get married.

"Where's Liam?" I ask, changing the subject. The house seems quiet. Usually, if Liam's around, he'll be blasting music or playing his video games at full volume.

Jules is busy wiping something off Ashton's cheek—probably remnants from lunch. She glances up at me when I ask my question. "Oh, he's at Bennett this afternoon. He's helping Ryan coach the soccer team. Since Ryan is out of town today, Liam's running practice."

I frown. There was a lot of information just unloaded in her statement. "Ryan's coaching at Bennett?" I choose to ask first.

Jules nods. "Yeah, practices started this week."

I had forgotten sports were due to begin this week. The first day of school is just a little over a month away. I have to be up at the school with the rest of the faculty starting next week for meetings and training a few hours each day. Perks of working for a highly prestigious private school is extra hours put in over the summer. The start of school is right around the corner, and I can't wait.

Teaching is one of my favorite things. Most kids hate history, but I enjoy telling them stories and making history more than textbook lessons.

"And you said Ryan's out of town today?" I ask her. Aside from being pissed at me, that would explain why he ignored all my calls.

"I think he's on site for one of his projects," Juliet says. She and Ryan aren't as close as he and Liam. They never have been. I know she gets all of her information secondhand.

I tap my toe on her carpeted floor. Well, this is sufficient news. Now I'll know where Ryan will be most afternoons. I can find a way to apologize to him and hopefully smooth things over. He can't avoid me forever.

God, do I sound crazy?

I don't think I do. I just need to clear the air. After that, if Ryan wants nothing to do with me again, I'll respect it. But I can't leave things the way they are now. There's a lot I would be willing to concede to in my life. I can deal with Mark's mom being the literal worst, and I can probably handle Mark's unchecked mood swings.

What I'm not prepared to deal with is Ryan hating me. The two of us got past that phase in our relationship years ago, and I'm not willing to take a step backward. I don't care if I never see him again—been there, done that—but I need to make sure he knows that I didn't stand him up on purpose. *Loathing* is no longer a word I associate with him, and I want to keep it that way.

Chapter 19

Ryan

"Alright, guys, keep moving! Let's go!" I shout at my team as they run their sprints.

After tryouts last week, I felt pretty confident in my selection until we did a practice shirt vs. skins scrimmage. That was when I woefully discovered my team doesn't know how to move their feet.

So now we're running and drilling, over and over again.

It's about three in the afternoon. The sun is beating down heavily on us, and we're all sweating. The boys are moaning and groaning in pain as they run. I figure I'll give them a break here in a minute, then we can go into some dribbling drills.

Liam is standing next to me, looking out at the players through his sunglasses. Every once in a while, I'll see him jot something down on his clipboard. The two of us were co-captains our senior year of high school. I feel like we'll make a great coaching team as well.

I eyeball one of the seniors on the team. Last week, he made waves at the tryouts, trying to show off with fancy moves and foot tricks. He's a talented player, and he sure knows it too.

"That Martin kid is one cocky little shit," I mutter to Liam. He looks up at me from his clipboard and smirks.

"Yeah, he reminds me of this kid I knew when I was his age. Called himself the King of Bennett. Can you believe that?"

I laugh and shove my friend away from me. "Fuck off, man."

Liam chuckles and comes back to stand by my side. "I'm just saying. You were a lot worse than him."

"I was not."

"Whatever, Ry, you got everything you wanted. The captain spot, the grades, the internship, the girl." The words fall out of Liam's mouth before he realizes what he's saying. His eyes go wide, and he looks at me as if I'm going to shatter before him.

I roll my eyes, letting the boys run for a little while longer before blowing my whistle. The team comes to a slamming halt. "Bring it in, guys!"

They all fall in and crowd around. Liam explains the next set of drills that we're going to be working on. We're just getting ready to break and split into groups, when one of the boys peers over at the bleachers, cupping his hand above his eyes to shade from the sun.

"Is that Miss Sanders?"

The rest of the gang whips around to see who it is. And I'm sorry to say, I do too. I have no willpower.

Sure enough, there's Miss Izabel Sanders, sitting on the bleachers, mulling over a binder in her lap, chewing on the end of a pen. As if she can tell we're looking at her, she peeks up, and I swear I can see the brilliance of her ocean eyes from across the field. Izabel gives a hesitant wave, and the boys go nuts.

"I didn't know she likes soccer," one of the boys says.

"Maybe she just came to see her favorite pupil," another one chimes in, stretching arrogantly.

"I wouldn't mind one bit if she sent me to detention."

I feel my face turn down into a scowl and blow my whistle again. "Get to work, guys." They set off and split into separate groups.

Liam looks at me with his eyebrows raised, and I clear my throat. "I'm just gonna, uh, go see what she wants," I say. "Can you run the drill for me?"

He gives me a knowing smirk. "Sure, man, take as long as you want."

We fist bump, and then I'm walking over to the bleachers. Bells sees me coming and sets her stuff down, coming closer to the edge of the stands to talk easier. It's hard for me to believe that our disaster of a "non-date" was already a week ago.

Since then, I've been walking the straight and narrow line. I've pretty much consumed myself with work, getting ready for the HQ presentation I've got to give the board of directors at Bates Industries tomorrow. Josie's been hot on my tail, making sure that I don't slip up with the stress and hit the bottle. She's even attended an AA meeting with me after basically bullying me into it, despite my reluctance. As we walked out together, I was humbled enough to admit that she was right.

Just like Josie said, it's best to nip this in the bud before it turns into anything more.

I'm biting my cheek so hard I can feel the skin break as I walk over to Bells. I know she's been trying to reach out; I've got the phone notifications to prove it. I just haven't been able to get myself to talk to her yet.

"Hey, Ryan," she says when I'm finally within earshot. "The team's looking good so far."

"Ah yeah," I respond, rubbing the back of my neck and

feeling the taut muscles bunch underneath my fingers. I'm feeling a sunburn coming on, I think. "We got a long way to go."

"I've been trying to call you."

"I know," I say, ignoring the pang of regret at the betrayed tone in her voice.

"I've just been getting your voicemail."

"Yup."

She sighs and purses her lips, aggravated. "You've been sending me straight to voicemail."

"I was just following your lead after you no-showed at Siriano's."

"It wasn't on purpose!" she shouts at me, and I snap my head around to her. I take her in, recognizing the way her eyes have that pleading look to them. Right away, I suspect I've made a mistake not being open to listening to her explanation. Izabel squares her shoulders and stares me down with a hard gaze. "I want to explain myself and apologize."

I wave my hand. "You don't have to."

"Yes, I do," she says. "You deserve to know the truth. Last week was a mess. I was getting ready to head out when Mark showed up and—"

I frown. "I don't need to hear it. It's fine, really."

"Would you just *let me finish?*" Bells all but growls at me. I jolt back in surprise. I haven't heard her use that tone of voice on me in years.

Stepping back, I cross my arms over my chest, giving her the space to say everything she wants to say.

"Mark showed up at my house unexpectedly, and so that's why I wasn't able to meet you. And we have this dumb rule," she tells me, shaking her head. "No cell phones during date nights, and every time I tried to sneak away to text you, Mark was right there watching me."

I narrow my eyes at the beautiful girl who consumes most

of my thoughts. I try not to let it hurt me that she ditched me for her fiancé, because that would just be *ridiculous*. But it stings anyway. I'm not sure what I was expecting. That is a perfectly valid excuse. After all, she is still planning on marrying the guy.

"I feel awful about it, really. I would have much rather been with you that night," she says, her voice breathy. Her fingers come up to graze the base of her neck, almost as if she has an itch, but she doesn't scratch it. The action has the rest of my defenses lowering and my shoulders dropping.

"Bells," I say her name hesitantly, fully aware that the whole truth might not be something I want to know.

She waves her hand, brushing off my concern before looking at me with hopeful eyes. "I'd like to make it up to you. Are you busy this weekend? We could get a coffee or something. I promise there won't be any type of interruption this time."

This weekend is the Fourth of July. I'm due to be in Nashville tomorrow afternoon for my presentation. Then I was planning on staying Saturday and Sunday just to be away.

My fingers fiddle with the whistle around my neck. "I won't be in town this weekend."

"Oh..." She frowns. "Where are you going?"

"Nashville. I have a meeting with Bates."

Her eyes light up. "You're going to Nashville? Will you be seeing Teddy and Sage?"

"Likely." What is running through her head right now? I can practically see the gears shifting in her brain, piecing something together.

"When are you leaving?"

"Sometime tomorrow morning, why?"

Izabel smiles and shrugs. "Oh, no reason. Okay. Well, I'll let you get back to practice! Bye, Ryan!"

She spins on her toe, grabs her stuff, and struts off. Scratching the back of my head, I mull over our strange encounter. She's definitely up to something, I just don't know what. My suspicions are on high alert, but I turn and head back to practice.

The following morning, as I'm heading out to my car, I'm not surprised to see Izabel leaning against it. I halt in my steps and stare at my favorite brunette. She has a duffel bag draped across her shoulder. Her hands are placed on her hips, and she's grinning at me from ear to ear.

I grip my keys in my hand. "What are you doing here?"

"I thought I'd come with you. It's been a while since I've seen Sage, and I need to get out of Cedar Ridge for the weekend."

My feet take a second before they decide to work again, but then I move fluidly towards my car and open the trunk to toss my bag in, then I hold out my hand for Izabel's. I could argue with her. I could tell her that I don't want her to come with me, that I don't want to be anywhere near her. But I don't. "What does your fiancé think about this?"

Izabel looks away from my inquisitive stare and frowns. "I don't really care what he thinks about this. We're not talking right now."

I raise my eyebrows, a little taken back. *Okay, then.*

I can't lie and say it isn't a little satisfying hearing her get all fiery and snarky in regard to him. A thread of curiosity unspools, and I wonder why they're not talking right now. Did something happen between them? I wouldn't mind one bit if she finally decided to kick him to the curb. In fact, I think I'd be right behind her, applauding her the whole way.

With that thought, I consider that maybe she has. Maybe she's finally had the earth-shattering epiphany that he's an absolute piece of shit and she deserves better.

I take in the way her lips pull off into a stubborn pout and my intrigue gets the best of me.

"Fine. Then get in."

I crouch down to get into my car, turning the key in the ignition and getting the AC blowing. Izabel follows suit only a moment later, settling into the passenger seat. She's wearing a pair of jean shorts and a loose-fitting tank top. I close my eyes for a second and inhale deeply.

Lord, help me.

What in the hell do I think I'm doing? Everything cell in my body is screaming that I'm making a mistake, and I shouldn't have given in so easily, and yet here I go, shifting the car in drive and pulling out of my parking lot.

When we hit the freeway, Izabel turns to look at me. "So, what's your meeting about?"

"I'm pitching a design idea for their new headquarters building. Teddy's all on board with me designing it, but the board of directors isn't so sure since I'm only a startup."

Izabel frowns. "But you worked for them for years."

I shrug and keep my eyes on the road. "That's business, I guess. But anyway, I have the whole thing drawn up and priced out. I just have to convince them to hire me."

"I'm sure it will be a walk in the park. You're good at what you do."

I glance over at her, but she's looking out the window now. I can see a slight blush playing on her cheeks at the compliment she just gave me. The corners of my lips turn up slightly, and then my attention is back on the road.

"Are you excited for school to start back up?" I ask her.

She grins and nods. "Oh, yes, I love teaching. It's one of my favorite things."

"Do you want to keep teaching high school forever?"

Izabel thinks about my question for a second before

answering. "I don't know. I love the boys at Bennett." She gives me a side glance, as if measuring me for the implication in her words. "But I think being a college professor would be really fun as well. High schoolers don't have much stake in history. But at the college level, aside from the core curriculum, you get students who actually want to hear what I'm teaching and explaining to them. I think that would be very stimulating."

"You're such a nerd," I tease her, shooting her a fond smirk. For a moment, my brain tricks me into believing that this is our life. That nothing ever changed between us, and we get to go through each day, playfully taking shots at each other and going on impromptu adventures.

What a life that would be.

She smiles again, her teeth shiny white. "I know. I just can't help it! Hey, speaking of. How long are we staying? Do you think we could go see the Parthenon?"

"I think that could be arranged. I have the hotel check-out set for Sunday. So we could find some fireworks Saturday night, too, if you want."

Izabel nods her head vigorously. "Yes! That sounds perfect! Thanks for letting me tag along. You're my favorite!"

I laugh under my breath as I glance at her again. Who is this woman and what has she done with the Izabel I've gotten to know recently? This version of her is so like the old Izabel that it's completely taken me off guard. Don't get me wrong, it's refreshing, seeing that the version of her I love so much is still inside of her somewhere. But at the same time, something about how quickly she's made the change has me watching her cautiously, as if I'm afraid she'll detonate right in front of me.

We fall into a comfortable silence as Izabel fiddles around with her phone. I keep my eye on her as I'm driving. We've always been good at being just Ryan and Izabel, but something still feels off. Like we're going through the motions, but not fully on the same page.

She takes in a deep breath and adjusts in her seat. Kicking off her flip-flops, she perches her feet up on the dashboard, still typing away at the device in her hands. I notice purple nail polish is painted on her dainty toenails.

"That's really unsafe," I mutter at her position. "You could break both your legs."

Izabel turns to me and sticks out her tongue. "Well, then good thing I trust your driving."

I chuckle again, shaking my head at her, but loving every second of this playful banter. I don't know for sure, but I'm about 90% certain that my weekend just got a hell of a lot more interesting.

Chapter 20

Izabel

RYAN PULLS INTO AN EMPTY SPACE IN THE HOTEL PARKING lot, then gets out to go check-in. I stay in the car, unsure if he wants me with him or not. Anytime I travel with Mark, he always has me stay in the car while he handles the business.

Mark. He's going to be so pissed at me when he finds out where I am. My stomach is already knotting up in anticipation of the fight that is likely to unfold between us. I meant what I said to Ryan; I don't really care if Mark will be mad, but I need to prepare for the worst when he does find out.

Unless I don't tell him.

I'll be back home by the time he returns from his trip with his dad. Really, if I keep my mouth shut, and Ryan doesn't mention it, there's no reason Mark would have to find out. I bite my lip and ponder that thought.

All I want is a weekend away, to be me and not worry about getting my head bit off for every little thing. Is that too much to ask for? Then, I can go back, fresh, and ready to work everything out with him. Hopefully, Mark will have a new perspective from his trip too. We don't have much longer before our wedding. So it's time to iron out these kinks now before it's too late.

It took a tremendous amount of effort to avoid touching my neck during the car ride with Ryan. The bruise has faded slightly from a deep angry purple into a more even-red, though it is still an angry reminder of the fight. I purchased the most expensive full-coverage makeup I could: concealers, color correctors, foundation, powders. The makeup works pretty well to cover the remaining redness, as long as you're not looking for the bruise. But I don't want to touch the skin since there's the risk of wiping the makeup away.

This weekend will be tricky, keeping that from Ryan, but I'm hopeful I can do it. He hasn't noticed anything off yet, so maybe I'll be in the clear.

I jump when I hear Ryan's knuckles tapping on my window and his muffled voice saying, "Are you coming or what?"

I smile to myself and then grab my duffle bag from the open trunk, slinging it over my shoulder and jogging to catch up to Ryan. Together, we stride into the hotel and up to the desk. Ryan puts his bag on the ground by his feet so he can pull out his wallet.

"Hi, I've got a reservation for the weekend under Miller," the receptionist starts typing on her keyboard, her fingernails clacking over the keys. "I was hoping I could change that from the single king to two side-by-side rooms. Queen beds will be fine if that's all you have."

The clerk looks over her glasses at Ryan and frowns. "I'm sorry, sir, it's a holiday weekend, and unfortunately, we do not have any other rooms left. I still have the one you reserved, but it's a king room."

Ryan looks at me, his emerald eyes wide with concern. He reaches up to rub the back of his neck, his tell for when he's feeling nervous or awkward. "Maybe somewhere else will have two—"

This is unacceptable. I step forward and place my hands on the counter, giving the receptionist my sweetest smile. "Listen, we need two rooms. Either you find a way to make it happen, or I'll be having words with your manager," I pause to peek at her nametag, "*Louisa.*"

God, I hate to be *that person*. But it gets shit done!

The woman stares at me blankly, and then types on her keyboard again. "I have a guest who hasn't checked in yet. I can upgrade them when they get here, and you can take their room."

I clap my hand against the counter and give Louisa a wide grin. "That would just be lovely. Thank you so much!"

Ryan presses his lips together. I can tell he's uncomfortable. I don't care, though, he can get over it. Because it's a holiday weekend, the rates at the other hotels are going to be outrageous. We might as well take what we have.

The receptionist gathers Ryan's information and hands us two small packets of key cards, then directs us to our rooms. We're on the fourth floor, rooms 421 and 422. We take the elevator and walk down the hall.

Ryan stops right in front of our doors, handing me the key card to mine. He looks at me and rubs the back of his neck again. So nervous today, Ry. "So uh, I guess we can just get settled in. I have to be at Bates in about an hour. Do you want to come with me or...?" He trails off, as if he's unsure where he's going with this conversation.

I offer him a small smile and grip the strap of my duffel bag over my shoulder. Why does this feel so awkward? I get I'm kind of throwing him for a loop with my abrupt change in outlook, but I figured he'd just be happy to go along with it. "You go ahead over to Bates, and I'll call Sage and see if she wants to do something this afternoon. Maybe we can reconvene for dinner or drinks tonight."

He nods at my suggestion. "Okay, that sounds good. Wanna meet at the bar downstairs around seven?"

I agree, and we each step into our separate bedrooms. It's the typical hotel aesthetic: two queen beds, a TV, a desk with a chair, and then an armchair. The room smells clean like fresh linens.

My duffle bag flops on the extra queen bed, and I sit next to it, glancing around. I can't believe I'm in Nashville with Ryan, and not at home with Mark. What an exciting change of events.

Mark has gratefully respected my request for distance. He sent me a few texts each day checking in—simplistic *good mornings* and *goodnights*, and the occasional *I love you*. Other than that, I haven't seen or heard from him since I kicked him out of my apartment. Cell service for him will be spotty at best up in the mountains, so I'm not expecting to hear from him any more for the next few days.

My heart is still bitter from everything that went down between us last week. It's hard for me to process. One second, we were curled up on the couch, sipping wine and watching a cheesy rom-com, and the next, I was pressed against a wall, gasping for breath.

Over the past week, I've been trying to gather my thoughts so that I can relay to Mark what will hopefully help him understand how I feel. But nothing has worked thus far. All I feel is anger and betrayal. I'm afraid to type out a text because I might say something impulsive and then actually send it. But I don't want to call him on the phone either, because then I know I'll just get flustered and end up flubbing what I really want to say.

My eyes fall to a pad of paper, sitting on top of the measly corner desk in the room. Next to it are a few stray pens bearing the logo of the hotel. I shuffle toward the desk, pull out the chair, and sit down. My fingers wrap around the pen, and I tap it against my hand.

Words are often so hard to come by in the moment. This is why, for centuries, people have always written out their thoughts, feelings, experiences. Some of the world's greatest novels are written out of heartbreak or tragedy. Knowing these calming benefits, I put pen to paper and start writing out my every thought over the last week. What makes me sad, angry, hurt. I begin to write it all down and allow myself to try to find some peace.

Dear Mark,

I can't begin to explain how it feels to have someone you hold so dear, hurt you so badly. I wish that we could go back in time, but we can't. I love you so much, but I have to wonder sometimes what that love means to you. Your jealousy and anger toward Ryan consume you, to the point where all you can see is red, and somehow, I end up with your hand against my throat, fighting for air.

It cannot be this way.

We can be better, do better. It won't be easy, but I love you, and I believe in you, and I'm willing to help you change. I know we have a long way to go, but maybe if we stand together for once, we can fix everything...

Barely over an hour later, I set the pen down and look at the pages of words I've written. I pile it neatly on the desk and turn away. Writing it all down was like ripping open a dam in my heart.

Now I'll step away, mull it over, and then come back to it.

Feelings can change quickly, which is why I think putting them into writing is more cathartic than just speaking.

I rummage through my duffle bag, finding a different set of clothes to wear, and then send my sister a quick message. I'll try to meet her for a late lunch; hopefully, she hasn't eaten yet. Then, I'll be done in time to meet Ryan this evening.

I head into the hotel bathroom to reapply the makeup to my neck. Luckily, it hasn't smudged yet, but I apply another concealer and powder coat around the area to keep it smooth.

Sage tells me to meet her at a small local café. After one last look over, I order an Uber and meet her there within half an hour. My sister looks every bit the business mogul's wife in her straight navy-blue dress and nude-colored heels. It's a different image than I usually conjure up of her. In my memories, she's always clad in sweatpants and an oversized t-shirt. Seeing my sister, the professional, is a pleasant change.

She gives me a big hug, and then leads me into the café and over to a small cozy table in the corner of the building. A waitress comes by, and we order two sweet teas and mozzarella sticks. Sage tells me she already had lunch but will never say no to appetizers. Once the order is in, she turns to me, crossing her arms over the table.

"So give me the dirty deets. You're here in *Nashville* with your hot ex-boyfriend?" Her blue eyes, exactly the same as mine, light up in anticipation of the gossip.

I shake my head and roll my eyes at her. "It is definitely not like that. Ryan mentioned that he was coming here for a meeting with Bates, and I tagged along. I needed a change of scenery. And I missed you."

"Aw, sis, I missed you too. How are the wedding plans coming? You still head over heels for the lawyer?"

"They're coming along."

Sage makes a face at me and dunks a mozzarella stick into

the red sauce. "Don't think I didn't miss your avoidance of that second question, but we'll let it slide for now."

She's just as bad as Juliet.

Sage tells me about life in Nashville. She and Teddy are taking the Bates world by storm. Teddy is still running the business as CEO, and Sage is working as the head of marketing. It sounds like she's living the dream.

I sit and chat with my sister for a while until she says she has to get going. Sage drops me off back at the hotel, and I wander up to my room to kill time before I have to meet Ryan down at the bar.

Before I go back downstairs, I stand in front of the mirror to make sure I look presentable. I fluff my hair a little bit and double-check that my makeup coverage is still good.

I realize I'm arriving a little early as I find a seat right at the bar. The bartender comes up to me with a big smile and asks for my order.

"I'll have a mojito," I say, setting my clutch wallet down on the bar.

"A mojito girl, huh?" a guy next to me says once the bartender's walked away. I glance over at him, and then avert my eyes.

"Um, yeah."

The guy scoots down a seat, coming closer to me. "Gotta say, I've never actually tried one for myself. Maybe I should."

My nose wrinkles in discomfort. I turn to the guy and hold out my hand, displaying my sparkly ring. "I'm waiting for my fiancé to meet me. Would you mind going back to your other seat?"

The guy glances down at the obnoxious rock on my finger, his eyes raised in surprise. He gives a low whistle. "He really wasn't playing around, huh. That thing must have cost a fortune."

I don't respond this time. The bartender returns with my mojito, and I take a big sip. My friend is still sitting next to me. He picks up his tumbler of whiskey and takes a small drink, keeping his eyes on me.

I breathe deeply, and then turn to him. "What do you want?"

"Oh nothing, darlin'. I'm just enjoying the view," he says, and the drawl in his voice makes my skin feel clammy. He reaches up and tries to tuck a strand of hair behind my ear, but I slap his hand away and glare at him.

"Why don't you go enjoy it somewhere else," a new, deeper voice says from the other side of me. I turn around and see Ryan sitting down next to me. He extends his arm across the back of the barstool, his fingers brushing against my arm. I feel a small smile threatening on my lips, and a wave of relief come over me.

"Who are you?" the rude man asks. He's frowning at Ryan, whose face is impassive but shows he's not playing around.

"The guy who's gonna rearrange your face if you don't leave the lady alone."

The other man leans back against the backrest of his stool and takes another drink. "Ah. the *fiancé*." I notice Ryan doesn't correct him, though his firm stare remains. The guy raises his hands in surrender. "Alright, alright. I know when to cut my losses. You better keep a close eye on this one, though," he drawls, shooting one last indecent grin at me. "She's quite the catch."

Ryan's face morphs into a scowl, and he mutters, "I'm aware."

The guy walks away from the bar, chuckling under his breath. I turn to look at Ryan. "Thank you, but I can take care of myself, you know."

He scoffs. "Right. All five-foot-three of you? That guy was

at *least* twice your size. Do you even know how to escape if he were to grab you?"

Images of Mark holding me against my apartment wall flash in my mind. My heart rate picks up slightly, and I have to restrain my fingers from fluttering up to the healing contusions on my neck. I take a sip of my beverage and shrug, doing my best to hide my impending panic. "It's a public place. Someone would have stopped him."

Ryan stares at me long and hard, those green eyes twinkling underneath the dim bar lights. "Seriously, Bells."

"Seriously, Ryan."

"Have you ever thought about taking self-defense classes?"

I hold his gaze for a long second before calling the bartender over. I'm questioning his motives here. This couldn't just be from the guy touching my hair. Suggesting self-defense classes is not exactly a topic of small talk. Did Ryan know something about the Mark thing last week? Has my makeup worn off, and he can see that bruise there? Maybe I should run to the bathroom to check, but I thought I saw that pervy guy head that way. No—Ryan would have definitely said something if he could see it.

He might be right, though. Thinking back to last week, I was utterly helpless against Mark and his anger. Maybe it wouldn't be such a terrible idea...

"I'll think about it," I tell Ryan right as the bartender walks over to us.

"What can I get you?" he asks.

Ryan stays quiet for a second, glancing down at the mojito sitting in front of me as if he's really pondering what kind of drink he wants tonight. "I think I'll just have water."

The bartender nods and heads off, tapping the top of the bar. I turn to Ryan with a frown. "You sure you don't want anything else? I'm buying."

Ryan smiles at me and leans back, the picture of ease. "Nah, I'm good tonight. I'll just stick to water."

We sit at the bar for what feels like forever, Ryan, with his water and me with my mojito. As we talk, he finally moves past whatever awkwardness he was holding on to. He starts to open up a bit, becoming more comfortable as he tells me everything that happened today at the Bates meeting, not leaving out even the smallest detail. He feels like he nailed the proposal and isn't too concerned they'll turn him down. I have no doubt he did a great job. Ryan succeeds at just about anything he puts his mind to.

"They would be crazy to do that, knowing what you're capable of," I tell him.

Ryan's eyes twinkle again, offering me one of those smiles that makes my insides flip around. "Thanks, Bells. That means a lot coming from you."

I blush and flick a crumb off of the bar top. "So, what's on the agenda for tomorrow?"

Ryan's eyebrows pull together slightly. "Well, we could check out the Parthenon for you in the morning, then we can hit those concerts downtown in the afternoon. Then, fireworks, of course."

"That would be great!" Excitement bubbles in my belly, knowing Ryan went out of his way to add something to our agenda that he knew I'd appreciate. I can't imagine Mark ever taking that extra step. If he found it even remotely boring, he wouldn't even bother.

"I figured you would have already been there," Ryan says, chuckling as he watches me. I can tell he's amused by my apparent excitement.

I shrug a shoulder, still smiling. Of course, I've already been to the Parthenon, but Ryan doesn't need to know that. I'm just grateful he's thought of me on this trip. It's nice being considered. It's something I've gotten out of the habit of expecting. But being back with Ryan, even if just in this platonic situation, reminds me of how good it feels.

"I like seeing you this happy," he says, his voice hesitant, as if he's worried saying it out loud might ruin the moment.

My smile lowers a bit, but I hold his gaze. My fingers knot together in my lap. "I like being this happy," I admit.

His familiar green eyes study my face before he changes the subject back into lighter topics. We chat a little bit longer before deciding to call it a night. Ryan picks up the tab for my mojitos despite my protests, and then we walk back to our hotel rooms. Though we walk side by side, he keeps his distance, respecting the boundary. When we get to our rooms, Ryan gives me a quick goodnight. He shoots me that boyish grin of his that has my heart skipping a beat, before disappearing into his room and leaving me alone in the hallway.

I can't help but smile as I slide my keycard into the slot, unlocking my room. I glance around at my stuff and then flop onto one of the beds, landing on my back. My head spins as I look at the ceiling, tracing the patterns of the popcorn detailing. It might be from the mojitos, but I think I'm just looking forward to tomorrow.

I get to run around Nashville all day, spending time with Ryan—a therapy I didn't know how badly I needed. I roll off the bed and work on getting ready to go to sleep. Slipping on my pajamas, I clean off all the makeup still coating my face, and then crawl back into the bed closest to the window. Once I'm settled under the covers, I smile to myself. I think this weekend away is just what the doctor ordered.

Chapter 21

Ryan

THE NEXT MORNING, I GET UP EARLY, HITTING THE HOTEL gym for an hour or so before I have to get Bells. I didn't sleep well, knowing she was in the room right next to me. She was so close but so far away, just like it has been for the last few months. It's something I'm slowly growing accustomed to, no matter how much I dislike it. At the very least, I'm choosing to focus on the fact that she's in my life at all. Even that is better than nothing. I finish styling my hair in the bathroom mirror, satisfied with how it looks. Grabbing my keys, wallet, and phone, I head out into the hallway and take a few steps to the room next to mine.

My knuckles rap on the door three times, but there's no answer. I knock again. "Bells?" I click on my phone screen, seeing it's already ten. There's no way she could still be asleep.

Right before I resort to kicking the door in, Izabel opens it up and smiles. She has a washcloth pressed against her neck and a hairbrush in her hand.

"Morning, Ryan!" She steps back and allows me to walk

into her room. I glance at her unsurely as I step in. "I just need a few more minutes. You can just hang out."

Izabel scrambles back into the bathroom, shutting the door and locking it. The bed that she chose to sleep in by the window is unmade, so I meander over and sit on the edge. She has the TV on to some kid's cartoon, and I mindlessly watch as she finishes getting ready.

My mind rushes as I try to think about everything I have planned for today. I can't deny that I'm feeling a bit of pressure to make sure that it's perfect. I keep recalling the way her face lit up last night when I mentioned going to the Parthenon, and I'd do anything to keep that kind of happiness on her face.

It's still a little jarring, getting to experience this side of her for the first time in what feels like ages, but I'm not about to look a gift horse in the mouth. I'll take what I can get, and do whatever I can to make sure that beautiful smile sticks around.

It reminds me of better days and better times. Times when she could be herself without fear of any type of retribution. Even if she just gets to experience that freedom for a few days, I'm more than willing to be the one to provide her that safe space to do it.

It's definitely more than just a "few minutes" before Izabel steps out of the bathroom. She gives me a big grin and does a little twirl, showing off her Fourth of July dress.

I can't help the smile that forms on my face when she spins again for me. She looks beautiful, as always. She has a little bit more makeup on than I'm used to. Her eyelids are coated with a shimmery shadow, her lips painted red. But she's gorgeous.

"Ready to go?" I ask, and she bobs her head, grabbing her purse from the dresser. "I thought we could stop for brunch since we missed the hotel breakfast." I'm starving, so I hope she says yes.

"That sounds good to me. Where do you think?"

I don't respond until we're standing in the elevator. I press the button for the lobby, and we start descending. "I was looking through the pamphlet in my room. I think there's a little breakfast joint down the road that we could check out."

We both head out of the building and over to my car. I drive us to the diner, and we are seated right away, which is somewhat surprising since it's a holiday. The waitress comes by, and we put in our orders: a slinger for me and French toast for Bells. It doesn't take long for the waitress to bring out the food. Our plates are piled high and steaming as if it's fresh off the griddle.

"Tell me something I don't know, Bells," I say as I take a big spoonful of potatoes, chili, and eggs.

Izabel looks at me wryly before stabbing a piece of her fancy toast. "I knew you were going to do this, so I came prepared." She dramatically clears her throat and looks me square in the eye. "Did you know that the first Fourth of July fireworks happened in 1777? On the first anniversary of our independence?"

I can't help the laugh that sneaks out at how serious her expression got. "I didn't know that. I guess I just thought that was a more recent tradition."

Bells shakes her head. "Nope, kind of makes it feel more sentimental, right? Like we're really celebrating something rather than just blowing stuff up."

I let my eyes trail over her face, a small smile playing on my lips. She's got that wistful expression that I love so much. Whenever she talks about something she's passionate about, her eyes get this dreamy look to them. Those blue depths illustrate how strongly she feels about the topic. I feel a knot in my throat, so I tear my eyes away from her before I do anything stupid like kiss her.

Yesterday afternoon I had a long phone conversation with Josie, explaining my situation. How infatuated I'm becoming with Bells again. How I'm feeling seeing that smile back on her face more often than it's not. I'm trying my damnedest to keep that boundary I've drawn between us, but I can feel my defenses weakening with every minute I spend with her. Having Bells here with me could be both a blessing and a curse. Only time will tell which one it turns out to be.

Josie was absolutely no help. She laughed and laughed when I told her that Bells commandeered my business trip—muttering something about how maybe we would finally be forced to face the music in Music City. It's a fine line, which Josie herself is toeing too with her suggestion. Sure, there's nothing I'd like better than to make a move on Izabel and help her move past the darkness that still follows her around, but I know that would be selfish of me to pretend that what she's dealing with could be solved with something so simple. And that could backfire on me. The last thing I'd want would be for me to push the limit and force her to retreat.

"So tell me something I don't know," Bells says, her tone light and airy. "What really brought you back home? You said it was a family matter. Is it your mom?"

I swallow thickly and push a piece of sausage around on my plate. "Uh, why would you say that?"

Izabel looks at me with sadness in her eyes. "I noticed that something was off with her after the gala. I didn't want to ask outright, though."

"You should've just asked me," I told her, though honestly, I'm not sure if I would have been open to telling her everything. Things are uncomfortable between us now, but they were even more strained right after the gala.

"I'm asking you now. Let me be here for you, Ry."

I study her face again and consider what I want to tell her. I could lie, tell her everything was fine. She wouldn't believe me, but she may accept the falsity, given our relationship. We haven't been that person for each other in years.

Or I could tell her the truth. This is Izabel, my Bells. For so long, the one person I could count on in any situation. We'd sacrificed for each other and have been through so much. And though life took us down different paths, that kind of trust runs deep, the roots still holding firm.

And so, I tell her. I tell her everything, from the first moment my mom thought something was off, to the many doctors' appointments, the tests, the biopsies, and finally the diagnosis. Then, I explained the realization I had that it was time for me to come back to the States.

Izabel listens, nodding, her eyes wide as she takes it all in. She doesn't say anything until I'm finished. Instead, she reaches across the table, offering me her hand.

I take it, wrapping my fingers together with hers, and it feels so *right* to have her here, sharing in my struggles, and offering her support silently. I'm struck then that this is what I miss the most about her. Not her laugh, or her kisses, or those sapphire blue eyes—though those are all things I love about her too. But her companionship. I miss my best friend. The closeness and intimacy that comes with knowing someone better than anyone else in the world. Having that relationship to fall back on in times like these, where you just want to know that they've got you. That they're with you.

That's why throughout the rest of the day, I don't let go of her hand. I let Izabel lead me around Nashville with her fingers entwined tightly in mine. We go visit the Parthenon and marvel at the vastness of the architecture. Bells is like a kid in a candy shop, reading every word on the descriptive plaques, soaking up all the fun facts.

After we're done with that, we head downtown and check out the music festival. A few big-name country artists perform, and Izabel loses herself in the music, dancing with me amongst the crowded street. I don't think I've laughed this much in years. We struggle through the crowds and have a late lunch by means of a food truck.

Izabel chooses a gyro truck, not my favorite food in the world, but I concede to make her Fourth of July trip all the better. I can't help myself when a dribble of tzatziki sauce slips down her chin; I reach out, catch it with my thumb, and then lick it off.

Izabel watches my actions with amused eyes before she bursts into laughter. I laugh with her before she goes back to demolishing her lunch.

All day, I'm fighting my instincts to just lean over and kiss her. It takes everything in me to control the urge. That blissful smile on her face is making me fall in love with her all over again. I need her like I need the air I'm breathing.

Once evening hits, we meander over to Vanderbilt University. I'd read online last night that the tops of the parking garages here make a perfect firework viewing site. They overlook downtown, and then we don't have to deal with the insane crowds.

There are a few cars here already, but I'm able to find a spot somewhat secluded. I'm sure the place will get busier as the evening drags on. I back my car into the spot, leaving plenty of room.

Izabel hops out of the car and scurries over to the edge of the parking garage, peeking over. She looks back at me with a weird expression on her face.

"What?" I ask, amused.

"We're really high up," she says, peering over the edge

again. I chuckle and open up the trunk of my car, grabbing the wrapped-up blanket I keep in there.

I give it a quick shake and then lay it out over the rear windshield and trunk. This will have to do for tonight since I don't have any chairs. I crawl up on top of my car and lean back, resting my head against the blanket. Not the most comfortable, but it will do.

The car dips a little bit as Izabel climbs up next to me. Her arm presses against mine as she settles in. Thankfully, the sun is starting to set. Otherwise, it would be hot as Hades on top of this garage. I tuck my arm under my head as a makeshift pillow and close my eyes. It's been a long day.

I feel Izabel shifting around beside me. When I crack an eye open to spy on her, she's wringing her fingers together on her stomach. She's looking up at the sky, but it's clear her mind is elsewhere.

"Where's your head, pretty girl?"

She turns her eyes to me, hitting me with their soul-searing blue. "I don't know. I've just got a lot on my mind."

"Anything I can help with?" She listened to my woes this morning, so the least I can do is return the favor.

Izabel tilts her head up, observing the sky silently, and shrugs her shoulders. "I don't know. I'm just thinking about everything I have to do when we get back. Lesson planning for school, wedding planning—I'm supposed to be meeting with Mark's mom and the planner next Wednesday, and I just..." She shakes her head. "I'd rather drown."

I bite down the sharp pain that stabs through my heart at her words. It's taken great strength for me to push the knowledge that Izabel is getting married to that bastard to the back of my brain. The image of her walking down the aisle to him makes me nauseous, and to hear her bring it up makes all of those feelings even worse.

On top of it, her verbalizing that she still intends to move forward with these plans—given everything that's happened between the two of them—has me fisting my hands in irritation.

I manage to keep my tone level as I question, "That bad, huh?"

Izabel lets out a breathy laugh. "You don't even know. She's nothing like your mom." We fall into a comfortable silence again, until Izabel asks me, "Are you scared? Of your mom being sick?"

"Of course. I don't know how I couldn't be." I think about it. "Not really even so much for me. I mean, she's the only parent I have left, but mostly for Thalia."

"Thalia is still so young."

I nod. "I know. I wasn't much older than she is when my dad died, and you know how much that affected me." Izabel is quiet, but I feel her gaze on me. "I just want her to be able to be a kid. She should be playing outside, getting dirty, having fun. She shouldn't have to worry about cancer or losing her mom this young."

Izabel reaches down beside us and retakes my hand, fitting it back to where it's been all day. I suck in a deep breath and squeeze her fingers.

"You're going to be an amazing dad someday, Ryan," she says, taking me by surprise. "I've always thought so."

Another laugh rolls out of my chest. "Yeah, we'll see. If I ever get to that point."

"Why wouldn't you?" she asks me naively. I shoot her a look with my eyebrows raised. "Oh."

The silence, this time, is awkward. I always feel that way whenever my feelings for her come up. She knows how I feel, how much she means to me. But it never changes anything. Who knows, maybe somewhere down the line, I'll find myself someone new... Someday, maybe.

For now, though, I'm just happy to be here with her. Content to hold her hand and talk. Even if this is the last time we ever get to do this, I'll be a happy man.

I still can't help the *what if* thoughts that spring up in my head. As we sit there, I let myself daydream that this is our life. That we can take weekend excursions whenever we want, and meander through cities for hours, hand-in-hand. I wonder what would have happened if we hadn't let the distance come between us all those years ago—where'd we be today.

The sky darkens as I'm still lost in thought. I could travel down this spiral for years, playing out the many scenarios in my head.

But I don't get a chance to as the first firework shoots off, making a trail of noise as it fires into the sky. A roar of cheers sounds from the nearby area, loud enough that we can hear it echoing from our post atop the parking garage.

Izabel sits up from our relaxed position and crosses her legs. Her eyes go wide with awe as she watches the colorful explosions. After a particularly impressive round, she looks at me to gauge my reaction, and I smile and nod. *Beautiful.*

I choose not to tell her that I don't even see the fireworks going off in the sky. My attention is on her, watching the colors dance across her face and reflecting in her eyes. Izabel looks back at me after the finale goes off. Her eyes are sparkling with joy, her face beaming.

We pack everything up and get in the car. Izabel buckles her seatbelt as we're driving off, and then looks at me sheepishly as her stomach growls loudly.

"Are you hungry?" I ask her, chuckling.

She shrugs and glances at me. "I wouldn't turn down a pizza if you wanted."

"Well, then I guess we're going for pizza."

We get a large carryout pizza from a small business close to our hotel. Izabel holds it as we get into the elevator and go to the fourth floor, turning to me with a questioning gaze. "Do you want to come to my room and eat? We could see if there's anything good on TV."

I stay quiet for a moment before I agree and follow her into her room. The line between friendship and something else is very clearly drawn in the sand in front of me, but eating pizza alone in my hotel room sounds way worse than crossing that boundary a little bit. Izabel sets the pizza down on the bed and then reaches for the TV remote, turning it on and handing it to me.

"Here, make yourself comfortable. See if you can find something to watch. I'll be right back!" She scurries into the bathroom and closes the door, locking it.

I stare at the brown door for a second before settling on the bed, flipping through channels. There really isn't much on for a Saturday night, but I decide on some chick flick that I know she likes.

A few minutes later, Bells comes out of the bathroom and sits down next to me. Both of us lean against the headboard and put the pizza box between us. We settled on pepperoni, though I know that's not her first choice. We each grab a slice and dig in, our attention on the movie.

Before too long, the pizza is gone, and we're still lounging on the bed. Izabel scooted closer to me once the box was out of the way. Now, she's cuddled into the crook of my arm, her head resting against my shoulder. I lean my cheek against her hair, feeling the softness tickle my cheek.

"Isn't it so dumb that movies do this?" she asks, pointing at the screen. "They make it seem like a girl's first time having sex is supposed to be all rainbows and sprinkles."

"What?" I exclaim out loud. "Yours wasn't like that?"

I glance down at her and see a sexy blush covering her cheeks. "I mean...no, it was perfect."

I wrap my arm tighter around her. Damn straight, it was perfect. Maybe not rose petals and dreamsicles like the movies show, but it was perfect. "Definitely glad it didn't happen in Old Mac's cabin, though," I say, gauging her reaction.

The blush deepens on her cheeks, and she covers her eyes with her hand. "Oh, God! He practically walked in on you having me for dessert. That was so embarrassing."

I throw my head back and laugh. She joins along with me until we both have tears in our eyes. I finally get a hold of myself, the movie long forgotten. Bells is curled up next to me, her knee bent and pressed against my thigh. She wipes at her eyes and then looks to me, the corners of her lips pulling up into a grin.

My gaze traces her features, flicking down to her lips, and then back up to her eyes. Her lips part slightly, bringing my focus back them. My pulse picks up as I lean in toward her. My mind wars with itself, equally knowing that what I'm about to do is breaking all the rules I've created for myself, and also not giving one flying fuck. The way she's staring at me right now draws me into her, her siren song too much for me to resist any longer.

I push my indecision and the hurt that I've felt for so long aside, choosing rather to focus on the twinkle of hope in her eyes, wishing that it means she feels how I am in this moment.

"Ryan?" she whispers, her breath fanning against my face, but it doesn't deter me. My eyes hare glued to her lips.

I finally close the distance between us, taking deep breaths through my nose as I meld my lips with hers, and my hand grips at her waist, pulling her into me. I manage to part from her lips, and give her a moment to push me away, slap me. Give me any type of signal that she doesn't want this. I hope with everything in me she doesn't pull away because, *God,* I want this. I want *her.*

Izabel opens her eyes a second later, her eyebrows furrowing. I brace myself for the rejection that is sure to come, but I'm surprised when she puts her hands on my cheeks and brings her lips to mine again, kissing me with everything she can give.

Chapter 22

Izabel

RYAN GROANS AS I STRADDLE ACROSS HIS HIPS IN ONE swift movement. He's still leaning against the headboard, his face tilted up to meet mine in a feverish kiss. Hands trace up my thighs, coming to rest on the bare skin. I rock my hips back and forth, loving the friction.

At this moment, all I can focus on is how it feels, knowing that Ryan desires me again. It's something I think I've always known, but now that we're here in this moment, it feels truer than ever. I didn't intend for this to happen when I asked to come with him. All I needed was an escape from reality, but little did I know that Ryan would be the one I would escape in.

And now that we're here together, facing this decision to do this, I can't seem to think straight. Some aspect of me is aware that we should put the brakes on, slow everything down, really *talk* before this all happens—there's still so much Ryan doesn't know. But I can't seem to make myself pull away from him. I can't stop, and I don't want to.

I'm quickly becoming intoxicated by his touch, by his kiss, and it's overwhelming all of my senses.

Ryan's hands grip the hem of my dress, pulling it up and over my head, leaving me in just my underwear. His emerald eyes trace the outline of my bra and down my bare stomach to my panties.

Then, I'm on my back and Ryan's hovering above me. He pulls his shirt off, and then devours my mouth with his, letting his hand explore lower. I let out a gasp as his fingers tickle my sides, and he emits a husky chuckle as his lips begin a trek down my jaw. When he tries to go lower to the base of my neck, I panic and use my hand to direct him back up to my lips.

I can't let him kiss my neck, he'll smudge the makeup I just reapplied, and the bruise will start peeking through. If he notices my jittery movement, he doesn't show it. He just moves his mouth with mine instead. When his hand brazenly dips underneath the hem of my underwear, I open my eyes, seeing his stare on me, gauging my reaction.

I arch my back up and reach behind me to unclasp my bra, pulling it off and shucking it across the room. Ryan's eyes are drawn to my chest, and he gently covers my right breast with his hand, giving a slight squeeze. Closing my eyes, I leave him to it. Gentle fingers trace my skin, the swell of my breasts, across my clavicle, and down my sternum.

Then he leans forward and presses his lips to my skin, trailing kisses until he's at the peak of my breast. His tongue swirls my nipple twice before his mouth engulfs the sensitive tip. His tongue flicks back and forth a few times, the movement making me squirm and moan. Then he's gone and continues on his journey down the center of my abdomen.

I catch his eyes as he circles around my navel, then dips lower to press a kiss against my underwear. The movement makes my legs shake, and I involuntarily thrust my hips up to meet his kiss. Giving me a wicked smirk, Ryan's fingers hook underneath the seam of my panties and work them down my legs, leaving me completely bare before him.

Once they're gone, Ryan takes a moment to lean back and admire me lying there. His eyes dilate, and then he's kissing me again. His fingers immediately find their mark and begin stroking the heat between my legs. I sigh against his mouth as one of his fingers slips inside of me, and he starts languidly thrusting it in and out, increasing my arousal.

It feels heavenly, being here again with Ryan, but I want *more*.

I grip my hands in his hair and tug slightly, pulling him away from me. His eyes find mine as he grins. My fingers make quick work of the belt around his shorts and pull the zipper down. Ryan helps, kicking the clothing off the rest of the way.

"Are you sure you want this?" he asks, nuzzling my cheek with his nose. I arch my back up into him, pressing my breasts against his chest. The feel of his bare skin on mine has my head spinning.

I nod fervently. "I want you." His eyes sear into mine as he shifts, his knee pushing my legs wider, so he can settle against me.

He's between my legs, and I can feel the length of his whole body against mine as he positions himself at my entrance. Before pushing forward, he captures my eyes with his again and moves up to kiss me. One of his hands braces near my head, and I wrap my hand around it, interlacing our fingers as he enters me.

I throw my head back once he reaches the deepest part of me. Ryan hisses between his teeth, feeling me clenching around him, and then starts moving. I meet his actions thrust for thrust until I'm not sure where I end and he begins. This is heaven, it must be.

I'd forgotten what it's like with him. The last time we were together was years ago. Ryan is the most attentive lover, finding his pleasure but chasing mine as well. I know from this point moving forward, I'll be ruined. There's just something about sharing this type of experience with the one person who knows you best. Who loves you for all your flaws, all your shortcomings. Someone you feel safe with. And it feels just as safe as the last time we were together.

Even if this is the last time I get to share this with Ryan, I will be happy. At least I have this moment with him now.

Ryan's fingers grip around my hip. He pulls out, flipping me over onto my stomach and adjusting my pelvis before entering me again at a new, deeper angle. Folding himself over my back, he lets out a moan in my ear that has me clenching even tighter around him. He thrusts into me hard, hitting every glorious spot within me. I feel him hovering against my back as I press my face into the pillow, crying out in pleasure.

His hand snakes around my front, finding my clit and stroking it expertly. As his fingers work me there, he continues to thrust into me. "Come for me, Bells," he says close to my ear. I let the sensations overwhelm me, starting at the base of my spine and shooting down to my toes as I shatter around him with a loud cry.

Ryan slows his movements as I come around him. When the pulsing stops, he pulls out and turns me back over onto my back. He kisses along my breasts, moving toward my neck. Again, I redirect his mouth back to mine, so he doesn't spend too much time there. It doesn't deter him.

He slides into me again, slower this time, letting me feel every inch of him. He keeps his mouth on mine, kissing me sensually as he makes love to me. My body starts to amp up again, the familiar tingle setting in as he speeds up, his movements quickly becoming erratic. Ryan tears away from my lips and buries his face in the pillow next to my head as he lets out a loud moan, losing control.

"Bells," he says my name over and over, his voice husky.

"I'm so close," I tell him. My fingers claw at his back, trying to get him impossibly closer to me. Every time he pulls out of me, all I want is him back inside. "Keep going, keep going."

"Fuck," he grinds out, kissing me again. "Bells, I'm gonna come."

The sound of his voice, teetering on the edge of ecstasy, pushes me over, and I orgasm hard around him, my voice turning raspy as I moan. Ryan follows close behind me, his thrusts getting deeper until he stills. His body collapses against mine as we both let the wave rush over us.

I can feel his heart beating through his chest. Running my fingers through his hair, I catch the sweat beads on his forehead. After a minute or two, Ryan pushes himself off of me with his hands and gives me a boyish grin. Then he slips out of me and strolls into the bathroom. I hear the water running before he returns with a wet washcloth, and he gently wipes me between my legs. The scratchy washcloth in that sensitive area makes me tremble. I force my body to relax at the gesture. With a kiss to my forehead, he gets rid of the washcloth.

I hop off the bed and prance into the bathroom to take care of business and make sure my neck is still covered. I'm pleased to find the makeup has held, and I let myself relax even more.

When I step back out into the room, Ryan is sprawled out in the bed, underneath the covers. He's lying on his back with one arm tucked behind his head. He peeks one eye at me and gives me a lazy smile.

"Can I sleep with you tonight?"

I can't fight the smile off my lips as I pull back the covers and crawl next to him. "I think you just did."

His arm shifts as I cuddle close to him. As his hand rests on my hip, he traces slow circles on my naked skin. Pressing his lips to mine softly, he flexes his arm, pulling me closer to him until we're flush together, skin-to-skin.

"I love you, Bells."

My heart sinks into my stomach.

There's something so delectable about hearing those words once again from Ryan's lips. It makes my soul sing in a way I never thought was possible. And yet...

I know I shouldn't be feeling this way, and that knowledge dampens the thrill of the moment. But I can't seem to help myself from basking in the euphoric sensation of his love.

I smile and lean my face against his chest, feeling the rhythmic beat of his heart. My fingers trace the outline of the scar on his stomach. Though it's faded over the years, it's still a distinct souvenir. Ryan shivers from my light touch, and I feel his lips on my forehead. He takes a deep breath and then exhales against me.

"I missed this. I miss *you*," he whispers into the darkness, hand tightening against my skin.

I snuggle against him and press my lips to his chest. "Me too," I say back. He makes a contented grunt, but then falls silent. I stay awake long enough to hear Ryan's breathing even out before I fall asleep, too.

The next morning, I wake up to the bed empty beside me. My hands feel around for Ryan, but I find I'm alone. Light is streaming in through the hotel room curtains, gently illuminating the space. I peek open one eye, not fully ready to be awake yet.

Ryan is sitting in the armchair near the window. He's got his shorts back on but no t-shirt, his skin glowing in the soft light from the window. He's glaring at the floor with his eyebrows pulled together, his eyes distant and unyielding, fist pressed against his mouth. I sit up slightly, looking at him with concern. Is he regretting last night? Is he mad?

"Ryan?" I whisper, not managing to hide the concern of rejection lacing my tone.

He looks at me at the sound of his name, staring at me for a minute before picking something up off of his lap. I didn't see it before. My stomach lurches into my throat when I recognize what it is.

"Want to explain what this is?"

I'm sitting up fully now, staring at the notepad that has my handwriting on it. The words I wrote to Mark glaring at me right in the face. "Where did you find that? Were you going through my things?"

Ryan scoffs and stands, tossing the notepad back on the desk. "No, I was trying to get coffee when I saw it sitting there. I was going to ignore it, but some part of my brain saw my name written on the page, so I looked. And I'm glad I did." He shakes his head, pinching the bridge of his nose. "I'm not mad," he says to me before looking up. "I just want to know the truth. Has he hurt you?"

My mind spins as I try to come up with a way out of this situation on the fly. I could lie. He wouldn't believe me—he knows me far too well, and would see right through it—but I could try.

The guilt eats me alive, though. I know how Ryan feels about the situation with Mark; he's made that very clear. But still, I can't seem to force the words of denial through my lips.

With his expectant expression, I know I'm caught. My stomach churns with the realization that I have to tell him. He won't let me out of this that easily. Not now that I'm sure the truth is written all over my face.

Maybe if I tell him and convince him that I have everything

under control, he'll drop it. He'll let me handle everything on my own and stop pushing his way into my business.

Throwing the covers back, I crawl out of bed and walk toward Ryan. My hands shake as I grab his hand and lead him to the bathroom. I can practically feel Ryan's confused stare on my back.

My feet find the cold tile of the bathroom, and I walk over to the shower, turning on the hot water, pulling the shower curtain across the rod, sealing in the hot water. The bathroom is already starting to steam up. The giant mirror above the sink gets foggy as the heat warms the room. Ryan's eyebrows furrow as I turn toward him, making quick work of the shorts he's wearing.

"What—" He tries to speak, but I place my finger over his lips. I don't want to lose my confidence. I have to do this now. I have no choice.

I grab Ryan's hand again as I pull back the shower curtain and step under the stream of water. The water cascades down my back, and Ryan follows behind me, sealing us into the tight space. His hands find my shoulders and trail down my skin. I know his eyes are on me, watching my every move.

The water pours down my neck, and I scrub at the makeup left from last night. Underneath the foundation and concealer, there will be the fading remnants of Mark's fingerprints on my skin. I close my eyes, trying to steady my heartbeat. This is uncharted territory. I don't know how he's going to react, but I know it won't be good.

I'm not scared of Ryan. I've never been scared of Ryan in my entire life. He won't hurt me, but I know what I'm about to reveal is going to hurt him.

Slowly, I turn around. My eyes are still closed, but I open them once I know the bruise is fully visible to him. I stand there for a second, vulnerably, letting my truth show, startling at the hardness in Ryan's facial features as he stares at the marks marring my skin. His jaw tightens as he looks at my clavicle, and my eyes start to burn with unshed tears.

His eyes trace the outline for what feels like hours. I finally reach for his hand, bringing it up to my neck. His fingers are gentle as I let him touch me, his shoulders trembling with controlled rage. I can see the fire behind those emerald eyes.

His touch against such a gruesome memory is therapeutic. I feel exposed. More explored than I did last night when he was making love to me and kissing every inch of my skin. Tears fall down my cheeks as he continues to stroke the still-tender spot.

Through the wetness clouding my eyes, I see his expression. It's brutal. Eyes hardened, jaw slack. He looks as if I've just shot him in the gut. Another stroke down my neck, then his hand comes up to cup my cheek.

"Bells," he whispers brokenly. Then his face contorts in anger as he pulls his hand away from me, turning to face the wall of the shower. He inhales sharply as he leans his forehead against the tile, squeezing his eyes shut. His fist comes up and slams against the wall.

The sheer physical pain I observe written across his features further triggers my tears. My hand flutters up to cover my mouth as a sob escapes. My knees are threatening to buckle underneath me.

Ryan whirls back around to face me, the anger dissolving right away. Strong arms wrap around my waist, and he pulls me into him right before I would have collapsed in this shower. His wet skin against mine warms some of the chill deep within my body from the truth of what I've just showed him. I let him hold me and lean my head against his chest. Ryan's grip is tight as he lets me cry against him.

The water from the shower still pelts against my back, but I don't care. I let it wash away all the hurt and embarrassment. It rolls down the drain as Ryan's lips press into my hair, replacing those shameful feelings with love and tenderness.

Chapter 23

Ryan

"Bells," I whisper. I feel the energy coursing through me. Spinning around, I pound my fist against the wall, feeling the hit radiate down my arm. I press my forehead onto the cold tile, letting the chilled ceramic calm down my anger.

I hear a strangled sob escape Izabel, and I turn to her. Tears are streaming down her face as I hold her. Our naked bodies are pressed together. It's an intimate moment, but more as if two souls are finally reconnecting. There's nothing inappropriate, nothing even remotely sexual about this moment.

All I want is to take away her pain. Take away the shame she must be feeling or the embarrassment. She hid this from me. I can't believe I didn't notice during all the time we've spent together on this trip. I told her I couldn't be that guy for her, and look what happened. Could things have gone differently if I had been around more?

After finding that letter and reading what she scribbled, I had to know if Mark hurt her in that way. If he pushed her up against the wall and pressed on her neck until she couldn't breathe. Her beautiful neck. I think back to last night when she wouldn't let me kiss her neck, and I suddenly feel sick to my stomach as the pieces come together.

The words she wrote whisper in the back of my mind as if she were saying them out loud:

"...and somehow, I end up with your hand against my throat, fighting for air."

"I don't want to be afraid of how badly you'll hurt me next time we disagree."

My body shakes I hold her tightly against me, afraid what will happen if I let her go. Her tears mix with the water from the shower. She settles down a few minutes later and pulls away from me, turning around to shut off the water. I step out first, grabbing a towel and wrapping it around my waist before handing her one. She steps into it, holding on to the edges tightly. As she turns to me, her eyes dart to the ground and her hand flies up to cover her neck, the bruises now hidden from my view.

"I'm sorry," she mutters.

I narrow my eyes at her. "What are *you* sorry for? You didn't do this." She shakes her head, not meeting my eyes, but doesn't respond. "When did this happen?"

"Last Wednesday, when I was supposed to meet you for dinner." She peeks up at me from under her eyelashes.

I stumble back a step and feel my heart constrict. "Last week? Why didn't you tell me, Bells? I could have helped you."

As the words leave my lips, I remember how many times I ignored her calls. Shame drapes over me like a cloak, and I clench my jaw, trying to push it back.

"I don't need your help," she says back. Suddenly, I see the fire in her eyes, and I'm relieved it still exists. Mark didn't extinguish it this time.

"I think you do."

Izabel throws her hands in the air with a gruff sigh. She

turns on her heel and storms out of the bathroom. "I never wanted this. I wasn't going to tell you, but I knew you wouldn't let me leave this room without spilling everything. So, now you know. What more do you want from me, Ryan? Was the sex not enough for you?"

"Of course it was," I tell her incredulously as I follow her back into the room, though even as I say the words, something tells me it's not the whole truth. "You are enough for me. You will always be enough for me. But you are so much more to me than sex. I want *you*, Bells. I want all of you and I want you safe. That's all I've ever wanted."

Another tear falls from the corner of her eye, but she swipes it away quickly. "I don't need your protection. I can handle this. I *am* going to handle this."

"How? By writing him a letter?" I ask, pointing at the pad of paper on the desk. "I don't think that's going to magically turn him into Prince Charming! I hate that you feel like you have to write him a letter instead of talking about it to his face. Some relationship, that is."

"It's fine, Ryan. It's none of your business." Going over to her duffle bag, she starts digging through it, looking for some clothes. She groans when she can't find anything, and then grabs my t-shirt off the ground, pulling it over her head. "Look, this has been fun and all, but I think we should go home."

I feel my shoulders sag as I watch her. I don't move an inch. We're going around in circles right now, not making any positive headway. I conclude that I have to change my strategy here if I want her to hear anything I'm trying to convey. She's got her weapons drawn defensively, but I'm not her enemy. I'm not even close to that, and I hate that she feels that way. I can see it clear as day by the gleam in her eye. She doesn't believe that I'm on her side, and that guts me.

Switching to a gentler tone, I plead, "Don't push me away anymore. Let me help you."

She pauses and covers her eyes with her hands, taking a few deep breaths. "I don't know what to do. Everything is falling apart."

I don't know what to say to her. The defensiveness fades into vulnerability as she stands there, focusing on her breathing. All I can do is *show* her that I'm here for her and that everything will be okay.

I cautiously take a few steps toward her, my hands coming to rest on her shoulders just like before. She exhales, leaning into my touch. I turn her around to face me, taking in her appearance. Her face is void of any makeup after our shower, making the bruising on her neck painfully obvious. Even with the bruised neck and the red-ringed eyes, she's beautiful to me.

Leaning down, I press my lips against hers. Izabel responds immediately, standing on her tiptoes to wrap her arms around my neck. I reach down, picking her up by her thighs, and she jumps and wraps her legs around me on instinct. Without breaking our kiss, I shuffle over to the bed. Dropping Izabel back on the mattress, I crawl on top of her.

My t-shirt comes off a few minutes later, the towel wrapped around my waist following suit. I kiss down her chest before moving back up to her neck. Izabel stills as I gently press my lips against the bruise. Once. Twice. Then I move to her breasts, then down to the apex of her thighs. I kiss and lick her until she's a moaning mess on the sheets. Climbing up her body, I position myself at her entrance.

Before I push inside of her, I look up at her face. Her eyes lock with mine and everything around us stills. It's so quiet I can hear my heartbeat in my ears and the gentle rhythm of her breaths. I find myself falling deep into those blue eyes. My chest aches as we stand on the precipice of this moment together. I wonder if she feels how I'm feeling right now. If her heart is yearning for more.

Still holding her gaze with mine, I thrust inside her, groaning at her silkiness around me. *Fuck,* I could stay here all day.

I start to grind against her, never breaking eye contact. Izabel's hands fist in my hair, gripping through her pleasure. I bring us both to completion, spilling myself into her and stilling. Once I catch my breath, I pull out, falling onto my side as I gather her close to me.

We lie there together for a while. The only sound in the room is the echo of our breathing and the air conditioner. I shift a little bit on my back, moving Izabel so she's settled on my chest.

"Focus on the moment, not the monsters that may or may not be up ahead," I quote. She looks up at me, and I meet her confused gaze.

"What's that from?"

"That book you gave me," I tell her. "*The Obstacle is the Way.*"

Izabel giggles, the sound vibrating against the skin of my chest. "Well, I'm glad to hear you're learning something."

I tickle her waist, making her squirm. "I'm a lot smarter than I look, you know." I laugh under my breath. "Focus on the moment, Bells."

She leans up with a smile, the tears from earlier forgotten as she presses her lips to mine. All I can think about is how happy I am right now. I want all of these moments: the heartaches, the hurt, the giggles, the love. I want them with her. I let her get lost in the kissing for a few minutes before pulling away.

The words are on the tip of my tongue, and before I can consider the possible repercussions, I blurt out, "Leave him."

Izabel pulls away from me with wide eyes. "What?"

"Leave him. Be with me again. Bells, you were meant for me, and I'm meant for you."

Her head is shaking even before I finish my sentence. She crawls out of the bed until she's standing in front of me. Her arms wrap around her middle as if she's trying to hold herself together. One hand raises up to her cheek, then falls to the base of her neck, absentmindedly covering her bruise. I follow her lead and stand up as well, taking a step toward her. Both of us are still without a stitch of clothing on, but if anything, that just makes the moment more intimate, more significant.

"I can't, Ryan."

"Why not?" My question comes out a little harsher than I intend, but I hate that she feels like she's trapped when she's not. I could help her, if only she'd let me.

"I just can't," she mumbles.

"Please, Bells. I'm begging you. Leave him," I say, softer this time. I take a step toward her, but she quickly backs away, as if she's frightened of my approach.

"I *can't!*"

"Why?" I plead with her. I feel helpless, and that feeling has panic starting to rise in my chest.

"Because I'm scared!" she shouts. The expression on her face shows me she's just as surprised by the admission as I am.

I let her words settle in the room around us. Izabel's eyes are wide, and her chest heaves with labored breaths. I step closer, my arms extended, but she steps away from me, out of my grasp. My arms drop to my sides, but I don't avert my gaze.

"Bells," I say softly, coaxing. "Let me help you."

Maybe it's the softness of my tone, or the way I'm looking at her, but without any warning, she breaks in front of me. Her knees buckle, and she falls to the floor. Her arms wrap around her middle as if she's trying to hold herself together as she sobs.

I don't hesitate. I close the distance between us and pull her into my arms. She leans her head against my shoulder and cries. The type of cry that guts me deep down to my core. I hold her and squeeze my eyes shut, my own eyes burning from the realization that this woman I love so dearly has been broken.

"He *choked* me, Ryan," she sobs.

Finally, my own tears fall. The thought of him holding her against her will and crushing her neck has a fury of different emotions exploding within me. I bury my face in her hair and breathe her in. This woman is so precious to me. I don't know how anyone could ever hurt her.

"You need to leave him," I tell her. "Please, let me help you. Or Juliet. I can't let you go back to him."

"I don't know if I can," she whispers. Her body trembles against my own, and I tighten my arms around her again.

"Do you want to?" I dare to ask.

She falls silent, but then says, "I don't want to feel like this anymore."

"Then, please. We can figure this out. We'll get you out, away from him. Bells, I love you. I will do anything for you. Just let me."

Izabel curls into me even more, but she doesn't say anything for several heartbeats until she says the last thing I want to hear. "I think we should go."

I clench my jaw, feeling the muscles protest, but I nod my acknowledgment to her. Izabel brushes past me, her shoulder hitting mine as she walks into the bathroom. The door shuts more forcefully than I think she intends, and I hear her flip the lock. My eyes close, and I let a breath out of my nose.

Why did I have to fuck everything up? We were blissfully happy, not even ten minutes ago. I should've known better than to ask her to leave him. Though the decision seems evident to me, I know Izabel isn't there yet. Or if she'll ever be.

The bathroom is silent for a minute before I hear her begin

to rustle around in her things. I decide that I'm not going to get anywhere else with her right now. So I find my clothes, then walk out of her room and into my room next door to start packing.

This weekend went by way too fast. A small part of me wants to storm back into Izabel's room and force her to listen. Force her to think about all that transpired between us. To ask her if she felt the same way I did. As if the missing part of me was found.

But I don't. Instead, I pack up my belongings and meet Izabel out in the hallway a little while later. She closes her door behind her, her duffle bag slung over her shoulder. I do a quick once-over of her. Her eyes aren't red from tears anymore. Her hair is pulled back from her face, thoroughly dried from our stint in the shower this morning. She's wearing a yellow sundress that goes just to her knees. She's stunning, as always.

But what shocks me more than I'm prepared to admit to her is her neck. Once again, it's entirely covered with makeup. No trace of her fiance's anger evident on her delicate skin. My mind recalls this morning and the soul-wrenching vulnerability of her showing me what he did to her. It was as if everything was stripped bare. It was just us, and she trusted me enough to reveal what Mark did.

And now she's hiding again.

My jaw clenches. Izabel looks at me sheepishly, giving me a small smile. Then her eyes dart to the elevators down the hall.

"Ready to go?" she asks, grabbing her bag and adjusting it over her shoulder.

I nod and follow her as she walks down the hallway. She stands quietly by me as I check out at the lobby desk, then still doesn't say anything as we settle in the car and pull onto the highway.

Home isn't far. It's only a few hours, but I wouldn't be

surprised if she doesn't say a word to me the whole car ride. A sick feeling settles into the pit of my stomach. My hands grip the steering wheel as I glare at the highway in front of me.

What if he's there, waiting for her? What if he loses control and goes after her again? What if I'm not there to save her?

What if she doesn't want me to be?

My mind is like a battlefield the entire drive home. Izabel's silence from the seat next to me doesn't seem to help. I can't stop my thoughts from spiraling into dangerous territory.

Though the drive is short, I feel exhausted by the time I pull up in front of her apartment complex. Izabel unbuckles her seatbelt and glances around the parking lot. Her shoulders stiffen slightly, and then she looks at me over her shoulder.

"Will you be okay?" I ask her carefully. "Do you want me to come up with you?

She gives me a sad smile. "I'll be fine."

"Okay," I say and rub the back of my neck. "Well, if you need me, don't hesitate to call. I'll be over."

"Thanks, Ryan. And thank you for letting me come with you. Sorry for ruining your weekend with all my drama."

"You didn't—" I start to say, but she opens the car door and hops out. It falls shut behind her, and I'm alone. I watch her run into her complex. She doesn't stop to turn around and wave to me. She just disappears inside the building.

I rub my first three fingers over my chin, feeling the rigidness of the stubble of my beard. I didn't bother shaving this morning. Frankly, I didn't have the energy after everything that happened. I sit in her parking lot for another minute before pulling out my cell phone and scrolling through my favorite contacts.

I give a gruff sigh under my breath and tap on Josie's number and lift the phone to my ear as it starts to ring. She picks up right away with a simple greeting.

"Are you busy?" I ask her. "'Cause Jack Daniel's is screaming my name, and I just cannot handle another blow this weekend."

"No, I'm not busy. I'll be over in a bit. Don't do anything stupid," Josie replies. I hang up with a groan, leaning my head back against my seat.

It is too fucking late for that. I've already done all the stupid things I could possibly do this weekend.

Chapter 24

Izabel

I PRESS MY HAND AGAINST THE DOOR OF MY APARTMENT AS it closes. The space is mostly dark, aside from the daylight streaming through my curtains. A few boxes are stacked in the other room, ready for moving day in a little over a week. It smells like home—just how I left it.

I hear my guest shift against the couch, and I finally turn around to face him. I noticed Mark's car sitting in the parking lot, so I'm not surprised. It was part of why I bolted out on Ryan without saying a proper goodbye after our memorable weekend. Mark is reclined on my couch. A blue Gatorade sits on the side table, half drank. I gave Mark a key to my apartment last year. Thankfully, he usually respects my space, so I don't have to worry about random drop-ins. But the possibility is always there.

Such as right now.

He observes me as I step into my home, then he stands up, putting his hands into his pockets. My eyes dart over his face, gauging his demeanor. He seems to be in an okay mood.

"You're back early," I speculate, still staring at him. "I didn't think you were coming back until tomorrow."

Mark's hands flex in his pockets, but he doesn't move. "We decided to cut the trip a little short. I was anxious to see you. To talk."

I nod as my hand grips the strap of my duffle bag. We both still stand there, neither of us brave enough to make the first move.

After a beat, Mark says, "I suppose I should say welcome back to you too. Where have you been?"

I bite my lip as I stare at him. "I was in Nashville. Visiting Sage. We went and watched the fireworks downtown."

"Did you go with someone? Your car was still here." I know the real question hidden beneath the formalities.

"I took a rental. I didn't want to put the miles on my car," I lie.

It appeases him, though. His warm brown eyes soften at my words, and he nods at my supposed smart decision. "Good, that's good. I guess we both needed some time away."

"What are you doing here, Mark?" I ask him.

"I was hoping we could talk," he says. "Things didn't exactly end well between us last time and—"

"They didn't end well?" I fire at him. "Mark, you choked me."

His face hardens again, and he looks down at the ground. "I know. I'm sorry, Izabel. You don't know how much I hate myself for what I did to you." Then he glances up, his eyes studying me. "It looks like it's all healed up. The bruise, I mean."

I stare at him for a minute, and then breeze past him to my bedroom to put away my things. "That's because I have it covered with makeup."

No, the bruise is definitely still there. Not as angry or

vibrant. But still there. The memory of Mark's hand holding me against the wall is still very apparent too.

Though it's less consuming than it was before.

I think back to this morning when Ryan's fingers grazed the tender spot. So gentle, so careful. The gut-wrenching pain and anger that flashed across his face will forever be etched in my mind. I know it wasn't directed at me, but rather at the man standing in the doorway of my bedroom, hands still in his pockets. That one simple action eased the emotional hurt enough.

"Izabel, what can I do to make you forget this?" he asks, watching me throw my duffle bag onto my bed and zip it open. I dump the contents out and start sorting through the clothes to determine what needs to be washed. "Please, baby, talk to me."

The tone in his voice is finally what breaks me. I can hear the dejection and the hurt, and I can tell he's really sorry. Memories of the past years of Mark opening up to me and showing me the side of him that no one else gets to see ricochets through my mind. It softens the part of me that has been defiant toward him these last few days. That doesn't excuse his actions, by any means, but I know he is sorry. I turn back to look at him and let my shoulders drop a little from my defensive position.

He sees the visible change in me and comes forward, extending his arms. I let him wrap me up in a hug. His hands rest on my waist as he pulls me against his body. Involuntarily, my hands circle around him. Burying his nose in my hair, he breathes me in, pressing his lips against my scalp.

"I missed you. I'm so sorry."

I press my head against his shirt, feeling the rhythm of his heart, but I stay quiet. I close my eyes, searching for those feelings that he elicited in me all those years ago. This is the man who convinced me to fall in love with him once upon a time—but still, I feel so disconnected from that version of him. He's like a ghost, a presence I can feel around me, but can't grasp onto.

Before, the beat of his pulse could calm me, but now it just sounds hollow. I don't know what to say to him. I kind of feel like we're starting from scratch. This is the man I said I would marry in only a few months. Shouldn't I know how to talk to him about these things?

It's just like Ryan said. I should be able to have conversations with my fiancé without having to write him a letter beforehand. I shouldn't have to be frightened of his reactions to my words.

I take a deep breath, and Mark tightens his hold around me as if he can tell something is coming. "I need you to be able to talk to me," I tell him hesitantly. Here goes nothing. If he loses his shit on me again, then I'll know there is no salvaging this. "And I want to be able to talk to you about things without you getting mad."

Mark exhales against my hair. "I think that's fair. I can work on that."

He steps away slightly, giving me a tender look. Bending down, he aims for my lips. His hands resting on my waist, travel around to the zipper of my dress. I squirm away from him, putting distance between us. He has a hurt expression on his face, but I don't care. Kissing Mark will lead to sex, and I have no interest in that with him right now. I'm still far too conflicted from the thoughts and emotions swirling inside of me to even consider sleeping with him.

Mark's hurt appearance slowly morphs into something else as his eyebrows pull together. It's not anger, but I'm unable to identify it. "If I'm going to make such a difference in our relationship, then you have to too."

My head spins from the quick change of tone. "What does that mean?"

"It means you're not completely innocent in this whole thing either. You need to start acting like my fiancée instead of running around trying to make me jealous all the time."

I pause. His harsh tone quickly pulls me out of any lingering dream-like feelings I was in after my weekend with Ryan. Right away, I go on the defense, feeling my muscles turn ridged as I face him.

"Mark, that's not—"

"What? That's not what you were trying to do? You know how I feel about him," he growls, pointing his finger at his chest. My pulse rises as I recognize the direction this conversation is headed. "And I know how he feels about you. So, stop acting like a slut and start focusing on the wedding we have coming up."

I feel my jaw drop at his words. He might as well have just slapped me again. "Mark," I gasp. I can't believe he just said that to me. As if that's the final straw, any sense of understanding flies out the window.

I know I should feel guilty for what transpired between me and Ryan over the weekend, but I don't. If anything, it was a reminder of what I deserve.

"No."

All it would take would be for me to leave this house, run to Ryan, and let him follow through on his offer to protect me. That's all it would take. Then I'd be free.

Like he can hear my line of thinking, Mark raises a challenging eyebrow at me, and his face morphs into a snide expression. "What do you mean, no?"

"I don't want to do this with you anymore. I can't. I won't."

Mark clenches his jaw, tight enough that the muscles tick. The silence is deafening as he mulls over the implications of my words. My fight-or-flight response is slowly going into overdrive, waiting for him to say something. "I don't think you're prepared to play this game, Izabel. You don't know who you're going up against."

I stand my ground and lift my chin, but don't say a word. There's an ominous streak to his words that has me second guessing talking back to him. The glint in his eye that tells me that he really isn't playing around, and I don't want to know what happens if I push him too far.

So I stay quiet. But my refusal to speak seems to send him over the edge. Before I know what's happening, he's raising his arm and striking the back of his hand against my cheek. The brunt force sends me flying into the wall. I cry out and clutch at my now burning face. Through my tears, I look up at him, hoping he can see how he is breaking me. But all I see is his fury.

"Let me make something clear," he sneers. "You. Are. Mine. Ryan had his chance to keep you, and he fucked it up. So now you belong to me. I get to decide when we're done and when we're not. And right now, I'm saying we're not."

I blink at him and swallow thickly. My throat feels tight. Sweat breaks out on my arms, and my stomach roils with the implications of what he's saying. I should have stayed with Ryan, point blank. I should have let him take me away far from here.

But I didn't.

And now I'm stuck here, with no end to this torture in sight. Mark isn't going to change. I know that now.

Mark leans back and laughs humorlessly. "See, I didn't want to do this. I came back early, hoping you would've gotten over what happened last week, but it seems you've just taken the time apart to blow it way out of proportion." He sighs as though he's disappointed with me, and then pinches the bridge of my nose. "Let's just drop it and move on. We both have a lot on our plate, and we need to focus."

Focus. All I have to do is play it cool, and let his temper run its course so he'll leave me alone.

"I got you this while I was out of town," Mark says, his voice taking on a lighter tone. "It's kind of a mix between an *I'm Sorry* gift and an *I Love You*."

I'm still cowered against the wall as he reaches into his back pocket and pulls out a small black box. He holds it out to me like a peace offering. I watch him warily but take the box, nonetheless. I'm scared to know what would happen if I refuse.

Inside the box is a heart necklace. It's made of silver, but in the center is a huge sparkling diamond. I blink a few times as I take it in, my eyes trying to process what they're seeing.

"Here, let me help you try it on," Mark says, holding out his hand for me. My heart is thundering in my ears as my eyes dart between his outstretched hand and his face. Mark's acting as if he has no recollection of what just transpired between us, my cheek burning from where he hit me.

With fear being my primary motivator, I place my hand in his and let him pull me up into a standing position. He puts his hands on my hips and spins me around so my back is facing him. Taking the box from me, he pulls the necklace out.

"Look at the back. I had them put an engraving on it," Mark says huskily as he holds the pendant in his hand, showing me the backside.

Mine Forever.

I stare at the engraving and feel the bile rising up in my throat. I don't trust myself to say anything, so I turn away and stare at the wall in front of me. Mark doesn't seem to notice my inability to speak, and he fastens the necklace around my neck. Once it's resting on my chest, he walks around and gives me a once-over.

"It looks perfect on you. I knew it would," he says, giving me a sardonic grin. I still cannot get myself to respond. Mark approaches me and raises his hands toward my face. I can't help but flinch away. He hesitates, but then runs his fingers gently across the side he hit. My skin feels like sandpaper as he touches me. I watch as his eyes grow sad, "I wish I didn't have to do this," he whispers.

"Then why do you?" I finally manage to ask.

He raises an eyebrow, and then cups my cheeks, drawing my gaze up to himself. "Because you don't give me any other option."

I squeeze my eyes shut and try to shake my head, but he's holding too tight.

"I want you to listen to what I'm about to tell you because I don't want there to be any type of misunderstanding between us, okay, baby?" I open my eyes and glare at him. His own eyes are cold as he looks down at me. "You are *mine*. Don't go getting any ideas of running away, because if I find out you're even *thinking* about calling off this wedding, I will go after your little boyfriend and kill him. And then no one will be able to save you. Do you understand?"

My voice catches in my throat as fear once again takes over me. As my body trembles in his hold, I manage to nod. The thought of Mark seeing through his threat has me paralyzed. The shock and terrible reality settle into my core and churns my stomach until I'm sure I'm going to be sick all over the floor.

I can't imagine living in a world that Ryan is no longer a part of.

Suddenly, every potential escape plan or possible liberation is stripped away from me. I can't risk challenging what he's suggested. I'd be putting Ryan's life at risk, and I'm not willing to do that.

Which means I'm trapped. Officially and utterly trapped.

A prisoner in my own life.

I don't mean to, but I cower in on myself, feeling the weight of the cage that has just slammed and locked into place around me. I feel cold, chilled to the bone. Feelings of despair assure me that there's no way out.

A smile erupts on Mark's face, and he leans down, pressing his lips to mine. Again, bile rises, but I don't try to fight him off. I'm at his mercy.

When he pulls away, he finally releases my face. I take a step back, trying to put some distance between us. My gaze falls to the floor as Mark continues to look me over. Every bit of humanity has disappeared, as though I'm a piece of his property.

Unaware of my inner turmoil, Mark hums and says, "That necklace really does suit you. Do you want to go out to dinner? Maybe show it off? Then we could come back here and finish packing your stuff. Moving day is coming soon. I can't wait to have you all to myself in our own house."

I know he's trying to lighten the mood and be funny and romantic, but it makes my skin itch. "Actually, Mark, I'm feeling kind of tired from the trip and all the driving. Do you think I could take a rain check?"

He looks disappointed, but he nods and gives my shoulders a squeeze. I fight the urge to rip myself out of his grip. "Of course, baby. You should rest."

Mark tilts my chin up with his fingers, and I see the challenge in his eyes, so I consent and let him press his lips against mine again. I close my eyes as he kisses me, trying to get myself to feel something, anything. But I don't. It's just lips against lips.

He pulls away, a lighthearted smile on his face, and he grabs my hand. "Okay, well, you just rest tonight, and maybe this week we can finish packing up your things."

Again, I force a smile. Mark leans down to kiss me one more time, and then turns, seeing himself out of the apartment.

Once I hear the door shut behind him, I fall onto the edge of my bed. My eyes close, and I take a few deep breaths. The necklace's weight is heavy on my neck, and I fumble with the clasp, trying to get it off of me.

Once it's off, I hold it in my hand, turning it over. The thing is a huge, gaudy disaster. What was he thinking? This isn't me. I stand up and walk over to my dresser, pulling the top drawer open. I sift through the different pieces of jewelry, looking for the necklace Ryan gave me. So simple, but it meant so much.

Where is it? I frown as I realize it's not in the drawer. I could have sworn I just saw it a few days ago. Weird.

I set my new necklace on top of my dresser. The diamond glints at me mockingly. I glare at it for a moment, feeling my eyes begin to burn before going into my bathroom. Even though Mark's gone, I close the door and lock it behind me.

Once in the privacy of my bathroom, I let the tears fall and crumble against the cool laminate cabinets, letting the weight of what just happened finally hit me. I was at the point where I was willing to finally put Mark in his place, telling him that everything was over and doing what I knew was right before running back to Ryan's side.

But then Mark threw down the gauntlet, squashing any remaining hope of freedom or happiness that I might have had.

It's hard for me to fully wrap my head around the fact that only a few hours ago, I was safe in Ryan's arms after making love. Everything seemed so perfect when I woke up this morning, and now it's tainted with the reminder that it's time to get back to real life. If I could rewind the clock and go back, I would. I would give anything to be back in Nashville, snuggled up next to Ryan's chest, with him whispering sweet nothings in my ear.

But I can't. If Mark knew that my heart was conflicted, I feel like there would be nothing stopping him from taking Ryan from me and physically ripping the traitorous organ straight out of my chest.

The thought brings more tears to my eyes and a heart-wrenching sob rips from my chest. I crumple even further into myself, holding my torso tightly as if I'm afraid that I'll fall to pieces if I don't.

With everything that just transpired with Mark in mind, and some of my conversations with Ryan echoing in my ears, when I've finally cried myself out, I leave my bedroom and walk into my little study. I sit down at my desk and open my laptop, pulling up a new browser window. My fingers fly over the keyboard as I type what I'm looking for into the search engine. Results come up, and I scroll through them.

Ryan suggested going through self-defense classes. And the more I think about it, the better that idea sounds to me. Even if just to learn a few basic escape maneuvers. Just in case Mark gets angry and tries to attack me again. I may be trapped for now, but I am not going to allow myself to be helpless.

The Cedar Ridge community college holds a class for women, and their next session starts next week. I click through the web page, reading more about what kinds of things they go over. After browsing for a few minutes, I find myself deciding to sign up. I can always leave if I don't like it. I enter all my personal information in the required boxes. But before I hit submit, I pause and chew on my thumbnail.

What would Mark think if he found out I'm doing this? I know Ryan would be proud. I can practically picture Ryan standing there with a half-smile on his face and approval etched over his features.

I do it before I can talk myself out of it. I don't know why I'm so hesitant. It's not like anyone really needs to know. The class takes place on Monday evenings at 7 o'clock. That's late enough that it won't interfere with work, and if I need to, I can grab dinner with Mark beforehand and just tell him I'm going to the gym.

The form submits, and I get a confirmation code that I'm supposed to bring with me. I print it out and set it on my desk next to my computer. This will be a good step for me.

At the very least, I'll hopefully get a few extra tools to keep in my toolbox just in case shit hits the fan. And these days, that seems like that's all it ever does.

Chapter 25

Ryan

"WELL, DON'T YOU LOOK LIKE DEATH WARMED OVER," Josie speculates as she leans against my apartment door. She beat me here. I grumble under my breath as I pull out my keys and unlock the door, walking in. I leave it open for my friend to follow me.

"Always a pleasure, Jos, always a pleasure."

"Hey, you called me here," she says, raising her hands in surrender. "Not that I'm mad about it, 'cause fuck, Ry, you look awful." Her eyes roam up and down my body, and she shakes her head. Not in disgust, but rather concern.

I groan as I drop the duffle bag to the floor and collapse onto the couch. I set my elbows on my knees, resting my head in the palms of my hands. "You have no idea."

Josie sits next to me a beat later, curling her legs up underneath her. She's wearing plain black leggings with a t-shirt. I love casual Josie. Her being comfortable makes me comfortable. She hesitantly places a hand on my shoulder and gives my muscle a friendly squeeze.

"Want to talk about it, buddy?"

"No, I just really want to drink," I tell her honestly. There's no point in lying to her. Josie's seen the best and the worst of me and has somehow stuck through it all.

"Well, that's not an option. So you can either talk to me about it, or we can sit here in silence. I'm fine with either."

I choose to sit there. I can't get the words to form appropriately out of my mouth, so I don't say anything. Josie sticks to her word and sits next to me. When I peek over at her, she's examining her nails, picking at a cuticle. She glances up, catching me staring at her, and sticks her tongue out at me.

"So, how was your weekend?" Josie asks casually. Smooth.

I groan and fall back onto the couch, resting my head on the top. "It was great. And it was awful. All at the same time."

"Wow. That sounds interesting. Did you see the fireworks?" I close my eyes and don't respond. Without missing a beat, Josie says, "Well, this is fun. While you stew, I'm going to order some food. You want anything?"

I sigh. "Whatever."

"Great, super helpful." I hear her fiddling with her phone, and a few minutes later, she gives a satisfied sigh. "It will be here in twenty to thirty minutes."

I tilt my head and look at her. She's staring right back at me, an understanding smile on her face. "Why couldn't I have just fallen in love with you?" I ask her miserably.

She laughs now. "Trust me, Ryan, I am not the best girlfriend material. I've got all sorts of baggage. You really dodged a bullet with me."

"Like what kind of baggage?" I prod. Josie is one of my best friends, but I really don't know much about her past other than her alcoholic brother. She keeps pretty tight-lipped about most things.

Josie huffs another laugh and shakes her head. "Nice try,

but I'm over here to help you deal with *your* baggage. Mine is a whole different story."

"It just would have been so much easier if you were the one I was hopelessly in love with. You're easy."

"Who said love was easy? I'm pretty sure it's not supposed to be easy. It gets messy and ugly, and it hurts. But, a lot of times, it's also the greatest thing to ever happen to a person."

"Have you ever been in love?" I ask her. "Like, really in love?"

Josie presses her lips together and gives me a brisk nod. "I've loved plenty of guys. But I've only actually been in love once. A long time ago. But, like I was just saying, it got messy. We couldn't work through it. But my issues are not the same as yours."

"Yeah," I respond. "I love her. Izabel. I'll always love her. No matter what."

"I know," Josie says softly. "Did you two get to talk at all this weekend?"

"We did a lot more than *talk*," I mutter.

Josie's hazel eyes go wide, and she scoots closer to me on the couch. "Oh, I like where this is going. Tell me everything."

So I do. Well, mostly, everything. I tell Josie about our day spent out and about Nashville, the food trucks, the concerts, the fireworks. Then I tell her about how I ended up in bed with Izabel, not once but twice.

I leave out the part about the bruises on Bells' neck. That was a secret she entrusted to me, and I'm not going to break that trust, even for Josie.

"So yeah, we hooked up. I fell even more in love with her if that was even possible, and I asked her to leave him," I spill.

Josie is biting on the knuckle of her pointer finger, eyes still wide. "And? What did she say?"

"She didn't really say either way. She's scared. I don't know what to do about it."

The doorbell rings, and I get up, needing a break. I pull out my wallet and hand the delivery guy money for the food and a tip, and then I head back to the couch. We dig into our food, each grabbing a healthy serving.

"Okay, so let me get this straight," Josie says between bites. She drops a bit of sauce on her leggings and slides it off with her finger. "You guys magically fall into bed together. Then out of the blue, you tell her to leave her fiancé and be with you, and she says she's scared, and you're mad at her for that?"

I look at my friend with a dumb expression on my face. "There's more to it than that."

Josie flips her dark curly hair around, tying it up into a bun on top of her head. "Like what?"

I glower at her. "I can't tell you."

Now Josie glares at me. "How am I supposed to help you if you can't tell me what's going on?"

"I just can't, okay?" I growl. "All that really matters is that I *love* her, and that piece of shit isn't even *close* to being good enough for her."

"That's not your decision to make," she says simply. I feel my blood pressure rising, so I stuff my face with another large bite. After a while, Josie tries again, "I'm just saying, you can't expect her to drop him just like that since she's slept with you." She snaps her fingers on "*that.*"

I turn away from her and glare daggers at the ground. "He is not a good guy, Josie. She needs to leave him. It has nothing to do with the fact that we slept together."

Josie is quiet for a few moments. I think she picks up on my tone of voice by the way that her shoulders tighten. But as usual, she reads the situation correctly and doesn't pry. I'm not going to say any more than that, and she's respecting it.

"Okay. So I see two pathways here. Let's discuss them," she says, adjusting herself on the couch again. She's sitting criss-cross, her feet tucked under her knees. "We know that, clearly, Izabel wants you just as much as you want her, but she's conflicted. So here are your options." She holds up a finger. "Option one, do not give up on her, no matter how bad you want to or how bad it hurts. You show her you love her and hope to God that's enough, and she'll realize it before it's too late.

"Or Option two, just move on. There are lots of—"

"There will never be anyone else," I cut her off, my voice firm. "So, I have to go with option one."

"Okay, then. There you go. Stick with it. If things are as bad as you're not telling me, she needs you now more than ever. Do not give up hope on her. At the very least, she'll need you as her friend."

The idea of being just friends with Izabel is the last thing I want. But I understand what Josie is saying. All I can do is let her know that I'm here. I'll always be here for her, no matter what. And maybe someday that will be enough. Or it won't.

I'm prepared for either. It would kill me if she marries Mark without a glance back, but I'm hoping that one day, hopefully soon, Izabel will be able to recognize that I'm what she needs. What she wants. Just like Josie said, love is messy, it's ugly. But I'm not going to give up on my love for Izabel. I can't. I'd move mountains for this girl.

"So now that we have that figured out, what now?" Josie asks. I'm still not trustworthy enough to be left on my own in a mood like this. Even though she's talked me through it, the idea of drowning out the pain in a bottle of Jack is still tremendously appealing.

I shrug and nod to the TV. "Want to play video games?"

That will help get my mind off of this whole situation. Maybe I could actually relax for a while.

A grin splits across Josie's face, and she nods. "That sounds great. You sure you're ready for me to whoop your ass?"

I throw my head back and laugh as I get up and grab the controllers. "You wish. I've been doing this way longer than you have."

"That's what you think," she says, giving my shoulder a shove as I sit down next to her. The game fires up, and soon our entire focus is on killing the enemy. I pretend all the bad guys are Mark.

Chapter 26

Izabel

My days seem to blur together before I can stop it from happening. As time passes after my trip with Ryan to Nashville, memories of that happiness I experienced there with Ryan fade with it.

Quickly, I fall into the routine of merely existing. I get up in the morning, I go to my workout classes, I eat a boring lunch to give me energy to get through the afternoon, and then I go home. On the weekends, I spend time with Mark, trying to pretend that everything is okay when it's really not.

Before I can wrap my head around it, we close on our new house. Mark is adamant that we move in as quickly as possible. He even helps me pack up all my boxes from my apartment and get everything settled. I think we might set the record for the fastest move-in time. The week after closing feels like a time warp. I hardly have the chance to breathe, let alone process the big changes we are going through.

Though all my boxes are unpacked, and all my clothes and accessories placed neatly in my closet, it still doesn't feel like home. As soon as we moved in, I claimed the guest bedroom as my own, much to Mark's annoyance. He finally let it go after I managed to convince him I wanted to wait until after the wedding to move into the primary bedroom, when really I just couldn't stand the thought of sharing a bed with him.

Even after moving in together, Mark has been in rare form lately, constantly asking me what I'm doing, or where I'm going. Even when I'm off to the grocery store, he's interrogating me before and afterwards, as if trying to make sure I'm telling him the truth. It's enough to make me dread going anywhere at all.

He is particularly suspicious whenever I tell him that I'm going to hang out with Juliet. And the questioning and overall lack of trust from him has me walking on eggshells at all hours of the day. I never know when he's going to fall into another one of his fits and lose his temper with me.

It's something that has me fearful to reach out to anyone, even the people closest to me. I haven't spoken to my parents or my sister in weeks, always shying away whenever they ask to come over and spend time with Mark and myself. I always have a number of excuses at the ready. I don't want them to see what my life has become. I can't imagine how disappointed they would be in me.

Sage already hates Mark. I'm sure she'd hate me just as much for going along with his games if she knew. Which is why she can never know.

The feeling of solitude is slowly settling in.

Made even worse by Mark's pretense that everything between us is okay.

That's the opposite of what it is. I'm skating around him as much as possible, trying to stay out of his path and any potential altercation.

I crave having my own space, away from him. He's too overbearing at all other times that the thought of falling asleep knowing he's in the next room sends a deep sense of unease careening through my body. The words he said to me after returning from Nashville still echo in my mind, festering and reminding me that any type of reprieve is hopeless.

I will go after your little boyfriend and kill him. And then no one will be able to save you.

Even now, as I walk down the sidewalk, toward my favorite little coffee shop, they play on repeat through my memories. I can still hear how vicious his tone was, as he ensured that I knew he wasn't bluffing.

Though the afternoon is warm, a shiver runs down my spine, but I try to dampen it, choosing to focus on my main mission for today.

Juliet and I are meeting up for coffee to discuss wedding details. Though she's still not the happiest camper about Mark and me getting married, she agreed to be my Matron of Honor. We're meeting up today to talk about some of the finer details that I'm expected to nail out. I haven't picked out a dress yet, but I figure worst-case scenario I can order something online.

It's depressing to think that I'm so uninterested in my impending wedding.

I have barely spoken to Ryan since we returned, though he's reached out a few times. I feel too guilty, and I'm scared to press the limits of Mark's patience. He already doesn't trust me to go to on measly errands. I'm afraid of what other small freedoms he'll take from me if he finds out that I'm going behind his back again.

It's not something I'm happy about. I regret now more than ever not listening to Ryan's and Juliet's concerns about Mark. I had been blinded by the performance he seemed to always put on when I was around, and now it's too late.

I feel completely and utterly trapped within my own life.

And it's miserable.

Hopefully, spending time with Juliet this afternoon will help brighten up my perspective—but I doubt it.

When I open the door to the coffee shop, the small bell jingles, announcing my entrance. I look around, not spotting Juliet here yet. I suspect she'll be here any minute, so instead of grabbing a table right away, I walk up to the counter, ordering our drinks so they'll be ready when she gets here.

I get a kind smile from the employee standing behind the counter as I rattle off my order and Juliet's, and then order us both a dessert as a special treat.

As I'm turning away from the counter, I'm stuffing the receipt into my wallet. My hair falls over my face like a curtain, blocking my line of sight in front of me. Before I have a chance to catch myself, I'm running right into someone.

"Shit," I mutter, mostly to myself. "I'm so sorry."

When I look up to make sure whoever I almost ran over is okay, my mouth goes dry.

Familiar green eyes stare down at me. His expression is unreadable as he traces the features of my face.

"I'm sorry," I say again, though this time it's a whisper as I find myself getting lost in Ryan's gaze.

His shoulders drop sightly as he lets out a long breath. "It's okay. You're not hurt, are you?"

I'm suddenly wondering if he's asking that question because I ran into him, or because he knows the dirty secrets that revolve around my relationship.

My cheeks heat and I drop my eyes away from him. "No. I'm not hurt."

At least not on the outside.

"Glad to hear it," he says. His tone is level, and I can't help but look up at him again, hoping to find some unspoken facial cue. But I get nothing. His face is still just as stoic as it was a moment ago. "Good to see you, Bells."

"You too," I say. He nods once, as if he's content with the pleasantries and is ready to move on already. Stepping aside, he gives me a tight smile. Panic explodes in my chest out of nowhere, and I realize I'm not ready to be done talking to him yet.

Not after I haven't seen him in weeks.

"Wait," I say before he has a chance to get too far away from me. He turns his head with a brow raised. I scramble for something, anything to say, to help relieve this awkwardness that is settling between us. It's such a foreign feeling I'm entirely unprepared to deal with it. "How's your mom doing?"

Ryan takes a deep breath. "Good...well, as good as she can be, I suppose."

I press my lips together. Out of my peripheral, I spot a couple leaving a table by the windows. I look over at it and then back to Ryan. "Want to sit and catch up for a minute?"

Ryan looks hesitant. "Are you sure that's a good idea?"

I shrug a shoulder in answer. Without saying anything else, I walk over to the vacated table and take a seat. A second later, Ryan follows me.

He slides into the seat and folds his hands on top of the table.

"So she's doing okay?"

"Yeah, she's just going through treatments, and praying that they're working. She's got a follow up in a few weeks with her main oncologist."

"I'm sure it will be nothing but good news," I say, hopeful.

Ryan rubs the back of his neck. "You and me both."

"If you ever need anything..." I start, but trail off. I know deep down I shouldn't be offering this. But at the same time, I can't not offer. "Just know I'm here for you."

Ryan is quiet a beat too long. It makes the already awkward atmosphere even more awkward. "Yeah, you too, Bells."

My cheeks heat, and I look down at the table. Thankfully, someone swings by and places Juliet and my coffees down. They swipe away the order number and disappear before I can even thank them. Ryan eyes the second coffee before his eyes catch on something outside.

"You meeting up with Juliet?" he asks, tilting his head to the front of the shop. I turn around in my seat to look out the windows, spotting Juliet pacing back and forth, phone stuck to her ear. I can tell she's annoyed by the way she's scowling at the cement in front of her.

"Oh yeah. We're um—" I hesitate. "Working on wedding things together."

Ryan's face instantly darkens. He stares at me a moment longer before giving me a curt nod. "Guess that's coming up soon, then, huh?"

I nod, and my throat feels dry. "Yes, on the eighth of next month."

"It's still on then? The wedding."

Words get caught now, so I settle on giving him a slow, regretful nod.

I want to beg and plead for him to understand, because I can see it all over his face that he doesn't. I wouldn't either, if I were him. But there's no way I can tell him. He means too much for me to risk putting him in direct harm like that.

So I don't say anything else.

Ryan's eyes crinkle in the corners and his jaw flexes. "Right. Well, enjoy. I'll see you around."

Before I have a chance to say anything, Ryan is getting up from his seat and taking a step toward me. He places his hand on my shoulder, giving me a meaningful look before letting me go and walking out of the shop. He waves a hand to Juliet, stopping to say a few quick words to her.

A few minutes later, Juliet gives Ryan a hug, and then jogs

into the shop. Ryan stands there on the sidewalk by himself, staring down.

"Sorry about that," Juliet says, as she stuffs her phone into her purse. "That was Liam having an absolute meltdown because Ashton won't go down for his nap. I swear you'd think *he* was the toddler sometimes."

I chuckle and slide her coffee across the table. She takes it gratefully and then gives me a quizzical look. "Alright, so let's get started so we can finish it."

I laugh again and reach for my bag, pulling out a notebook that has a checklist of things I need to finish before the wedding. My eyes travel back up from the table to the window, where Ryan's still standing. Juliet is talking about something, but I'm distracted by him. Now he has his head turned up to the sky, as if taking in the rays from the sun. My chest aches as I watch him, and I yearn to go grab him and bring him back inside so I can spend more time with him.

But I know how terrible an idea that would be.

When he's finally ready, Ryan's shoulders drop a little, and he walks out of my line of sight. And the minute he's gone, I feel his distance in every cell of my body. As soon as that happens, the loneliness and solitude seep back into me and my throat feels tight.

But I swallow it down and turn my attention back toward my friend, knowing that this is just the way things have to be now.

That doesn't mean I have to like it.

Chapter 27

Izabel

THE LAST FEW WEEKS OF SUMMER FLY BY, AND BEFORE I know it, it's the first day of school. I'm up before the sun to get to the high school about an hour before classes start. I head out of our guest bedroom and into our kitchen, adjusting my blouse tucked into a modest pencil skirt. Mark is seated at the breakfast bar watching me, a grin etched over his face. I stop in my tracks and look at him.

"Good morning, sexy," he says, eyeing me up and down.

I offer him a timid smile and move into the kitchen. Opening the refrigerator, I grab a bottle of water. "I wasn't expecting to see you this morning."

Usually, Mark is gone by the time I get up. I've got it timed down to the minute. He goes to the gym and then straight to his law firm to get started for the day, and he doesn't typically get home until close to six in the evening. Then we'll sit and have dinner before each heading to our respective bedrooms for the night. We barely speak to each other. I can't find it inside myself to make any additional effort. His threat lingers over my head like a storm cloud, and until I can figure out a way to get out from under his control, I toe the line, hoping that's enough.

"I decided to go in late today. I wanted to see you off on your first day of classes. Also, I got you something." He eyes a black box sitting on the counter in front of him.

My stomach tightens as I near him. It's another jewelry box. The rock around my neck already feels heavy to me. Mark has insisted that I wear it for my first day, and I'm not sure if I'm emotionally prepared for another extravagant gift. I reluctantly reach for the box and open it, my mouth going dry at its contents.

Inside is a gorgeous diamond tennis bracelet. I run my fingers over it and glance up at Mark, who looks like a child on Christmas. "Do you like it?" he asks. "I thought it would match well with your necklace."

"Mark," I say, at a loss for words. "This is too much."

"Nonsense," he responds, standing up from the breakfast bar. He walks over to me and takes the bracelet from me. Working the clasp, he reaches for my wrist so he can fasten it. "You should be dripping in diamonds, because that's how much you mean to me. There, look at that," he says, holding out my hand for me to see. "This is perfect. You're perfect." He leans down and kisses me on the tip of my nose.

I twist my wrist around, examining the new jewelry. It *is* pretty. I force a smile, hoping that it comes off as appreciative. "Thank you, Mark."

"You're welcome, baby," he says with a grin. "Okay, now you better head out. Don't want to be tardy for your first day." He gives my ass a swat, and I jump. I'm still not comfortable with this version of playful Mark. He is delusional if he thinks that things between us are fine, but that seems to be the way he's acting.

I find the rest of my things and head out the door without saying much more to him. Communication has been somewhat forced between us, mostly by my doing. Mark keeps chalking it up to stress about the wedding, but it's not. I have nothing I want to talk to him about. We make small talk over dinners. I'll ask him about his day, and then he goes off on long tangents, telling me all the gritty details. But he never asks about my day. Not that I even want him to. When he does ask, it usually ends with him admonishing me for something I said or did.

I'm playing the role of a perfect housewife. I haven't been able to figure out a way to escape him without there being severe repercussions. Until I can, this is what I have to do.

I listen to my favorite podcast on the drive to work. Our new house is relatively close to Bennett, so it's not a long drive. I park in my designated staff spot and reach for my purse and school bag. A few of my colleagues are heading into the building as I am, and we chat on our way. I've seen them all a few times over the summer, but today is fresh and exciting. It's the first day of school!

The hallways are empty; we likely won't see any of the boys until closer to eight. Bennett is a boarding school with dorms. The majority of our students stay on campus in the dormitories, but a few commute. Once they show up, though, these halls will be echoing with laughter.

I settle in my room and boot up my computer. While waiting, I pull out my lesson plan book and go over my first few plans again. Today we'll just be talking about the syllabus and course expectations. Still, I want to be prepared just in case my students have questions about what is to come this semester.

The room has that first-day-of-school scent—like waxed floors, Clorox wipes, and freshly sharpened pencils. My stomach is still somewhat unsettled from my encounter with my fiancé earlier this morning, so much so that it's making it hard to focus. The words of my lesson plans keep running together, making me feel kind of queasy. I should have grabbed breakfast on the way, but I was more than ready to get out of that house this morning. I rest my forehead in the palm of my hand and close my eyes for a second.

A knock on my door has me startling as I push back my chair and stand up. The door cracks open, and a head of messy blonde-brown hair peeks through. Familiar green eyes gaze at me. The corners of my lips instinctually twitch up into a hesitant smile. I'm reminded of how awkward it was to see Ryan at the coffee shop a few weeks ago, but the way he's looking at me now is as if that never happened.

"Knock, knock," he says, opening the door wider until I can see all of him. Ryan is dressed in his work clothes, navy-blue slacks and a white button-down shirt. He has a brown paper bag in his hand and a to-go cup of coffee. He holds it up like a peace offering. "Are you busy, Miss Sanders?"

"I'm never too busy for my new favorite soccer coach," I say, putting my hands on my hips, playing along. "What are you doing here?"

"I brought you a special first-day breakfast. And coffee. I hope you haven't eaten yet," he replies, holding up the bag to show me.

"Actually, no. I haven't," I say, surprised. "Thank you." I reach for the bag and sit down at my desk, setting it in my lap. Ryan comes closer and places the coffee gingerly on my desk in front of me. I unfold the paper bag and pull out a blueberry scone wrapped in a smaller bag. "Oh, these are my favorite! You remembered!"

Ryan sticks his hands in his pockets and gives me a soft smile. "I remember everything about you, Bells. You're hard to forget."

"And is this..." I trail off, reaching for my coffee, and taking a sip. Warm silky caramel heaven hits my tongue, and I give Ryan an appreciative grin. "A caramel macchiato. You are amazing."

He shrugs, "I try. I don't understand the hype, though. That's more sugar and milk than coffee."

"Mmm, but it's so good," I say, taking another sip and closing my eyes with a soft moan. When I open them, I see Ryan staring at me. His eyes are heated, a small smirk playing on his lips.

"Did the boys have practice this morning?" I ask, changing the subject before breaking off a piece of my scone.

"Ah, no. I knew you'd be here today, so I just wanted to drop by on my way to work to bring you a treat. We have practice this afternoon, though."

My heart flutters in my chest. Ryan's office isn't close to Bennett. He drove all the way across town just to bring me breakfast on my first day of school. How sweet of him.

"Does it feel weird being back here?"

Ryan looks around my room with a half-smile. "Yeah, kind of. I spent a lot of time in these classrooms. It feels different, but still familiar."

I nod, knowing exactly what he's talking about. I have only been back to my alma mater—Bennett's sister school—Hawthorne Academy, a few times since graduating. But it felt exactly like that.

I reach up and tuck a strand of hair behind my ear with my right hand. Ryan's eyes immediately go to my wrist, and he whistles lowly, "That's a statement piece if I've ever seen one."

Rolling my eyes, I give a huff and don't bother responding. Instead, I pop a crumbly piece of scone in my mouth and chew it, giving Ryan a pointed stare. Ryan sees my non-existent enthusiasm for my gift from Mark and gives me a tight smile, like he's not sure what to do with this information.

"Okay, well, I better get going. I probably have a million emails to sort through," he says. Then he nods toward my breakfast. "Enjoy. Maybe I'll catch you at the end of the day."

"Thank you again, Ryan. This made my whole day."

Ryan shoots me a wink before stepping out of my room and closing the door. I settle back into my chair and scarf down the rest of my scone and coffee. This was exactly what I needed.

I lean back with a sigh. My fingers absentmindedly fiddle with the tennis bracelet on my wrist, and I glance down at it. It is definitely beautiful, but it feels like a shackle. My necklace feels like a constricting collar, as if Mark is staking his claim by throwing expensive jewelry at me and holding me hostage.

I have no interest in expensive jewelry. I don't need to be adorned or worshipped with diamonds and jewels. My thoughts dart to the simple scone and coffee Ryan brought me this morning. That all probably cost him under $10. That's the kind of gift I want. Simplistic, meaningful. I've never had to pretend to like any of Ryan's gifts. He always knew exactly what I would like. He just *knows* me.

Though my morning was greatly improved by Ryan stopping by, the last thought quickly brings down my mood.

I keep catching myself comparing Ryan to Mark, which I know is unfair because the two of them are so different.

The familiar feeling of regret settles in my chest and squeezes around my heart. Before I can talk myself out of it, I undo the clasp of the bracelet and then my necklace. Opening the top drawer of my desk, I lay the pieces inside with care and then close it. I'll just have to remember to grab them before I leave work today. The minute the jewelry is off, my chest feels lighter, as if I can breathe again.

Now feeling free, I reach for my coffee again and take a sip, letting myself pretend just for the morning that I'm a girl who was brought a special first day of school treat by a man who cares about her deeply.

I ignore the pain in my chest telling me that's exactly what happened, but I'm just too stupid to do anything to make it last.

Chapter 28

Ryan

"What! How did you do that?" my little sister asks me over our lunch of grilled cheese and tomato soup. It's early September now, so the weather is starting to cool off. My mom always celebrates fall by introducing soups and stews to the menu. I've been showing Thalia a few basic magic tricks, and they are blowing her mind. Her green eyes are wide, with a mixture of confusion and awe.

"*Magic*," I say, wiggling my fingers in front of her.

Thalia pouts, looking at the deck of cards in front of us. It was a simple trick, one I just learned off of a video last night. But I don't tell her that. Let her be a kid and believe in the magic for a little while longer.

My mom watches us fondly before turning around and working on the dishes. Thalia picks up the deck of cards and attempts to shuffle them. She hasn't perfected this skill yet, and one card falls into her tomato soup. She quickly picks it up, glancing at me from the corner of her eye to see if I noticed.

I chuckle under my breath, but pretend I didn't see, taking a big bite of my grilled cheese instead. Can never go wrong with grilled cheese. I don't care that I'm almost thirty years old. I'll admit it.

"Can you teach me, Ryno? Please!" she begs me, grabbing a hold of my arm. "I want to be able to show all my friends that I can do magic. Tyler will love it!"

I rub the side of my jaw. "Hm, I don't know Thalia. Are you sure you can even *do* magic?"

She nods fervently. "I can do it! You just have to show me. If you can do it, I can do it!"

I open my mouth to agree, when I hear a crash. My attention is immediately drawn to my mom, standing at the sink. Her hands are braced on the counter, head bowed. I narrow my eyes at her, seeing her sway where she stands.

"Thalia, go to your room for a few minutes," I instruct. I expect a certain level of refusal from my eight-year-old sister, but she listens to me, to my surprise. Maybe she can hear the desperation in my voice or see that something is definitely not right with our mom.

Her feet patter out of the kitchen, and I stand up, walking over to my mom, right as her knees buckle under her weight. I take a few hurried steps to her, catching her so that she doesn't crack her head against the floor or a sharp edge.

"Mom!" I exclaim as she collapses into my arms. I carefully lower her to the ground. Her face is pale, eyes closed. I gently pat her cheeks, trying to rouse her. She hasn't had chemo since Wednesday, so I have no idea if it's a direct side effect or not. "Mom, wake up!"

I hold her for a few minutes, but she doesn't rouse. Bending over her, I put my ear next to her nose to ensure she's still breathing. My fingers find her pulse point on her wrist, then on her neck to double-check. There, but weak. I shift to reach my phone out of my back pocket.

I dial 911 and wait for the operator to pick up. "911, what's your location?" I give her my mom's address and explain the situation. The operator tells me she's dispatching an ambulance to my mom's house, and it should just be a few minutes.

Once the call ends, I look down at my mom and stroke her cheek, using the back of my fingers. "Please, be okay."

The paramedics arrive within a few minutes and shuffle me out of the way to do their exams. They ask me questions about her condition, how long she's been sick or if she's ever lost consciousness before. I do my best to answer, but it's hard since I don't live with her full time anymore. My hands are shaking, and I'm trying not to pass out myself.

The crew decides they need to take her to the hospital, so they load her up on a stretcher and give me the details for which hospital they're taking her to. I nod and walk with them as they wheel my mom out to the ambulance. A few minutes later, the rig pulls away, and I bolt back inside.

Thalia has come back downstairs. She's standing in the kitchen, looking at the place where our mom was just standing. Her little hands are wrung together in front of her, and when she turns her green eyes to me, I can see her fear.

"What happened to Mommy?" she asks me in her little girl voice.

I crouch down, so I'm not talking down to her, placing a hand on her shoulder. "Mommy wasn't feeling well. Probably from the disease she has. They're taking her to go see her doctor."

"Can we go too?" she asks.

I stare at my sister, contemplating, and then nod, knowing that I don't want to stay here either. "Yeah, go get your shoes. We'll meet her there."

Thalia hurries off to find some shoes, and I pull my phone out again to call Derek. He picks up quickly. "Ryan, what's going on?"

In normal circumstances, I would've chuckled—not the warmest greeting from my stepfather. But I never call him. He must know it's something serious.

"Mom collapsed while doing the dishes," I tell him. "I caught her before she fell, so she didn't hit her head, but she wouldn't wake up. I called an ambulance, and they're taking her to St. John's."

Derek asks a few more questions, and then mumbles a thank you and informs me he will be there shortly. He's out golfing with his buddies at the club on the other side of town. Even with Thalia and me just leaving now, we'll probably still beat him there.

Thalia rounds the corner, her pink tennis shoes on, gripping onto a stuffed animal. I don't say anything as I grab my wallet and keys and load her into my car. She clutches to her animal as we drive. I don't turn any music on or say much. I know I should try to put on a brave face for my sister, but I can't. I'm scared too.

I park the car in the visitor's lot and help Thalia out. Grabbing her hand, we walk into the emergency department. I'm greeted by the desk, and they direct me to the bed that my mother is in. She still hasn't woken up yet, but she's hooked up to a bunch of medical machines, measuring her oxygen levels, heart rate, and blood pressure.

Thalia grips my hand tightly, and I curse myself. *Jesus*, this is no place for a little girl. She doesn't need to see her mom like this.

For the third time, I pull my phone out and call the only person I can trust in this kind of situation. I've only spoken to Izabel a few times since I ran into her at the coffee shop. Occasionally, I'll wake up at night in a cold sweat thinking about her, wondering if I'm making the right decision with my actions. I've been trying to keep a healthy distance but still be open to any communication she initiates. Just like Josie told me, at the very least, I can be here for her if she needs me. Her wedding is coming up quick, and every time I think about it, I feel sick to my stomach.

"Hello?"

"Bells?" I ask, and damn me to hell, my voice cracks.

"Ryan? What's wrong?" Her voice is sweet like honey. I close my eyes tightly.

"Could you come to St. John's? My mom collapsed, and I'm here with Thalia, but I don't think she—"

"Oh, God. Yes, I'll be right there. Are you in the ER?" Izabel asks. I can hear her shuffling around on her end of the line, grabbing her purse. A door slams and she starts breathing harder.

"Yeah," I mutter. "Thank you."

"I'll see you soon, Ry."

Once she hangs up, I look down at Thalia, who can't tear her eyes off our mom. I tug on her hand, and she looks up at me. "Hey, my friend Izabel is going to come and sit with you. You guys can go get some snacks or something if you want. Then your dad and I can make sure Mom is okay."

Thalia nods silently and then looks around the emergency department. Nurses are hustling around. There are a few doctors talking to a nurse or checking chart notes before going in with a patient. This place is scary, even for me. Especially when someone you love is here.

Izabel is quick on her arrival. She flies through the doors of the ER only fifteen minutes later. Her eyes land on me, and she rushes over to us. I let go of Thalia's hand so I can catch Izabel as she throws herself at me in a hug.

My arms wrap around her waist as I hold her, burying my face in her neck and breathing her in. She's still the woman I love, and I'm still...whatever I am to her.

Izabel pulls away first, her hands coming up to my cheeks so she can look me dead in the eye. "Are you okay?"

I nod sullenly. "I'm fine. We're still waiting on some doctors to check her out. She hasn't woken up yet."

"Okay, well, hopefully, we'll know more soon. They don't look too busy here today, so that's a good sign," she says. Then, Izabel looks down at Thalia, who is peering around my legs at her. "Hey, lady, want to come with me? We can head to the cafeteria and see if they have anything good there. This place is boring."

Izabel offers my sister her hand, and Thalia takes it, her other hand still gripping her animal tightly. Then changing her mind, she runs back and hugs me, her short arms wrapping around my waist. I pat my sister's back and run my hand over her hair.

"It will be okay, Thal. Just go with Bells, and I'll come find you when I know something," I tell her. I look up at Izabel. She's watching the two of us with a weird expression on her face. "I'll text you when I know something."

Bells takes a step toward me, putting her hand on my cheek again. Then she gently pulls me down to press her lips to mine, like she's letting me know that she's here for me. I kiss her back, hard, pouring everything I can into that kiss and letting her take it. She pulls away, her clear blue eyes shining.

"We'll see you soon," Bells says, offering Thalia her hand again. The two of them walk off toward the central part of the hospital.

I release a deep breath of relief, knowing that Thalia is with someone safe. I'm a terrible brother for even bringing her here. But I didn't know what else to do. I walk into the bay where my mom is and sit in the plastic armchair next to her bed. It's not comfortable, but I don't care.

My mom's face is peaceful, like she's asleep, and I can see

her chest rising and falling with her breathing. The tube across her nose *whirrs* as it delivers more oxygen to her body. I reach out and grab her hand, holding on to it. I know she'll be fine. This whole thing is probably just a side effect from her chemo-therapy, but it's still nerve-wracking. She's my mom. She's the only parent I have left.

I hear a deep voice rumbling near the front desk. Glancing over, I see Derek storming past the nurses to get to his wife. A hilarious scene with him in a baby blue golf t-shirt and white shorts. But I have to admire him for his persistence. If Bells were laid up in a hospital, nothing could keep me away from her.

Derek steps into the bay, his eyes first going to my mom and then to me. I stand up and accept the hug he offers. The older man wraps his arms around me, clapping my back.

"Everything's going to be okay, Ryan," he says lowly. I nod and pull away from him. It's comforting to have him here. Derek isn't my dad, but he's the closest thing I have. "Has the doctor come by yet?"

I shake my head. "No, I haven't seen a white coat in a while. I think they're running a few tests, or waiting for a phone call from her oncologist or something."

"Where's Thalia?"

I motion my head to the main hospital building. "Bells came and got her. I think they're in the cafeteria having a snack."

"Good, that's good," Derek says, rubbing his jaw. He takes a few steps toward my mom and brushes his hand across her head, leaning down and pressing a kiss to her forehead. He whispers something to her that I can't hear, but then he comes back to stand next to me. He's quiet for a moment, then he looks pointedly at me. "So Izabel's been around a lot more recently."

"I guess," I say with a shrug. "She's a good friend."

"Right, a friend. Your mom was my *friend* for a long time," Derek says, smirking at me.

"I really don't want to hear this right now," I reply, a hint of disgust lacing my tone.

Derek laughs. "All I'm saying, Son, is don't get ahead of yourself. You never know what might come out of a friendship. Especially given your history."

I choose not to continue this conversation and go back over to sit next to my mom. A doctor strolls by a few minutes later, tablet in hand, with my mom's chart notes pulled up. He goes over the preliminary test results.

"We spoke with her oncologist, and he believes that it's an adverse side effect to the chemo treatment. He said they switched her regimen this week?" Derek confirms, and the doctor continues. "We're expecting that she will be just fine, but we're going to keep her overnight for observation to monitor her blood pressure levels. We'll have a nurse come by soon to get her situated once we can transfer her."

The doctor heads off, leaving Derek and me alone with Mom once again. We sit for a while before, finally, she starts to stir. First, it's her fingers twitching, then her eyelids flutter before she takes a deep breath and comes to.

She sees me first. Her eyebrows pull together, and she tries to shift on the bed. "Ryno? What's going on?"

Derek is on the other side of her bed. He runs his hand across her head like he did earlier. "You collapsed this afternoon. Ryan called the ambulance, and now you're in the emergency room. Everything's fine," he adds quickly when he sees my mom start to panic. "But they're going to keep you overnight just to make sure."

"I can stay with Thalia tonight so you can stay with Mom,"

I offer to both Derek and my mom. Mom grabs my hand, giving me a slight, appreciative squeeze.

"That would be great, thank you, Ryan," Derek replies. Then he looks behind him. "Do you want to call Izabel and have her bring Thalia back?"

I agree, pulling out my phone and typing a quick text to Izabel. She responds right away, letting me know they're heading back. I tuck the phone back into my pocket and turn around to my mom.

"How are you feeling?"

Mom shrugs. "Kinda tired, but I'm okay. I'm sorry you had to deal with that, Ry."

I shake my head with a chuckle. "Don't be. I'm just glad you're okay."

She smiles at me. Her face is thin, so much more delicate than it used to be. Her hair is completely gone, but her eyes still hold fire behind them that I love about her. She's a fighter, and I have no doubt she'll beat this. It's just a little bump in the road.

That's what families are for, though—the bumps in the road, both big and small. We stand by each other through thick and thin. My mom is one of the most influential people in my life.

Thalia comes back with Izabel, and she talks to Mom for a few minutes before we head out. Izabel follows us, waiting until I've got Thalia all buckled in the backseat before grabbing my hand.

We stare at each other for a few minutes before she says simply, "Let me know if you need anything, Ryan. I'll be happy to help in any way I can."

I acknowledge her, and she starts to walk away. I grip her hand once more, pulling her back. She spins toward me until she's pressed against my chest. I wrap my arms around her slim body, holding her tightly to me. She sighs and leans into me, pressing her chest against mine. I think I could hold this woman for an eternity if she would let me.

I release her a moment later, but we don't entirely part. Her eyes are dancing as I gaze into them. "Thank you," I whisper. I raise my hand to brush my thumb tenderly across her cheek. Something I can't decipher flashes in her eyes but disappears just as quickly as it came. "Hey," I whisper, bringing her back to me. Her eyebrow hitches up. "I love you, Bells."

Izabel stares at me with a smile, her cheeks turning a bright red and her eyes softening. Then her expression hardens, and a flash of sadness overtakes whatever feeling she was experiencing before. She gives me one last wary glance before lifting her hand in a wave and leaving. After watching her walk away, I finally get into the car, glancing at Thalia in the back seat. She's staring at me with a smirk on her face. The same smirk that I so often display.

"What?" I ask her.

She shrugs and looks out the window. "Nothing. I just think that Bells would make a really good big sister."

Chapter 29

Izabel

"Do you think they have Doritos?" The little girl holding my hand asks me as we walk into the cafeteria.

I glance around at the sterile environment smothered in blues and beiges and grays. You would think they would make hospitals more inviting and friendly, considering the hours that many families have to spend here waiting for their loved ones. My job today is to occupy Thalia so the reality of her mom being so sick doesn't hit too hard.

"I don't know, Thalia," I tell her. "Maybe we can find a vending machine that has some Doritos. Which kind do you like?"

"I like the blue ones," she tells me with confidence. I smile. The blue ones are my favorite, too.

We wander around until I find a vending machine with Cool Ranch Doritos. I pull out my wallet, handing Thalia a few dollars to put it in the machine and type in the letters. I help her, and soon enough, we're sitting at a table, munching on Doritos and drinking Sprite.

"Do you think my mommy's going to be okay?" Thalia asks me after a moment of silence.

I watch her closely. Her green eyes hold a sadness that I hate to see in a girl so young. I nod my head fervently. "I think she's going to be just fine." I hope that I'm not made out to be a liar. "The doctors here are very smart. They're going to take good care of her."

"I'm scared," Thalia whispers, almost as if she's afraid to say it aloud.

My heart shatters as I observe her. Of course, she's frightened. I reach across the table and hold her hand. "I know. It's okay to be scared. But it's important that you don't let that fear consume you. You have to be strong."

I'm not sure if my words are more for her or for me, but they do the trick. Thalia nods and offers me a smile before going back to her chips, taking tiny bites out of one like a chipmunk. "I saw you kiss Ryan. Did you break up with your other boyfriend?"

I nearly choke. Talk about a topic change. Thalia is always good at leaving me speechless. She asks so many direct questions. "Um, no, Thalia. We haven't broken up."

"Oh. Then why did you kiss Ryan? Do you love him?"

I bite my lip as I contemplate how to answer her. I want to shout *Yes*, and explain that I'm trapped in a life I don't want anymore, but I don't. I can't. "Your brother means a lot to me. We were in love for a long time. But sometimes things happen, and people go their separate ways. Just because we're not together like that anymore doesn't mean I don't care about him."

"What's it like to be in love?"

"Well," I say, setting down my bag of chips. How do I explain this to an eight-year-old? "It's like finding the missing piece to your puzzle or coloring a picture in the brightest colors possible. Loving someone is the brightest star in the sky or seeing a rainbow after a storm." Thalia's eyes are glued to me as I keep going. I hope I'm making sense to her.

"The person you love becomes one of the most important things in your life. You feel incomplete without the other person, but when they're around, everything is better again. You want to be with them, live a happy life with them, and grow old together."

My voice cuts out as my throat dries with the realization that I'm describing my feelings toward her brother to a T.

"I think I might love Tyler," the little girl announces to me, brushing a few chip crumbs around the table. "But don't tell Ryan, 'cause he said he'll bash his face in."

"Who's Tyler?" I ask her, curious.

"He's this boy at my school. I don't know if he's going to be in the same 4th-grade class with me this year or not, 'cause we haven't gotten our teachers yet. He used to be really mean to me last year, and I hated him. But then he got nicer, and I started to like him more."

"Have you told him you like him?"

Thalia looks at me with wide green eyes and shakes her head vehemently. "No! That would be super embarrassing. And besides," she says, going back to her crumbs, "he likes the other girls more." I look at Ryan's little sister and think about how unlikely that is. Even at eight years old, Thalia is beautiful. She's going to break some hearts someday.

"Well, how will he know if you don't tell him? Sometimes with love, you have to take a risk," I explain to her. My phone buzzes on the table, and I see a text from Ryan come through. "Ryan says we can head back." I type out a quick response and hit send.

Thalia cleans up her mess, and then we walk hand-in-hand

back to the emergency department. She runs over when she sees her mom is awake. I lock eyes with Ryan for a second, but I look away quickly, feeling a blush form on my cheeks.

My heart aches. All I want is to be with him, feel his strong arms wrap around me, and let him keep me safe. Every time I let myself fall into these fantasies, Mark's threat rings loud in my mind. *"If I find out you're even thinking about calling off this wedding and running back to him, I will go after your little boyfriend and kill him. And then no one will be able to save you. Do you understand?"*

A cold shiver travels down my spine and goosebumps erupt on my arms at the mere thought of Mark following through on his threat. I shake my head, trying to clear it.

Thalia and Ryan both say goodbye to their mom and then head out to the car. I follow close behind them. I watch as Ryan gets Thalia all situated, then turns to me. We stare at each other awkwardly for a few minutes before I get myself to say something.

"Let me know if you need anything, Ryan. I'll be happy to help in any way I can."

He nods at me, and I head to my car, assuming that's that. I'm surprised when he grabs my hand. His fingers are warm on my palm as he pulls me back to him. I bump into his chest and his arms wrap tightly around me. Pressing my cheek against his pectoral muscle, I listen to his heartbeat thumping in my ear.

Ryan pulls away slightly, fitting his hand along the curve of my jaw. His thumb gently traces over the cheek Mark struck when we returned from Nashville. The difference between Mark's heavy hand and Ryan's gentle touch is a stark reminder that I am not living the life I should be.

Everything in my brain tells me that this is wrong, that I shouldn't be risking Ryan's life like this. But my heart screams that this is right. So right.

A few seconds later, Ryan steps away and offers me a small smile. He thanks me, then pulls me back into him. "Hey," he says. I look at him with an eyebrow raised, unsure of where he's going with this. "I love you, Bells."

I smile at him, my face now burning with a mixture of embarrassment and desire. Then I turn and head to my car. I rub my fist over my chest, trying to relieve the ache in my heart. In one week, I'm supposed to be walking down the aisle toward Mark, and then I'll be stuck with him forever. If this were any other man, I would simply leave, but the fear is still seated deeply within me.

When Monday rolls around, I head into the community college gym for my self-defense class. I'm still a little shaken from the events of the weekend with Ryan's mom.

I've texted Ryan a few times, and he informed me that his mom is fine and that she was able to come home. But I still can't get Thalia's and my conversation out of my head. "I'm scared," is what she said. Those words stay with me as I set down my bag and get ready for the class. Fear is what drove me to look into self-defense in the first place. I am no stranger to being scared.

Tonight is our sixth session of the self-defense course. This evening is a checkpoint, and we are being evaluated on our skills that we've acquired thus far. We started off the whole thing sitting down and talking with our classmates and instructors about what to expect and any past experiences that might have influenced us to achieve this self-defense certification. I stayed quiet, but I was amazed to hear the women in my class share their stories. A few of them explained situations that sounded similar to mine.

Tonight, we are going to be working with the instructors hands-on. Both the women and the instructors will have an assortment of protective padding to wear. This helps safeguard our heads, fists, elbows, and knees. Then we will work with the instructors one on one. They will try to take us off guard by grabbing or attacking us, and we need to use our skills to fight them off or maneuver out of their grip to run away.

I am nervous about this evaluation. I know the "attackers" won't actually hurt me, but still. The thought of someone grabbing at me has me on edge. So much so that my stomach feels tight and is teetering on the edge of making me feel nauseous.

After I get my personal items situated, I find a chair on the edge of the room and wait for the class to get started. The officers go over a few things before we begin and then ask for volunteers to go first. I keep my hands firmly planted in my lap. No way am I going first.

Someone does volunteer, and I watch with interest as she dons the gear and then starts her test. The two instructors walking close to her are also clad in gear. They walk back and forth beside her. The idea is that she won't know which one will make an attempt to grab her, so she has to be alert at all times.

Finally, it happens. The instructor on her left makes the reach for her, and she springs into action. "NO!" she shouts as she hits his hand away. He tries again, making a move to grab for her waist. "NO!" she yells again. She throws kicks and punches at him and then knocks the guy flat on his back.

The women in the room all stand up and cheer. I even find myself on my feet, clapping. She did really well. That didn't look so bad.

They go through a few more demonstrations until, finally, it's my turn. I stand up, my hands shaking, and walk toward the instructors to get my gear. They help me put on the helmet and the pads that will cover my elbows and knees. The female officer catches my eye and gives me a quick pep talk.

"You can do this, Izabel. Just think back to everything

you've learned so far. You've practiced the moves enough that you know how to perform them. You can get out of his grip. Fight like your life depends on it, and don't forget to yell 'No!' Use your voice. Sometimes that's your most powerful weapon." I nod, glancing at her through the prongs in the helmet. "Okay, do you have any health conditions that we should know about before we get started?"

I shake my head, but then pause. "I haven't really been feeling good the last few days. I think I've been anxious about this test."

The woman gives me a kind smile and places her hand on my shoulder. "It's normal to be nervous about this. That's okay. Our goal is to prepare you to identify situations and then know how to react without hesitation. But fear is always okay."

She says a few more words to me before sending me out into the middle of the room. My classmates cheer me on, hollering my name and clapping. The instructors in their body-suits come up right next to me. The scenario I'm running is that I'm standing at an ATM, and these guys want my money, so they attack me. I turn and face the wall, aware of the two instructors who come up right behind me, their shoulders uncomfortably close to mine.

They're throwing taunts at me left and right, but I force myself to not listen. My stomach is still feeling like it wants to come up through my throat, but I hold it in. I turn my head, making eye contact with the guy on my left. "Leave me alone," I say firmly. I don't let my stare waver. Finally, the guy on my left makes a move, reaching for my wrist to grab me.

"No!" I yell and come down on his hand with a forceful blow. He lets go, but then quickly comes back at me, reaching around my shoulders to hold me. "No!" I shout again as I struggle against him.

It's not working. He's holding on too tight. His forearm is

placed against my sternum in an unrelenting hold. I kick back with my feet, trying to strike a blow on his shins. Then I throw my elbow around, trying to land him in the gut. Nothing. I wrestle and struggle.

"Use what you have," the female instructor yells from across the room.

My classmates are all still cheering me on. It's loud. There's too much going on. I'm stuck. I'm trapped. My breathing is labored, my breasts rising and falling with the exertion, heart threatening to beat out of my chest. I hear everyone shouting support from the sidelines, but I can't do it. I'm not strong enough.

His arms are still wrapped around my chest as I struggle, and I finally realize what I can do.

"No!" I yell one more time as I drop my weight, letting my body go limp and falling to the ground. I slip right out of his grip and scramble away from him. I try to run over to the other end of the room, but the second instructor gets in my way. After being able to escape the first instructor, I feel a little more confident, and I throw kicks and punches in an attempt to thwart the second attacker. I'm able to get away, and I now stand across from them, panting.

The instructors stand up and nod with satisfaction, my classmates cheering. I'm done.

My hands are still shaking, and my skin is breaking out in a clammy cold sweat. I need to get this gear off of me right now. I hurry in, taking the pads and the helmet off, tossing them on the ground before running out of the gym toward the women's bathroom. I enter the first open stall and fall to my knees right before I heave into the toilet.

I throw up twice before I'm steady enough to stand. Flushing the toilet, I then step out of the stall, dragging myself to the sink to clean up. I first wash my hands and then scoop water in my palms, bringing it up to my mouth to swish and spit out the bile taste. My throat is burning, and my eyes are watery. I risk a glance in the mirror and want to be sick again. I look like a mess.

I knew I could get away from the instructor in there, but I still froze up. How am I going to do this if it happens in real life? Mark is a lot bigger than I am and—

I catch the thought before it can fully form, squashing the fear and anxiety in my gut before it amplifies. It's too depressing a thought, regardless of how necessary it might be.

After collecting myself for another minute, I head back into the gym to grab my things. I meet the female instructor's eyes, and she gives me a nod. Once I find my bag, I head out. I don't have the energy to stay and watch my classmates struggle or succeed faster than I could. I want to go home and crawl under the covers of my bed.

When I get to my car, I lean forward and press my forehead to the steering wheel. I focus on my breathing, trying to steady my heart rate. In, two-three-four, out, two-three-four.

I jolt when the ring of my phone sounds off in my purse. I rummage through my bag, trying to find it. When my fingers grasp onto the phone, I see it's my mother who's calling. I steel myself and swipe the green button to answer. I've managed to keep them at an arm's distance, but I know I can't do that forever.

"Hi, Mom."

"Izzie? We haven't talked in ages. How are you? How did your test go? I wasn't sure if you'd be done yet, but I thought I'd call and ask," she says. I told my mom about the self-defense classes only because she was pestering me about getting dinner together a few weeks ago. She's under the impression that Bennett requires all its staff to take continuing education—not wholly false—and I chose self-defense this year. It was the quickest excuse I could come up with on the fly.

"I'm fine, Mom. I just finished. I did okay, but it was a lot harder than I thought."

"I'm sure you did great, honey!" Mom praises me. I stare outside my windshield, seeing a few drops of rain hitting the window. "I also wanted to check in and make sure you're all ready for this week. It's hard to believe in just a few days you'll be a married woman!"

I clench my jaw, not loving the way that sounds. "I know it's crazy. But yeah, pretty much everything is good to go. Mark's mom has been planning like crazy. Now it's just a waiting game."

"Your father and I are so proud of you, Izabel. I hope you know that. We couldn't have wished anything better for you," my mom says. I can hear the pride laced in her voice.

If only she knew...but that was Mark's whole game. Mark's a professional at appearing like the perfect fiancé. The only exceptions are Juliet, who never liked him to begin with, and Ryan, who has seen the bruises Mark has left on me. He won over my parents right away, and they haven't doubted him since. I know they would come to my defense the minute I said otherwise, but they had no reason to question Mark. I haven't ever given them a reason. And Mark would quickly throw me up against a wall if I even thought about ruining that perfect image of his.

My stomach churns as I finish our conversation and then hang up the call. I close my eyes and lean my head back one more time, letting the sound of the raindrops on the windshield soothe me. I'm still concerned that I could throw up again.

Your father and I are proud of you. Will they still be proud of the woman I'm slowly becoming? The woman who feels like a prisoner in her own life? Who's about to marry a man who is holding her in shackles? No, I don't think they would be proud of me if they knew everything that was going on behind the scenes. But I've always been good at putting up a front—just like Mark. You could say I learned from the best.

It's exhausting, though. Pretending that everything is perfect when it's not.

I finally put the car into drive with a sigh and stop at a gas station to get a Sprite before going home. I take baby sips and let it settle my stomach.

Dropping my bag by the garage door, I walk into the house. Mark is waiting for me in the kitchen with his arms crossed. His eyes are hard as he takes in my rumpled appearance.

"Where the hell were you?" he grits out.

I look at him with a weak expression. God, please, not tonight. "I was at the gym."

He scoffs. "Right. The gym. Is that codeword for Ryan's bed?"

I close my eyes and shake my head, uncertain if I heard him correctly. "What?"

"I know you've been hooking up with him."

My eyes are wide as I stare at him, at a loss for words. "H-how?"

My words fall flat, and I can see the consequence before it even happens.

That was indubitably the wrong response.

Mark pushes off the counter with his hips and takes a few steps toward me. His hand grips my jaw too tight, his fingers digging into the soft skin as he forces my eyes to his. "If you're going to lie, you might want to make sure your accomplice is on the same page. Nashville? His secretary told me he had a meeting in Nashville over the Fourth of July. Convenient, seeing as you happened to be there too. Do you think I'm an idiot, Izabel?"

"N-no," I fumble. My brain feels fuzzy, and my ears begin to ring with the implications of Mark knowing I was with Ryan in Nashville. I don't have the energy for this.

"And how about this weekend at the hospital, hmm?" he growls, turning and walking a few steps away. "You know one of my clients is an ER nurse there? She stopped by today for a meeting and saw your picture sitting on my desk. Imagine her confusion since she saw you lovey-dovey with Ryan and his family there this weekend. I had to practically pry it out of her, but she said you were making out as if you were horny teenagers."

"I-I'm sorry," I squeak. "P-please, don't hurt him."

In a swift motion, Mark picks up a glass flower vase and throws it at me. His arm strains as he puts all his strength into hurling the glass piece. I skirt to my left, and the vase hits the wall, shattering into a million pieces. "You're sorry?" He laughs darkly and goosebumps erupt over my skin, my palms growing clammy. "This kind of behavior is unacceptable. I've never been more disgusted with you. I can barely even look at you right now. You're so fucking lucky I'm the one marrying you, 'cause any other guy wouldn't put up with this kind of behavior. I should go over to Ryan's house and put a bullet through his head right now. At least *then* you might actually show up for our wedding on Saturday. I've never met such a sad excuse for a woman as you."

My hands are shaking again, my stomach roiling. Mark already made this threat, and now he's reinforcing it. I have no doubt he means business, and that thought is frightening. I don't think I could live with myself if something happened to him because of me.

"You've had your fun with him, but this shit's gotta stop. Do you understand me? I'm not going to have my wife make a fool of me," he snarls. "If you don't get your shit together, I'm going to do it for you, starting with that sad excuse of a boyfriend of yours. And trust me, baby, I'm not bluffing. I'm doing you a favor right now. Don't fucking mess it up. Got it?" I nod, keeping my eyes trained on the ground like a scolded child. The corners of my eyes sting with tears. "Good. Clean this shit up."

Then he stalks out of the living room, leaving me alone. The master bedroom door closes with a loud slam, making me jump from the loud noise. I lean against the wall and let my back slide down until I'm sitting. Pulling my knees up to my chest, I take a few steadying breaths. Then I turn to the shards of glass beside me. I pick a couple of pieces up with my fingers and set them in the palm of my hand. I need a dustpan and a broom.

Standing up, I walk over to the closet where we keep cleaning supplies, but my right foot gets tangled up with my other one and I start falling. My hands go out to brace myself, and as I fall, my palm lands directly on one of those glass shards. I feel it slice into my skin, and I cry out. I slowly turn my hand around to observe the damage. I gasp when I see the huge gash across my palm that is bleeding profusely. Blood pools in the palm of my hand and drips onto our hardwood floor beneath me.

"Shit," I whisper. It's deep. I scramble to my feet and grab a paper towel, pressing it to the wound. "Mark!" I call out. He doesn't respond. "Mark, I need you!" He still ignores me.

I swear and then pull the towel away. I get a quick glimpse of the injury before it starts bleeding again. I'm going to need stitches to close this. I make myself a temporary bandage, so I won't bleed all over my car and grab my keys. There's an Urgent Care right down the road from us I can go to.

My hands shake as I pull out of the garage and drive to Urgent Care. I keep glancing down at the paper towel covering the gash. It's slowly turning from white to red. This is now the third time Mark's hurt me. This time, it ended with me needing stitches. He didn't directly hit me, but he is responsible for this injury just as much as the others.

As I drive, I start to question myself: how much longer can I survive living this way?

Chapter 30

Izabel

Before I know it, the whole week has passed by. I've been living in some kind of time warp, barely existing and going through the motions. With each day, I've begun to hate myself more and more. It's the small sneers from Mark, or his snide comments about how I'm under his control, that keep me feeling like I'm insignificant.

When Friday evening rolls around, I'm standing in the back of the church Mark and I selected for our wedding ceremony, staring straight ahead but barely seeing anything. My dad is standing next to me, waiting for our cue. It's only the rehearsal, aimed toward working out any kinks in the program. According to Mark's mom, though, we might as well be really getting married tonight.

"It's just formalities," his mom boasts as she waves her hand this way and that, barking orders and making our wedding planner cower in her wake.

My hand is tucked in the crook of my dad's arm. I stare straight ahead of me, unfeeling, unthinking, numb. Juliet and Sage stand at the end of the aisle, each holding a paper towel roll as a stand-in bouquet. They got creative and balled up some colored tissue paper to look like flowers. Mark is across from them with his two groomsmen. Even though the wedding planner is hustling about this way and that, explaining what needs to happen, Mark's eyes are locked on me. A menacing smile paints his face, one that screams that he's winning—he's getting everything he wants. All I can muster back is a grimace, at best.

I grip my dad's arm like a lifeline, begging for him to lend me strength. The wedding planner cues me, and my song starts playing. The song that Mark's mother has picked for my procession. My dad leads me down the aisle, practicing his tempo to the beat of the song. I can hear him counting his steps under his breath. I dig my fingernails so tightly into his arm that he slightly flinches away from me.

This is my wedding weekend. I should be over the moon with happiness and whimsical anticipation for the next chapter of my life. I should be so in love with the man I want to marry that all I feel is motivation to get down that aisle to him. But all I feel is dread. Every cell in my body is begging me to turn and run away. I don't want to be here. I *can't* be here.

I get halfway down the aisle before I skirt to a stop. Everyone freezes and all eyes are on me. I gasp as if I've been underwater for years, and I'm finally resurfacing. Air fills my lungs, and I can breathe again, at last. My dad looks at me in worried surprise, but my attention is only on Mark. His cold brown eyes and his ever-increasing aggressive posture. I know he knows what I'm about to do, and he takes a step forward, his dark eyes daring me.

I've been continuously thinking about my conversation with Thalia about love. I told her the person you love is supposed to be the most important person to you, your missing piece, someone who makes you whole. I can't get over how much that *isn't* Mark. It will *never* be Mark.

When I close my eyes and imagine my future, I can see it all: the house, the babies, the dog. But I don't see it with Mark. It's Ryan. It always has been. These last few years I've been living in an alternate reality, but the truth remains: Ryan Miller is everything to me. He's the missing piece.

My chest rises and falls with labored breaths. Juliet's eyes widen, moving closer, noticing that something is very wrong.

Mark takes another aggressive step toward me and growls a warning, "Izabel."

I step back, and Mark's face erupts with anger, but for the first time in what feels like forever, I feel no fear. The shackles have fallen away—I am taking my freedom back. I tear my eyes away and look at my dad.

Dad is watching me closely, gauging my every move. I squeeze my eyes shut for a second and then look at him. "No." My dad stiffens and tilts his head. I say it louder this time, loud enough that everyone can hear it. That Mark can hear me. "No. Do whatever you need to do, Mark. But I will *not* marry you. I could never love a monster like you."

I risk one more look at Mark, recognizing the murderous expression that has taken over his face before I release my dad's arm and reach for the gaudy engagement ring on my left hand. I hold Mark's gaze as I take it off and throw it at him down the aisle. I'm not going to risk handing it to him and having him grab me. Before anyone has a chance to stop me, I turn and run back down the aisle, leaving everyone in the dust. I hear the confusion and questions, and Juliet calls my name as I run into the women's powder room and grab my purse and my overnight bag. I was supposed to spend my last night as an unmarried woman with Jules, my best friend.

I bolt out of the church before I lose my nerve, tearing out of the parking lot in my car before even putting on my seatbelt. My phone keeps lighting up with calls and messages, so I turn it off right as I pull into the driveway of our house. I run inside to the guest bedroom where I've been staying, quickly pulling a handful of clothes out of my closet and sticking them in a suitcase. My eyes keep darting over my shoulder to make sure no one has followed me.

I only stay long enough to grab some essentials before running back out to my car. Driving across town, I don't stop until I've reached the parking lot of my destination. I grab my bags and head up the stairs, taking them two at a time.

I knock on the door rapidly, still feeling numb. Scared. Excited. Nervous. Overjoyed. Liberated. My heart is thrumming and adrenaline courses through my veins.

Please, be home. Please, be home.

I hear a thump and a round of laughter before the door opens to reveal Ryan grinning wide. His face morphs into confusion as he takes in my flushed appearance and the suitcase propped up beside my legs. "Bells?"

"Can I come in?" I ask him. I'm out of breath from running up the stairs.

Ryan stares at me for a moment before sidestepping and opening the door wider, allowing me to enter. My body is vibrating from the events of the evening, and I wonder if he can see it. I glance around and see Josie sitting on the couch. She's got chopsticks full of some kind of chicken halfway up to her mouth as we lock eyes.

Ryan comes and stands behind me, sticking his hands in his jean pockets. Josie looks back and forth between Ryan and me, and then puts down her chopsticks and folds up the white takeout box. She clears her throat as she stands and brushes off her lap.

"I'm just gonna go...but I'm taking this with me," she

mutters before grabbing her takeout and heading toward the door. She pats Ryan on the shoulder as she passes him, and I hear her mutter, "Don't screw this up, Charming."

Ryan chuckles under his breath at his friend, and then she's gone. He turns to me with an eyebrow raised. "What's going on, Bells?"

I hesitate for only a second as my eyes roam over him. He's looking at me expectantly, his hands still in his pockets. A defensive stance. His shoulders are tight, broad.

"I did it," I breathe out.

"You did what?"

"I escaped. I called it off." I say, nervously. Ryan's eyes go wide, but then they narrow in confusion. He knows the wedding was supposed to be tomorrow. Talk about last-minute adjustments.

"You called it off?"

I sink my teeth into my lower lip and nod, observing Ryan. He doesn't seem to know what to do with this information. I can't hold his wariness against him, as I've completely caught him off guard. It's an unusual occurrence, but Ryan looks...nervous.

"Ever since our trip, I've known the truth of what needed to happen, but I was too scared to follow through on that. And I'm sorry." I shake my head, feeling my eyes prick with tears at the admission. I look at him sincerely, taking in those green eyes that sparkle when he's happy, and the strong jaw that makes my knees go weak. Ryan is everything to me, and I can't believe I've been so blind. "I'm so sorry. Mark was threatening me, trying to control me. I know that what I want is you. It's been you this whole time and I—"

Ryan cuts me off with a strangled noise as he lurches forward and claims my lips with his. His hands come up to cup my face tenderly as he kisses me senseless. When we're both breathing hard, he breaks our kiss and leans his forehead against mine. His eyes are closed, and he takes a few deep breaths in and out.

"Tell me this is real. I don't want to wake up from this dream." Ryan's words are broken. Every ounce of hurt and pain over the last eight years is now evident in his tone. He isn't hiding, and neither am I. Tears leak from the corners of my eyes as I pull away slightly.

"It's real. It's all real," I whisper. I offer Ryan a smile, and for the first time in a long, long time, I feel like I can finally relax. I stand up on my tiptoes, wrapping my arms around his neck. I kiss his cheek, feeling the scratchy stubble of his five o'clock shadow.

Ryan's eyes open, meeting mine with vivid green. "So you've left him," he says out loud, not really to me. "What do we do now?"

I bite the inside of my cheek for a moment. "I don't know. My head is spinning. I don't know how Mark is going to react. I'm scared he might actually follow through on his threat. I don't know him anymore... I don't know what he's capable of."

I thought I did. I thought I knew that man so well that nothing could surprise me. I was going to spend the rest of my life with him. But then the bruises started happening. And I felt like I was holding my breath around him every second, afraid to piss him off.

Ryan tucks some hair behind my ear and frowns. "Are you planning on staying here?"

"If that's okay," I say hesitantly. "I don't know where else to go?"

"Of course, it's okay. I would have insisted otherwise. Do you think Mark will come looking for you here? Or me, if that's who he's after?"

I feel my stomach clench with anxiety. "He did threaten you."

He blinks twice and then his expression morphs into something grim. It's an intimidating look that I've never seen on his face before. "Did he?"

I nod, squeezing my eyes shut and wishing this wasn't my reality. But it is.

"I didn't want to risk—I couldn't." My voice breaks, and I shake my head, looking down at the floor. "I wanted to leave sooner, but I couldn't."

I look at Ryan, hesitant, only to find him studying me. His expression is expectant, like he knows there's more to the story. But behind that expectation, I recognize the familiar understanding that is *so Ryan*. And a sense of comfort settles over me, realizing that he's on the same page. He understands—at least to some degree—of why it took me so long to get here.

As if he can sense my line of thinking, Ryan reaches to grab my hand to comfort me, but then feels the rigid stitches still embedded in my palm. I'm supposed to wait a few more days before I get them out. Ryan lifts my hand and tilts it, observing the cut.

When he glances back up with me, I can see the anger etched across his face. "What happened?" he asks, even though I'm pretty sure he has a good idea. But he surprises me again when he says, "Tell me everything."

My instinct is to snatch my hand back and hide it, but I force myself not to. This is Ryan. And I don't want to live like that anymore. I'm ready to face the truth head-on and address it. I'm not naive enough to believe it will be an overnight thing, but I'm ready to move on.

"After I got back, Mark confronted me. I told him no. I swear, Ryan, I was fully set on leaving him and going back to you," I say, conviction in my tone. Ryan's expression is still firmly set, his eyes watching me closely. I take a deep breath and continue with a shaky voice. "I told him *No*, and then he hit me again. After that, I tried to lay low, stay out of his way. But it was no use. When he finally found out about everything between us, he threw a vase at me. When I tried to clean it up, I sliced my hand open. It wouldn't stop bleeding, so I had to go get stitches."

"He hit you? *Again?*" Ryan growls, and the severity of his tone has my heart racing, though in a different way than what I've grown accustomed to. Even though I know Ryan's raging with anger, I'm assured that none of it is directed toward me.

"Yes. I'm sor—"

Ryan's expression darkens even further, and he swears, cutting off my backwards apology, before pulling me into his chest in one swift motion. "He will never hurt you again. I swear." He pauses, and then squeezes me tighter. "Fuck, Bells, you don't know how relieved I am right now that you're here, away from him."

His arms tighten around my shoulders until he's almost crushing me. I don't feel uncomfortable, though. I feel cherished. It makes me feel inadequate, undeserving. "I'm so sorry, Ryan. How can you be so understanding? How can you still want me?"

Ryan leans down and presses his lips against my hair in a firm kiss. "Stop apologizing. You have nothing to be sorry for. And I'll always want you. When you love someone as much as I love you, it doesn't just go away. You don't just stop loving them."

"Even after everything I've done? Even though people told you, you were crazy for not moving on?"

"Especially then," he says, his voice a low rumble in his chest.

I snuggle into his chest, feeling a smile stretch across my face. Finally, this is where I'm supposed to be. This feels right.

We stay there for a few moments before Ryan releases me and reaches down to grab my suitcase. He heads down the hall toward the bedrooms, and I follow him. Stepping into the master bedroom, he puts my suitcase down by the dresser.

I stand in the doorway and wring my hands together. He notices my movement and pauses, raising an eyebrow. "What's wrong?"

"Do you think I could sleep in the guest room?" I ask him timidly. I don't know why I'm suddenly so nervous.

Ryan's eyebrows now pull together in confusion. "If that's what you want, of course."

I twist my fingers together tightly and bite my lip. "I just don't want to jump in too deep, too fast," I say. It sounds a little absurd, but I don't want to rush things.

Ryan's expression softens, and he nods. "Bells, you've been through a lot. I don't ever want you to feel like you have to meet any expectations with me. You call the shots here, okay? We'll go at whatever pace you want."

I'm shocked at how easily Ryan is willing to drop everything to let me into his life. Ever since he returned, I feel like I've been nothing but a burden to him, but now, here he is, willing to lay everything down to make sure I feel safe and comfortable.

"You're amazing, Ryan. And I feel like I've really not been fair to you over the last few years, but I want to be better for you. I want to be someone who deserves your kindness and your love. Do you think we could start over? A clean slate?"

Ryan moves toward me and puts a finger under my chin, locking our eyes. "Whatever you need, Bells, I'll be here for you."

"I really don't deserve you."

He gives me a wry smile and presses his lips to mine in a tender kiss. "That's not your call. And I say you do. We belong together. The rest doesn't matter."

Ryan turns around and picks up my suitcase again, giving me a wink before walking into the guest bedroom right next door. He sets it down and then turns to me. "I'll let you rest. You've had a long day." He presses another kiss to my forehead. "Let me know if you need anything, I'll just be out here."

When he makes a move to close the door, I stop him. "Ryan?" He pauses and looks at me. "Thank you."

Ryan gives me a gentle smile. "Get some rest, Bells." He closes the door all the way then, leaving me alone.

I get my things settled, and then crawl into bed. I'm suddenly exhausted. The events over the last week have wiped me out. I curl up under the covers and situate my pillows so they're perfect.

From out in the living room, I hear Ryan answer his phone. He's trying to be quiet, but his deep voice travels down the hall-way. "Hello? Yes, she's here with me. She's fine. Yeah, Juliet, don't worry. I'll keep her safe."

I press my head into my pillow and smile. Ryan's words wrap around me like a blanket. I don't think I've felt this kind of contentment in a long, long time. Though I know Mark is still out there somewhere, I feel a sense of ease that is unfamiliar. There's something about being here with Ryan just around the corner that assures me everything will be okay.

Mark may come after me, or even Ryan, still. That's a very real possibility. But for now, all that matters is that I'm away from him. For now, I can let my mind and defenses rest. I have every confidence in the man down the hall following through on his promise to my best friend.

I'm safe. I'm finally safe.

Chapter 31

Ryan

I JOLT AWAKE AT THE SOUND OF LOUD SOUND ECHOING throughout my apartment. Sitting up quickly, I throw the covers off and run out of my bedroom. My feet hit the floor, propelling me forward. My heartbeat thrums with anxiety. *Bells.*

I knew I should have insisted she sleep with me last night. What if Mark broke in? What if he got to her? I checked and triple checked the apartment locks before going to sleep; I was so paranoid. When I step out into the hallway, I see the guest bedroom door open, the bed made. Where is she?

I find her in the kitchen, picking up the pans that are scattered across the tile floor. My heart stutters, and I allow myself to take a deep breath. Izabel stands up and looks at me with wide blue eyes before they roam across my chest. I didn't have time to throw on a shirt in my initial panic.

"What are you doing?" I ask her.

Izabel looks at the counter where she has a few ingredients laid out, and then looks at me again before dropping her eyes to the ground. "I thought I'd make breakfast. I'm sorry. I should have asked you first. I can just clean this up." She brings her hands around in front of her, wringing her fingers together.

I narrow my eyes and move toward her. "Hey…" She looks back up at me. "Don't apologize. Do you need help cooking?"

She looks down at the floor again. "No. Your pots and pans were just all crammed into the cabinet, and I couldn't get them out. And then they went everywhere. I'm sorry. I didn't mean to wake you."

I rub the back of my neck. "Don't be. What are you making?"

"French toast. Is that okay? I can make something else if you want," she says quickly.

I give her a reassuring smile and shake my head. "No, French toast sounds great." I move to sit down at the breakfast bar in my kitchen. "Did you sleep okay?" I glance at the clock on the microwave—nine a.m.

Izabel nods her head and goes to her mixing bowl, dropping a slice of bread into her concoction. "Honestly? I slept better than I have in years. Despite everything."

"Has Mark tried to contact you yet?" I ask hesitantly.

Bells' clear sapphire eyes meet mine, and she frowns. "Actually, no. I turned my phone on this morning, and I had a lot of missed calls from my parents and Jules. And a nasty-gram from his mom about all the money I'm wasting. But nothing from him."

"That's…concerning," I respond. Given his track record, I would have thought Mark would be on a full rampage trying to find her. Or get to me to follow through on the threat he was holding over her head.

"I know. It's almost worse this way. I don't know what his angle is."

I clear my throat and consider my next words carefully. "Do you think he's plotting something?

"I don't know. He sounded like he meant it when he said he would hurt you if I didn't follow his rules. That was finally what helped me realize I needed to get out. I shouldn't be *afraid* of the man I'm supposed to marry."

"In every situation, life is asking us a question, and our actions are the answer," I say softly. Izabel raises an eyebrow. "Another quote from my book," I tell her. "But it definitely applies."

She chuckles. "That book is proving to be more beneficial than I thought it would be. I just picked it up as an excuse to see you."

I smile, the admission making my heart swell. "Well, I'm glad you did."

"Me too," she whispers, her eyes sparkling as she gazes at me. Then she turns and flips her French toast to the other side.

I still don't feel like this is real life. This domestic scene has me feeling all warm and fuzzy. I hope I get to experience a lifetime of this: Izabel making breakfast, talking about our future, being pregnant with our babies someday. It's a dream come true.

Standing up, I walk over to her. I press her back into my chest and wrap my arms around her. She stiffens briefly—something which makes my heart ache—but then relaxes into my embrace. The knowledge that Bells is going to have to face this trauma one way or the other nags at me, but I don't push the issue today.

She flips a few pieces of French toast onto a plate and then offers it to me. I take it with a grateful smile. "Breakfast is served."

I find my syrup in the pantry and then sit back down and dig in. Izabel works on finishing the rest of the toast and then comes and sits beside me with her own plate. She takes a few small bites but doesn't finish hers.

"You sure you're feeling okay?" I ask, concerned.

She gives me a reassuring smile. "Yeah, I think it's still just the aftermath of everything. I'm fine." Izabel laughs at my expression. "Really, Ryan. I'm not going to break."

I clear my throat and try to change the subject. "So, what's the plan here?"

"How do you mean?" she asks.

"Well, I assume you'll be wanting to move in. I can stop by a furniture store and get you a better dresser for your room. And a mirror or something. It's pretty bare in there."

Izabel looks down at her fingers and picks at her cuticles. "I think it's fine. Do you want me to look for a different place? I don't want to infringe on your privacy."

"No," I say quickly. "I want you here."

"Okay," Izabel responds with a smile, and for the first time in a really long time, I feel fully content.

The rest of the weekend flies by. I spend a lot of quiet time with her. We snuggle on the couch, watching old movies while stuffing our faces with popcorn, playing board games, or just talking. We take it slow. I often catch her looking at me longingly, but she never takes things further.

I keep catching her apologizing to me for the littlest things, and it breaks my heart. Or I reach up to brush a strand of hair behind her ear, and she flinches away from me, wincing. It's like she's walking on eggshells around me without even realizing it. As if she's waiting for the next ball to drop. Every time I check in with her, she brushes me off and tells me everything's fine. It's not fine, though. That much is obvious. I wish Mark would show up, just so I could clock him in the face for doing this to Bells.

Juliet and Liam come by on Sunday afternoon with Ashton. Juliet wraps her arms around Izabel tightly and tells her how proud she is. Liam stands beside me, holding their son.

He claps me on the shoulder approvingly, but doesn't say a word.

"How was everything after I left?" Izabel asks her friend quietly.

Juliet frowns. "Well, Mark's mom completely lost her mind. She was screaming at the wedding planner, and then got into a pissing match with your dad."

"My dad?" Bells questions.

"Yeah, Mark's mom was really railing on you, going on and on about nothing. I think your dad finally had enough and stood up for you, saying that he supported whatever decision you made."

Bells' lips curve up into a soft smile, but then it drops from her face. "What about Mark?"

Liam and Juliet look at each other uncomfortably, and Liam clears his throat. "Mark didn't react. He just stared after you as you ran out with a dark expression on his face. Then he left. We haven't heard anything from him since."

Izabel looks at me, her eyebrows pulled together. I frown. That can't be a good sign. But I'm not sure what to make of the whole thing.

Our friends hang out for a while longer before taking off. Once again, Izabel and I are alone in my apartment. I can tell she's not quite sure how she's supposed to act. She's struggling, but I'm not sure how to help her.

I'm just biding my time. We'll take this at her pace. I'm not in any type of rush. I've waited eight years to have her back, so what's a few more months while she establishes her new normal?

Monday morning I'm getting ready for work, and Bells is sitting on my bed cross-legged, watching me. Her chin rests in her hand.

I pull on my suit jacket and turn to her. "Are you *sure* you're going to be okay by yourself?"

I've asked her this a hundred times. I'm hoping she'll ask me to stay. I wouldn't mind calling into work. If Bells says she'll be okay, I have to take her word for it. She needs to be able to make decisions on her own and be assured that I'm not going to turn on her like Mark did.

Izabel stands up off the bed and stands right in front of me. Her fingers grip the edges of my jacket, and she straightens it. "I'll be okay, Ryno. I'll just stay inside and watch movies, or read a book or something. Don't worry about me."

With a sigh, I reach a hand around her waist, pulling her into me. "That's an impossible request, you know."

I feel her smile against me, and she trails her hands up my back, clutching me to her in a hug. "That's why I feel so safe."

I reluctantly let her go and grab the rest of my things, and Izabel remains the highlight of my musings as I drive to work.

Josie is waiting for me when I get there. She's leaning against the edge of my desk, her arms crossed in front of her. A few weeks ago, I offered Josie a more permanent place at my firm. She now has her own office and contracts out as part of my team.

I step into the office and shake off my suit jacket as I stare at her in silence. She widens her hazel eyes at me, begging me to spill the beans.

"Well?" she asks.

"Well, what?"

"Are you gonna tell me what happened or not?"

I straighten my tie around my neck and walk toward my desk. "Izabel dropped by the other night to let me know that she called off the wedding." I look at her with a grin. "And she left Mark, officially."

Josie's face splits into a smile, and she throws a friendly

punch at my shoulder. "See, I told you everything would work out! That's great, Ryan. I'm so happy for you both." I rub at the spot and chuckle. Josie plants her hands on the surface of my desk and leans over. "So then what happened?"

I glance at her as I pull my emails up. Shit, there's a ton. Just another day in the life. "Uh, nothing really. She's been staying with me all weekend. She'll probably officially move in once things settle down. We're not sure how Mark is going to react. He's been eerily absent all weekend." I frown at the subject line of one email. *Great, this call will take all day.*

"Well, hopefully, he'll just disappear into the shadows and leave you alone."

I chuckle under my breath, hoping we'll get that lucky. "Yeah, we'll see. I'm just glad she's away from him."

Josie pats my shoulder in solidarity, and then leaves me to the mess of an email I need to get to work on.

It's no surprise that I run late that evening, and it's almost nine by the time I get home. My condo is dark, and I see Izabel's door is closed. I set my briefcase by the door and shuffle to my own room, treading carefully to not wake her up. I was hoping to see her tonight, but I guess that's my own fault. Life of a business owner.

I take a quick shower and then fall onto my bed, clicking on the TV and looking for something to watch. Tucking one arm behind my head, I let my mind wander as I stare at the images flashing across the screen.

I think about how I want things to progress with Izabel. The idea of counseling flashes through my mind, but I'm not sure how she would respond if I brought it up. She needs to talk to someone about everything that she went through with Mark. She keeps telling me she's okay and that she's over it, but based on the reactions and mannerisms I've observed over the last few days, I don't think that's genuinely the case. I wish she would talk to me. She's probably worried about being a burden to me, but that's what I'm here for. I have to get her to realize that I have her back for better or for worse.

I don't know how we're going to move forward if she's repressing everything she's been through in the last few years. Maybe I'll approach the topic tomorrow. I wish there was something I could do to help her, but I don't know where to start. I'm entirely helpless in this situation. All I can do is make myself available. She'll come to me when she's ready.

I jump a little when I hear my door crack open. Bells peeks her head through the gap and looks at me sheepishly. "Hey," I say softly, sitting up a little straighter. "Everything okay?"

She opens the door wider and pulls her hands together in front of her. "Um. I was wondering if I could sleep in here tonight?"

"What happened?" I ask her, my spine going ramrod straight. My pulse quickens. Did Mark come here? Did he threaten her? Is she hurt?

Izabel shakes her head and moves closer to me. "Nothing, I'm just feeling a little—I just wanted to be near you."

Yeah. Everything is most definitely *not* okay with her.

"But if you want your space, that's fine. I'll be fine," she says quickly. "Sorry to bother you."

She makes a move to leave, pulling the door closed behind her. "Bells, wait." Stopping, she peers at me again, biting her lip. "Come here, pretty girl. Let me hold you."

I lift my arm, creating a space for her. Izabel prances across the room to the other side of the bed and crawls under the covers. She snuggles up against my side and nuzzles her cheek on my chest. Pressing a kiss to her hair, I let my arm fall around her shoulders. I breathe in, smelling her shampoo.

"Tell me something I don't know," I murmur against her head after a moment of silence.

Her hand is resting on my chest, and she runs her fingers through the hair there. I jolt a little at the feel of her fingernails, but she doesn't notice. "I started taking self-defense classes."

I raise my eyebrows in surprise. I remember suggesting that while we were in Nashville, but I never actually thought she would pursue it. Maybe she wouldn't completely object to my suggestion of talking to someone then. "That's great, Bells. How are they going?"

Her shoulder shrugs underneath my hand, and her fingers make random patterns against my chest, forming goosebumps. "Fine, I guess. I don't know if I want to continue. We had an evaluation where we had to escape from some attackers last week."

"How'd you do?"

"Not that great. It ended with me throwing up in the women's bathroom," she says with a sigh. "It was supposed to be empowering, but mostly, I felt weak."

"You're not weak, Bells," I tell her. "You gotta give yourself more credit."

"How can I do that? This whole situation is my fault. If I would've just left at the first sign of trouble, I wouldn't even be in this mess," Izabel grumbles. "I don't deserve any type of break, or credit, or forgiveness."

"That's not true at all. Look at me," she doesn't, so I put a finger under her chin. "Look at me, Bells." Finally, those blues meet mine, and I see they're glittering with unshed tears. My heart shatters at her pain, and I wish there was something I could do to ease it. "Toxic situations like this are hard to escape. But you did. It's only been a few days. Maybe—" I pause. "Maybe you should talk to someone."

Izabel's lips turn down, but I continue before she can protest. "Talk to a professional who has dealt with situations like this before. I want to help you through this, but I'm concerned I might be too close to the situation to be much help. I care about you far too much to be objective."

She presses her cheek against my pectoral and wraps her arm around my waist. "I'll think about it. I'm not opposed to it, but I'm ready to move on. I can't keep living like this. I feel like any second, everything is going to come crumbling down. He'll find me and hurt me—hurt us. And the last thing I want is to have a therapist look at me like I'm a victim."

"Okay," I say, my heart constricting at her honesty. "Maybe just think about it. It could help you move past everything once and for all."

She exhales, and though I can tell she's still not on board, she nods. "I don't want to be like this anymore."

"I know," I say, tightening my hold around her. "We'll get through this. I promise."

I reach for the remote to the TV and shut it off, before scooting down and lying on my side. We face each other in the dark. Her arm is still resting on my hipbone as I lean forward and capture her mouth with mine.

Izabel responds by arching her back and pressing herself into me. She's wearing a skimpy tank top, so I can feel her breasts pressing through the fabric against my chest. She mewls quietly against my mouth as I pull her closer to me.

I call it quits before we get too carried away, though. We're not there yet. I know it, she knows it. She has a lot of healing to do before we get to that point, and I'm not about to take advantage of the situation.

Running my hands down her back, I let out a contented sigh. "You know I love you, Bells. Right?" I feel her nod, and she snuggles in closer to me. "Good, don't ever forget it."

Chapter 32

Izabel

"Are you *sure* you feel up to going today? You can always call in another day," Ryan pleads with me over breakfast.

I take a sip of my hot tea and offer him a smile that I hope is reassuring. "I'm sure, Ryan. I have to get out of this house. And I can't call in another day, or Todd will have my ass."

"He'll understand," he says, then pauses and grumbles, "I'll make him understand."

I place my hand on his cheek, smooth after shaving this morning, and force him to look at me. "Everything will be fine. Mark's been radio silent for the last few days. I don't think he's going to pull anything."

Ryan clenches his jaw, making the muscles pop out on his cheek. "I hope you're right. Are you sure you need to go back?"

"Ryan, I've been cooped up in this house for four days. I need to get out of here. I miss my students and the sun. I promise I'll be fine." I give him a wry smile. "And besides, I have some secret defense moves tucked up my sleeve if it comes to it."

I don't know why I'm joking right now. If Mark were to show up, I don't think I would have the guts to fight him off. The threat of him lurking around is still very real. The thought of going out still scares me—not that I'll tell Ryan that—but I can't stay hidden away anymore. I have to get on with my life.

He doesn't smile back. "This is serious, Bells. If he shows up, you need to get the hell out of there, call the cops, and then call me as soon as you're safe."

"I will. It will be fine." I'm touched by his order. Ryan puts my safety above himself. That much is clear.

"Promise me," he presses. "Please."

"I promise."

Ryan exhales heavily and takes a sip of his coffee. "I don't like it. But if you think it will be okay, I'll get over it."

I smile at him again and take a bite of my muffin. We finish breakfast and then work on getting ready for the day. After brushing my teeth, I meet Ryan back in the living room. He asks if I'm ready before we both head out to the parking lot. Ryan informs me that his soccer team has a game after school. He invites me to come by and watch if I want, then he gives me a kiss before getting in his car and driving away. I start my car and head across town toward school.

Such a mundane routine that we've established in our day, but I love every little bit of it. It's small moments like these, where we've settled into a new normal of co-existing, when I forget all that trauma I've been through. How difficult it was for me to finally get to this moment.

And with thoughts of how I love how my life has turned out, come along feelings of trepidation that it all might be taken from me.

I wonder if my students are going to ask questions. They all were under the impression—along with the rest of the world— that my wedding was this weekend. Maybe they won't notice the obnoxious diamond missing from my finger, or the lack of the matching wedding band.

I arrive at Bennett, and then make my way into my classroom. A few minutes later, I hear a knock on my door, and I stiffen. My shoulders tighten, and my spine straightens. I relax immediately when I see the headmaster stick his head in.

"Hey, Izabel," Todd says as he steps into my room. He closes the door behind him. "I spoke with Ryan this morning, and he filled me in on everything."

Of course, he did. I can't be mad at Ryan for that, though. Everything with him comes from a place of caring and concern —virtually the opposite of where Mark's intentions rose from.

"It's been an interesting weekend, to say the least." I attempt to make light of the situation.

"Look, if you need more time off, we can figure it out. I don't want you to stress yourself by being here," he offers. Todd is one of Ryan's oldest friends. They attended Bennett Academy together and stayed tight throughout the years. I know he cares about me because Ryan does, but Todd would do this for any of his faculty. He's a sweet guy.

"I think I need to get back to work," I tell him. "I miss my students, and honestly, it will help take my mind off of everything."

Todd nods. "I understand. Well, I just wanted to check in with you. If there's anything I can do to help, my door is always open."

"Thanks, Todd," I say with a smile.

He taps his knuckles on the door and then steps out, leaving me alone again. About half an hour later, the students start filing in. The boys in my first class seem happy to have me back, and we dive into the lesson.

The day passes uneventfully, but I am ready to call it a day when the release bell rings. I have a raging headache, and I could use a nap. My final class gathers their bookbags and note-books, and they shuffle out of the room. A few say goodbye, and I give them small waves.

Once everyone is gone, I sit down at my desk to submit attendance for the day and close everything out. By the time I gather up my things and shut everything down, the hallways are mostly empty. This is usual. The boys typically bolt as quickly as they can to head back to their dorms or their sports.

My shoes make a soft noise against the tile floors as I steer toward the staff parking lot. I take a deep breath of the fresh fall air once I step outside and let it fill my lungs. I love fall. I had to park on the opposite end of the lot this morning. Ryan's apart-ment is farther than Mark's and my place was, and I didn't take the extra drive time into account this morning.

A short distance behind me, my ears pick up on unusual movement. I think it's footsteps hitting the pavement, heading in the exact direction I'm going. I pick up my pace, trying to get to the car quicker, but they keep following me. I have the creepy-crawling feeling someone is watching my every move. My heart strums away, and my palms start to sweat.

It's nothing, just take a deep breath, I tell myself. *It's not Mark.*

But what if it is? I haven't heard from Mark since the rehearsal. What if he's been biding his time, waiting for me to come back to work? He knows which car is mine. He could have been waiting for me to leave the building to confront me in the parking lot. Maybe I was too quick to jump on freedom. Mark could have been plotting this whole time.

My mind immediately starts working out scenarios. If Mark grabs me, what am I going to do? How am I going to respond? I have to have a game plan to protect myself. My fingers grip onto the strap of my bag, and I keep walking. Why did I have to park so far away? The footsteps get faster; they're getting closer. I squeeze my eyes shut and muster all my courage.

Okay, I can do this. I can do this. I can protect us.

I *have* to protect us.

In one swift movement, I spin around, extending my bag out in a big sweep. My body goes into the self-defense stance I learned at classes: a wide stance with my legs, one foot slightly back, my arms raised in defensive fists, ready to strike or deflect if needed.

"Stay away from me!" I yell at the top of my lungs. Maybe if Mark hears me scream, he'll abort his attempt to attack me.

A few Bennett boys dodge out of the way, shooting weird looks at my stance. They slide by me and continue on with their run.

The cross-country team.

I feel my face heat up in embarrassment as I drop my arms. My heart is still racing, my breathing slightly hitched. My eyes roam the area to make sure Mark isn't still lurking anywhere. As I turn around, I see Ryan's friend, Josie, standing at the parking lot's edge. She's looking at me with a concerned expression. Her hair is pulled into a high ponytail, and she's wearing leggings with a Bennett Soccer shirt. She's here for Ryan's game.

Josie jogs over to me, her eyebrows still bunched together in worry. "Hey, are you okay?"

I nod and brush my hair away from my face. I feel unbelievably vulnerable, and all I want to do is go curl up in my bed and cry. "I'm fine."

"Those were some impressive moves. You look like you've been training."

"Yeah," I admit, shrugging sheepishly. "I guess I'm still a little paranoid after everything." I keep my eye on her to gauge her reaction. I wonder how much of the situation Ryan has deemed appropriate to share.

"Well, I'd hate to be the guy on the receiving end," Josie teases while shooting me a big grin. She doesn't make fun of me for my apparent misunderstanding. Instead, she glances over toward the soccer fields. "I was just going to go catch the game. Do you want to tag along, Rhonda Rousey?"

I was planning on heading back to Ryan's house. My head is still throbbing, even worse now that the adrenaline from my non-stalker is wearing off. But despite all that, the idea of being alone doesn't appeal to me at all. I'd like to go home and rest, but being around people feels like a smarter choice.

I shift my bag up on my shoulder. "Yeah, I think I will. You don't mind?"

"Not at all! Do you want to drop that stuff off in your car?" Josie offers. I nod, and she walks with me over to the car, where I deposit my bag and grab my sunglasses out of the console.

We walk side by side into the stadium and make a pit stop at the concession stand. Josie orders a big soda and some nachos, and I get a water bottle and a giant pretzel. We locate a few open seats on the metal bleachers and turn our attention towards the fields. The boys are running a few drills before the game, and Ryan is deep in a conversation with Liam, going over a sheet of paper on a clipboard.

"So, you sure you're good?" Josie asks me after a minute. I can tell she's hesitant. She's Ryan's best friend, not mine.

But he trusts her. So maybe I should too.

I pick at the pieces of salt on my pretzel, and then answer her honestly. "I don't know."

Josie nods and dips one of her chips into the cheese. "It's okay to not be okay. But you should know that you have a good network of people who would be happy to help you. Myself, included. If you ever need to talk, just let me know. I'm pretty good at lending an ear here and there. Or, I could give you the name of a therapist I've been working with. She's amazing."

I turn and look at her, surprised. "Thank you, Josie. That really means a lot."

"Of course, just let me know. I'm glad everything is working out, though. Ryan deserves things to go his way for once."

I press my lips together, suddenly embarrassed again. "He is pretty great."

Josie stares at me for a second and then clears her throat. "Look, I'm just gonna get this serious-talk out of the way, and then we can never speak of it again. I like you, Izabel, but Ryan is my best friend. He worships the ground you walk on, which inadvertently makes you important to me too. I'm happy that you two are working on things... Just promise me that you won't hurt him again. I'm not sure if he could take it."

I give Josie a resolute look. Her hazel eyes are firm as she holds my gaze. "I promise."

She lets out a breath, and then bites into a chip. "Good. Oh, look, they're calling captains!"

I turn my attention to the field. The two captains walk to the center of the green to meet the referee. Ryan's team is donned in Bennett Blue, and the other team wears green jerseys. The captains quickly shake hands and then step slightly apart. The ref tosses a coin into the air and motions toward the Bennett side of the field. Josie and I cheer and clap along with the crowd.

Ryan is on the field, clapping his hands and directing his team into a huddle. They surround him and listen to his game plan. The boys pile their hands into the middle and let out a chant before breaking and getting into their positions. Ryan turns around toward the stands. His eyes scan the crowd until they fall on Josie and me. I give him a small wave, and a big smile splits across his face before he turns back to his team.

Josie nudges me with her elbow, and I glance at her. She wiggles her eyebrows up and down and shoots me a wink before clapping her hands and cheering.

The game gets started, and I get sucked into watching the teams dribble the ball back and forth. So much so that I almost forget the headache pounding at the back of my head. Bennett scores a goal. Then the other team does. Then Bennett gets another, taking the lead!

Ryan is pacing back and forth along the sidelines, shouting instructions to the teams. I watch him just as much as I watch the game. He's in his element out there. Soccer has always been one of his favorite things. I wish things would have taken off for us as a couple earlier when we were younger. I would have liked to see him in the glory days, scoring all the goals and leading his team. I'm sure the crowds went crazy for him whenever he took the field.

As the second quarter flies by, the other team scores another goal, but Bennett pulls ahead with two, keeping the lead. The scoreboard buzzes, announcing half time. Crowd cheering, people disperse to get refreshments or use the restroom.

Josie stretches her arms above her head and sighs, then she turns to me. "Woo, that was exciting."

I grin at her. "It was!"

We both then turn back to the field. A few minutes later, the second half picks up, and the game resumes. In between plays, Ryan will occasionally turn around to glance at me. He'll shoot me a wink or blow a kiss, and every time my belly tightens in response.

This man is everything I could ever want. I can't believe it took me this long to take matters into my own hands and stand up for myself and what I deserve.

The game ends in a sweep. Bennett shut out the other team from getting any goals in the second half, and the boys walked away with a win. Josie and I cheered the whole time, and my throat feels slightly scratchy from the exertion, but at least my headache has eased.

After the game finishes, Ryan runs over to the fence blocking off the stands from the field. He leans over, locking his eyes on me as I walk down the steps toward him. I trot over to where he's standing, and he reaches an arm across the fence, locating my waist and pulling me into him. My body lights up with energy the minute his hand comes into contact with me.

Ryan captures my lips with his and kisses me like he hasn't seen me in ten years. I knot my fingers in his hair and let him devour me. The kiss awakens some part of me that has been dormant for weeks. I moan into his mouth, and his fingers tighten around me in response.

"Okay, lovebirds, break it up before you scar these teenagers for life," Josie teases next to us.

Ryan pulls away and looks at his friend wryly. "Cock-blocker."

Josie sticks her tongue out at him and then steps forward. "Nice game, Ry. Those guys looked great out there."

Ryan runs a hand across the back of his neck and grins. *Good Lord, this man is attractive.* "Yeah, they did really well today. I'm glad you both could make it." He glances back toward the team, who are starting their trek to the locker rooms. "I better get going," he says, his voice low. He turns to me, his vivid green eyes meeting mine. "I'll see you at home?"

My insides clench, and I force myself to acknowledge his question. I love the way that sounds—*home.* Ryan is home. He leans over the fence and kisses me again. His arm wraps around my waist, his hand resting above my rear. As he pulls away, he leaves me all hot and bothered again. His eyes spark as if he knows what he's doing to me. Looking me up and down, he winks at me and turns to jog off after his team.

Josie walks with me to my car and then gives me a hug before trekking off to find hers. I hop in and settle my things before starting the engine and pulling out. Ryan would probably be another hour or so before he makes it home.

I press my legs together as I drive, feeling the ache between my thighs ease slightly. I'm not sure what it was about seeing Ryan this afternoon after his victory, but it ignited every molecule in my body to the point that I would have jumped that fence and ravished him then and there if he would have let me.

Things have been going slow for us. I didn't feel right about falling straight into bed with Ryan immediately following everything that happened with Mark. It hasn't even been a week yet, but I'm not sure how much longer I can hold out. Even though my logical side says wait, the rising heat of the moment is telling me that getting naked in bed with Ryan is *exactly* what needs to happen.

Tonight should be special. We haven't really had a chance to celebrate together. My mind begins plotting all the ways I could seduce him tonight. Not that I think I really need to do much, as I seemed to have the same effect on Ryan that he did with me. I just have to make sure he knows that this is what I want. Ryan would never put me into a situation where I felt uncomfortable.

Up ahead, I see a flashing sign for a local Tennessee Distillery outlet. I'm immediately struck with the idea of getting him a little congratulatory present. I pull into the parking lot and hurry inside, scouring the shelves and looking for the perfect one. I finally choose one and then head up to the cash register to pay. The clerk sticks the whiskey into a brown paper bag and hands it to me with a smile.

I stop by the drugstore too and buy a nice bow. When I'm on the road again, my eyes dart to my passenger's seat where the items are sitting, and smile to myself. He'll love this.

Once I get home, I set the bottle on the counter and position the bow just right. I glance at the clock on my cell phone. Ryan should be home shortly. Hurrying into the bathroom, I hop into the shower. I run my loofah over my body, the sweet strawberry scent of my soap flooding my senses. I keep my hair out of the water, so it doesn't get soaked. When I'm done, I walk into the guest bedroom where all my clothes are still stashed.

I rummage through my drawers, trying to find my sexiest pair of underwear. Most of my sexiest lingerie is still at Mark's house. I was initially in too much of a rush to think about what clothes I would need when I left. It didn't occur to me that I would want to look sexy for Ryan in the immediate future.

But I need this. Tonight.

I settle on a purple lacy set. And turn back and forth in the mirror, making sure that everything is exactly where it needs to be.

I hear the lock click, signaling Ryan's return. Quickly, I reach for the silk nightgown I found in my drawer and pull it over my lacy underwear set. Giving myself one last turn in the mirror, I feel satisfied.

My bare feet pad against the wood floors of the hallway, and I step out to meet Ryan. He's still standing by the door, setting his things down on the floor. I pull my hands behind my back and watch him. He stands up and looks around, his eyes falling on my figure in the entrance to the living room.

Ryan goes stock still as his eyes roam over my appearance. I see his jaw clench and his eyes smolder. "Well, hello there, gorgeous," he mutters in a low voice.

My knees go weak as he takes three long strides across the living room, coming to stand right in front of me. His hands wrap around my waist, holding me up as he lines our bodies together. He crushes his lips to mine in a sensual kiss and runs his fingers up my sides. They tease along the edges of my sensitive breasts, and I gasp into his mouth. Even through the material, I can feel the sensations of his touch.

He devours me for a few minutes before breathlessly pulling away. His eyes are lit up like embers. Looking me over, his lips turn up in a wicked smile. "I could get used to this. What's the occasion?"

I wrap my arms around his neck and press the length of my body against his. "You won tonight."

He chuckles and kisses me. "This wasn't our first win, but I'll take it anyway."

"I got you something, too. Kind of a victory present," I say softly.

Ryan looks at me with tender eyes. "You didn't have to do that."

"I know, but I wanted to," I tell him. "You've done so much for me. I wanted to do something nice for you."

I pull away from him and move over to where the whiskey bottle is sitting on the counter. I pick it up and show it to him, a big smile on my face. "It was one of the nicest ones they had. They told me it's their most popular blend."

Ryan's eyes go wide, and he presses his lips together. He's frozen in place for a minute before he clears his throat awkwardly. His eyes flick from the bottle to me, and he rubs the back of his neck. I can tell he's uncomfortable, and I immediately feel embarrassed.

My brain kicks into overdrive as anxiety washes over me.

What was I thinking? I shouldn't have assumed that we were at this point. He's clearly not on the same page as I am. I should've tested the waters first before diving into the deep end.

"Sorry," I whisper, setting the bottle back on the counter. "I shouldn't have assumed anything. It was stupid. I'll just go to my room."

I try to walk by him, but he catches my hand, halting my movements. Ryan lets out a forced sigh and turns me around to face him. His hand comes up to cup my cheek, and he kisses me tenderly.

When he pulls away, his eyes are gentle. "Thank you, Bells. I know you were trying to be sweet. This means a lot to me." I can feel the *but* coming, and I brace myself for the easy letdown. "But there's something I've been keeping from you. I should've been honest."

"What is it?" I ask, panic setting in. Does he have someone else? Is he going to ask me to leave?

Ryan takes a deep breath and runs his hand through my hair. "I'm sober." At my blank expression, he elaborates, "Things this year were...rough, to say the least. I resorted to some not so healthy habits any time something had me down."

"Because of me?" I ask, mortified.

He shakes his head and pulls me closer. "No, it wasn't your fault. It was the situation. It was me. I was weak, and I turned to the first available vice to numb everything out. Josie's been helping me work through it, but I haven't touched the stuff since."

I feel so embarrassed I'm not quite entirely sure what to say. Now I know what Josie meant earlier when she said she wasn't sure if Ryan could handle another blow. I can't believe he didn't say anything earlier.

I untangle from his grasp and walk over to the sink. The

bottle is still in my hands, and I unscrew the cap. Ryan follows me into the kitchen, hot on my heels.

"What are you doing?" he asks, confused.

I shake my head and start pouring the amber liquid down the drain. "Well, if you're sober, then we're not even going to keep this here as a temptation. I don't want to be the reason you turn to that again."

Ryan steps behind me and wraps his hands around my waist. He leans over and presses his lips to my neck. I suck in a breath and lean back into his embrace.

"I love you, Bells," he whispers against my skin.

The whiskey is all gone, and I drop the bottle on the counter before turning to him. "Thank you for telling me. I want to support you like you support me. We're a team," I say hesitantly with a smile. Ryan stares at me for a second before grabbing my hand and pulling me behind him. A laugh bubbles out of me. "Where are you taking me?"

Ryan glances over his shoulder and gives me a heated look, promising me exactly what he's planning. His eyes roam over my body, leaving a trail of longing where they land. "I'm going to unwrap my present."

Chapter 33

Ryan

I GLANCE UP FROM MY TABLET SCREEN WHEN I HEAR THEIR voices. Izabel's words are timid, but the therapist speaks to her in a soothing tone. I pull my glasses off as I watch them emerge into the waiting room.

"Don't worry, Izabel," the therapist smiles at her. "We'll touch base next week and pick up where we left off." Then she pats Izabel's arm and turns around to head back into her office.

Bells walks over to me and collapses in the seat next to mine with a sigh. "How'd it go?" I ask her as I hand her the coffee I picked up from the cafe next door.

Her face lights up as she takes it and sips gingerly. "Mm, this is amazing," she moans, taking another drink.

"It's a caramel macchiato," I say with a shrug.

"Thank you. It went okay. The therapist rationalized a lot of my fears and paranoia. She says that's perfectly normal for someone to be experiencing after being in a relationship like I was."

I rub my hand over my jaw. I don't want to push Izabel on anything; if she wants to talk further about her session with me,

I'll listen. But honestly, it's not really my business. All I care about is that she has someone to work through all this with.

I all but insisted that Izabel get in with someone as soon as possible a few days ago. We were at the grocery store, and Izabel went into a full-on panic attack because she thought she saw Mark. She completely shut down and froze right there in the checkout line.

It wasn't him. It was some other tall guy with brown hair, but that was enough to convince me that she needed to talk to someone about all that had transpired. Then Izabel reluctantly told me about what happened at school on Wednesday with the cross-country team. That sealed the deal for me.

On top of her terror going about her day-to-day life, I think she still has a lot of things to work through before she's back to her usual self. There's still a part of Izabel that seems to be stuck in that submissive state, worried about speaking too loudly or taking up too much space. It seems that every time something happens, she's apologizing, as if that will solve it. It's almost like a reflex. Something goes awry and Izabel begins profusely apologizing.

Josie gave us the name of a therapist that she'd spoken to before, and I made Izabel an appointment for this morning. Izabel asked me to come with her, which I was more than willing to do. But I still made sure she had her privacy in session.

We'll get through this. I know we will.

"I think I really like her," Bells says, looking at me over the rim of her coffee cup. "She's really gentle and easy to talk to. I hope she'll be able to help me work through this." She sighs audibly. "I'm tired of being scared."

I reach my hand over the edge of her seat and rub her back. Izabel leans into my touch and closes her eyes. "Do you want to go home?" I ask.

She gives me a small nod, and I gather up our things. Bells is quiet on the car ride home, and I can tell she must be contemplating whatever they spoke about while in session. "When does she want you back?" I ask when we're settled in the car.

"She said she'd like to see me two times a week for a while," Bells says, looking out at the passing trees and houses.

"How do you feel about that?"

She shoots me an amused look. "I think it's good. I've never really done therapy just for myself before—I went a few times to couple's counseling with Mark, but I know regular therapy helps a lot of people. I'm willing to do whatever it takes."

"You're so brave, Bells," I say.

Izabel scoffs. "No, I'm not. Not even a little bit."

I frown at her. "Why do you say that?"

"I let him control me," she replies sadly. "I didn't see what was happening right under my nose. I alienated my family, my friends, you. And I just let it happen, for so long."

"Maybe that's true," I say carefully. "But from my perspective, I see a beautiful, strong woman who broke free from a manipulative situation. The timeline doesn't matter. What matters is that you're out. You're free."

Izabel still has a forlorn expression on her face. She grips her coffee between her hands and stares out the window. My heart aches. I wish there was more I could do to help her through this, but I know this is something she needs to work out on her own.

I watch her from the corner of my eye and suddenly can't resist. "Tell me something I don't know, Bells."

She looks up at me, and a second later, a huge smile splits across her face. "I love you, Ryan."

I nearly swerve the car, but luckily, we make it to the stoplight. "Really?" I ask her once we're at a complete stop. I hate that I sound so surprised, but it doesn't seem to faze her.

She fiddles with her fingers in her lap and looks up at me from under her eyelashes. "Really. You know you've always been important to me, but these last few days, it's just hit me that I don't want to go another minute of the day without you knowing exactly how I feel about you."

While we're still stopped, I cross the console in a swift movement, capturing her face in my hands. I kiss her like a madman, pouring every bit of how I feel into it. She lets out a little moan and kisses me back with just as much fervor.

We're both breathless when the light turns green. "I love you too, Bells," I say softly. I can't wipe the smile off my face for the rest of the drive.

We head back into the condo, and Izabel goes straight to my bedroom rather than the guest room. She's been sleeping with me every night this week, so I think it's safe to assume she's moved out of guest status. Most of her personal items are still stashed in there, but maybe I could convince her to move those today or tomorrow.

I stand door frame and cross my arms as I watch her get settled on the bed. When she sees me watching her, she gives me a smile. "What?"

"I just like the sight of you in my bed," I say as my chest swells with warmth. I cross the room, closing the distance between us. When I'm on the bed, I wrap my arms around her, pulling her closer to me. Izabel presses her cheek against my chest and wraps her arms around my waist. We hold each other for a few quiet moments before she takes in a shaky breath.

"What is it?"

"My therapist said that I should consider getting the rest of my things from Mark's house," Izabel recounts to me hesitantly. "She says that as long as I still have part of my life there, I won't be able to fully move on."

I frown, even though she can't see my face. "Have you told

her he's hurt you? I don't know if it's safe..." I trail off. I hope I haven't crossed a line.

"She suggested going at a time when I know he won't be there. Like a weekday, during work hours." Izabel nuzzles into my t-shirt. "I know what she's saying, though. I want my life to continue to move forward on this path, but a part of me still feels like I'm stuck back where I was."

I exhale, frustrated. "Well, I need to go with you. I don't want you there alone." I feel her nod against me, and I tighten my hold. "Maybe we could go Thursday. I want to give it another week," I tell her. "Does Mark work Thursdays? Can you wait that long?"

"I have plenty of things I can wash until then. And yes, he's usually at the office all week until late."

"How much stuff do you have?" I ask. "I could get a truck if we need it."

She nods again. "That would be good. I never unpacked all my stuff from my apartment, so it's all still in boxes. But I don't think it will fit in your car."

I rest my chin on top of her hair. "Okay, then I'll let Josie know I'm taking off Thursday and Friday. She can hold down the fort. We'll get the rest of your things from over there and then get you settled here. Then you'll be done with him, for good."

Izabel presses herself against me tighter and her body relaxes. I plant a kiss on her head. "I can't even begin to tell you how amazing that sounds."

Chapter 34

Izabel

Thursday morning comes far too quickly.

Ryan and I wake up around the same time, taking a few extra minutes to ourselves while we lie in bed together. Ryan's big hand runs over my body's length, the rough edges of his fingers scraping my sensitive bare skin. He gives me a sultry look and then rolls me onto my back, shifting his body on top of mine, nudging my knees apart with his, and entering me in a swift, practiced movement. I let myself get lost in him, knowing that the outcome of today is up in the air.

A while later, we emerge into the kitchen, still glowing in post-coital bliss, but even that is not enough to ease the wariness of what is looming. Ryan instructs me to sit at the breakfast bar, and he whips up some eggs, toast, and breakfast sausage. He makes a cup of coffee for himself and then pulls the gallon of decaf iced coffee for me out of the fridge, pouring a glass.

We eat our breakfasts, making awkward small talk. We're just wasting time. We could go whenever, as Mark leaves for work early, so the house will be empty. I know Ryan is dreading this just as much as I am.

I spoke with Todd yesterday after classes, explaining what was going on today. He assured me that given the circumstances, I could take as much time as I needed, and they would hold my position for me. It was a massive weight off my chest to have that assurance, but I still felt guilty about skipping class *again*.

At least Ryan is self-employed. He can work from anywhere most of the time. As long as he has Lori or Josie in the office to answer phones, he doesn't have to be there full time.

Ryan sets down his fork with a clatter and then peeks over at me. He stretches his arms above his head and groans. Then he checks the watch resting on his wrist. "Think we're good to go? We still have to pick up a rental truck too."

I nod and wipe the edge of my mouth with a napkin. "Yeah, let me go brush my teeth, and I'll be ready."

Ryan doesn't follow me back to the bedroom. Instead, he grabs our dishes and works on cleaning up the kitchen. I wander into the bathroom and shut the door, making sure it's locked behind me. Then I turn on my reflection in the mirror. The woman staring back at me has dark circles under her eyes, and her face is narrow, like she hasn't had a decent meal in months.

I know it's the stress of the situation. The anxiety that Mark will come after me or show up in my new everyday life. I'll be happy when this is all over. But a part of me is questioning if it even *will* be over after this.

So I get my personal items from his house. Then what? Does he officially get over the fact that I ran out on him the night before our wedding? My therapist says that I won't fully move on until everything from my life with him is non-existent. But does that translate that way for him as well? Will he move on once I'm out of his life?

I shudder as the questions and what-ifs roll through my brain on repeat. I make quick work of brushing my teeth and then swish with mouthwash. Once I'm done, I find my shoes and then walk out to the living room to meet Ryan again.

He's scrolling through his phone, but looks up when he hears me enter. His eyes look me over appreciatively, and my body tingles where his gaze lingers. I'm wearing a simple white shirt and capri pants today, but Ryan looks at me like I'm in the sexiest little back dress I own. I feel incredibly wanted, desired. My mind floods with images of him hovering above me, moving inside me. I flush and look down at the floor, a smile playing on the corners of my lips.

Ryan stands and grabs his keys, leading us down to his car. We stop at the rental place, and Ryan gets out to go talk to the teller inside. He comes bounding out a few minutes later and leads me to a decent-sized pickup truck.

I don't have much stuff still at Mark's, but Ryan's little sedan is not going to cut it. We both hop in and cumulatively take a steadying deep breath before he starts the engine and heads toward Mark's house.

The cabin of the truck is silent as Ryan pulls into the driveway and shifts the vehicle into park. He stares at the house for a brief moment before reaching into his pocket and pulling out his phone. Sending a quick text, he puts it away and turns to look at me. Ryan's green eyes are grave as he reaches out a hand and trails the back of his fingers over my cheek.

"Ready?" he asks me gently. I nod, lacking any type of enthusiasm.

All I need to do is go inside and get my stuff. It should be easy. Then I'll be done with Mark and done with this chapter of my life. I plan on moving forward without a single glance back.

I can't believe I let myself live that way for so long. But no one ever thinks about their future and sees an abusive partner. I didn't want this. I didn't ask for this.

I let myself observe the house. This was supposed to be my home, where I lived with my husband and built a family. Now it represents a jail sentence.

"Let's just get this over with," I mutter to Ryan, still looking at the house. I push open the truck door and hop out.

Ryan follows my lead over to the garage door, where I flip open the hatch and punch in the code. Hopefully, Mark didn't change it on me. The garage door whines in protest when I press the enter button and then rises slowly. I reach for Ryan's hand, gripping it in mine as I watch the garage open.

It's empty. Mark's gone.

I breathe a sigh of relief, and Ryan gives my hand a squeeze. Together, we walk through the garage and then into the house. The place is dark and quiet. It's almost eerie. My eyes roam over every surface, looking for anything out of the ordinary. I'm on edge.

The kitchen is immaculately clean. It looks like it hasn't been used, though the garbage can next to the counter is over-flowing with carryout and fast-food bags. The couch in the living room has a rumpled blanket and a few pillows scattered on the floor. It looks as if Mark's been sleeping there. His safe is bolted into the wall next to the TV stand, shut and locked.

The warmth of Ryan's palm on my own gives me the courage I need to get through the first central part of the house. I trek on toward the bedrooms where my things are going to be. My first goal is to empty out the master bedroom, where I had been in the process of moving my stuff to.

Because I was supposed to marry him. Until I didn't.

The giant king bed in the master bedroom looks lonely, like it hasn't been slept in for months. Pillows are fluffed perfectly, and there isn't a single wrinkle on the comforter. It leaves a sour feeling in my stomach, and I turn my eyes elsewhere. The tops of the dressers are organized, and the room faintly still smells like Mark's cologne.

I let go of Ryan's hand and open a few drawers, pulling the clothes out and throwing them onto the bed to pack them. Ryan stands in the doorframe, watching me. He looks around the room but doesn't say anything. It takes me only ten minutes, and then I send Ryan out to grab some boxes and bags from the trucks. While he's getting those, I hurry into the guest bedroom and set to work, pulling out the rest of my personal items.

He returns a moment later with a frown etched on his face. My heart skips a beat. "What's wrong?" I ask.

Ryan shakes his head like it's nothing and sets the boxes down on the guest room floor, before going to lean in the frame of the door. "I'm not sure." He looks puzzled. I look back down at the pile of clothes I've been accumulating "I thought I saw—"

Ryan's sentence is cut off with a grunt, and then I hear a thump as he hits the ground. I spin around, my hands coming up to cover my mouth in a muffled scream. Mark stands over Ryan's crumpled body, his dark eyes observing the man on the ground, a gun held up in his hand. He's holding on to the barrel, exposing the base he used to hit Ryan over the head. He turns his attention to me, a sneer painting his face.

"*Fuck*, I've wanted to do that for a long time," he growls as he sticks the gun in the waistband of his pants.

"Ryan!" I scream as I drop to the ground and try to get to him. Mark catches me and hauls me back up to my feet.

His hand comes to cup my cheek, and he steps into the guest bedroom, getting in my personal space. Mark runs his nose along my jawline and takes a deep breath. "God, I've missed you, baby. Don't worry, you're safe now."

I struggle to get away from him, but his hands grip me tight.

"Let go of me!" I shout at him. I hear my pulse thrumming in my ears. "Ryan! Ryan, wake up!"

Ryan's still crumpled on the ground. Mark's blow to his head knocked him out cold. I'm on my own.

"Shhh," Mark soothes as he runs his thumb over my bottom lip. "It's okay. By the time he wakes up, we'll be long gone."

I turn my head away from his fingers and glare at him. "I'm not going *anywhere* with you."

Mark's face hardens, and he pulls me closer into him. "I don't think you really have a choice in the matter, baby. You are *mine*, remember?" He captures my mouth, and pries open my lips with his tongue, invading me, taking what's his.

I sink my teeth into his bottom lip in a desperate move to get him off of me. Mark pulls away with a roar, and his fingers come up to touch his mouth. When he pulls them away, there's a spot of blood. He gives a dark chuckle, and then spins me around so that my back is pressed against his front. His thick forearm comes across my chest, holding me captive, as his other hand comes up to cup my throat. Tilting my head back, he exposes my neck to him.

"I was wondering when you'd come back," he whispers in my ear. His warm breath against my skin makes my skin crawl. "I've been waiting for you."

"How'd you know we were here?" I gasp, his hand slightly pressing into my windpipe, making it difficult to breathe, but not entirely blocking my airway.

"Hmm," he murmurs. "Security cameras. I got the notification the minute you showed up here, and I hurried right over. I didn't want to risk missing you."

I thrash my body, trying to break free from his grip. My eyes dart to Ryan, but he's still out cold. Seeing him helpless like that makes my stomach churn, and I have to tear my eyes away. Mark continues to speak nonsense, telling me that he knew I would return to him and that everything will be okay. My mind is spinning, trying to think of an escape route. First thing's first, I need to get out of his grip.

I think back to how I escaped when the instructors grabbed me during my self-defense class. This was why I took that course in the first place. It's time to utilize what I learned. I take a deep breath, ignoring the slimy words Mark's muttering to me and focusing on my body's position in relation to his.

In one swift move, I throw my heel back, connecting with Mark's shin. It doesn't even faze him. He continues to keep a tight grip on me. I squeeze my eyes shut and pray to whatever God or deity is listening to please let us get through this. I muster up all my strength and raise my heel again, coming down on his foot as hard as I possibly can.

Mark startles, just enough for me to wiggle away from him. I turn to face him and swing my fist, connecting with his jaw. He groans in pain and clutches at his face. While he's distracted, I aim another hit at his gut, hitting my target with enough power to force him to double over.

"You fucking *bitch*," he growls, bent over at the waist.

I see my opportunity, and I take it, leaping over Ryan's crumpled form and running out to the living room. I'm in the living room, the front door in my sights, when he grabs my wrist, forcing me to spin around and face him. Mark pushes me against the wall harshly, and I cry out when my spine hits the drywall. The force momentarily knocks the wind out of me.

"You really shouldn't have done that," he grits out. "Looks like you forgot how to behave like a good little wife. Do I need to remind you?"

"Let me go!" I spit at him and throw my hand out, connecting with his face. Flexing my fingers, I dig my nails into his cheek.

He roars in pain and lets go of my neck, his hand flying up

to grip my fingers clawing at his skin. With an incredible force of strength, he throws me away from him. I stay on my feet when he throws me, but then lose my balance as I'm trying to right myself. As I crash to the ground, my hands sprawl around me.

When I hear Mark's thunderous footsteps coming up behind me, I scramble onto my back, not wanting to have him out of my sights. I push myself into a sitting position and crowd into a corner in the living room. Making myself small, I curl my knees up into my chest.

Mark's face is murderous as he glares at me. He reaches behind him and removes the gun from his waistband. As he pulls the slide back, the unmistakable noise of the bullet moving into place sends a wave of panic throughout my whole body, and then he aims it at me. My stomach flips like I'm on a roller-coaster, heart kicking into overdrive as I stare into the barrel.

"Mark," I whisper, defeated. I raise my hands in surrender.

"You think you can get away with making a fool of me like that?" he snarls. "I *love* you, Izabel. I've given you everything you could possibly hope for, and *this* is how you repay me?" Mark takes a step closer, keeping the gun trained on my face.

"Please," I plead with him. I'm scouring my mind for something I could use as leverage. My eyes dart around, looking for a weapon. But I have nothing.

"Why?" he asks, anger etched on his face. "Why should I let you go? You are *mine*."

Tears stream down my cheeks, and I squeeze my eyes shut. "I'm sorry, please, Mark. Please, please don't," I sob.

"You did this to yourself," he says darkly.

"Stop!"

I snap my head to the entryway to the living room. Ryan stands there, his hands balled into fists and his green eyes wide on the situation he just walked into. He takes a slightly wobbly step toward us, and Mark quickly turns the gun to point at him. With the weapon no longer directed at me, I scramble to my feet, another sob escaping my lips as I do so.

Ryan holds out a hand to me, his eyes never leaving Mark or the gun directed at him. I reach out and grab Ryan's hand as he shuffles me behind him, shielding me with his body. I grip onto his shirt, feeling his strong back beneath my fingers.

"You," Mark spits at him, holding the gun firmly, aiming at Ryan's head. "This is all your fault."

I can't see Ryan's face, but I'm sure he's glaring at my ex-fiancé with malice. "I'm the one you want. You leave her out of it."

Ryan takes a small side-step toward the connecting garage door. I go with him, still firmly gripping his shirt.

"Oh, trust me," Mark grits. "Nothing would make me happier than to get rid of you. You've been a nuisance in my life from the very first time we met."

Ryan takes another step.

"Then what are you waiting for?" he taunts Mark. Then he takes another step. "I'm right here. Or are you too scared, Marky Mark? You're not going to do it."

Another step.

I peek around Ryan's body and see Mark's eyes flare. "I'm not *scared.*"

One more step. Mark follows the movement, keeping the gun trained on Ryan.

"I think you are. You're in way over your head," Ryan says. His words are firm but calm. Meanwhile, I feel like I may pass out any second. My fingers shake while still gripping into his t-shirt.

"Ryan, what are you doing?" I ask incredulously. I can't

believe he's so brazenly poking the bear. We need to focus on getting out of here.

"Just do it and be done." Ryan ignores me and continues taunting Mark. Nausea swirls in my belly, and my whole body shakes with uncontrollable adrenaline. Ryan takes one more step, and I see I have a clear pathway to the door. Three strides are all it would take.

Ryan's plan becomes clear. He's trying to distract, keep Mark occupied while he gives me a clear shot to the door so that Mark can't get me. His body stands between me and Mark, fully intercepting Mark's path.

Ryan reaches behind his back and finds my fingers. He pries me off of him and then softly instructs me, "Go. Now."

"I don't want to leave you," I cry into his back, pressing my face against him. My muscles are coiled so tightly, I'm not sure if I could run even if I wanted to. Which I don't. I want to stay *here*, with Ryan.

"Bells, I love you. Now go," Ryan urges, taking a step backward, pushing me toward the door.

"Do *not* take a single move," Mark growls. I squeeze my eyes shut, a sob escaping me.

"GO!" Ryan now yells at me. He doesn't give me an option as his hand shoves me into motion.

Tears blur my vision, but I move. Though I stumble a few times, I sprint as fast as I can toward the door, throwing it open and rushing out into the fresh air. I run and run, not stopping even when I hear the gunshot echo through the house.

Chapter 35

Ryan

I watch Izabel run out the door, a brief moment of relief gripping my heart the minute she disappears. But that feeling is rapidly squashed by Mark's sneering voice reminding me of the imminent danger I'm in.

Mark told Izabel he wouldn't hesitate to kill me, and now we're here. I face him head on, hoping that I come off braver than I'm feeling right now. Time seems to slow down as my brain jolts into overdrive.

I don't want to die. Especially not now that Izabel and I have finally found our footing together. Distantly, I think about what will happen to my family—my mom will be devastated. Thalia, though young, will still feel the lasting effects of this for the rest of her life.

No, I don't want to die. I won't.

Not today.

"You've had this coming," Mark growls at me and moves his finger to the trigger. The fear coursing through my body amplifies, and I know if I don't act now, everything will be over.

Everything happens in a split second. I see Mark's finger

flex, and I lunge myself off to the right as the gun fires. Searing pain shoots through the side of my arm as I fall onto the ground. I don't take the time to observe the damage, but keep my eye on Mark.

He's glaring at me, his expression even more murderous than it was before. Then he laughs humorlessly. "You're a real piece of shit, you know that, Ryan?" He raises the gun to me again as he steps closer.

I push to my feet, ignoring the pain in my shoulder. We're facing off, but I don't offer him any type of reaction at this point.

"The *King of Bennett*," Mark taunts me. "Everything always works out for you, doesn't it. You got the career, the job, the girl." He shakes his head, strands of dark hair falling over his forehead. "And what do I get? My fiancée left me at the altar because you manipulated her into thinking she loves you."

"I'm not the manipulator here," I finally say, hoping my voice comes out firmly rather than shaky.

"I HAD IT ALL!" Mark shouts. He's unhinged. His face is red with emotion as he shakes the gun in my face. "Everything was perfect. After so many years of trying to show her how perfect we are together, I finally had Izabel. Everything was going the way it was supposed to until *you* showed up again, and now I have nothing. NOTHING." He laughs again, a manic sound. "This is all your fault."

"Put the gun down," I instruct as I take a step toward him. I raise my hands as if in surrender, hoping he doesn't see the way they're trembling. "And we can figure this out."

"Take another step, Miller. I dare you," Mark sneers and returns the gun to my face. I freeze as I stare down the dark abyss of the barrel. Apprehension crashes through me with the wild glint in his eye as he moves his finger to the trigger once again.

My arm aches and my head is throbbing from where he clocked me over the head earlier, but I shove it down. I can't let myself get distracted. "Mark, put the gun down."

His eyes narrow at me, and then he shakes his head, his nose wrinkling up in disgust. "I *hate* you, Ryan Miller. You've ruined my life. I don't even have anything left to live for. She's gone. You win."

"I didn't *win* anything," I say.

But Mark does not hear it. He's still shaking his head. Tears spill out of his eyes, and he finally drops the gun away from me, but then raises it to his temple. "You won. You always win."

A new type of dread settles deep in my gut and my blood turns to ice.

I observe Mark, our eyes locking. Body thrumming, I ready myself to move. He's not going to do it, but I can't take that risk. My leg muscles coil together as I get ready to lunge. Sirens echo faintly in the distance. Mark hesitates for only a second when he hears them, giving me the perfect opportunity to make my move.

I throw myself at Mark, catching his arm holding the gun to his head, and maneuver it away from his body. The shot goes off, a chain reaction to me grabbing him. Mark howls out as I tackle him to the ground and kick the gun out of his hand. We tussle and fight until I bring my fist back, clocking him in the jaw. Mark is stunned for long enough for me to scramble off of him and grab the gun. I release the magazine and pull back the slide to quickly remove the bullet from the chamber. I tuck both safely into my pocket while I place the gun in my belt.

A loud exhale escapes me, and I slouch against the wall. It's over. Mark is still sprawled on the floor, lying there without moving. I hear the sirens shut off, and then car doors slamming outside.

The police shout their arrival, and I push myself up, staggering over to the door and slowly pulling it open. I hear guns cocking and aiming at me as I step out into the light and put my hands up behind my head in surrender. My eyes immediately latch on to Izabel, who is collapsed against the grass.

Her face is a mess, blotchy and red from crying. Still, I see the relief overwhelm her at my appearance, and she collapses against the elderly woman next to her.

The police officers move up to me and pull my hands behind my back, securing my wrists in handcuffs. I hiss through my teeth as the forced movement sends shoots of pain through my injured arm. "There's an unloaded gun in my waistband," I explain to the one who's locking me up. "The magazine and spare bullet are in my pocket. The man in the house tried to murder my girlfriend and me."

"Do you know of any other weapons?" the cop asks me as he removes the gun from my belt.

"No, but there's a safe in the living room. There might be another one in there," I tell him. The safe is what tipped me off that something wasn't right in the first place. When I was bringing the boxes to Izabel, I noticed that the door was wide open, and I could have sworn it wasn't that way when we first walked in. But before I had gotten the chance to explain to Izabel, Mark clonked me over the head and everything went black.

The police maneuver into the house in their tactical formation, and my eyes go back to Izabel. I can see she's a mess. I give her a small nod, trying to let her know everything will be okay. She falls into another round of hysterics, and all I want is to go to her. I need to feel her in my arms, know that she's safe. Know that I still have the other half of my heart on this earth with me.

"You get shot?" one of the cops asks me, motioning towards my arm.

"I guess," I say blandly as I look down at my arm. Sure

enough, there's blood seeping through the fabric of my shirt. A humorless laugh escapes as I stare down at my shoulder. That fucker shot me. "It burns something fierce. And he knocked me over the head with a gun."

Even though I know the words I say are an accurate depiction of what happened in that house, it still feels surreal. Like something out of a soap opera TV show. How did this become my life?

He moves toward me and rolls up the sleeve of my shirt. There, through the belly of my deltoid muscle, is a clear path. It's superficial, so the bullet didn't pierce, just grazed by.

"We'll have the paramedics take a look at you."

I sit there, letting the adrenaline settle in my body. As the minutes tick by, my shoulder starts to ache more and more. My body trembles uncontrollably and my head pounds. Finally, a paramedic comes by and patches me up. He cleans the wound, determines it isn't anything serious, and then throws a bandage over it, giving me brief instructions on when to change it. Then he does a quick head exam, using a light to check my pupil response, and asks me a ton of questions about symptoms before concluding that I don't have a severe concussion.

The paramedics gather their things together and then pile into the ambulance before driving off. The cops inside the house make their appearance again, pushing Mark ahead of them. He's handcuffed as well, and he shoots me a glare as he walks by. They direct him to one of their patrol cars and secure him in the backseat. The officer tears out of the neighborhood, taking Mark with him.

"You can let your guy go," one female cop says to the officer babysitting me.

The officer helps me stand up and then unlocks the cuffs from around my wrists. I rub at the skin and offer him thanks.

He pats me on my good shoulder and tells me to hang tight. My eyes find Izabel again, who stands when she sees me free.

Izabel runs at me full speed, and then launches herself into my arms as soon as I'm close enough. Her legs wrap around my waist, and she locks her ankles above my hips. I hold her tightly to me, closing my eyes and breathing a sigh of relief that she's not hurt. Izabel's face buries into my neck, and I feel my skin moisten with her tears.

After a few moments, I set her down on her feet, but she still grips onto my shirt, not wanting distance between us. My hands come up to cup her face, and I look her over, making sure she's not injured. Her sapphire blue eyes are still brimming with tears, but they sparkle at me. Moving my hands from her cheek up to her scalp, I thread my fingers through her hair. I smash our lips together, finally. Izabel moans into my mouth as if she's been yearning for this too.

As I kiss her, the world around us seems to disappear. All that matters now is that she's in my arms, and she's safe. Somehow, we made it through, and now, we can finally start our lives together.

Chapter 36

Izabel

THE ROOM IS SILENT AS I STARE AT MY THERAPIST. SHE looks right back at me, a soft smile on her lips. She hasn't pushed me yet this session, but she's there observing my every move, and I can tell she knows something's not right—the clock ticks by the seconds.

"Ryan and I are supposed to go to see my parents today," I finally tell her, fingering the threads of a blanket that is draped over the couch. "We're having a sit-down so I can break the news to them about what happened. The truth."

She gives me a sympathetic smile. "That sounds like it might not be the easiest conversation to have."

"Yeah, well, I think we have to have it. I mean, if I'm going to still be invited to family events like Thanksgiving or Christmas." I grimace, remembering how once upon a time, I had no qualms being open with my parents, but now the thought makes me want to vomit.

The therapist smiles and waits for me to continue as if she knows this is just a preamble.

"Do you have plans for Thanksgiving this year?" she asks me when I don't offer anything else up.

I pick at a piece of lint and nod my head. "Yeah, I think we're all going to Ryan's parents' house. My family will be over as well."

"That sounds like a lot of fun. Things must be going well, then."

I take a deep breath and shake my head. "I just keep feeling like I'm waiting for the second shoe to drop."

"What do you mean by that?"

"It just seems like it was too easy," I correct my statement when she raises an eyebrow. "I mean, I can't believe it's all over. I still keep waiting for Mark to show up at work. Or jump me when I turn a corner." I take a deep breath. "I'm terrified that he's going to hurt Ryan or me, or any of the people I love."

Mark was able to pay the amount that was posted as bail. At his first arraignment hearing, Mark pleaded "not guilty," of course, though the judge still hit him with a temporary order of protection so he couldn't contact me. And we haven't heard anything since then. Somehow, that's even more frightening than if he were still lurking around.

"How are your nightmares?"

I scoff under my breath. How are they? They're terrible. For the past seven weeks, ever since the showdown at Mark's, I've woken up each night to Ryan shaking me awake, trying to convince me that everything's okay. Each night after I wake up drenched in a cold sweat, he wraps me up tightly in his arms and whispers that he's here, he's got me. It takes a few moments of me lying there against him, his hand running over my hair, to fully recenter myself.

It's always the same dream.

Mark holding a gun to Ryan's head, and Ryan telling me to run, go. I turn to leave, but then the gun goes off, and I spin back around. Ryan's crumpled on the ground. I know he's dead, but there's no gunshot. Then Mark turns the gun around on me.

That's usually when Ryan wakes me up. The searing pain of him dying in my dreams has me screaming at the top of my lungs and thrashing through the sheets. It's gotten to the point where I'm afraid to go to sleep at night because I know within a few hours I'll be screaming my head off. And I feel bad for waking Ryan up every night.

Ryan's started developing dark circles under his eyes, and I hate that they're because of me. He always soothes me when I apologize, saying he's glad he's here with me. That I have nothing to apologize for.

"I still get them," I tell my therapist. "Every night."

"Do you think part of that is not being back at work? Do you feel like you're missing a purpose?"

I shake my head. "No, that hasn't bothered me as much as I thought it would. I think it helps to be back to a regular routine. And," I pause, taking a deep breath, "I don't know. Everything in my life feels different now, but sometimes it's not in a good way."

"Izabel," my therapist begins, and then hesitates. My gut tightens with anxiety.

"Just say it."

"Have you ever thought about finding closure with Mark?" She hurries on when I frown. "I know we discussed that moving your items out would serve as a sort of closure, but Mark has made such a strong negative impact on your life. I'm not terribly surprised that the idea of simply moving on isn't working for you."

I bunch my eyebrows together. "So then what would you suggest?"

She shrugs noncommittally. "I can't really answer that for

you. Closure can come in many different forms; it just depends on what you need to close this chapter."

The buzzer on her alarm clock goes off, signaling that our time is up. My therapist scratches something on a piece of paper and then hands it to me. "Here, I would highly recommend making an appointment with a primary care doctor to get something to aid with your sleep. You need to get some good rest. I think we're all set up for next week, so I look forward to meeting with you then."

She hands me the referral, and then I shuffle out of her office. Ryan's waiting for me in the waiting room, just like he has every session since I've started. He's still scrolling through emails—he tells me 70% of his job is email correspondence, the other 30% is paperwork. Green eyes meet mine when he hears me come out, and he offers me a crooked smile.

"How'd it go?" Ryan asks, standing up as I walk over to him.

First thing's first: I stand on my tiptoes once I reach him and press my lips to his in a scorching kiss. Ryan sighs happily as his hand snakes around my waist.

I pull back with a smile. "Hi."

"Hey, pretty girl," he says, smirking before leaning down and pecking me again. When he pulls back, one eyebrow is raised. "So?"

I shrug and hitch my purse over my shoulder. "It was okay. She gave me a lot to think about."

"Good things?"

I shrug. "I'm not really sure. She thinks I need closure."

There's no sense in hiding anything from Ryan. He's seen me at my best and at my worst, and all the spots in between. I give him the rundown of our therapy sessions each time. He's the protecting, providing type. And by letting him in on where

I'm at mentally, I know that he feels like we're on even ground. He can be exactly what I need him to be.

"Closure," he mutters softly. "How do you do that?"

"I'm not sure," I say again. "I guess I need to figure it out."

He leans forward and kisses my cheek, before pulling my purse off my arm and shouldering it himself. "Well, whatever you need, I'll do it."

My stomach flutters, and I grin at him. "I love you."

Ryan looks at me tenderly, reaching up to tuck a strand of loose hair behind my ear. "I love you too, Bells. More than you could ever know."

He offers me his hand, and I take it, holding tightly to him as we walk down to the car. "Well, you ready to do this? Face the parents?"

My stomach tightens, and I clench my jaw, feeling the joint pop from the added tension.

"I don't know if I'll ever be ready, but I know it's what we need to do. I'll go with you on one condition," I say, making my voice sound light. Ryan's lips twitch as he waits for the punch-line. "I could really use a chocolate milkshake to cheer me up."

He tosses his head back with a laugh, and then drapes his arm across my shoulder, pulling my body close into his. "I think I can make that happen, just for you, Bells."

Once we get settled in the car, Ryan finds a McDonald's to drive through. He buys me my large chocolate milkshake and some fries after I insisted. Then he gets a double cheeseburger for himself and an unsweet tea for us to share.

I don't waste any time being polite; I take a big sip of the milkshake and moan happily.

"Good?" Ryan teases me.

"This is exactly what I needed. A little confidence booster," I say, looking at the milkshake cup for a second before popping off the top. I reach for two or three fries and then dip it in the chocolatey goodness before popping them in my mouth. Ryan makes a noise next to me, and I turn on him.

"Don't knock it till you try it, Ryno!" I reach for another few fries, dip them in the shake, and then offer them up. He looks wary for a second before accepting. He eats it and doesn't spit it out, which is a good sign. "Well?"

His eyes dart to mine before looking out the windshield. I can see he's really trying to cover up a smirk on his face. "Okay. It wasn't *as* gross as I'd thought it would be."

I laugh and then hand him another fry, which he takes without argument. My chest feels warm and bubbly. We're just sitting in the drive-thru, but everything feels normal. As if the last few years never happened, and it's only been Ryan and me this whole time. I often forget that aside from being the man I was in love with all those years ago, he was one of my favorite people to be around. Ryan could make me laugh easier than anyone else on the planet.

I missed it. I missed him.

As soon as he pulls into the driveway of my parents' house, my body freezes. I stare up at the house I grew up in, feeling an unmeasurable amount of distance.

I'm a completely different girl than I used to be when I lived in the second room upstairs. Anxiety bursts through me as I wonder if my parents will still love me the same way they did before I let all of this happen.

Ryan helps me get out of the car when we arrive. Ever the gentleman, he likes to hold the door open for me and then takes my hand right away so we can walk up to the front door together. Before he rings the doorbell, he tugs on my hand, pulling me into him. I don't hesitate, wrapping my arms around his middle, and burying my face into his strong chest.

"I'm scared," I admit against his t-shirt.

His hands tighten around me. "I know. But your parents love you. They're going to be on your side."

I take a deep breath and then let go of him. Bracing myself, I nod, and Ryan reaches forward, pressing the doorbell. It takes no time at all for the front door to be thrown open and the warm smile of my dad to greet me.

"Izabel! Ryan! So glad you two made it. Come in, come in." He opens the door for us to step into the foyer. A moment later, my mom hurries into the hall and wraps me in a hug.

"Oh, sweetie, we were so glad you called. We've missed you so much."

That sentiment, coming from my mother, and the comforting feel of her arms wrapped around me, is enough to break the dam. Before I can stop it, tears are streaming down my face. She grips me tighter, knowing that I need her strength right now.

The rest of the world slips away as I hold on to my mother for dear life. Her hand soothingly runs up and down my back as I cry against her. Her calm words echo in my ears as the crushing reality of everything I've been through in the last few months—years—suffocates me.

When I finally have myself pulled together, I swipe at my face, wiping away the evidence. My mother studies me closely as I gather myself, waiting for me to break the ice. My father steps next to her, his arm wrapping around my mom's waist as they wait patiently for me to share my truth.

"Mom, Dad," I say, my voice breaking as I address them. "There's something we need to talk about."

The minute we cross the threshold into our own home, the weight of the events of the day seems to amplify tenfold. My muscles tighten, but my body feels weak. I keep replaying the memories of how my parents reacted to everything I shared with them. There was a symphony of emotions all raining down at once—shock, disbelief, heartbreak, anger, helplessness.

All of that sticks to me like something I'll never be able to get off. I desperately want to shower, to erase the stains of this reality, but the exhaustion is too much.

"I'm gonna..." I point toward our bedroom. "I'm just gonna go lay down for a little bit."

Ryan gives me a sympathetic smile and steps forward, cupping my cheeks before giving me a tender kiss. "I'm so proud of you, Bells."

I close my eyes and allow myself to soak up his love for a few precious moments. When he releases me, I shuffle into the bedroom and collapse on our bed, yanking the covers over myself and burying deep into the comfort of the blankets.

I don't even realize that I fall asleep—it comes fast and hard, exhaustion overwhelming any other possible function.

When I jolt awake, it takes me a moment to orient myself. How long was I sleeping? Where am I, even?

From down the hall, I can hear the familiar murmur of Ryan's deep voice. I throw back the covers and pad down the hallway, wondering who he's talking to.

"Yeah, Mom, we're trying," Ryan says. I freeze outside the door frame to the office where he can't see me, leaning against the hallway wall and listening to his conversation. His voice sounds tired and worn out. "She's doing okay. Every day is a little bit better."

He falls silent as he listens to whatever his mom says on the other line.

"I know.

I step into the door frame, and rest my shoulder against one edge, looking in on him. He's got his head buried in his hands and his broad shoulders rise and fall with deep breaths. Even distressed, Ryan Miller is a sight to behold. I can't believe this man is all mine. That I get to build my life with him. The path was difficult, but all that matters is that it led me here.

As if he can hear me thinking about him, Ryan glances up at me. He's startled only for a second before a content smile curves on his lips. "What are you doing?"

"Just admiring the view," I tease him. "You're adorable, you know that?"

"*Adorable?*" He scoffs. "You could have gone with any other word."

I bite my bottom lip between my teeth and let my eyes roam over him. The apprehension surges to the front of my mind again. "Were you talking to your mom just now?"

He leans back in his chair and nods. Suddenly, he looks even more tired than he did a few seconds ago. Maybe Ryan needs a nap too. "Yeah, she wanted to know how you were doing. How *we* were doing."

"Did you tell her I'm still a trainwreck?" I ask him, trying to put on a teasing tone.

Ryan doesn't laugh or even smile at my joke. "Of course not." He sighs and then swivels in his chair before patting his knee. "Come here, Bells."

I do as he asks, closing the distance between us and settling myself on his lap. His arms circle around my waist and he holds me close, leaning over and pressing a kiss to the side of my neck. I close my eyes, relishing the contact and wrap my arms around his neck.

"I just want to be better," I whisper.

"We'll get there. I know we will."

"Sometimes it just feels impossible," I say. A tear leaks out of the corner of my eye and down my cheek. I swipe it away before he can see it.

"What can I do? Tell me and I'll do it. Anything."

This is something Ryan's said to me over and over the last few weeks. I know he feels helpless a lot of the time, trying to be supportive without overbearing when I need space.

Sometimes I feel selfish, knowing that Ryan went through trauma that day just the same as I did. Yet still it seems that I'm always the one needing more attention, more care, always *more*.

"I don't know how to answer that question, Ryan. I think it's just going to take time," I tell him. It's not the answer either of us wants, but I think it's the truth.

He's quiet for a moment. His hand trails up and down my back, finally settling on my hip. "I just want you to know how much I admire your strength, and your will to keep going through each day."

I swallow thickly, trying not to cry more at Ryan's tender words.

He presses a kiss on my forehead. "We're going to get through this, Bells. I promise you. And we'll do it together."

Chapter 37

Izabel

"Bells, wake up," Ryan murmurs in my ear before pressing feather-light kisses against my cheeks, my eyelids, my mouth. I groan and clutch the pillow I'm holding closer to me.

"I don't want to," I complain.

I hear Ryan's throaty chuckle from above me. He climbs up onto the bed and hovers over my body. Slowly, he peels back the covers until I'm not underneath them anymore. As he runs his hand up the length of my spine, and through my thin t-shirt, I can feel the heat of his touch.

"I've got a surprise for you," he taunts me. I peek one eye open at him, making him laugh again. "Come on, Bells, up and at 'em. I've already packed a bag for you."

"What? Why are you home from work so early? Where are we going?" I ask, the questions rolling out of me. I'm still groggy from my nap.

I snuggle the side of my face into my pillow, take a glance at the clock, and then do a double-take. How is it already one o'clock? I was just planning on taking a late-morning cat nap, and here we are, three hours later. With a sigh, I struggle up into a sitting position. Ryan is still on the bed, and he offers me a hand to support myself.

"I thought we could get away for a long weekend. We both need a break, so I took off early today. What do you think?"

I stretch my arms up above my head, feeling the muscles in my back and sides protest with the movement. "I think that sounds nice. Where were you thinking?"

"Probably up towards the mountains," he tells me, bouncing off the bed and getting my shoes for me. "I only got a few days off, so we can't go much farther than that."

I nod. "I love the mountains. Are we leaving right now?"

Ryan's green eyes shine as they observe me. He shoots me a wry smile. "If that's okay with you?"

I nod again and then run into the bathroom to freshen up before we go. When I wander out of our bedroom, I see Ryan standing next to our bags on the floor. He's holding my coat for me to slip into. It's February now, and pretty chilly outside. Thankfully, Cedar Ridge is far enough south that we have more mild winters, but it's definitely not tank top weather these days.

I slip my arms into the coat and secure the buttons around my middle, feeling very cozy. Ryan straightens the collar on my jacket and then pulls me into him, pressing a steamy kiss on my lips. I feel a surge of electricity run through me until it hits my toes, and I shiver. He pulls back, making me sigh in frustration at the distance now between us. Giving me an understanding purse of his lips, he opens the door for me.

He already has the car running, so I settle in the front seat while he situates our bags in the trunk. Once he slides into the car, he fiddles with the dash for a second, setting up his road trip music. I frown and look at him.

"How long of a drive is this?" Usually, to get up to the

Smokies, it's around an hour and a half to two hours, that's doable.

"Not bad, about four hours," he tells me. "We're actually up in the mountains, so a lot of it is back roads. Don't worry, I packed the Dramamine and ginger chews in case you start feeling gross."

I smile at him affectionately. Ryan, always thinking ahead, hands the small pill bottle over, and I take one pill now preemptively, stashing the bag of ginger chews nearby just in case. Hopefully, this pill will keep me one step ahead of the motion sickness.

We drive, singing along to his playlist, and making mindless small talk. My life has been relatively quiet since I'm not working right now, so Ryan tells me more about some of the projects he and Josie are working on. A lot of what he says goes over my head, just like it always used to, but I still listen with a smile on my face. I could listen to Ryan talk for hours about absolutely nothing. He's always so passionate about everything, and the deep timbre of his voice is soothing to my senses.

We stop twice for bathroom breaks, but then we hit the road right after that. I'm leaning my head against the window, watching the trees fly by when Ryan pulls off the main highway onto the back roads. I sit up with a questioning look.

"Are we almost there?" I ask him, hopeful.

He turns his head and winks at me. "Almost."

I lean across the center console and rest my head against his shoulder. Ryan twists enough to press a side-kiss onto my forehead. The roads get windy, and I find myself sitting back up straight and closing my eyes, so I don't have to see the car's motion.

Ryan catches my hand across the console and gives me a reassuring squeeze. He tilts my hand and then straightens out my fingers. "That's a pretty color. Did you just get them done?"

I peek one eye open to look at the fresh coat of nail polish. "Yes, I went with Jules last night. She practically dragged me out of the house to go with her. I guess she has a conference this weekend, so she wanted to go before then."

"Hm, looks nice," Ryan muses before turning his attention back to driving. He fiddles with my fingers for a while, and I close my eyes again, trying my best to not get nauseous. Thankfully, the Dramamine seems to be helping, but I unwrap a ginger chew and pop it into my mouth for added comfort. The spicy flavor overwhelms my senses but eases my stomach.

Finally, after another hour or so, Ryan slows the car down to a stop. I sit up, blinking my eyes back into focus, and look around. Immediately, I recognize where we are. My mouth drops open when I lock eyes on our destination just in front of the car.

"Wha—How?" I ask, flabbergasted.

Ryan smirks wryly, before getting out of the vehicle and jogging around to my side. He opens my door and offers me a hand, which I gratefully take. I can't take my eyes off of the little cabin standing before me. It's different, new, but still the same. It is unmistakably *our* cabin.

My heart starts beating wildly in excitement as I turn to Ryan in shock and ask again, "How?"

"I bought it," he says proudly, standing up straighter. "Mac passed away about a year and a half ago. I saw the ad for it online, and I jumped on it as quickly as I could. Josie helped me completely redesign the architecture."

"But it looks the same," I whisper as my eyes trace over the outline of the cabin that completely changed my life.

"From the outside," Ryan teases. "But, the inside is suitable for occupancy now."

I take a few steps towards the cabin, wanting to see more. I glance back at Ryan, and he motions me forward, a broad smile on his face.

The cabin is made of the same cherry-wood that the old one was. But where Mac's cabin was barely standing, this new cabin looks sturdy. Like it was built to last. The windows aren't shattered, and the door seems wholly attached to its hinges. I can see that Ryan expanded the cabin off the backside, hopefully giving it more than just one main room.

I take the few steps up to the porch and look around. The porch was extended to wrap around the front of the house. Underneath one of the front windows are two rocking chairs, and off to the other side is a pile of neatly stacked firewood.

I turn to Ryan, who has come to stand right next to me. He places his hand at the small of my back, letting me know of his presence. "What do you think?"

"Can we go inside?" I ask him. My blood is humming with anticipation to see the interior.

"Of course," he says, stepping forward and pulling the screen door open to unlock the front door. He throws it wide open for me to go inside first.

I scurry inside and pause the minute I'm in the main room. The cabin definitely got a facelift. The integrity of the old one is still here, but this floor plan is so much more functional. The front door opens directly into the living room, where there's a cozy-looking couch and a TV. My eyes land on the original wood-burning fireplace, cleaned and ready to use.

When I turn my head to the right, I see the kitchen, exactly where it was before but so much bigger, with a full-size refrigerator and a modern stove lining the far wall. The kitchen sink is massive, a window placed right above it to look outside while washing dishes.

"I can't believe you did all this," I breathe as I spin in a circle, taking it all in.

Ryan's still standing by the front door, watching with amusement. "Do you want to go see the rest of the house?"

I nod fervently, and then follow him as he heads down the hall. I peek in the first bathroom, then the two extra bedrooms. One has a queen-size bed in it, and the other is set up as an office. I stare at the office space and feel a smile play on my lips as I imagine it set up as a playroom or a child's bedroom.

My head spins as plans start running through my mind. We won't live here full time; it's much too far from both our jobs. But as I look around, I can picture long weekends, summers, holidays. I let myself dream for a moment, and I feel a bubble of happiness settle in my stomach.

"Want to see our room?" Ryan asks, coming up behind me. He presses a kiss into my neck and wraps his hands around my waist. I nod, and he takes my hand, leading me to the farthest bedroom.

I cover my mouth when we cross the threshold of the master bedroom. Its rustic design makes it feel warm and welcoming. A large king bed with a wooden frame sits against the wall. The pillows on top of the bed are an off-white canvas and have the words *"They Lived Happily Ever After"* inked on them.

I turn to Ryan with an eyebrow raised, and he chuckles. "Josie did most of the decorating for us. Turns out, she's just as good at designing the insides as she is at designing actual buildings." He's still holding my hand as he drags me across the room towards the far wall. "Except this was my idea," he says proudly, pointing to a wall hanging.

My jaw goes slack again as I take in the piece. It's a black shadow box with a familiar silver dog tag mounted inside. On it are the engraved words that ran through my head countless times in the earlier days of our relationship, *"Distance means so little when someone means so much.*" A heart is punched out of the right corner.

My chest tightens, and I bite my lower lip. As much as I love the sentiment, guilt laces through me, knowing that I lost my piece of the necklace. I don't look at him as I take a deep breath and prepare to admit my fault. "Ryan, I'm so sorry, but I lost—"

He cuts me off by clearing his throat. My eyes dart to his, and he's grinning mischievously. Ryan holds up his hand at my eye level and doesn't say a thing.

"Mine," I gasp. My silver engraved heart hangs over his hand, dangling off his fingers. I reach up for it and place it in my palm. "Where did you find this? I thought it was lost."

"Mark had stashed it in his safe at his house," Ryan tells me carefully. "I found it when I was going through, gathering the rest of your stuff."

"That bastard," I mutter as I run my thumb over the little heart. "I was so worried it was lost forever."

"I'm glad I found it. We were always meant to be together, and I think part of Mark knew that. He was doing everything he could to erase me from your life."

My eyes meet his, and I feel them sting with emotion. Ryan doesn't make it a habit to speak this candidly about the situation. His primary goal is to help us move forward, not be stuck in the past. But his words stir something in me that makes me so grateful. "Thank you, Ryan. For finding my necklace, and for building me a cabin, and for loving me in a way I never knew I could be loved," I say with a tearful chuckle. "You altered my life again. But I couldn't be happier."

Ryan brushes a few strands of hair off my face and gives me a content look. "I'd do anything for you, Bells." He presses a kiss to my forehead and then leans away. "Now, do you want to keep exploring a little? I need to run to the grocery store to get some food for the weekend. You can stay here and look around or come with me."

"There's no food here?" I ask him.

He chuckles. "Why don't you go look for yourself?"

I narrow my eyes at him but wander back out to the kitchen. Opening the fridge, I am met with absolutely nothing in there, not even ketchup. Then I turn to the cabinets, and all of them are empty too, except for one. I snort a laugh when I see a few stacks of canned peaches.

I turn around and glare at Ryan, who barks out a laugh at my expression. "You're hilarious."

"Couldn't resist, gorgeous," Ryan says as he wraps his arm around my shoulders. "So as you can see, we're going to starve if I don't make a grocery run. And while it was fun the first time, I really don't feel like reliving our past to that extreme."

I roll my eyes and shove him off of me. "Okay, fine. You go ahead to the store, and I'll stay here."

"You sure?"

"Yeah, Ry, I'll be fine. I don't feel like having to sit through those awful gravel roads again. I'll find a book or something to read," I tell him.

"Okay," he says. Then he presses a kiss to my cheek and tells me he's going to head out. I wave at him as he walks out the door, hearing him lock the deadbolt behind him before driving off.

Maybe it's because we're so far away from everything, or because I'm so used to being by myself these days, but I have no qualms about being here alone. This cabin is in the middle of nowhere. The only people who even know it's here are me, Ryan, and Josie, since she helped design it.

Besides, Mark's still out of the picture, and we haven't heard anything from him. I do my best to try to pretend that he's gone for good. At some point, I'm sure I'll get asked to testify whenever he gets scheduled for his hearing, but until then, I try to keep him as far from my thoughts as possible.

I do fine with that notion during the day, but still, at night, Mark often lurks. They're getting better. I only have them a few times a week versus every night. The medication I got from my new doctor helps, but I hate using it because it makes me groggy in the mornings.

Ryan is still as understanding as ever. He doesn't hesitate when I'm in the throes of a nightmare. He wraps me up in his arms, gently coaxing me back into consciousness, whispering soothing words. He'll hold me until the tremors subside, and my heart rate is back to normal, then he'll stay as close to me as possible throughout the remainder of the night so that I know he's there.

I honestly couldn't be any luckier than I am with him.

With that thought in mind, I look around the cabin, and that warm fuzzy feeling settles in my heart again. I can't believe Ryan did all this. I never thought I'd see this place again, but now it's ours. It feels like a part of us that was missing.

This is where it all started for the two of us. It makes sense that it would continue to be a part of our future. I imagine our kids being here, our friends, and family. There are years of memories that we'll make here that I can already picture.

I meander through the house and wind up in the office space. The room is made up of a desk with a chair, a computer setup, and a few bookshelves stacked with books. My eyes scan the spines of the books before I find one and pull it out of its place. I settle in on the living room couch and pull a blanket over me.

I get lost in the story, and before long, I hear the sound of a car door slamming outside. The front door unlocks, and Ryan comes barreling in with plastic grocery bags in his hands.

"Do you need help?" I ask him, sitting up straight.

He waves me off. "No, go back to your book. I got it."

I lean back into my seat and watch him. "Are you feeding an army?" I question when he comes in from his second trip, his hands full of bags again.

Ryan laughs. "I thought I'd stock up on some necessities while I was there. That way, we'll be a little better off next time." He sets the bags on the counter and starts putting things away. "I just got some simple things to cook this weekend: eggs, hamburger meat, chicken. And then the staples: eggs, bread, milk, cheese."

"Much better than fish and canned peaches for every meal," I tease him.

He winks at me. "Much. Not that I'm complaining. That was better than nothing at that point."

"I still don't like canned peaches," I say, my lips pulling up into a smile.

He grins back. "Me neither."

"Well, then I guess it's bad luck that our cabinet is full of them."

"I'll give them to a food bank. No reason to put perfectly good food to waste," Ryan says before going back to the groceries. "Go back to your book, Bells. I'll come bother you when I'm done."

I laugh under my breath, but adjust my legs and open my book to where I left off. Ryan mutters to himself while he works, and I continue to read with a smile on my face. After a while, Ryan comes over to stand in front of me. He kneels on the floor and looks at me with a warm smile. He's got one of his hands behind his back. I look at him, confused.

"I got something for you, Bells," he says, reaching for my hand.

Oh my God, is he going to propose?

The thought flashes through my mind, unwarranted, and

my heart skips a beat. My body lights up with excitement. We've skirted around the topic for weeks now, but I know Ryan plans to marry me at some point. He has always wanted me to be his wife.

Ryan turns my hand, palm side up, and then pulls whatever he's hiding from behind his back. He sets it in my hand, and my spirits drop.

"Surprise!" he exclaims with an elated expression.

In my hand rests a pint of Edy's slow-churned cookie dough ice cream. I try to keep my face as light as possible, feigning a look of surprise. But I can't help the feeling of disappointment that's settling in my gut.

Why do I even feel disappointed? I have everything I could ever want. I have an incredible man who fought for me with everything in him, who built me this stunning cabin, who bought me ice cream.

I guess I never realized how badly *I* wanted to be his wife until this moment.

I bottle up the emotion and shove it deep. There's no sense in marinating in this sour feeling. It will happen someday. It's not a matter of if, but when.

But until then, I guess I'll take what I can get because he's worth every second.

Chapter 38

Ryan

I WAKE UP TO AN EMPTY BED. MY HAND EXTENDS, LOOKING for Izabel's form next to me. When I don't find her, I sit up slightly, looking around the room. I'm met with silence. Sunlight is just barely streaming through the bedroom curtains. Maybe she got up early.

Miraculously, Izabel had no nightmares last night. She didn't make a single peep all night long. I hope, for once, she felt rested enough to get up early and enjoy the day. Tossing the covers back from the bed, I roll out, finding my sweatpants and slipping them on, not worrying about any boxers.

I pad my way out of the bedroom and into the main living area of the cabin. *There she is.* Izabel is curled up on the couch, her feet tucked underneath her. She's wrapped up in one of the fluffy blue robes from our bathroom, a mug of warm steaming liquid is in her hands. As I step closer, I see it's hot chocolate.

She doesn't hear me sneaking up behind her. Her eyes are gazing out the front window. As I look over that way, I can see why. Snow is gently falling from the sky in big flakes, dusting the ground, creating a cozy "Cabin-in-the-mountains" aesthetic.

I come up close behind Izabel and then lean over, pressing a sloppy kiss to her cheek. She startles a little bit and squeaks, a dribble of her hot cocoa slipping down the side of the mug.

"Heya, Bells," I say with a smile, capturing her lips with mine and parting her mouth so I can give her a proper good morning. Morning breath, be damned. Izabel tastes like chocolate.

"Hi, yourself," she responds against my mouth before slipping away from me.

I settle down again next to her, draping my arm across the back of the couch. Izabel sets her hot chocolate down on the side table and then snuggles in closer to my side. Her hand comes to rest on my thigh, and her head lolls against my chest. I wrap my arm tighter around her, drawing designs with my fingertips on the nape of her neck, making her shiver.

"You looked lost in thought. What's on your mind, pretty girl?"

"I was thinking about all the years we're going to spend here. All the good times we're going to have."

I tighten my hold. "I can't wait."

"I can picture it now. You and me waking up early in the morning and having coffee together out on the porch, listening to the trees rustle in the wind." She pauses and gives me a shy smile. "And maybe, someday, sharing it with our children—if that's what you want."

I don't like the way she tacked on the last bit so quickly, as if she's worried that's not something I want with her. I kiss her temple and give her a warm smile. *Of course*, I want to have children with her someday. Hopefully, someday soon. "Bells, you fill this home with as babies as you want. I'm more than willing to go along with the ride. Especially the part where we get to make them together." My teeth nibble at her earlobe suggestively.

She beams at me, her eyes twinkling. "Yes, that part is especially thrilling."

I let out a low rumble of a laugh and run my fingers through her hair. "So, what do you want to do today?"

"Just stay here," Izabel says, snuggling her face farther into my chest. She takes a deep breath and then melts against me. "I just want to do nothing with you. That sounds perfect."

"Okay," I say, a smile playing on my lips. "Let's do a whole lot of nothing, then."

And we sure excel at it. We snuggle on the couch for a while longer, musing about every little thing. Izabel asks me all kinds of questions about the cabin and the process with which it came to be what it is. I explained as best as I could, though I know a lot of my job goes over her head.

Then we get up and go take a shower together. I can't help myself from roaming over every inch of her body. I love every dip and curve, and I can barely get enough of her. We wash each other, paying careful attention to, and tenderly appreciating, every inch of one another. When I can't take it anymore, I gently spin her around so she's facing the tile wall. I guide her hands up on the tile, giving her something to brace herself on. Then I slip into her from behind, letting out a groan when I feel her heat surrounding me.

Izabel moans, feeling me taking her inch by inch. I sigh as I move within her. My hand traces down her spine, watching her back arch in an instinctual response. Then I move my hands around to her front. I roam over her abdomen and cup her breasts, pulling her back into me so my chest is pressed against her bare back. Then my hand snakes down to her thighs, and I expertly maneuver my fingers, doing precisely what she needs to go over the edge.

When we're both dried and fully satisfied, we dress in lounging clothes—sweatpants and long sleeve t-shirts. Then we snuggle back up on the couch and watch a few movies. Izabel makes us lunch, simple PBJs, and fruit.

Once the movie's over, I shut off the TV and turn my attention to my girl. She's tucked against my side, just like earlier. Her eyes are closed, leaving her expression peaceful. She has one hand curled up underneath her cheek, with her lips parted slightly. Light breath escapes her mouth in a steady rhythm, telling me she is very much asleep.

I softly brush my fingers over her hair and appreciate the fact that I get a life full of moments like this. As if reading my train of thought, my phone dings with a text message coming through. One quick glance tells me it's from Josie, confirming the plans I had laid out for this evening.

Carefully, so I don't jostle Izabel, I reach for my phone and type out a quick response to Josie. She lets me know everything is going according to plan, and she'll touch base with me later today when everything is all set. I put my phone down with a smile, feeling my heart twang, knowing that today is officially the first day of the rest of my life.

Once Bells wake up, we find a few board games to play. As we're battling over an intense game of checkers, Izabel hits me with those blue eyes. My body heats under her searing gaze, but I don't move, wondering what she'll do next.

She surprises me and throws herself at me, wrapping her arms around my neck. I catch her, our checkers game going everywhere. I laugh as she grips me to her.

"Guess we'll never know who's the Checker Master," I whisper in her ear. Her arms tighten before she pulls away with a wry grin, and then crashes her lips to mine, effectively pulling my mind away from checkers.

When we finally get around to resetting our game, Izabel

beats me, bad. We play another few times before Izabel's stomach growls, and she gets up to go make dinner. She hums to herself in the kitchen while she works, as I stay in the living room and watch her. Though when she's distracted, I sneak away to the bedroom.

Making sure the door is closed behind me, I wander over to my side of the room. I dig through my duffle bag until my fingers brush against the smooth velvet box. Pulling it out, I sit back on my heels. The box pops open easily, and I'm met with the sparkle of the diamond ring I picked out for her all those years ago.

I was a poor pathetic bastard for keeping it for eight long years, but I just couldn't get myself to sell it. At least the thing is now fully paid off. This is Izabel's ring; it has always been hers. I couldn't fathom the idea of someone else wearing it.

It's not much, but it's everything that I can't put into words. The solitaire diamond sits in the middle, proudly, no other bling distracting from its brilliance. Straight and to the point. The white gold band is smooth and simple. Though I've already planned what wedding band I'll give her to match, and that will give her the extra sparkle the engagement ring is lacking.

I snap the box closed and stick it in my pocket. My heart rams around in my chest as I walk back out to the living room. I want to kick myself. Why do I feel so nervous? I know she'll say yes. There's not a doubt in my mind. There's just something so *vulnerable* about proposing marriage to the woman who makes your world turn.

"Hey, there you are," Izabel says, looking up from where she's setting steaming plates of Hamburger Helper and garlic bread on the table. "It's all ready."

"Great, looks good, Bells," I tell her with a smile, settling into my seat.

She grabs two glasses of water and then joins me. We make mindless talk while we shovel our faces full of the cheesy noodles. I catch Bells giving me some weird looks, and finally, I can't take it anymore.

"Why are you looking at me like that?"

Her eyes dart away, and she digs her fork into her dinner. "I don't know. You just seem weird all of a sudden."

"Weird how?" *Shit.* Gotta get it together, man.

Izabel shrugs and offers me a smile. "I'm not sure. I'm probably just imagining it."

"Maybe I'm just enthralled with your cooking skills. This is really good."

She laughs and raises an eyebrow. "It's out of a box, Ryan. But thanks, I'll take the compliment."

Smooth.

Thankfully, she drops the subject, and we finish our meal. When we're done. I watch her put away the dishes. I'm perched at the table, my chin in my hand, perfectly content, when my phone chimes. My eyes dart down to my screen, and I see Josie has sent me a thumbs-up emoji.

Here goes nothing.

I scoot my chair back, the feet squeaking against the hardwood floors of the cabin. Strolling over to where Izabel is standing at the sink, I wrap my arms around her waist. My hands come to rest on the slight swell of her lower abdomen, and I smile. Leaning down, I press my lips to her neck. Izabel tilts her head off to the side, giving me better access.

"Want to go for a walk with me?" I ask her.

She turns around with wide blue eyes. "It's dark outside."

"So?" I ask her with a wry grin.

"So, what if there are bears?"

"I'll protect you, Bells," I murmur against her neck with a chuckle.

"It's cold out, though."

Jesus, just take the bait, woman!

"We'll bundle up. We've been cooped up all day. I need to get out and roam a little bit," I tell her. "Here, how about you go on a walk with me, then we can come back and take a nice warm bath, hm?"

Bells turns around to face me, my hands now resting above her rear. Her arms wrap around my neck as she looks at me. "You sure know the way to a girl's heart."

"Just this girl's," I say, leaning forward and kissing the tip of her nose.

"Fine," she says with a sigh. "Let me get my coat."

She strides toward our bedroom and emerges with her coat only a minute later, giving me a grin. "Let's go."

I reach for her hand, and she gratefully takes it, lacing her fingers with mine. We walk out of the cabin and are hit with a brisk breeze on the front porch. Bells steps closer to me, burrowing deeper into her coat. It is definitely colder than I thought it was.

The daylight hours got much warmer, hovering in the low fifties, and effectively melting the snow we got last night. But now that the sun is gone, the chill is back in full force. The night is clear, though, and the stars up in the sky are vast and twinkling. One of my favorite parts about being out here is seeing the stars without any interference from the city.

The underbrush crushes underneath our feet as we walk. Bells keeps her hand in mine, seeking warmth, but she doesn't say anything. I glance over at her a few times and am relieved when she looks content. The ring box burns in my back pocket as we walk a little farther.

I lead her over to the clearing where Josie and the gang got everything set up. As we round the corner, Bells gasps next to me, her hand coming up to cover her mouth.

The trees surrounding the small clearing are wrapped in white fairy lights, making their trunks look like they're glowing. On the path in front of us are paper bag lanterns. The white candles inside the bags illuminate the direction we're supposed to follow. The whole scene looks utterly enchanting. Josie and Jules were able to pull it off exactly how I wanted them too.

Izabel grips my hand harder and looks at me with wide, confused eyes. "What's happening, Ryan?"

I stay quiet until we reach a spacious area. White rose petals are strewn across the ground, making it look like the snow that was there this morning. My heart is about to burst with anticipation and love for this woman. If I don't get this over with, I might die. This is years in the making, and though it's miraculous I waited that long, I don't think I can hold out another second. I turn to Izabel and take her other hand in mine, holding her awed gaze. My pulse is skyrocketing with nerves and adrenaline.

Then slowly, so that I don't fall over, I bend down to one knee in front of the woman I plan to love for as long as I'm alive.

Chapter 39

Izabel

My lips part as I watch Ryan take a knee in front of me, letting out a little gasp. I knew the moment I saw the lanterns and the trees that this was happening tonight, but still. Nothing could have fully prepared me for the moment Ryan got down on one knee.

I've dreamed about this moment for so long; now that it's finally happening, it almost doesn't feel real. My chest aches with love for this man, the kind of love I can't wait to feel for the rest of my life.

"Izabel Marie Sanders," Ryan whispers, his green eyes locked on mine, unwavering. "I didn't think it was possible to love a person as much as I love you.

"We have come a long way since we hated each other as kids. We started as enemies, loathing each other's existence. Then, when all we had was each other, we came to rely upon and trust one another. I knew then that this was meant to happen between us. We were meant to be together. And even though it took a few obstacles, here we are. We've overcome so much, and I want to be everything you need in your life and more."

"Ryan," I whisper, feeling my whole body alight with his words.

"Bells, I love you more than anything," he says, his voice shaky as he reaches into his pocket and pulls out a box. My heart hammers in my chest as he opens it, displaying the most gorgeous diamond ring I've ever seen.

He holds it up for me and gives me a sultry smile. "Would you please do me the extreme honor of becoming my wife?"

I feel my face split with a giant smile. Lowering myself to the ground, so I can be closer to him, I nod eagerly. "Yes. Yes, Ryan, of course, I'll be your wife!"

He grins back at me and lifts my left hand, sliding the ring onto my fourth finger. Once the ring is where it's supposed to be, his lips claim mine in a soul-searing kiss. "I'm the happiest man in the world right now, you don't even know."

"I believe you," I whisper against him. My arms trail up and around his neck, and I hold him to me while I kiss him sense-less. When I pull away, I give him a wry smile. "I'm the happiest woman in the world."

Ryan brushes a strand of hair behind my ear and lets his eyes roam my face. "You're beautiful and kind, and strong, and everything I could ever want in a partner to go through life with. It's always been you, Bells."

My smile only grows as I press myself against Ryan, letting him hug me. I meant what I said a few minutes ago; I don't think I have ever been this happy in my entire life. This moment trumps everything else, every ceremony, every event, every-thing. I get to be Ryan's *wife,* and he gets to be my *husband.*

I picture myself hosting all the historical society galas in the future, making rounds and thanking people for attending. Ryan goes with me, with my hand tucked carefully into the crook of his elbow. Every time I stop to say hello, I introduce the man next to me. "This is Ryan, my husband."

Energy is tingling through my body with the thoughts, and I hold him tighter, closing my eyes and letting out a happy sigh.

When I open my eyes again, I glance around the clearing, taking in the setup again. The fairy lights are twinkling in the dark, illuminating the trees they're wrapped around. And paper lanterns! Something so simple shouldn't be so magical. It's the most beautiful proposal I've ever seen, and he did it all for me.

"How did you pull all of this off?" I mumble into his chest. He was with me all day. I don't think we were apart for more than five minutes.

"Josie and Juliet did it."

I pull away and look up at him in surprise. "They're here?" I turn to the left and right to make sure they're not going to jump out at me any second.

He chuckles. "No, they're not *here*, here. Liam rented a cabin about thirty minutes away, and they're all staying there. They even brought Ashton with them. They'll be by tomorrow morning for a celebratory brunch."

"So, they knew this whole time?" I ask, pieces now falling into place. I extend my hand in front of me, straightening my fingers out. I look at the engagement ring and tilt it, making it sparkle in the fairy light. "That's why Jules was so insistent on getting manicures this week."

"Ha, yeah, she told me that was nonnegotiable," Ryan laughed. "Your best friend can be very persistent." He grabs my hand and looks at the ring sitting on it. A satisfied smirk settles on his lips; he likes what he sees.

"No, I definitely don't. But I mean it. Seeing my ring on

your finger does things to me," he says darkly, laughing under his breath.

My body lights up. "What kinds of things?"

Ryan gets a devilish smirk on his face, and he leans toward me so he can whisper in my ear. "Hot, dirty, unspeakable things."

I suck in a sharp breath and meet his smoldering eyes with mine. It doesn't matter that we had steamy shower sex earlier today, I'm ready to go again. All night if he's up for it. "I think you promised me a bath if I went on this stupid walk with you."

Ryan's eyes flare, and he grabs my hand. "You're right, and I always deliver on my promises."

He gives my hand a yank, pulling me behind him. I yelp out a laugh and follow his footsteps. He doesn't stop until we're back in the cabin right in front of the master bathroom. Ryan's hands go to my coat and make quick work of undoing all the buttons before he pushes it down my shoulders and then does the same for his. Then they're tossed off to the side, forgotten.

The big bathtub starts filling up with warm water as our lips stay connected in a languid, passionate kiss. Once it's full, Ryan instructs me to get in first. I feel my cheeks heating as I try to maneuver my body into the tub. Water sloshes over the sides. After I'm finally settled, Ryan sinks behind me. He gently pulls on my shoulders, leaning me back, allowing my back to rest against his front. His hands circle my waist and rest on my abdomen.

He leans forward and presses hot kisses to my cheek and neck. I tilt my head, giving him better access, and moan at his impeccable work. Ryan's hands trace over the outline of my body, over the curvature hips, then up until his hands cup underneath my aching breasts. I lean my head back and sigh as his fingers gently dance over my nipples.

I can feel his arousal poking against my lower back, but I let him continue his exploration. We sit there in the tub for about fifteen minutes before I think he loses the rest of his self-control. He flicks the drain with his foot, and the water level starts receding.

Ryan slips out from behind me and grabs a towel. My eyes watch his every movement, my heart rate increasing as I observe his handsome figure. Ryan is an attractive man—he always has been. But now, there's something about the way his strong legs flex, and his abs tighten as he reaches for the towel, which instills a proud, possessive feeling in me. Maybe it's still the excitement of our engagement, but I just can't ever seem to get enough of him.

Ryan comes back to the tub and holds out a towel for me. When I stand, he wraps me up as I step over the edge. The towel covers my body, enveloping me in a fuzzy cocoon of warmth. Ryan's arms wrap around me next, and he shuffles the two of us into our conjoining bedroom. He rubs his hands up and down the length of my arms, trying to warm me and get all the water droplets dried off.

Stepping around to face me, his eyes are tender as they trace over my face. His hand comes up and fits itself in the crevice of my jawbone and my neck. He extends his thumb, rubbing the pad over my bottom lip. His eyes flare when I dart my tongue out, licking the edge of his finger.

As he leans forward, he takes my mouth in his, prying my lips open and not leaving any room for mercy. He kisses me heatedly, tangling his tongue with mine and walking us over to the edge of the bed without breaking our connection.

When he reaches the bed, he sits down on the mattress. His hands go to where mine are grasping the edge of the towel, and he pulls them away. A smirk plays gently on my lips as I let the towel slip from my body. The cold air hits my bare skin, making me shiver. Ryan's hands are on me then, discovering and exploring my silhouette. He leans forward and presses kisses between my breasts, trailing up my chest until he reaches my collarbone. Ryan dots kisses along the length of my chest, his hands notching against my hips and pulling me toward him.

In one swift movement, Ryan arranges himself, so he's lying on his back, his head resting on the pillow. He reaches for my hand and guides me on top of him. I adjust to a comfortable position and let him retake the lead.

He captures my mouth and kisses me, letting me know exactly where he wants this to go. I shift my hips and feel the rigidity of his length running along my center. Arousal flows through me like molten lava, my body burning for him. I rock back and forth against his body and feel the energy spark at my movements. Ryan pulls away from our kiss and throws his head back in a noisy groan, his hands locating my hips as he helps me find my rhythm.

"Just like that, Bells," he murmurs, his deep voice making me tremble. "Take what you need. *Jesus.*" He groans, then as I shift my hips a little more.

Ryan adjusts me a little, lifting my hips and then reaching down to position himself at my entrance. A hiss escapes his teeth the minute he enters me, closing his eyes in ecstasy. He sinks into me as deep as he can, and I pause for a second, letting my body adjust to the incredible feeling of how he fills me.

I brace my hands against his chest and move my hips up and down his length. Ryan matches me thrust for thrust, locking his green eyes on me to gauge my reaction. I feel myself climbing higher and higher as I grind my hips harder against him. Ryan's hands curve toward my backside, angling my hips downward slightly against him. The slight change is all it takes to reach the peak of pleasure. I cry out, feeling my body erupt.

When I open my eyes, Ryan looks like he could devour me. He moves then, slipping out, making me groan at the loss of contact. He carefully adjusts us, so we're standing, me leaning over the bed. As he enters me swiftly from behind, I sigh in happiness, and he starts thrusting again.

His hips piston into me, and my hands claw at the sheets. The sounds of my moans and his heavy breaths fill the room, and I feel myself falling over the edge again. My body shudders, and my hands stiffen.

"That's it," Ryan gasps as he bends over my back, pressing our heated skin together. "You gorgeous, wonderful woman. I love you so much."

He's still moving in me, though I can tell he's getting closer to finishing. His thrusts are becoming more erratic, and he's panting hard. With a sigh, I tilt my head a little so he can see my face. Ryan's tempo speeds up.

I give a happy, blissful smile and then murmur, "I can't wait for you to be my husband."

He gives a strangled moan behind me, my words pushing him over the edge. Collapsing against me, he presses his forehead between my shoulder blades as he climaxes. His body jerks a few times, and then he stills.

We stay there for a moment longer before he pulls out of me. I stand up straight, my legs wobbling. Ryan notices, his hands jolting to my hips to hold me steady while I regain my bearings. Draping an arm across my chest, he pulls my back into his front. He presses open-mouthed kisses against my neck before sucking my earlobe between his teeth.

"I love you, Bells," he whispers in my ear.

I scrape my nails against his arm on my chest gently, making his skin break out in goosebumps. "I love you too, Ry."

He kisses my cheek again before letting me go and jogging to the bathroom to grab a wet washcloth. Handing it to me when he comes out, he allows me to clean myself up while he gets a glass of water.

I put the cloth back in the bathroom, and then settle in bed underneath the covers. Ryan joins me a moment later, letting me curl up against his body. I tuck my cheek against his chest. My eyes fall shut when his hands wrap around me protectively.

"It's always so good with you," he mumbles against my hair.

I pull back, giving him a shit-eating grin. "Yeah?"

"Mhmm. No one else compares to you, Bells. Not ever."

My toes tingle with happiness, and I snuggle into his warmth more. My heart feels full. "Well, I think we have effectively christened our little love-shack, what do you think?"

A laugh rumbles out of his chest, and his arm flexes. "Thank God no one walked in on us this time."

I chuckle as I remember how mortifying it was when Mac interrupted us as teenagers. It was such an awkward mix of relief that another human had found us, and frustration because he found us in the throes of passion.

With a relaxed sigh, I close my eyes, suddenly feeling exhausted. Ryan's hand rubs soothing circles on my lower back, and the movements start lulling me to sleep.

"I meant what I said," I mumble, my words slurring. He presses his lips to my forehead.

"Hm?"

"I really can't wait for you to be my husband," I say.

Happiness blooms through me at the outcome of our life. It took a while to get to where we are, but at this moment, I'd do it all again. Because though the path might have been absolute torture, what I have now is a dream come true, and I'll never take it for granted.

Chapter 40

Ryan

"Are you excited?" I ask Izabel. She's sitting in the passenger seat of my car, fiddling with her engagement ring on her finger.

Izabel turns those striking blue eyes on me and gives a reassuring smile. "I'm so excited I can barely handle it."

I grin at her as I pull into my parents' subdivision. When we arrive, she meets me at the front of the car, and we stroll hand-in-hand up to the door. I don't bother ringing the doorbell and just push the front door open. The house is warm and welcoming against the chilly evening air. I hear laughter coming from the living room, and a delicious smell wafting from the kitchen.

Bells wiggles out of her jacket and then hands it to me. I take it and drop it on the bench by the door before bobbing my head toward the kitchen. "I'm going to go say hi to my mom." Bells gives me an encouraging smile and nods as I tip forward and press a kiss to her temple, then wander off towards the kitchen.

My mom looks up with a grin when she sees me enter her

domain. I stick my hands into the pockets of my slacks and smile back. "Hey, Mom."

"Hey, Ryno! Glad you could make it." She lifts a big pot off of the stove and steps toward the sink, dumping the water out of it.

"It's kind of our party," I chuckle as I peer into the many different dishes she has going. She insisted on throwing us this engagement celebration dinner as soon as I told her I was planning on proposing. "What are you making? Can I help you with anything?"

My mom presses her lips together and glances around. "I think I have it pretty much handled right now, hun, but thank you."

"Okay." I spy a tray of veggies sitting on the breakfast bar and reach for a carrot, crunching it between my teeth. "Where's Thals?"

"She went to go see a movie with her friend Nora. She should be back in a little bit. She was really looking forward to seeing Izabel's ring."

I laugh and pop a cherry tomato in my mouth. "She's such a little hopeless romantic."

Mom tosses her head back and laughs. "Don't I know it. Although you were like that too."

I crinkle up my nose. "I was not."

She gives me a look. "Please. You still are. You have a big heart, Ryan. Don't you remember one of the first things you said to me when I got to the hospital after you all were stranded in the woods?"

"No...?" I'm sure I said a lot of things right after that whole situation. At the time, all I could think about was Izabel and that we weren't together anymore. After being together and relying on each other so much, it was a definite shock to the system to be alone in that hospital room.

Mom puts the pot back on the stove, and then turns to face me. Her hand rests on her hip, and she has a sly smile on her lips. "You looked me dead in the eyes and said, 'Mom, I'm going to marry her.' I had no clue who you were even talking about! All I knew at that point was that that dumb camp let my baby get stranded in the woods, and here he was talking about marriage." She laughs and shakes her head. "I didn't even know how to respond."

I go for the celery this time. "I think you paused for a second, and then told me you were going to go get me a burger."

She chuckles again. "That sounds about right. But here we are, celebrating an engagement, how long in the making?"

"Too long," I say firmly, leaning against the edge of the counter. "Far too long."

"Things usually have a way of working themselves out," Mom speculates. She reaches for her oven mitts before pulling open the oven and reaching for the pan sitting inside. "It's hard for me to believe that my baby is getting married, and maybe soon, you'll have babies of your own."

I grab the shredded mozzarella cheese sitting on the counter and sprinkle some over the steaming pan of lasagna. "It blows my mind too." I peer around my mom to still make sure we're still alone, then I let out a breath, feeling comfortable to admit to her what's on my mind. "In fact, I'm a little nervous."

"What are you nervous about?"

I shrug. "I don't know. I kind of feel like all of this is too good to be true. That I'll wake up and it will all just have been a dream. Or if it's not a dream, that I'll be a terrible husband or a worse father."

Mom turns her attention back to me, her eyebrows raised in surprise. "Oh, honey, trust me, you have absolutely nothing to be nervous about."

"How do I know if I'm doing it right?"

"You don't. You just do the best you can," she says tenderly, patting me on the shoulder. "You will be a great husband and an amazing father when the time comes, I have no doubt in my mind. And you'll have Izabel to help you as well. She'll keep you in line."

I seal up the cheese and give her a sly smile. "Yeah, I know she will."

Once the lasagna is back in the oven, I reach for another carrot stick. I trust that my mom is right, but regardless, I put on a brave face for everyone else to see the majority of the time. But I'd be lying if I didn't admit that I had some worries about my future knocking at my doorstep.

Instead of lingering in this uncomfortable topic, I switch to a different one. "Have you gotten the results back from your test this week?"

Mom is still going through chemo treatments. The last time they did a check-up, they found that the cancer had shrunk a little bit. They adjusted her regimen, and now we're waiting to hear the results from that alteration. We're hoping it's good news again.

She smiles softly, but shakes her head. "No, they called and said they're still waiting on some labs to come back. It usually takes a few days."

"How are you feeling?"

"I'm okay. Great, actually," Mom says. "I have lots to keep me preoccupied. Thalia is always a handful, and you have so many exciting milestones coming up. I don't have time to sit around and worry."

I watch her as I chew on my veggies. This woman is amazing. Even now, she's making a nice dinner for a bunch of people despite probably being exhausted from treatment. My mom always puts others first. It's a rule she's lived by her whole life.

If I can be even a fraction of the parent that she was to me, I'd consider myself a successful father.

We chat while the lasagna finishes cooking, then I help her set everything up on the table. Right before we're about to sit down and eat, Thalia comes bounding through the door and throws herself at me, giving me a big hug before wrapping her arms around Izabel too. She whispers a quiet hello and settles in the seat next to Bells.

Mom sets the basket of garlic bread down and then sits. She gives the table a once-over before she says a quick grace and allows us all to dig in. We pass around our plates to Derek, who serves up the lasagna. Then we go for the garlic bread, veggies, and salad that my mom did up as well.

Thalia is chattering about the movie that she got to see today. We all listen aptly to her retelling of the entire plot. I watch my little sister in amusement as I devour my mom's cooking.

The table is alight with jokes and laughter. Izabel's parents are sitting across from us, my mom and Derek at either end. Izabel's sister Sage and her husband Teddy weren't able to make it in for this little get-together, but we'll see them in a few months.

"So, do you all have a date picked out yet?" Derek asks us.

I turn to Bells. We've been engaged for almost two weeks, but we've spent a lot of time since then dreaming and talking. She meets my gaze, and then nods toward my stepfather. "We're thinking probably sometime in October."

"It will be small," I add in, knowing they're going to comment on how we're going to pull a wedding together in only eight months. "Probably just close friends and family." She peers at me from underneath her eyelashes, and my heart swells with love and happiness.

After we're finished eating, my mom and Izabel's mom

stand to get everything cleaned up. Derek catches my eye and motions his head toward the garage. I nod silently and then get up to head that way. Vince trails behind us, curious about what kind of secret club we have going on.

Derek steps into the garage and hits the light illuminating his tool bench and work area. Vince gives a low whistle as he observes everything. "This is great work. I didn't know you were into carpentry, Derek?"

My stepfather gives a noncommittal shrug and digs into the garage refrigerator, pulling out three beers. "I do it more as a hobby." He offers a beer to Vince, who gratefully takes it and then to me. I shake my head and raise my hand up in no thanks. Derek frowns. "Right, sorry."

Vince raises an eyebrow at me. "Not one for beer? Are you more of a whiskey guy?"

Definitely more of a whiskey guy.

"I don't drink anything right now," I tell him. "Was hitting it a little too hard and had to get back on track." I leave it at that. I don't need to admit to my future father-in-law that I was bordering on alcoholism. Not a good look.

Vince just nods and offers his beer to me in a miniature toast. "Good man."

The three of us chat for a little while longer as we finish our beers. We don't want to be out here for too long and cause the women to come searching. The evening comes to a close a while later, and Izabel and I give the round of hugs and then head home.

As we're lying in bed that night, she releases a satisfied sigh against my chest. "That wasn't so bad."

I run my fingers over her bare shoulder. "Not bad at all."

"I love our family," she murmurs.

I get caught up on her statement, *our family*, and my thoughts go back to my conversation with my mom. I press my lips to Izabel's forehead and take in a deep breath, the smell of her shampoo hitting my nose. The scent assures me that this isn't a dream, but the actual reality. I pull her closer to me and close my eyes, settling into warmth. Even though it seems too good to be true, I'm not going to waste it.

The following day, I stop at the office for a while and do my daily tasks of going through emails and returning phone calls. Izabel comes with me and lies on my office couch, reading a book. We spend the rest of the day running around.

When we arrive back at the condo, I motion for Izabel to go ahead of me. I see the mailman distributing mail in the boxes by the stairs. I step over to him and wait until he gets to our box before holding my hand out.

"That's me," I say.

"Oh, you have a certified piece. Is there an Izabel Sanders in your unit?" he asks, reading off the address label.

I frown. "Yes, that's my fiancée."

"She has certified mail. Will you sign for this, please?" He holds out the letter and then the piece of green cardstock he pulled off of it.

I scribble my signature on the line and then take the remaining mail from him. Then I hurry up the stairs, following after Bells. She's just unlocking our front door when I come up beside her.

Izabel throws the door open, dropping her keys on the entry table, then she kicks her shoes off, giving a groan as she flops down on the couch. "I'm exhausted."

I watch her amusedly and sit down beside her. "You got mail."

Izabel sits up straighter and reaches for the envelope. Her eyes meet mine, and I can see the uncertainty hidden behind those sparkling blues. Her fingers sneak under the seal, and she tears it open, pulling out the letter and reading it. I notice her hands shaking as she holds the piece of paper.

When she's done, she releases the letter, letting it fall into her lap and then sits back against the cushions. I scoot closer and put my hand on her thigh. Whatever it was, it's not good. I reach for the letter and then read it over. The big, bold word *subpoena* stands out in front of my eyes, and that's all I need to know.

White-hot anger burns through me, and I give her leg a quick squeeze. "Everything will be okay," I whisper to her, unsure if I'm comforting her or myself more. A minute later, she takes a deep breath and sits up.

She faces me, and her expression is resolute. "They want me to testify in court against Mark."

I frown. "But you gave your statement to the police already."

Izabel stands up and runs her fingers through her hair. "I guess that wasn't enough."

"You don't have to go. We can get a lawyer and figure a way out of this."

She laughs under her breath, humorlessly, as she paces. "It's a subpoena, Ryan. I have to go. I don't think playing hooky is an option."

I stand up now too and cross my arms over my chest. I'm not sure why we're even discussing this. "That man has trauma-tized you enough already," I growl. "If you don't want to go, I'll make sure you don't have to."

"I don't think so. It's not worth the risk," I tell her, standing firm.

"I'll be perfectly safe. We have the order of protection. He won't be able to get to me. Or probably even say anything to me."

My pulse is thrumming with anxiety. Why is she being so

adamant about this? I'm giving her an out here, so why won't she take it? All I can picture right now is that moment in Nashville when the water washed away her makeup, revealing the bruises on her neck. The image in my mind leaves my stomach churning. "I don't care if they have him locked in a cage. I don't want you anywhere near him."

Izabel straightens her shoulders and hits me with an icy glare. "Well, then good thing you weren't the one who was subpoenaed. It's not up to you."

"The hell it isn't," I spit, my anxiousness ramping up. "Bells, I'm trying to protect you here. Why don't you see that?"

"Because I don't need protection. I *need* to do this. If I don't, they'll hold me in contempt or whatever. Put me in jail. That would be worse, don't you think?" she snarks.

I glare at her for a second, annoyed that she's not taking this seriously. "I'll call the lawyer. You're not going, and that's final. We'll figure out the details later." I turn on my heel, making a move to leave. I'm completely over this conversation and her random spurt of hero complex. But I falter when I hear the force behind her next word.

"*No.*"

I turn around to face her and frown. "Excuse me?"

Her expression is now riddled with anger. "No. You do not get to make these types of decisions for me. You can't bully me into something I don't want. The minute you start doing that, you are no better than *him.*"

Those words hit me in the chest like a sack of bricks. The frustration and stress whoosh out of me. I let out a wounded sound and then collapse back onto the couch, putting my hands over my face. "Fuck."

Izabel stays silent for a moment before she tiptoes over to me. I feel her settle on the couch beside me, her hand gingerly coming to rest on my shoulder. She hesitates before whispering, "It's okay, Ryan."

"No, it's not," I say, shaking my head. My heart hurts from the weight of her words. Comparing me to her ex-fiancé hurts. But she's right. She's definitely right.

Izabel rubs my shoulder through my shirt and takes a deep breath. "You are the king of my heart, Ryan Miller. But we are a team. This ring you gave me means we work together. We make decisions together."

I pick up my head and meet her eyes, letting out a shaky sigh. "When did you become so strong?"

"I'm not strong." She chuckles, brushing off my compliment.

I reach for her hand and tangle our fingers together. "You are. You are one of the strongest women I've met."

Her eyes are soft as they trace over my face. "I owe a lot of it to you, honestly. But I need to hear that you understand what I'm saying."

"I do, Bells. I'm sorry."

Her lips pull up at the corners, and she leans forward, giving me a kiss. "I love you. Promise me that, moving forward, we'll always make decisions together."

I cup her jaw with my other hand, pulling her to me in another kiss. "I promise."

She leans away and gives me a hard stare. "Okay, then. I'll go testify, and then we'll just be done with this whole mess."

"Can I come with you?" I ask her hesitantly. "At the very least, I don't want you to be alone."

"Of course. Honestly, it will make me feel better knowing you're there anyway," she admits.

I bite my tongue to keep myself from saying anything. Izabel made her point very clear. We're in this together. I'm not going to put her in the same situation she was in with Mark. That's the last thing I want to do.

I let my eyes trace over her, but I don't say anything. I really hit the jackpot with her. My mom was joking yesterday about me saying I'd marry her from the very start of our relationship. I knew, though, even then.

I'd be a fool to do anything to jeopardize that. So I let her words sink into me. Sometimes I get lost in the urge to protect her. That's just who I am by nature. But she's right. She doesn't need me to *protect* her. Izabel isn't some porcelain doll that I can set up in a china cabinet. She needs my support, my trust.

"When is it?"

Izabel picks up the official letter and checks the date. "A month from now."

I close my eyes and sigh. "I'll put it on the calendar."

She gives me a grateful squeeze of the hand. "Thank you."

I wrap an arm around Izabel again and bring her closer to me. "You're welcome," I concede with a breath. "Maybe this will be the closure you need to fully move on."

"God, I hope so," Bells admits against me. "I'm so ready to be done with him."

"Well, then let's just get this over with and send the bastard to jail."

A laugh bubbles out of Izabel, and she sits up, meeting her gaze with mine. "That's the best idea I've ever heard."

Chapter 41

Izabel

"Bells?" Ryan's hesitant voice snaps me out of my thoughts. We're standing on the sidewalk in front of the Cedar Ridge courthouse. It's a beautiful day, fluffy white clouds dotting the clear blue sky. A perfect day to put my nightmares to rest.

I was staring at the courthouse, thinking through everything the lawyer and I talked about over these last few weeks. I just wanted to get this whole thing over and done with.

The process of going through a court hearing and having to face Mark again was exhausting. Now that we're standing in front of this building, knowing we're about to hear what's going to be the final decision, makes my stomach churn with nerves.

Ryan comes up behind me, resting his large hand on the small of my back. The warmth from his hand seeps into my skin, and I let out a shaky breath before turning my gaze to him. He's wearing a suit that does wonders for his physique. The white button-down shirt hugs his broad shoulders, and the suit jacket emphasizes his back and waist. His eyes roam my face, checking to see if I'm okay. We're not even in there yet, and Ryan's as on edge as I am right now.

He tried his best to distract me all morning. We went on a nice walk through our neighborhood, and he even took me to an early lunch at my favorite café, but I think he and I both knew that nothing was going to take my mind off this afternoon.

"Are you ready?" he asks me gently.

I nod and try to give him a reassuring smile. "Let's get this over with."

He smiles wryly and offers his hand to me. "Couldn't agree with you more."

I tangle my fingers with his and let him lead me up the white concrete stairs to the big wooden courthouse doors. When I hesitate before we go inside, Ryan turns to me, his eyes flaring in concern.

"What's wrong?"

"Nothing." I brush him off and take a deep breath. "Let's go."

The minute we walk in the courtroom and take our seats next to our attorney, time seems to go at double speed. The judge comes up to the stand, and the jurors take their place. The judge accepts the verdict and begins to read it.

With each charge brought forward, only one word stands out from the buzzing I'm experiencing all around me.

Guilty.

And with each verdict, I seem to regain a piece of myself.

Fuck. Him.

This is my closure. After today, I don't ever have to see him again. I've said what I needed to say, and he proved to me that he is every bit the horrible man I believed him to be. The ball of worry in my belly eases slightly as I realize that it's over. He will never rule any part of my life anymore. I have a bright future ahead of me, full of love and family. Mark Snyder has absolutely no place in that.

After today, I'm done with him. I'm done being scared. I'm done holding on to our past. Mark will serve his time in prison, and this part of my life will officially be a closed book. I'm not wasting any more energy on this poor excuse of a man.

I don't even realize when it's over. I'm being dragged into a standing position and strong, familiar arms are wrapping me up tight.

"Bells," Ryan breathes into my neck as he hugs me close. "It's over. We won. We're safe."

When I don't respond right away, Ryan pulls back, staring at me in concern. "Are you okay?" I really wish that question would stop popping up today.

"No," I exhale. "I need to leave. Am I done? Can we go?"

It must be something that he sees on my face because Ryan's expression sombers and he nods quickly. With a hand on my lower back, he shuffles me out of the courtroom. I don't look up at Mark as we pass him, or even his family sitting in their seats.

Ryan, thankfully, doesn't say anything else until we're in the car. He looks over at me from the driver's side with an eyebrow raised. "What's going on, Bells?"

I lean my head against the headrest of the seat and take a big breath in through my nose and out through my mouth. "I'm done. I don't want to give Mark any more of my energy than I have to. We got the verdict we wanted, so can we please go home and move on from this?"

A wide grin takes over Ryan's face, and he nods, putting the car into reverse to pull out of his parking spot. "Absolutely. I love the sound of that."

I reach across the console and take his hand again, giving it a squeeze. As Ryan drives farther and farther away from the courthouse, I feel the tension start to leave from my body. There will still be lots to work through in the aftermath of this for me, I'm aware of that. But for today, I'm just happy to be free.

I never have to worry about him again. All that matters now is the man sitting next to me and our life that we get to build. Together.

Chapter 42

Ryan

"Gosh, she's beautiful," Josie whispers beside me. Though I agree with her, I don't turn to acknowledge her remark. My gaze is glued on Izabel, gliding down the aisle with her dad by her side.

My throat feels thick as I watch her take each confident step. She is beautiful, more beautiful than I could have ever dreamed. Her blue eyes are fixed on me, too, a soft smile playing on her lips. Even though I had the chance to see her in her wedding gown earlier, I still feel my eyes burning as I watch her walk down toward me as my bride. The significance of this day rests heavily on my heart, but I don't feel nervous or worried. Instead, I feel like I'm buzzing with anticipation. This is an event I've been waiting my whole life for. When Izabel will finally become my wife.

When she gets close enough, I take a few steps toward her and her father. Izabel's father, Vince, looks at me, extending his hand. I take it and give him a firm shake, and he grins at me. Then he turns to his daughter, leaning forward and pressing a kiss to her cheek before going to sit by his wife.

Izabel places her hand in mine and lets me lead her to the front of the altar. I can't help but give her a hard time as we finally stop right in front of the officiant. "You better not run this time 'cause I'm faster than you. I'll catch you."

She chuckles under her breath and rolls her eyes. "Trust me, Ryan. I'll be running *to* you, not *away* from you. And I have no intention of changing that."

I squeeze her hand in mine and then give a slight nod to the officiant. He smiles at us and then he begins the ceremony. My ears are buzzing, and I can barely make out what he's saying. All I can focus on is Izabel beaming up at me.

"Ryan, Izabel," the officiant says, pulling me out of my daydream of my wife-to-be. "Now is a chance for you to share your vows with each other."

Bells passes her bouquet off to Juliet, and then takes my other hand in hers. When we're facing each other, I give her hands an encouraging squeeze. The officiant gives Bells the go-ahead.

Her eyes don't leave mine, but she squeezes my hands right back. "Ryan Miller. I can't believe that I'm here right now, getting ready to profess my love for you and to commit myself to be your wife. If eighteen-year-old me was told that *you* would be the man standing up with me today, I probably would have keeled over and died," she says. A soft murmur of chuckles rises from our guests in the pews. I grin at her.

"You, Ryan Miller, were the utter bane of my existence. And I *loathed* you. You were so arrogant and confident and handsome all at the same time. I couldn't imagine that you would have any other interest in me other than to make fun of me and ruin my summers.

"But then I got to know you. The *real* you. And I saw the man who is now standing right before me: the kind, strong protector of a man who I would eventually choose to build my life with. You have proven to me time and time again how much you love me and how much you're willing to sacrifice for me.

"I can't think of anyone else I would want to grow old with. When I think of my future and every dream coming true, I always see you standing next to me, cheering me on, supporting me through thick and thin. I can't wait to start our lives together as husband and wife. I promise to honor you, cherish, and appreciate everything you do as my husband and the father to my children.

"I *loathe* you, Ryan Miller. But I also love you, more than I ever thought was humanly possible."

The officiant says a quick thank you to Bells, and then acknowledges me to give my vows.

"Izabel," I address her, and then make a quick adjustment. "Bells, I knew from the first time I watched you step off that bus at camp that you were going to play a big part in my life. Little did I know that you would turn out to be a massive pain in my ass.

"When I think back to our camp days, I have to roll my eyes at teenage me. I had no idea what I was doing. All I knew was that this gorgeous, witty, brilliant girl was driving me nuts, and I had to figure out how to stop her. I had to regain control over the situation." I chuckle and shake my head.

"We sure did have a lot of fun at camp, didn't we?" Izabel snorts, and the place erupts in laughter. "Okay, well, maybe not. But I would go back and do it all over again. I'd hang your underwear up on that flagpole for everyone to see a million times over because, in the long run, it brought us together.

"I've lived a life without you, and I can honestly say that I'd rather die than do that again. Throughout all those years we were apart, I always felt like a piece of me was missing. You're my second half, Bells. My equal. I never want to experience life without you. Because without you, I'm not me. For the rest of my life, I promise to be a good husband. You are my whole world. And I'll do whatever it takes to ensure that you smile like this every day of our lives together," I say as I reach up to brush my fingers against her cheek. A tear slips out of her eye and falls against my hand.

"Izabel Sanders, I love you with everything in me. And I can't wait to be your husband, for now, for eternity."

"Thank you, Ryan," the officiant says. "We'll now do the exchanging of the rings." Josie steps to my side and gives me the ring she's been keeping for me. Juliet does the same for Bells.

The officiant has Izabel go first. She repeats the phrases he says to her. "Ryan, I give you this ring as a sign of our love and commitment to each other, signifying a bond that is stronger than any obstacle." Izabel's lower lip trembles as she slips the wedding band onto my left ring finger and finishes off the vows. "I promise to love, support, and stand beside you for all the days of our lives."

"Ryan, please place your ring onto Izabel's finger and then repeat after me," the officiant says before launching into my promises to Izabel.

"Bells, I give you this ring as a sign of our love and commitment to each other and as a symbol of our united strength," I say as I put the wedding band on her finger, where it will stay forever. I try to keep my voice as level as possible, but I hear the emotion thick in my tone. "There is nothing that we can't conquer as long as we face it together. I promise to love, support, and stand beside you for all the days of our lives."

Once our rings are in place, we grip each other's hands tightly. I trace her face with my eyes, committing this moment to memory. It looks like she's doing the same thing. The church is silent for a moment, in reverence of the intimate promises we just made to each other.

"Love is when two people touch each other's souls," the officiant says a beat later. "Love is honesty and trust. Love is helping and respecting one another and being there when the other has fallen. Love is differences that can always be worked out. Love is reaching your dreams together.

"Ryan and Izabel, I hope you always remember the promises you made to each other today and hold this moment close to your hearts. It is with great pleasure that I now announce you husband and wife. Ryan, you may now kiss your bride."

Finally, I think as I pull Izabel toward me, my hands holding tightly to hers so she doesn't fall over. I raise one hand up and settle it against where her jaw and her neck collide. Then, in one swift movement, I have my lips pressed against hers.

I hear the cheers and hoots of our guests and our friends. I kiss Izabel as if it's the very first and last time, combined into one. Izabel presses her body up against mine as my mouth moves with hers.

When we finally break apart, her cheeks are flushed, and her lips swollen. Those sapphire blue eyes are sparkling with unbridled joy, and I feel my heart rate increase.

Izabel Miller. My wife.

Izabel's face lights up as she meets my eyes with hers. "It all went flawlessly, didn't it?"

"I think so. We still have the whole evening left. I'm sure someone will find a way to cause trouble."

Izabel urges toward me, wrapping her arms around my middle and resting her head against my chest. "I hope not. Today is just too perfect. I never want it to end."

I bend my head and press a kiss to the top of her hair. "Me neither, but we have a whole life of perfect days to look forward to."

All of our guests are still cheering and clapping as we make our way down the aisle. I wave at my mom and Derek, who are sitting in the front row. My mom has tears in her eyes as she watches me walk with my new wife down the aisle. It's something that means so much that she's able to be here with us. Her latest follow-up with her doctor was nothing but good news, which was such a relief. It's crazy to think that there was a time where we wondered how long we'd get to have her with us. And always by my mother's side, Derek gives me a thumbs-up as we pass, his face beaming with pride.

I make eye contact with a few of our other friends as we make our way out of the church. Everyone looks elated that we've made it to this moment. And that all means so much.

After we do a greeting line, Izabel and I are shuffled away to do private pictures with just the two of us. Shortly after that, we're brought back into the church to take family photos. Thalia is beside herself, demanding that she get to stand next to Izabel in her "princess dress" in every single photo. We oblige her, because why could we not?

"You two are just too cute," one of the photographers says as she takes a few last pictures. "I think we're all set here. You all can get your things, and we'll meet you at the reception hall."

"Thank you so much," Izabel tells her. The photographers nod and start collecting all their equipment.

I turn to my new bride and take a step back, admiring her dress fully now that we're in private. "You are absolutely stunning," I tell her. "I love this dress on you."

I move closer, wrapping my hands around her hips and pulling her into me. She arches against me, her arms falling over my shoulders. "I think I might love it more if it was piled on our bedroom floor, though," I tease her, leaning down and nipping at her earlobe.

Out of the corner of my eye, I see her arms erupt in goosebumps. Her fingers play with the ends of my hair on my neck, and she takes a shaky breath. "So impatient."

I laugh and pull away, shooting her a wry grin. "What? I can't be excited about our wedding night?"

Izabel looks at me in amusement. "It's not like this is new territory for you."

"That doesn't matter; you're my wife now. I've never done it with my wife before," I murmur, pulling her closer to me.

"Your wife," she hums. "I do like the sound of that."

"Trust me, I do too," I tell her, feeling the effect those words have on my body.

"I'll tell you what, husband. Let's go to the reception, and dance, and eat all the wedding cake, and then at the end of the evening, I promise to let you unfasten every single button on this dress. Then you can do with me as you please."

"Deal," I confirm. "I guess we better get going then. Don't want to keep our guests waiting."

I release her but still keep a hold of her hand. Then we grab whatever we need to and head outside. A limo is waiting for us, and I let Izabel climb in first, helping her arrange all the skirts and layers of her fluffy dress. As we settle into the back seat, I wrap my arms around Izabel's shoulders, and she leans against me for our drive.

Once we arrive at our reception, we take the elevator up to the first floor and then hang out outside in the hallway for a moment. I send a text to Juliet and Josie that we're here, and before long, they're with us out in the hallway.

"Mind if I steal your bride, Ryan?" Jules asks, taking hold of Izabel's hand. "We're just going to go freshen up before you make your grand entrance."

"Just make sure you bring her back," I say, only half-pretending to be serious.

Jules whisks her away to a bathroom down the hallway as Josie stands next to me with her arms crossed over her chest. I gotta say, my best friend can rock a suit. I was astonished when she showed up dressed to the nines today. I was expecting her to wear a dress similar to the bridesmaids.

But that's not Josie, and I'm glad she decided to be herself.

Her suit is the same as mine, though without the fancy boutonniere pinned to her front. She has a black bow tie secured around her neck and a pressed white shirt. Her slacks are black, though they only come down to her ankles in a fitted style. She's strutting around in a pair of strappy heels like she owns the place.

"Are you all ready to give your speech?" I ask her.

Josie's eyes meet mine, and she huffs out a breath. "Don't remind me. I'm not so great at public speaking. I'll probably throw up everywhere."

"You'll do great, I'm sure," I tell her. "Did you bring anyone with you today?"

"Nope, flying solo. How could I have succeeded at my Best Man duties when I have another man hanging off my arms? You're my primary focus today, buddy."

"I'm so glad you agreed to do this," I tell her honestly.

"Please, it's an honor. Really, Ryan. I know I'm late to this story, but I got to see it all come together. I wouldn't have missed this wedding for the world."

"Okay, we are all spruced up and looking beautiful again!" Juliet announces as she and Bells step out into the hallway. "Josie, why don't you go let the DJ know that they're here so he can announce their entrance?"

Josie scurries off as Izabel comes and takes my hand, Juliet straightening out her skirts. Inside the reception hall, I hear the DJ ask for everyone's attention.

"It's my extreme honor to introduce for the very first time, Mr. and Mrs. Ryan Miller!"

"Ready?" I ask Bells.

She grins back. "Ready."

We throw open the doors to the hall and step inside. All of our guests are standing at their tables, clapping and cheering for us. We walk hand-in-hand through the hall until we get to the bridal party table at the front.

The space has the industrial feel of a warehouse, but the twinkle lights on the ceiling and the gossamer streamers draped across the windows make it feel otherworldly. Round tables are spread out across the floor, surrounding the big dance area.

The tables are set up elegantly with cream-colored table-cloths and intricate centerpieces consisting of white and burgundy carnations. In between the bigger flowers are small blush-colored roses and pieces of greenery. Around the vases full of flowers are small votive candles, giving the tables a soft glow.

Izabel and I settle into our seats. As everyone else sits down, we hear the clattering of knives against champagne flutes and glasses. I look at Bells and give her a crooked grin before claiming her lips with mine. Our guests applause as we kiss.

Before too long, the event staff come out and serve dinner. It's a delicious spread of either chicken or filet mignon served with mashed potatoes and roasted veggies. The room is alive with laughter and conversation as we all dig into our dinner.

After we're all stuffed, and the plates are cleared away, the DJ announces that we're going to go ahead with the toasts. I hear Josie groan next to me, and I laugh under my breath. The staff hurries about, delivering flutes of champagne, and a micro-phone is provided to our table.

Juliet goes first and gives everyone her biggest smile. "Izabel is my best friend. I remember when we first met each other at Hawthorne Academy, all those years ago. We were assigned as roommates in the dorms. I took one look at the skinny blue-eyed girl wearing bright purple leggings and a pink turtleneck shirt. I knew right away that she needed my professional help." Everyone chuckles. "Since then, I've acted as Izabel's personal stylist and official advisor."

Jules launches into memories and anecdotes that have everyone laughing. Izabel wipes the corner of her eye with her napkin and smiles at her friend. Juliet raises her glass to us, and our guests follow their lead. I lean over and press another warm kiss to my new bride's lips, and the room erupts in cheers again.

Josie stands and then smooths out her suit when it's her turn. She holds the microphone up and begins her speech. "When I was little, I used to dream about what happily ever after would look like. I never imagined that I would get to witness it happen right in front of my eyes, but here we are. Ryan and Izabel are a real-life fairytale that has finally reached its happy ending.

"I'm new to this friend group, so I don't have the repertoire of embarrassing stories that Juliet has graciously shared with us. But there is one thing that I know to be true with every ounce of my being: there is no more genuine love than what Ryan and Izabel have for each other.

"In the short time that I've known the couple, I've witnessed what it means to truly be in love. They've each over-come so many obstacles to get to this point, and I'm thrilled that they have found their happy ending in each other." Josie gives me a wide smile. "I once told Ryan that love wasn't supposed to be easy. It can be messy, ugly, complicated. It can simultane-ously bring out the worst and the best in a person. But it is also the greatest thing that you can ever experience. Love is always worth fighting for.

"Ryan and Izabel have been through the messy and the ugly, and they came out better and stronger for it. They've fought and clawed and conquered. So now all that's left is their happy ending." Josie holds up her champagne glass. "Ryan, Izabel, I am so happy to be part of this special day with you. I wish you all the happiness, and I can't wait to see where life brings you. Just know that whatever comes your way, you can handle it together. Because honestly, I've never seen a love like yours, and that will see you through anything. Cheers!"

I give Josie an appreciative smile and then lean over to kiss Izabel again. Her hand comes up to my cheek, and she leans her forehead against mine. I look into her eyes and grin, my heart feeling like it's going to overflow with tenderness: blue and green, the perfect match.

After the other toasts are made, Izabel and I take the floor for our first dance. The gentle melody of our song comes through the speakers, and I draw her in close to me. We sway slowly to the music. The violin and piano notes echo throughout the hall.

"Today was everything I hoped it would be," Izabel says against my shoulder. She draws back and then looks into my eyes. "I can't believe we made it."

"I can," I tell her. "And now we have our whole lives ahead of us."

Bells leans her head against my chest again. "I can't wait."

Epilogue

Izabel - 7 Years Later

I LOOK UP, STARTLED WHEN I HEAR THE FRONT DOOR crash open. My eyes dart out to the backyard where Amy and Ashton play their favorite game of "princes and princesses" in the jungle gym. Amelia is dressed up in a sparkly princess costume, and Ashton is swinging a plastic sword around.

Juliet and Liam are spending the day together at the winery, much to Amy's pleasure, their son Ashton is hanging out with us all day.

Our oldest child, Amelia, was born less than a year following our wedding. Ryan and I didn't waste any time. He wanted to be a dad more than anything. I'll never forget the moment we found out together. I've never seen Ryan cry so many tears of joy before. Until nine months later, when he held his daughter for the first time.

I get back to cutting up the apple slices I'm working on.

Those kids have been playing hard for a few hours, so they'll be wanting a snack soon. Amy absolutely *adores* Ashton. Almost as much as she loves her father. Ashton is two years older than her, so he tolerates her at best. I enjoy watching them play together. Ashton is always so patient and lets Amy dress him up or boss him around to do her bidding.

As I watch the kids play outside, I hear the unmistakable sound of grocery bags crinkling as they're set on the counter. Then a pair of large muscular arms wind around my middle. My lips pull up into a smile as my husband presses his lips in the hollow spot right behind my jaw.

"Heya, Bells," he whispers in my ears, giving me goose-bumps even all these years later.

I spin around and face him, resting my hips against the edge of the counter. My arms wrap around his neck, and I stand up on my tiptoes to give him a proper kiss. When I pull away, I rub my nose against his. "Hey, yourself."

"How are the munchkins today?" he asks, glancing out the door to watch Amy and Ashton play.

Ryan was out of town all day yesterday and overnight. He had a few out-of-town clients he had to check on, so he and his partner slash best friend, Josie, went on a small business excursion. They got back into town this morning and did a little work at the office before heading home.

"They've been good. Your daughter is bullying Ashton into playing Princes and Princesses with her."

Ryan gives a deep laugh and then shakes his head. "She's too headstrong for her own good."

"Poor Ashton doesn't stand a chance," I tease. "She'll be excited to see you, though. You should go say hi."

"I think I might say hello to the boy first; where is that little rascal?"

I smile softly when I think of our littlest member of our

family. At Ryan's suggestion, we started trying for another baby shortly after Amelia turned six months old. It didn't happen right away, but I found out I was pregnant right around when Amelia was a year old. Nine months later, Daniel joined our family, and we've been a happy family of four ever since.

"Danny's up playing Legos in his room." At almost five years old, Danny was always busy and always chatty.

Ryan leans down and presses a kiss against my cheek. "I'll be back."

I watch my husband saunter off toward our son's room and then turn my attention back to the apples I'm slicing. I give each plate a few cheese cubes, five apple slices, and then a dollop of peanut butter. Then, when that looks good, I slide open the window above my kitchen sink and holler outside.

"Kids, come on in for a snack!"

Amy and Ashton both pause before dropping their props and running inside. They settle in the barstools at the breakfast peninsula and then get to work on their plates I set in front of them.

Ryan clambers down the stairs, with Danny settled into the crook of his arm. The little boy has my blue eyes and the blonde hair Ryan had when he was younger. Danny is unmistakably Ryan's son, with that mischievous smirk and trouble-maker attitude.

I grin at the sight of the two of them, then tap the counter in front of Amy to get her attention. She looks up at me, hitting me with those green eyes she got from her father. I point behind her, and she turns before letting out a high pitch squeal.

"DADDY!"

Amelia bolts off the stool and runs at Ryan full speed before attaching herself to his leg. He crouches down, still keeping Daniel in one arm, but wraps Amelia up in the other, drawing her in close.

I watch the three of them with a smile. The kids are chattering at him, asking if he had a good trip and if he brought back presents. He's only been gone for a day, but they're acting like they haven't seen him in years.

I chuckle and then look over at Ashton, who's watching them as well. "That Amelia is a handful, huh?"

He scowls, his dark eyebrows pulling over his bright silver-blue eyes. "She's a pipsqueak."

"She sure does love playing with you, though. You're very nice to let her play what she wants," I observe. Ashton shrugs noncommittally, and then stuffs an apple slice into his mouth.

I chuckle under my breath again and head over to the other counter to put away some of the groceries Ryan brought home. In the living room, I hear Ryan let out a theatrical roar, and I turn to see what they're doing to him.

Ryan's lying flat on his back, his hands and legs splayed out. Amy and Danny are climbing on top of him and giggling like hyenas.

I turn back to the groceries and smile to myself. The sound of my family playing in the background has my heart feeling full. I used to dream about what my life would be like all those years ago, and honestly, it turned out better than I could have ever imagined.

Ryan

Later that evening, once the kids are in bed and Ashton is back at his own home, Bells and I sit on the couch in our living room, watching the flames in our fireplace dance around. The night is quiet, perfect.

Her feet are resting in my lap as I rub the arch of her foot with my thumb, glancing up at her here and there, appreciating the view. Bells is still the most beautiful woman I've ever laid eyes on. The way the shadows from our fire paint her face makes her look enchanting.

"How was your trip?" she asks, after a bit of silence. We haven't had much time to be *us* since I got home. Danny and Amy keep us on our toes at all hours of the day. But once they're asleep in their beds, Bells and I get a chance to be us again. These quiet moments in the evening are spent just appreciating each other's company.

"It was good," I say, thinking back over the last twenty-four hours. "Everything seems to be on track with the projects, so I have no complaints. Either that or they just made it look like it because they knew I was coming to visit."

Izabel chuckles, and then stretches her arms lazily over her head. "That was probably it. You are pretty scary, you know."

I laugh with her. My business skyrocketed over the last few years. Josie and I are continually working and checking on projects these days. "Oh, for sure. How was your day yesterday?"

She shrugs. "It was fine. My class took a history exam and grumbled about it the whole time. Amelia is really excited about her field trip to the apple orchard next week. And Danny brought home some artwork he wants to show you. I'll remind him about it tomorrow."

Bells went back to teaching at Bennett the year we got married and has been at it ever since. She still loves teaching history almost as much as she likes learning about it herself.

"I got you something," I tell her slyly as I tickle the pad of her foot. She squirms away from me, and then shoots me a confused stare.

"For what?"

"For our anniversary," I say. I maneuver how I'm sitting and reach into my back pocket, pulling out a small black box.

Izabel makes a weird face that's something between a frown and a smile. "But that's not till next week."

"Well, I saw this, and I knew I had to get it for you. And I didn't want to wait for you to see it. So open it already."

Bells follows my instructions and pulls off the top of the little black box. She gasps when she sees what's inside and then looks at me with tears in her eyes. Pulling out the ring, she holds it up to see better. The dark gold ring has diamonds set into the outer edge, giving it a bright sparkle.

"The seventh-anniversary gift is supposed to be copper," I explain. "This is gold, but we can just pretend it's copper."

Her eyes meet mine again. "It's gorgeous, Ryan. Thank you."

"You can wear it with your other bands or alone. It might stand out more since your wedding rings are silver," I tell her. "But I thought it was perfect."

"It is," she says with a smile. Izabel slips it onto her right ring finger and holds her hand up, admiring it. Then she wiggles her feet out of my lap and then crawls on top of me, fitting her knees around my hips. Her hands come up to my cheeks, and she holds my face, locking our eyes together. "I love it. I love you."

I smile at her. "I love you too. Happy anniversary."

"Early anniversary," she corrects as she leans down to press our lips together. "You're not feeling that seven-year itch, are you?"

"Absolutely not. You're everything to me."

"Good," Bells murmurs before giving me a warm kiss. Her mouth parts with my own, and she kisses me tenderly. I groan into her mouth, and she presses closer.

After a few minutes, she pulls away and settles her head on

my shoulder. My arms wrap around her, holding her tightly to me. We stay there for a few minutes, quietly basking in each other's presence.

Izabel sighs happily as we snuggle. "Mm, I like it here. You're my new pillow."

I chuckle and run my hand up the length of her spine, feeling her shiver from the action. "Happy to oblige, pretty girl." After another moment, I break the silence, "Tell me something I don't know, Bells."

She pulls back, sitting straight up on my lap. Her cheeks look flushed in the firelight, her eyes sparkling mischievously. Then she leans forward, putting her lips at my ear. "I'm not wearing any underwear."

My whole body responds to that secret, and in one swift move, I'm scooping her up in my arms. "Now *that* is one hell of a fun fact," I say before capturing her lips in mine. She giggles against my lips as I walk us up the stairs to our bedroom.

Izabel and I have been married seven whole years. In that time, we've built our home together, built our family. As each day goes by, I fall more and more in love with her. Our promises to each other still hold true. We are stronger together, and there's nothing that will come between us. Ever.

Want to read what's next?
Click HERE to read the third book in the Cedar Ridge Series, "Just Josie," available now

Acknowledgments

Thank you so much to everyone who has been involved with creating and perfecting The *Loathing Ryan* Duet!

Ryan and Bells are two of my OG characters who have been with me for so long, I hardly know who I am without them. It's so satisfying to finally give them the story they deserve and get the chance to share them with the world.

Ryan and Izabel first came to me in 2011, and now all these years later, I finally get to see it all come full circle.

I have many people to thank for assisting me in this process:

Thank you to one of my oldest writing friends AnnRea, who reached out when Ryan and Bells were first introduced to the writing world on Wattpad. I can't believe we have been friends as long as we have. She was there when it was first written, and when I choose to pick this story up again in 2019, and in 2020 when I fully committed to rewriting the Duet. I can't have done it without you, your initial feedback and help really made these stories into what they are today. Thank you!

Thank you to my dear friend Kris Wood who has helped so much in this final stage of revision and editing to perfect this story. Thank you for loving Ryan and Izabel just as much as I do.

Thank you to my lovely beta-readers who gave me such great feedback.

And thank you to my editor Mckenzie who helped me in all the grueling stages of the editing process.

Another big thank you to Nicole with IndieSage for designing these beautiful covers for the paperback and ebook versions of this Duet.

And as always thank you to my husband for always being a support for me with my passion for writing. I can't imagine life without you!

About the Author

Aria Harding is an up-and-coming romance novelist from the Midwest, USA. Aria has been a long-time lover of romance novels and is excited to join the ranks as a romance author. Her first book, "Chasing Infinity" was published in May of 2023 and there are many more exciting projects to come. Her goal is to write stories that make readers feel as though they are immersed in the world and experiencing the same highs and lows as the characters on the pages. Her favorite tropes to write include slow burn, enemies-to-lovers and second-chance romances. Aria always looks forward to hearing from readers, so feel free to reach out on social media and have a chat!

Instagram: @ariaharding_author